OATLANDS

THROUGH CLOSED DOORS

OATLANDS

THROUGH CLOSED DOORS

Jill Rutherford

Little Wren Press

Published by Little Wren Press 2023

ISBN

Paperback 978-1-9996133-1-0

E book 978-1-9996133-2-7

A CIP catalogue record for this book is available from the British Library

Book Cover: Watercolour of rear view of Oatlands painted by C Brauns 1810 and reproduced here by kind permission of the Royal Collection Trust
©King Charles III 2022

For Jan, always ...
and for my ancestors who were
allowed through the closed doors of royalty

PROLOGUE

His footsteps echoed loudly on the flagstones as he increased his pace through the stone archway. The parade of the Coldstream Guards had finished and most soldiers had gone inside the barracks. He thought he was alone but stopped suddenly and stepped back into the shadows as he saw the Duke of York, flanked by two officers, striding across the large parade ground towards him. Damn, he thought. Jack's maxim had always been to keep a low profile around officers. But it was too late.

'Sergeant Dresser,' one of the officers barked out.

Jack marched out of the shadows onto the dust-covered ground and stopped in front of the duke and saluted smartly. He had never been so close to his commanding officer before and it disconcerted him to have to look up as he had always been the tallest in his regiment. He wondered why he had been singled out for special attention. The duke looked him up and down in appraisal.

'You have served your country for well over twenty years, I hear, Sergeant,' the duke said in his strong, rich voice. 'But now you are forced to retire through gout, I understand.'

'Yes, sir,' Jack replied a little too loudly in his effort to sound confident. It was the first time he had spoken to royalty. He tried not to shiver as the December cold penetrated his uniform.

'You fought in the Americas, I've been told.'

'Yes, sir,' Jack said more naturally, 'I had that honour.'

'And served us well. You have a high reputation amongst your men. They respect you.'

Surprised the duke would take an interest in him Jack was at a loss how to reply so looked ahead, silently standing to attention.

The duke scrutinised him. 'Very well, Sergeant, I'll see you tomorrow. Nine of the clock prompt. In my office.' He saluted and Jack returned it.

As the duke strode away one of the officers stayed behind. 'Don't look so worried, Sergeant.'

'No, sir.'

'You've been awarded your disability pension by the Chelsea Hospital, I understand.'

'Yes, sir, that has been approved. I leave the regiment next week. But sir, can you tell me why the duke wants to see me?'

'He needs servants for his new country estate and he's very particular who he employs. He favours retiring soldiers of good reputation who are reliable and loyal. Even though you suffer from the gout, you have been recommended as fit for the position of porter. He will see three retiring soldiers recommended to him and you are one.' He looked hard at Jack. 'If you are interested of course, Sergeant,' he barked. 'You may have other plans. Please let me know, now, if you have.'

Porter? Jack's mind was reeling. He was going

to be interviewed for position of gatekeeper at the duke's new country estate? That would mean a lodge …. somewhere to live. My God! This would answer all my prayers, he thought. He swallowed hard. 'No, sir,' he replied decisively. 'No other plans at all. I'd be honoured to serve the duke.'

He thought of his wife, Hannah. She'd been distraught when he'd seen her last week. His pension wouldn't be enough to keep them and their three small children and with Jack's gout how was he going to get steady work? They'd have to leave their accommodation and find a cheaper place – and there weren't many cheaper places that he would consider decent to lodge his family.

'You don't object to living in the country, Sergeant? Your family too? It's very different to London life.'

A country place. Out of the stink of London – and with a job too! Jack couldn't believe his luck. 'No, sir. No objections at all,' he grinned.

'Don't get too fixed on the idea. Remember, you will be one of three candidates. Nine of the clock prompt.'

'Yes, sir.' Jack saluted and the officer returned it before he marched off in the direction the duke had taken.

Jack stood in the vast parade ground his heart beating faster as his excitement grew. He had to tell Hannah. She needed to know. Some of his fellow soldiers misunderstood his devotion to his wife and children. They took it as a weakness in him, but he knew it meant that he'd been lucky in life. He'd been born into a poor family of tanners in Derbyshire who worked hard for the little they got. He'd taken the King's shilling at eighteen and joined the Coldstream

3

Guards and loved the army from the start. It gave him everything he needed to survive, a job, confidence and skills he could only have dreamed of as a tanner.

He knew his uniform had first attracted his wife to him: the pure white waistcoat and breeches that dazzled against the bright red tailcoat that defined the soldier of the Coldstream Guards. Jack was good-looking in a rugged way. His features were a little irregular with a slight crook to his nose, broken a long time ago. He had good, strong teeth and attractive lips, which his wife always told him were irresistible. But it was his eyes that lit up his face. Mid-blue in colour and clear, full of life and humour, but they could turn dark when he was angry. He was not a man to be trifled with.

He'd made sure his light brown hair was powdered an even white today and his queue well secured with its ribbon. The men had looked their best that morning during the parade. The duke had recently taken command and every man wanted to shine to support him. He'd taken an army of undisciplined, rough and complaining soldiers who were viewed as low–level scum by the population at large and was turning them into confident soldiers taking pride in their skills, abilities and appearance. Making the country realise that these men were all that stood between them and the threat of social unrest France was experiencing. The men were loyal to him and everyone marvelled that he had achieved so much in only a few months. The duke was an exceptional man.

Jack looked around. A few soldiers walked here and there but mostly the parade ground was empty as meal-time was looming. He'd just have time if he hurried. He walked swiftly past the buildings of the barracks until he came to a small side gate in the high railings surrounding the grounds. He took another furtive look around and slipped through the gate. Soldiers like Jack were obliged to live in barracks and many men with families gave money to their wives and left them to fend for themselves, but Jack needed to know that Hannah and the children were comfortable and protected. The two rooms he rented for them were nearby and more expensive because of their close proximity to the barracks.

Five minutes later, he was running up the stairs to the second floor of a respectable lodging house. He opened a door to the left of the corridor and called out, 'Hannah, it's me.'

A six-year-old girl sat at a scrubbed table in the middle of a large, cosy room, the coldness taken off by a mean-looking fire burning in the grate. She was drawing shapes with a slate and chalk while a four-year-old boy was making his own squiggles on another slate. 'Daddy, Daddy,' they shouted as they scrambled off the chairs and flung themselves at him. They clutched a leg each and jumped up and down in excitement.

'Hello, my little people,' he said, laughing. They shrieked with glee as he picked them up, one in each arm, and kissed them both extravagantly, which made them shriek even more.

Then he saw Hannah in the doorway of the bedroom pushing back a long strand of her blonde hair. Her features were delicate but her strength was apparent in her bearing and speech. It was clear she stood no nonsense. Her dress was faded and wrinkled but still accentuated her natural curves. Her back was straight and strong. She was frowning.

'Jack! What on earth's happened? Why are you

here? Did something go wrong with the inspection parade?'

He smiled, feeling those same emotions of love, desire and contentment he always felt when he saw her. Neither the years, nor children, had diminished her loveliness and to Jack she looked even more beautiful as time went by.

'Don't worry, Hannah love. It's nothing bad. The opposite if things turn out well.'

'What do you mean? Only you getting a job will make me stop worrying about how we pay our bills once we have only your pension to rely on. You know the price of bread continues to rise. It's become a luxury not the necessity it surely is.' Her voice broke. 'We'll die without bread. I despair every time I go to market and find myself with only enough money to buy a stale loaf. We won't even be able to do that once you are out of the army.' She swiped at the tears filling her eyes. 'Oh, Jack, I'm not criticising you I know you do your best. It's just bad luck you have to leave the army at this particular time.'

'I know. But don't forget William and Anne have got good jobs with Sir Arthur. It's a respectable house for our two eldest and we don't need to worry about them anymore. That's good luck, is it not? And now ...' he paused dramatically, looking at each one of them in turn, 'and now ... something else has happened. That's why I took the chance to come and tell you.' He laughed, pleased with his theatrical prose.

'Tell me what?' Hannah demanded, still frowning. 'You'll get thrown out before you get your pension if you're not careful. You know you are not allowed out of barracks today.' She sounded fierce, but there was a twinkle in her eye.

6

Jack put down the children and took her in his arms, 'You know I can't stay away from you, regardless of the consequences.'

She laughed as she pushed him away, 'Yes, and that's why we've had so many children. Now come on, tell me what has happened and get back to barracks. You'll see enough of me in the time to come that you'll be struggling to get away.'

'Never,' he said, laughing too. The children hugged his legs again and he ruffled their hair as he steadied himself. He put his hands on Hannah's shoulders. 'You'll never guess . . . I spoke to the duke today.'

Hannah's mouth dropped open. '*You!* You spoke to the *duke? The Duke of York?*'

'Well, more accurately, he spoke to me . . . but I did reply.' He held her gaze, his eyes sparkling.

'Well, come on man, spit it out. I'll be old before you tell—' a baby's cry pierced the air.

Jack looked towards the bedroom. 'Is it the gripe again?'

Hannah nodded. 'He's bad today and in a lot of pain. I've tried everything. Oh, Jack, I don't know what to do,' she said as she disappeared into the bedroom. She came back with the baby over her shoulder. 'He's not happy,' she said, patting his back and jiggling him into a grizzle rather than a cry. 'I wish we could afford a good doctor. I couldn't bear to lose another child.'

'That's why I've come to see you. I know it's been hard on you, but there's a chance things might improve. The duke has chosen me as one of three candidates for a job as porter at his country house.' He gave a single nod as if it was confirmation that the

7

job was his.

Hannah's mouth fell open again. She looked at her husband for a long time as she continued to jiggle the baby. 'A royal servant you mean . . . in their house . . . living in a royal household?'

Jack nodded, smiling broadly. 'There, I knew you'd be pleased.' He paused, 'although, not in the actual household but in the porter's lodge.'

'But just wait a minute. You said one of *three* candidates?'

He nodded again, still smiling.

'But that means you may not get the job. You have a one in three chance.'

'Good odds.'

'But three of you for one position . . . oh, Jack, what if you don't get it? Is this really good news? I think I'd rather have waited until you knew for sure. Did you risk leaving barracks to tell me something that *might* happen? And what if you're caught out of barracks, you definitely wouldn't get the job then.'

'They won't catch me. I'm too wily for them. That's why I'm such a good soldier. But don't you see, it's hope, my darling.' He smiled and his eyes shone as he looked deep into Hannah's. 'Hope and love make the world go round. We can't live without hope.' He took a step back, unsure. 'I thought you'd be pleased.'

'I will not be pleased until you come running in here to say they have given the position to you. *Then*, I will be pleased.'

Hannah was tall amongst women but only just came up to her husband's shoulder. Her eyes softened as she looked up at him. 'You, my dear husband,' she said stroking his cheek with her fingertips, 'you have much experience but have never met royalty before, how will you conduct yourself?' She wiped away a tear. 'Oh, Jack, I don't want to raise my hopes.'

He stroked her hair, charmed as always by its softness and gold highlights. 'The Coldstream Guards, as you well know, is the Royal Regiment. We guard royalty – that's our job. I've been in the king's company many times – and taken orders from earls and dukes and the like. You worry too much.'

'Ha! Yes, you've been in the king's company with all the other troops on parade, and taken orders, but not been applying for jobs with them. They're another breed.'

'Calm yourself,' he soothed. 'I'll do my best, that's all I can do. The duke has a reputation for being very approachable to all. He shows respect to men who do their jobs well, regardless of their status in life. He's unusual in that way.'

Hannah took a breath to reply but was cut off when the baby screamed again. Jack grinned and dislodged the two little ones still clinging to his legs. He kneeled down and kissed them on the cheek, rising to kiss Hannah full on the lips.

He walked to the door. 'If I get the job, I'll come running all right. I must get back. Take care of yourself,' he shouted over the baby's distress, and blew her a kiss.

Hannah frowned as the baby's screams increased.

*

Jack was nervous as he made his way to the duke's office the following morning. He'd been up early, making sure his uniform was immaculate and that he didn't cut himself shaving. I've a one in three chance, he kept saying to himself as he approached the office door. He swallowed his nervousness thinking how stupid it was. He'd been in bad situations throughout his career, but none had affected his nerves as much as this. It was because Hannah had put so much store by this, he thought. He couldn't let her down.

He took a deep breath and knocked sharply on the door, stepping smartly into the duke's outer office. The duke's secretary, a distinguished-looking officer looked up. 'Sergeant John Dresser,' Jack announced in a loud voice and saluted. He looked straight ahead in the sparse office but from the corner of his eye he could see two men sitting on wooden chairs set against a wall opposite the secretary's desk. Hell! I'm the last to arrive, damn it. *Damn it!*

He knew the last to arrive meant last to be seen therefore the duke would know he was the straggler. They must have arrived too early, he thought, because I'm exactly on time, as I should be. That's the way of the army, on time, not early. Early could get you into difficult situations, seeing things you were not intended to see.

'Sit down, Sergeant,' the officer said gruffly returning the salute.

Jack sat down on the third chair – the one furthest away from the duke's office door. After a considerable wait, the door to the office opened from the inside, although no one came out.

'Sergeant Morgan,' the duke's secretary barked. 'The duke is ready for you.' The first man jumped up and went in.

As Jack waited he tried to stop his foot from tapping with impatience. He was not good at waiting and knew he'd created a bad impression. Oh, God forgive me if I don't get this position because Hannah surely won't. He stifled a groan as the first man came out some ten minutes later, and as the next man went in, Jack started to feel bilious. This was worse than facing the fiercest enemy. At least then he could shoot and fight back. Things he knew how to do.

The second man came out and as he walked past Jack, the secretary called out, 'Sergeant Dresser,' so loudly it made Jack jump. He stood up and marched into the room. The duke was standing with his back to Jack in front of a long, ornate window. The strong sunlight cast him in a spotlight and lit up his red colonel's uniform making him look more muscular than he was and his gold epaulettes and buttons more extravagant than they were.

Jack stood at full attention feeling lost in the high-ceilinged room which was sparsely furnished in military functionality. A large mahogany desk and chair dominated the room, a map table, a couple of cabinets full of official-looking books. Two red velvet, high-backed armchairs either side of the marble fireplace was the only attempt at comfort. Jack didn't think he'd be asked to sit down.

The duke kept Jack waiting and finally swung around to face him. He looked him in the eye in a penetrating stare. Jack felt his soul had been searched.

'At ease, Sergeant. According to your records you joined the Coldstream Guards from Derbyshire,' the duke said, looking down at Jack's record sheet on his desk.

'Yes, sir,' Jack answered, relieved to hear his voice sounded confident.

'The south of England differs from the Midlands,

how have you felt living in the south, sergeant? Has it suited you?'

'Yes, sir, it's suited very well.' Jack decided to risk an aside. 'The weather is much better, sir.'

The duke laughed, much to Jack's relief. 'And army life? How has that suited you?'

'Very well, sir. It's given a man like me,' Jack hesitated, he didn't want to sound as if he were a peasant, but he needed the duke to know how much he had improved during his army life, 'from a poor working family, well, it's given me a chance to learn. I am grateful to the army.'

'And what have you learned?'

Jack knew he had to think quickly and show confidence if he was to get this job. He squared his shoulders and looked straight ahead. 'How to discipline men, sir; how to build them into an effective force and co-operate with each other and gain loyalty and watch your back and your fellows' backs; how to follow orders and implement them.' He hesitated momentarily. 'I can read and write much better than when I joined, too.'

The duke nodded.

'You've been a sergeant for the past twelve years. How has that been?'

'I cannot deny that sometimes it's been hard. When you become a sergeant you become a leader: a disciplinarian. But I took to it.'

The duke smiled and it encouraged Jack to relax more. He felt that the other two candidates would have been stiff and very proper in their meeting and he wasn't sure that would win the duke over. He'd heard stories about the duke's goodwill and charity to his servants and how relaxed he was with them. To hell with it, he thought, I either get this job or I don't, I have to be myself. 'And, if I may be so bold, sir, it's all been so much better since you became our colonel. The men now look up to a sergeant much more than before. I've been grateful for my promotion and done my best to uphold the position as best I can.'

'Yes, I see there are many good reports about you. You served in the Americas for,' the duke looked down at Jack's record, 'five years.'

'Yes, sir.'

'Your report says you acquitted yourself well, and you were respected by your men. You saved your commanding officer's life, I see.'

'Yes, sir.'

'It says here, you killed four enemy soldiers and carried your officer to safety.'

'Yes, sir. It was my honour to assist him.'

'And now you are to be invalided out because of,' the duke looked at his notes, looked back up at Jack, and smiled raising an eyebrow: 'Ah, yes, I remember now … gout!'

'Yes, sir.' Jack felt a prickle of embarrassment.

'And how does this – gout – affect you?'

'It's intermittent, sir. But I cannot be relied upon to be able to do what is expected of me if it should take me during a battle or a march. It's very painful. I cannot walk without the aid of a crutch when it's upon me.'

'And how often does it come upon you?'

'That's why I left the Americas, sir. It built up and disabled me in my fifth year and I was sent home. As is the way with gout, sir, I had no repeat attacks until this year. What with my advancing age and the gout, I'm afraid I am no longer fit for the army.'

There was a pause and Jack's words hung in the air and seemed to accuse him.

The duke shuffled his notes. 'You've been given a pension by the Chelsea Hospital I see.'

'Yes, sir, and very grateful I am. But I am capable of work – lots of work,' he added hurriedly. 'I am very fit when the gout is not upon me.' He hesitated. 'I can work as a porter, sir, without problems as even if the gout prevailed, I can still move about with my crutch and open gates and fight my corner.' He took a chance at humour. 'If I had to, I could hit any undesirables with my crutch!'

The duke laughed and his eyes softened. 'The country air will probably cure your gout. It's so clean in Weybridge, Sergeant. Do you know the county of Surrey?'

'No, sir. I haven't had the pleasure.'

'And pleasure it is. Eighteen miles from London and it could be a different country. Clean country air, good people.'

The duke was thoughtful and walked back to the window. He looked out with his back to Jack. 'There are two porter's lodges and there will, eventually, be two porters. I have arranged for one of my men, who has served under me for many a year, to be a porter in a few weeks' time. Until then, there will only be the porter I appoint now.'

He swung around to face Jack. 'As I am not living at the house yet, there will be few visitors, but you would need to be on duty constantly all day and night, every day, until the other man arrives. That means you cannot leave the lodge. Could you cope with that, Sergeant?'

Jack knew he had to prove himself. 'I'm an army

14

man, sir, used to campaigns and battles necessitating long periods on duty. And if there was any movement at night I would be awake at the snap of a twig or the rustle of cloth. Long hours are of no moment to me.'

The duke walked back to his desk and tapped his finger on Jack's record sheets, pondering. 'So,' he said so loudly, Jack jumped, 'you would like to be a royal servant, would you?'

'Yes, sir. I would deem it a great honour,' Jack said in a confident voice, pretending he was somewhere else and not facing the king's second son.

'So would most of the population, Sergeant. Tell me why it would be such a great honour to you.'

Jack was at a loss. He decided on honesty before his hesitation was taken advantage of. Hesitation on the battlefield meant death and he felt sure the same applied here, death to his dreams and his pleasant relationship with his wife.

He looked straight ahead, not daring to look at the duke. 'If I may be so bold as to say that since you took charge the life of the soldier has changed for the better. I've been proud to serve my country and proud to be a soldier but, well, excuse me, sir, but soldiers in general have not had much respect from the population. They see us as rogues and undisciplined and officers, again, please excuse my boldness sir, did nothing to alleviate this. Decent, serving men were demoralised and stopped caring.' He risked a glance at the duke who was studying him intently. Jack squashed down his rising nerves. 'When you took over, you changed all that by increasing discipline and fairness, not only to the men but among the officers too. This has meant the officers now respect the men more than before. You gave us pride, sir.' Jack stood up straighter. 'Pride in being a foot soldier instead of shame that a man could not get something better for his life. And that pride shows itself to the population and they are beginning to respect us more too. And I like that, sir. I like being respected for the job I do and it is all down to you, sir.' Jack risked another look at the duke who was still studying him.

He wondered if he'd gone too far and his nerves rose up again, but he had to finish, to make his meaning clear. 'You are the only leader we have had who has had the courage, if I may be so bold again sir, to change things in such a way. I will serve you to the very best of my ability in whatever way that helps you best. And if that is as a porter at your country home, I would welcome that wholeheartedly . . . and so would my wife.'

'Your *wife*? You take notice of your *wife*? You are unusual for a soldier … or you have a sense of humour, Sergeant?'

'Sorry, sir. My apologies. I always see the humour in things. But yes, truth be told, I do take notice of my wife. I know it is unusual, but I like to include my wife in my decisions for she is a woman of intelligence and common sense. I see no profit in keeping her lowly as do many men, sir.'

'Most men, Sergeant. But I like your attitude.'

'In that case, sir, my wife told me last night that she would be most honoured if her husband became a royal servant. Her eyes went huge at the prospect.' He suddenly stopped speaking, realising his mistake. *Damn! Damn! Damn! Stupid!* What was I thinking of telling him that? Jack broke out in a sweat.

'You *left* barracks and told your *wife?*' the duke snapped. 'You are well aware that no one was to leave barracks during manoeuvres and the parade. Are you not?'

Jack cringed inwardly. He took a deep breath to steady himself and try to redeem the situation as best he could. 'Yes, sir. I am aware of that rule and yes, I did leave barracks to tell my wife.' He had to think fast. 'She has been worrying so much about what will happen to us and our children that she is fraught. I wanted to reassure her. Give her some hope to hold on to. I … I didn't see the harm sir, as I'll be leaving the army soon and I was not on duty.'

The duke stared at him, frowning, but eventually said, 'You are your own man, I think, Dresser.' the duke studied him some more. 'It is obvious that you also love your wife.'

'Very much, sir,' Jack smiled. 'We have been married many years and I love her more now than ever before.' Jack knew he was babbling but couldn't stop. The duke had that knack of getting the truth out of people without them realising. 'It is a miracle that someone like her would marry someone like me. I have been blessed, sir.'

'I see,' the duke said slowly, as he considered Jack. 'You are an unusual man, Sergeant. A man not afraid of his feelings or speaking of them when others would hesitate. And such loyalty and commitment to your wife and family. Would you show such loyalty and commitment to me?'

Jack looked the duke in the eye. 'I would defend you, your family and your property with my life, sir.'

The duke looked at him long and hard and then slapped his hand down on his desk. 'I like you, Sergeant,' he said in his loud voice. 'You are a man who can redeem situations, something I need. You can charm and think fast on your feet. You'll get into some tricky situations at the porters' lodge; people determined to gain entry who may be people I don't wish to see but are important and have status in the community. I can see you coping with that; being diplomatic but also firm. You're confident and know your own worth. The job is yours, man,' he said with a smile. 'Go home and tell your wife.'

Jack's heart was beating hard and his knees were in danger of buckling as he saluted and said loudly, 'Yes, sir,' and grinned.

'By the way, how many children do you have, Sergeant?'

'I have two grown-up children in service in London, in good houses and two little ones and a baby but I'm not sure how long we may have baby Simon.'

'He is ill?'

'I'm afraid so, sir. We are sore worried as he cries all the time and can't keep his food down.'

'Indeed. We cannot have you distracted by a sick baby, Sergeant. I will send my physician to your home today.'

Jack gasped.

'Give my secretary your wife's address and ask him to arrange it on your way out. I look after my staff. My staff are my family.' He made eye contact with Jack, his voice full of authority. 'I expect total commitment, Sergeant. Total commitment.' His eyes hardened. 'You look after me and I'll look after you. That's what I like – my servants to be like my family. That way, we keep loyalty. And I'm willing to earn that loyalty by treating my servants well. Help them with their welfare and health. Do you understand me, Sergeant? I want total commitment from your wife too. Loyalty and commitment to me, my own family and the family of servants I gather around me. It's most important.'

'Yes, sir, I understand. And thank you. I am most grateful and my wife will be too. We will be loyal, I guarantee.'

'Good. Understood then.'

'Understood, sir.' Jack saluted and the duke acknowledged it.

*

Jack slipped out of barracks at the earliest opportunity. His heart raced fast as hurried to see Hannah. He ran up the stairs and threw open the door. 'I've got it, Hannah. I've got it,' he shouted, barely able to suppress his excitement.

Hannah looked up from her pie making at the kitchen table. She put a floured hand to her face, rubbed her forehead and frowned as she looked at Jack. 'Shh, be quiet or you'll wake the little ones and don't joke, please, not about this.'

'Hannah, ye of little faith. Believe it. It is true.' He couldn't stop grinning.

'True?' She frowned, unsure.

'Yes, how many times do I have to say it? Look, here is the document the duke's secretary gave me.' He rolled it out and held it up for her to see.

'Oh, I cannot let myself believe it, are you sure? There is no mistake?'

He took hold of Hannah's hands and looked into her eyes. 'Would I joke about a thing like this? Believe me, my darling wife, it is true. Look at the document,' he added gently.

'My hands are covered with flour. Put it on the table, Jack. Let me see.' Hannah looked at the document; her reading was not as good as her husband's but she could make out the letters clearly enough. 'It *is* true,' she said in such a low voice, Jack hardly heard her. 'Oh my guardian angel – you are to be a royal servant! It is a miracle. Oh, Jack!' She cried into his shoulder and clutched him tightly. He held her close and stroked her back until she regained her composure.

She looked at the document again. 'It says you start from the fifth day of January – two weeks – my goodness! I'll never be ready.'

'Oh, Hannah, dearest Hannah, you complain about me losing my job in the army and now you complain that my new job – my new *royal* job – is coming too soon.'

She laughed. And then couldn't stop her tears flowing. 'Oh, I'm in such a turmoil, I don't know what to do. It's marvellous, of course it's marvellous.' She hugged Jack again.

'Be careful. Watch my uniform with all that flour,' he said smiling.

'I don't care, I'll hug my husband, uniform or not, flour or not.' And she hugged him harder.

He bent his head and kissed her with passion and she responded with equal passion. Then she pushed him away. 'That's enough of that, Jack Dresser, or we'll end up with yet another little one. I can't cope with another little one just yet.'

His face turned serious. 'How is Simon today?'

'Much the same.'

'I have good news on that count too. The duke is sending his physician to see him today.'

Hannah stood back, shocked. 'The duke is sending his physician to see our son?' she repeated, incredulous.

'Yes,' Jack said in a soothing voice. 'I told you he had a good reputation for treating his staff well. He wants us to start our new life being happy and contented and not worrying about our baby. He wants us all to be like family to him.'

'Like family?'

Jack laughed. 'Don't look so shocked. I told you before that the duke is extraordinary; so unlike others in many ways. He's his own man. He makes his own rules as dictated by his conscience. He doesn't care that others think him strange or cannot understand him.'

'Oh, Jack,' Hannah said, sinking into a chair. 'Oh Jack,' she repeated and burst into tears.

CHAPTER ONE

The London to Weybridge coach hit a hole in the rough road and the children bellowed in delight. 'That's number thirty nine,' Jack said as he kept them occupied on the long coach journey. They counted the times the coach swayed dangerously from side to side as one wheel went into a pothole with a bump and came out the other side with another bump.

Sarah and Arthur had been learning to count with their mother. When he was a child, Jack had been taught his letters and numbers and the army had increased his knowledge. He had taught Hannah so that she, in turn, could teach their children. They wanted them to have every advantage they could give.

'It's good baby Simon has been cured of the gripe,' Jack said. 'It would be awful to travel with him crying all the time.'

'Good for him too.' Hannah tickled his chin as he gurgled good naturedly on her lap. 'He's a new boy since he had that medicine the duke's doctor made up for him.' She rubbed his tummy as the doctor had recommended. 'He loves having his tummy rubbed. It is a wonder what a simple thing like that can do for a baby with the gripe.'

She unbuttoned her blouse. 'Time for his feed.'

'Already?'

'I know, but remember the doctor said to feed him more often. He could be taking in too much air with the nipple if he's too hungry. Now he sucks more contentedly and slowly. He's a good boy.'

'He is that,' Jack said, smiling as his wife lifted the baby to her breast. 'It gives me great pleasure to see you both thus . . . and to know that I am the cause of it.'

Hannah raised an eyebrow but couldn't hide her smile.

The coach went over another hole in the road and the baby clamped his gums on her nipple.

'Number forty,' Jack and the children shouted out, laughing.

'God kept teeth away from babies for a very good reason,' Hannah said with feeling.

The coach finally pulled up and stopped. Jack looked around, ready for trouble. 'What's up' he asked Hannah, 'we're in the middle of a forest. Why have we stopped?'

The coach driver shouted out, 'Oatlands,' as his assistant scuttled up onto the roof of the carriage to get their boxes.

Jack got out and looked around. 'Well, it's a true country residence, not a house or anything can be seen, only trees, a high wall and a gate.'

'What did you expect?' Hannah said as she handed the baby to Jack and climbed down. 'Oh, look at that sky … it's huge! And so blue! And there's no fog here!' She breathed in deeply. 'Our children can breathe clean air. Just smell the goodness in it.'

'Aye, the stink of London is not here, that's for sure,' he said lifting the other children down. 'You two are strangely quiet,' he said, looking at the youngsters who were gazing around in awe.

'They have never seen a forest before, they are just babies. Give them time and they will love it.'

The coach disappeared into the distance in a storm of dust thrown up from the earthen road as they stood and shivered in the raw wind.

'Big gates, Daddy. Frightened, Daddy,' said Sarah as she clutched his well-muscled leg and hugged it to her.

He rubbed his hand over the top of her head. 'It is all right, my lovely girl. There is nothing to be afraid of. They are just gates, but as you say,' he looked up, 'big gates.' There was a sign attached to each of the brick pillars supporting the gates. 'Oatlands' was written in gold lettering on smooth slate.

'Well, this is the place, all right. But how do we get in?' He rattled the gates but they didn't budge. He could see a large lock on the inside of them and no key. 'Mmm, they are indeed in need of a porter I see. There is no one here to unlock them for us.'

He looked around at the high stone wall surrounding the property as far as his eye could see and was on the verge of thinking he would have to scale it, when he heard a voice.

'Hello there,' a breathless youth called out from inside the gates as he ran the last few yards. He was muffled up in a long coat and scarf. 'So sorry, we didn't expect you just yet, the coach made good time,' he said, unlocking the gates.

'Well, young man,' Hannah said, 'four hours in a coach is long enough, I think. My bones have all been rattled out of place and rattled back in again.'

He laughed and relaxed. 'Please excuse our tardiness. The house is working with few people at the moment.' He paused. 'I suppose you are the Dresser family?'

'We are indeed, young man,' Jack said stepping through the gates and taking charge. He held out his hand to the lad. 'I am Jack Dresser and this is my wife, Hannah and our children,' he added, making a sweep with his arm.

'And I am Walter, steward's room boy.'

'Well, Walter, very pleased to make your acquaintance, I'm sure.'

'There are two lodges as you can see and yours is this one,' he indicated with his arm. 'Oatlands house is behind us, through the trees.' He pointed his thumb over his shoulder to indicate the direction.

Hannah stood with her back to the house. 'Mmm, we have been given the right-hand lodge when your back is to the house.' She smiled at her husband. 'That's lucky, I think,' she nodded to herself, 'it's always good to be on the right side of your employer.'

Jack smiled indulgently.

'Well then,' Hannah said, becoming all business like. 'Let's see what condition it's in.'

'So be it,' Jack said as he walked to the front door. As he entered the lad said, 'It is a bit musty and damp inside, I'm afraid. But I opened the windows this morning to air it. It hasn't been in use for quite a while.'

'I can see that, lad. Mmm, it is the length of three horses and the width of two, I would say.'

'Thank goodness it doesn't smell of horses,' Hannah said, following them in. The two children held onto her skirts looking frightened. 'It's smaller than I thought but very light with lovely large windows, and I'm pleased to say, shutters for cold nights.' She looked around. 'What a large fireplace, look Jack, it has a small range too. That's splendid. We shall be very comfortable here.' She turned around. 'Was it you who lit the fire for us, Walter?'

'I did, Mrs Dresser, and also the one upstairs.' He nodded towards a narrow, steep staircase abutting the side wall. 'I thought you would be in need of some warmth after the coach from London. It gets chilly on them in winter.'

Hannah smiled. 'That's kind of you.'

'Mr Dresser,' Walter said, looking at Jack and pushing the front door to. 'This is your uniform, sir.' He indicated a uniform hanging from the door on a hanger.

'Ah, yes. Thank you. I was measured for it in London and was expecting it to be here for when I arrived.'

Hannah fingered the thick wool of the deep red tailcoat. 'It is true quality that and the stockings are woollen too, and soft wool at that. They will caress your legs like featherlike fingertips,' she said, laughing as she exchanged a look with her husband. 'So unlike your scratchy army stockings.' Walter started to blush.

'I will show you where the well and the woodshed is, Mr Dresser,' he blustered. 'If you will follow me, sir.' He looked at Hannah, shyly. 'I am hopeful you will be happy here, Mrs Dresser,' and bowed.

'Thank you. I am sure we will be.'

Jack returned with an armful of wood. 'These are well seasoned, they will burn very warm soon,' he said setting them down by the fireplace.

'When do you think the cart with our furniture will arrive?' Hannah asked, unpacking some bread and cheese and small beer.

'Should be here about two hours after us.'

'Well then, let's eat quickly and get to work on this house. Someone has obviously swept it and washed down the windows, but it could do with a bit more work, I think.'

'It needs Hannah's touch,' Jack said, smiling.

'Well, I like it very clean, as you know. 'It is important for the children. I don't want any roaches or mice sharing space with us.'

'As you say.' He gathered the children to him as he sat on the floor. 'Let's eat quickly and then start work.'

The house was swept and washed down thoroughly when a steady clip-clop alerted them to their cart arriving.

'We've finished just in time,' Hannah said as the children ran out to see the excitement.

'Before the carters come in,' Jack took hold of Hannah's hands, 'I just wanted to say something . . . you know, something to welcome us to our new life.' He cleared his throat. 'As you know,' he started rather formally, 'and I've told you this before, many times, but I thought I should say it again. That it is worth saying again now, as we are just starting out in our new life.' He squeezed her hands, gently. 'I've been a common soldier for all of my adult life, it was the only way I knew of bettering myself when I was young ... getting a decent job with regular money.' He kissed her cheek, lightly, and smiled. 'I wanted to confirm to you that what kept me going, what made my life bearable, was you. I am the luckiest man in the world. And now we'll be together always, no more going off to fight and leaving you and the children. I ... I just wanted to say we'll have a good life now. Better than before. I promise.'

Hannah's eyes filled with tears. 'I know that, Jack, love. But I am the lucky one. I've been blessed with a husband I'm proud of. You say you were a common soldier, but there is nothing common or ordinary about you. You are the best man I've ever known. The sweetest and gentlest and I thank God that you came my way. And thank you, Jack, thank you for saying what you've just said. That makes you special, the fact that you even thought to say such things.'

'I could say much more, Hannah, love, but maybe that's for later.'

'Oh, you and your twinkling eyes, I know those twinkles and what they mean. I never could resist them.' She laughed. 'Yes, later, we'll continue this–.'

'Hello, Mr Dresser, sir,' the carter called through the door.

They jumped. 'We've been so involved with ourselves,' Hannah said, 'we forgot about the carters.' They went outside to find their things were already being unloaded. As the kitchen table was taken off and set down Hannah said, 'Oh, no. The table's too big for the room. We'll never get the table and sideboard and dresser in. Oh, I can't believe it, I need that table.'

'Don't fret,' Jack said. 'Let's leave it outside for the moment and I'll cut it down to a smaller size. You'll see, it will be all right.'

'I hadn't expected the house would be quite so small,' said Hannah, 'but never mind, it's a minor point. We have a home and you have a job. That's the main thing.'

'That's my girl,' Jack said. 'And it's a brick-built house, that's a major point, it will be watertight and secure. We'll be all right.'

*

A few weeks later, on a stormy day where the wind whipped up debris sending it flying through the air and the cold turned puddles to ice, the second porter arrived with his family. Hannah quickly put on her coat, bonnet and gloves and went out to welcome them. Jack, similarly encumbered by clothing, was already opening the gates to let in their cart. A bedraggled looking man, a little younger than Jack, his wife and six children climbed off the cart stiff, wet and frozen to the bone.

'Oh, you poor things come inside our lodge and get warmed up. I've got a stew on the fire for you,' Hannah said, as she helped the children into her home. The eldest, a girl of about ten she guessed, another girl and four boys including a baby. Poor woman, she thought.

'You must be Mrs White,' Hannah said, taking in the small woman's gaunt looks and vacant eyes. She hid her concerns with joviality. 'I am Hannah Dresser and this is my husband, Jack. Our two children are at school in the village and baby Simon is asleep upstairs. You will meet them all in due course.'

'Thank you so much for your kindness, Mrs Dresser,' the woman said in a thin, quiet, voice. She tried a smile but it died on her face as her husband and Jack came inside, stamping the rain off their boots on the thick mat by the door.

'Come in and warm yourself, Mr White,' Jack said. 'Your house, as you may have guessed, is the other lodge house opposite and we have lit the fires and prepared things for you. It is nice and clean, but you need food to warm you first of all. Hannah, put out the stew for our guests.'

'We don't need your charity, sir,' the man said, his voice croaky from the cold.

Hannah noticed Mrs White looked frightened as did the children who avoided looking at their father.

"It is no charity, my friend,' answered Jack, 'but common decency when souls need food in their bellies and warmth through their bones.'

'Aye, well, I'm a proud man, Mr Dresser. I like to keep my family hardy.'

Hannah kept her voice sweet. 'Well, the children and your wife need food and warmth after that journey in this awful weather.' Ladling stew into bowls, she added, 'you, however, can decide for yourself whether you partake of our goodwill or not.'

Jack looked at Hannah in amazement, and then smiled. 'Come, man,' he said, 'we have to work and live together for many years, let's be decent to each other. I would hope you would do the same for me and my family in similar circumstances. It's not charity, far from it, for we would have to take care of you if you took sick, being your nearest neighbours and all.' Jack ladled some stew into two bowls and gave one to the man. 'Let's eat together, two old soldiers, servants of the Duke of York.'

The man looked Jack in the eye and nodded. 'Yes, well . . . you're right, man. I've been a bit hasty, maybe.'

The children and Mrs White took this as a sign to start eating and were obviously ravenous as they cleared their bowls quickly but with good manners. Hannah took her time eating and smiled at the little

31

ones offering them more bread which they turned to their father for permission to take. He nodded and they ate with frightened eyes. When they'd finished, Hannah said, 'I've also made a cake and I can't possibly eat it all myself.'

The children looked at her with longing but made no sound or movement.

'Come, my little ones,' she said, 'come and see what I have in my cupboard and help me cut the cake. Don't be shy, we're going to be great friends, I can see.' She offered her hand to the smallest boy. He hesitated and looked at his father, who nodded. He then took Hannah's offered hand and the other children followed Hannah the short distance to the sideboard.

Jack studied the man without seeming too, a trick he'd learned in the army; dour, humourless, stern, inhuman almost. He'd seen many a man before who'd experienced too much brutality to recover their humanity, if they ever had it, for some of them the brutality was their reason for living.

'You are a long-standing army man, I feel, Mr White; a man of experience.'

'Indeed, you are right, sir, but I have been invalided out for some time now after a broken leg failed to heal properly. As you see, I limp.'

Jack nodded. 'Painful, I should think.'

'As you say, but I can bear it and have no need of anyone's sympathy.'

Jack took note of his hostility. A stupid man, he thought. A man who doesn't learn from his mistakes or is too bitter about his misfortune to get on with a worthwhile life. A man with an attitude is a man to be wary of. But out loud he said, 'I can see that, Mr

White.'

'I have a debt of gratitude to the duke as he has been good to me and given me employment when others may have turned their backs. In turn, I am loyal and steadfast to him.'

'Where have you been employed, if I may presume to ask?'

'I see no benefit in talking of my life story. You are here yourself under the duke's patronage. He is a canny man and looks after his people and we in turn look after him. There are not many who understand his ways, they call him soft but he has so many men loyal to him which is more than can be said of others.' He looked uncomfortable suddenly. 'But I talk out of turn, Mr Dresser. I mean no criticism of anyone.'

Jack was unsure of this man. And he didn't like the way he treated his family. There was something wrong here. But the duke had chosen him for a servant, so who was Jack to challenge his judgement?

*

The months went by quickly in a flurry of work and autumn began playing cat and mouse with the end of summer. Jack and Mr White had worked out an agreeable arrangement of duties splitting the day in half. One man was on gate duty for the first twelve hours of the day and then the other took over. They alternated every week and it was working well. Jack had found the other man, despite his own misgivings, a good, conscientious worker and so he ignored any harshness he witnessed towards his wife and children and his propensity to drink hard when off-duty. Hannah, however, was more critical. 'Jack, he is cruel to them. I have seen some things I do not like.'

'But we cannot interfere between a man and his family. It is just not done. Not unless we see something really bad.'

'I cannot prove anything, it's just that they are so afraid of him and he speaks to them so sharply. Mrs White will not confide in me. She keeps me at a distance.'

'Well, no bad thing, maybe. It's best sometimes to be distant from close neighbours; then there is no chance of falling out. We cannot afford to, we may come off worse if there was a dispute and the duke favoured White over me. We could lose everything. No, Hannah, please, you must keep out of their business.'

'You are right, of course. We must put ourselves first.'

'That's the way, dear Hannah. And remember, we have Anne coming next week.'

'How could I forget? I am looking forward to that. We have had some great good luck this year and getting this job for Anne in the big house is a godsend.'

'I agree. Her letter of recommendation from her present employer together with her successful interview has secured her a most enviable post. Our daughter, housemaid to the Duke of York,' he said with great pride. 'Just think that when he marries he will need many more staff, maybe we can get William a post here.'

'Is the duke getting married?' Hannah looked puzzled. 'I hadn't heard.'

'Not to my knowledge, but he must, don't you see. He is the king's second son. He must marry soon and have children. If anything happened to his older brother, he would be king.'

'But the Prince of Wales is in fine health, is he not?'

'Indeed. But accidents do happen. As you know, he's a wild young man, drinking and gambling and womanising as if his life depends on it. It's causing scandal. I know the duke is no angel but he is in no way as profligate as his brother. I would not like to work for the prince.'

'I agree, Jack. Our children have a good life here – as do we. I want Anne and William to benefit from our good fortune.'

'As it happens I was speaking to Mr Tucker this very morning about William. He told me that it was hard to find really good, loyal servants, it is the curse of the rich, he said.'

'Ha! I should have such a curse,' Hannah retorted.

Jack laughed. 'Indeed, but it is not for us, I'm afraid. We are destined to be the servers of this world, but I am happy with our lot. I don't think we could have done better and Mr Tucker says that as William is already employed as a steward's room boy with Sir Arthur, he will be well placed for a vacancy of footman here when it arises. He will ask me to bring William to see him at that time. If he has a good recommendation from Sir Arthur as Anne has done and Mr Tucker approves of him, William will meet with the duke, and if he approves, William will be appointed.'

'Oh, Jack, that's excellent news. Let's hope it happens soon. I do worry about him living in London by himself now Anne is to come here. She, at least, could keep an eye on him. Who knows what he will get up to?'

'He has little time for himself, so do not fret about that. Sir Arthur keeps a close household, I understand.'

'But young men can always get into mischief no matter how close they are kept.'

'Has he done so?'

'Well . . . no … not that we know of.'

'So don't worry. He's a sensible lad.'

'Mmm, I'm not so sure. He's such a handsome young man women will encourage his attentions. He's of an age now.'

'You worry too much,' Jack smiled, 'and maybe you are just a little bit biased towards his good looks? Nonetheless, I will write to him and make sure he understands that if he gets into any trouble, including the female sort, he will not be allowed to work at Oatlands. That should do it.'

'Yes, do that. It will help.'

CHAPTER TWO

Anne was the only passenger on the London to Weybridge coach that October day of 1788. As it finally left the city behind she breathed in the fresh country air through the open window and realised just how polluted the air in London was. She'd always lived there and had no experience of country life. She had another three hours to go before they reached Weybridge, another three hours to feed her nerves, she thought. She so wanted to do well and make her parents proud of her. She knew how lucky she was to have secured this position, but her nerves increased with every mile of green fields and woodland with a cottage dotted here and there and a few small villages. What did people do for enjoyment in such surroundings? She'd been used to the bustle and vitality of the big city and even though she'd not had the luxury of time or money to enjoy what was on offer she soaked up the energy of the place and thrived on it.

She thought back to her interview with the duke at his London house. Her parents had recommended her for a position as housemaid at Oatlands but it was a long and frustrating wait before a vacancy presented itself. the duke had been charm itself but Mr Tucker, the steward at Oatlands who had made a special trip to London for the interview, was more down to earth and practical. She wouldn't want to cross him. But then, she thought, he did represent the duke's interests and took charge of all the details of daily life and the running of the house and could be as fierce as he liked which left the duke to be as charming as he cared to be.

The duke had made it clear he liked her good looks and, although he didn't exactly flirt with her, he gave her a lot of attention. She often felt she was too pretty for her own good, and this, coupled with her fine figure, clear skin and long blonde hair was more of a curse than a blessing for it meant that men desired her and often women disliked her seeing her as unfair competition. Little did they know that she abhorred the attentions she got from men. It wasn't what she wanted from life. She was full of hope that Oatlands, especially as her parents were there too, would prevent this kind of thing happening again.

She pulled herself together. Too much introspection was bad for the soul. It was a dream come true for them all, to work together and if, by some miracle, her brother William could come too that would make things perfect.

A few passengers had joined the coach during the journey and left again at other villages but by the time the coach approached Weybridge she was alone and bored with the journey. A loud voice made her jump.

'One mile to Oatlands, miss,' the driver called down to her which set her nerves tingling again. She smoothed down her best dress with its voluminous deep blue skirts, long sleeves and high buttoned front. It kept the cold at bay but she did wonder at the wisdom of wearing it for travelling but then she wanted to arrive looking her best for her parents.

'Oatlands, miss,' the driver called as he pulled up the horses. Anne smoothed her hair, catching a few fine strands and tucking them back into the ribbon tied at the base of her neck. She picked up her hat and carefully placed it on her head, setting it just right with her hatpin. She took a deep breath. 'Right,' she said out loud, 'what will be, will be.'

Hannah ran out of the lodge and shouted, 'Jack, where are you? The stage is here.'

He appeared carrying a pile of wood, unable to control his beaming smile. 'So it is. Let me put these down.'

'Smarten yourself up. Do you want our daughter to think her father is a scruff?'

Jack laughed as he brushed himself down.

'It feels like forever since we last saw her,' Hannah said to Jack as he opened the gates. The coachman secured the reins and the dust from the road settled. They both struggled to catch a glimpse of Anne as the driver jumped down and opened the door and placed a small set of steps in front of it. He gave his hand to Anne to help her down. Hannah put her arm in Jack's and squeezed it as she whispered, 'She's gained poise and confidence since we last saw her. She's grown more beautiful.'

'Well, she's nineteen now and is a beauty like her mother.'

'Oh, you old flatterer,' Hannah said over her shoulder as she ran to embrace her daughter. Jack followed and watched with pleasure as the two women hugged, kissed and laughed.

Anne looked over her mother's shoulder and said, 'Papa!' She walked to him and he took her in his arms as if she was the most delicate and precious piece of glass. She kissed his cheek. 'It's good to be here, a family once more. I've missed you and Mama so much.'

'My darling girl, not half as much as we've missed you. Welcome. Welcome to Oatlands, your new home,' he said as he helped the driver unload Anne's two boxes from the roof of the coach.

Anne looked around and her eye rested on the massive gates every visitor had to pass through to gain admittance. Then she took in the two lodge houses either side of the gates and the trees stretching into the distance. Jack followed her gaze. 'Our house is this one here,' he gestured with his arm, 'and Oatlands itself is straight ahead though it is hidden by the trees.'

'But enough of that,' Hannah interrupted, 'you will see it all later. First, let's go inside and have something to eat. You must be starving.'

Hannah put her arm around Anne and led her towards the lodge. 'We have prepared something special. It's not every day our daughter comes home.'

'Home,' Anne repeated. 'It sounds strange, we haven't all lived in the same place for such a long time.' She wiped away a tear. 'Oh, I am too sentimental.'

'And that is good in one so young. Come, your father will sort out your boxes.'

'But where are the children, Mama?' Anne looked around. 'I expected excited little people getting in the way and making a lot of noise.'

'They're at school in the village but are very excited to see you. I don't think the teacher will get any attention from them today.' They walked through the gates laughing at Hannah's joke when a woman suddenly appeared through the front door of the other lodge. Anne felt her mother's hand tighten on her shoulder. 'Ah, Mrs White, meet our daughter, Anne. Anne, this is Mrs White, the wife of the other porter here. He shares duties with your father.'

The woman looked frightened as she bobbed a curtsey and Anne curtsied back. She looks half-starved, thought Anne. And unkempt. She smelt bad too, which Anne tried to ignore.

A boy of about three ran out of the open door and ran into his mother's skirts when he saw Anne. Another boy ran after him and then another. All were close in age. The older boy stared rudely at Anne and this upset Mrs White, who looked embarrassed by her boys.

'I'm sorry, Mrs Dresser, the boys are energetic today.' Her shoulders slumped. She looked exhausted and unwell. 'I will try and keep them in order,' she said but her voice lost momentum.

'You really should put them into the school in the village, Mrs White. They accept the little one's too in a nursery class. It will give you some respite.'

Mrs White looked horrified at the suggestion and glanced towards her front door as her husband appeared in the doorway. Anne could see he was powerfully built but had a pronounced limp. He was well turned out, freshly shaved and looked well in his porter's uniform.

'Get in the house and keep those boys in order,' he hissed at his wife who looked terrified as she ushered them indoors. 'I told you to keep them inside today.'

Anne's hackles rose at the way this man spoke to his wife in public. She'd seen it many times before, of course, but she didn't expect it at Oatlands.

She bobbed an abrupt curtsy to him and mumbled, 'Pleased to meet you,' not meaning a word of it.

'Aye, you too, daughter of the house.'

Anne didn't like the way his eyes lingered over her and said, 'Come, Mama. Let's go inside.'

As they entered Anne whispered, 'What an awful man. And I am shocked to find such a strange and pathetic woman here. She looks more like a street woman worn down before her time than the wife of a servant here. I thought the duke only employed the best and looked after his staff?'

'Indeed. We are wondering the same. The poor woman is mistreated by her husband, nothing new there, but not here at Oatlands. I worry for her and the children's health. I feel obliged to help her but your father says we must not interfere between a man and his wife. But I do worry that she needs someone to help her.'

'But not us, Hannah, my love,' Jack said struggling in with Anne's large box and a smaller one balanced on the top. He set them down in a corner and looked at his wife and daughter. 'We must stay out of it. We cannot afford to become involved in anything that might jeopardise our position here. The duke has his own reasons for employing White. It is not for us to reason why. We must protect ourselves first and foremost. Now, let's forget about them, at least for today.'

Anne became aware of the most delicious aroma and took a deep breath. 'My, that smells good.'

'Beef and kidney pie and thick pea soup – your favourites,' her mother said.

'And there is fruit cake for afterwards,' her father added giving Anne a surreptitious wink.

She laughed. 'Your favourite, too, I seem to remember.' She gave him a kiss on the cheek. 'It's so good to be here. I've missed you all so much.'

'And we've missed you too, my darling girl.'

Jack put an arm over each woman's shoulder. 'It is a dream come true for us, to have you here. I want to pinch myself.'

'Well don't waste time doing that,' Hannah said lightly. 'Take Anne's cape and hat and sit her down while I dish out the soup.'

Time passed in a haze of good humour with everyone tripping over each others' conversation in their eagerness to chat.

'That was delicious,' Anne said mopping the last of her soup with a hunk of bread.

'Wait until you taste your mother's pie, she has been fussing over it for hours,' Jack said with wry amusement.

'Oh, you.' Hannah gave an ineffectual swipe of her arm at Jack as she hardly contained her grin of total pleasure.

As they ate the rest of the meal Anne asked about Oatlands.

'Well, you will work for Mrs Harley, she is the housekeeper,' said Jack. 'She is a strong disciplinarian but I believe she is fair.'

'I like her,' Hannah said. 'She has an air of a lady and she keeps everyone in their place and that is how it should be in a house of this kind. You don't want it too lax as people take advantage. A soft housekeeper means a badly run house, in my opinion,' she added with a nod.

'I agree,' Anne said. 'I like a strong housekeeper, but sometimes they put the fear of God into one.'

43

She paused. 'I have to admit to feeling nervous.' She looked at both her parents. 'I so want to do well.'

'And you will,' Jack said.

'Yes, indeed you will,' her mother confirmed, taking her hand. 'Don't worry it will be strange until you get to know everyone. But they are all nice here, on the whole, don't you think, Jack?'

'Mmm, maybe, but there are one or two I wouldn't give rope to.'

'Oh!'

'Don't take any notice of your father, it's his army experience. He sees things in people that I do not see.'

'Well, your mother may be right. But if you have any trouble – any at all – you come to me.' He looked at her. 'You understand?'

'I will. Thank you, that is reassuring.'

Jack looked at his fob watch. 'They'll be finishing up their dinner in the servants' hall soon and I'd like to show you a bit of the grounds as we walk to the house. The housekeeper said she would see you after dinner so we have time. It's only a five-minute walk from here to the house.'

As they came out of the lodge they veered left, passing the group of oak trees that hid the house from view and followed the winding driveway. Anne breathed in the clear air of the expansive gardens and before long the house came into view. The sun shone down on it accentuating the classical symmetry and strict proportions of a Palladian style manor house. Flat fronted with no decoration.

Anne gasped. 'Oh, Papa, it's so beautiful. It's like a gem of civilisation in the naturalness of the surrounding parkland.'

Jack laughed. 'You're like a poet. I didn't know

you had that talent.'

Anne frowned with concentration. 'What I mean is that we are surrounded by nothing but dense woodland and here is something made by man that is exquisite in architecture … the Palladian style is so elegant … plain, but by its very plainness, elegant. But it is much smaller than I had imagined.'

'It's big enough when you get closer. There is a lot of it at the rear and sides which you cannot see from here. But small or not the duke liked it enough to want to live here and for that we should be grateful.'

'Oh, I am, Papa, I am. Be in no doubt.'

Jack strode over to a large tree that grew as wide as it was high. Its thick, long, low branches seemed to reach out as if they wanted to shake your hand. 'Look here. King Charles the first's youngest son was born here at Oatlands well over one hundred years ago and the king planted this tree to commemorate his birth and thereafter the son was known as Henry of Oatlands. It is real history that, although the Oatlands in those days was a real palace, fit for a king. Henry the eighth built it and hunted here on the vast estate and so did Queen Elizabeth, she loved it here so I understand, and then the Stuarts and then Charles the first was kept prisoner here before his execution, and … oh, I could go on, but in brief, Anne my sweet, I can see you are looking a little bored by my enthusiasm,' he laughed, 'in a nutshell Oatlands Palace was demolished just after Charles was executed and then Oliver Cromwell and his Protectorate destroyed anything that remained except for a hunting lodge. The estate was sold to a Robert Turbridge and went through various owners until the Duke of Newcastle rebuilt it as you see here keeping the name of Oatlands.' He looked at Anne and smiled. 'A grand house but not a palace.'

She nodded smiling at her father. 'You always did love history, you make things so interesting. And indeed, the tree is unusual. The leaves are – well – not quite like leaves I've ever seen before … like needles, I suppose.' She looked at it more closely. 'And the bark is unusual too: sort of knobbly.'

'A cedar tree from Lebanon, so I understand.'

'I've never heard of such a tree.'

'Well, you are at Oatlands, now, my darling girl. It's likely you will see many unusual things.'

Anne looked from the tree to the house and back to her father who was leaning with his hand on the trunk. 'You look like a man of substance, as if you belong here,' she said smiling. 'I can see you are proud of this place.'

'I am. I never forget my poor beginnings and hope you will not either. Your mother and I have worked hard for our family, pushed ourselves and improved ourselves as best we could. And look where we are now: serving royalty. I think that's something to be proud of.'

Anne stood on tiptoe and kissed him on the cheek. 'I'll never forget it, Papa, don't fret.'

They walked on and came to another bend in the driveway opening out into a vista of green grassy banks. The rear of the house stood on top of the banks looking down to a large lake, its waters stretching into the distance.

Anne gasped. 'It's magnificent: so calm. The water is so smooth … like a mirror.'

'Aye, and look, can you see?' he said pointing. 'There are fairy sunbeams dancing on the top of the water.'

Anne laughed. 'It's magic all right.'

'The River Thames is just over there,' he said pointing, 'and there,' he pointed again, 'is the grotto. Now, that *is* a magic building. I'm sure you'll agree when you see it. But we cannot go today as we have no time, and it's not encouraged for staff to go there. But we'll go one day.'

Anne squinted into the distance. A strange, rickety looking building stood atop a knoll, squat, round, with mullioned windows that didn't match. Sunlight glistened off the water surrounding it. 'What a strange place, I'll look forward to exploring it. But I have to admit something to you.'

'Oh?'

'I cannot take my eyes away from this beauty around us. I want to look at it forever!'

'You and me both, but never fear, your home is here now and you will have many years to feast on it.'

'My nerves are being soothed already by this place. I'm so grateful to you for getting me this position.'

'We only recommended you, remember. You got the position yourself.'

A servant came hurrying along the pathway from the house, 'Mr Dresser,' she said, 'quickly, please. Mrs Harley is ready to receive the young lady. She's waiting.'

Father and daughter exchanged a look, pride from Jack and anxiety from Anne. 'You'll be all right,' he said as they hastened to the side of the house and Jack left Anne at the servants' entrance. 'You go with Joyce here,' he said, 'she'll take care of you – you will, won't you, Joyce? You know, show her what's what.'

'Yes, Mr Dresser, but Mrs Harley is waiting, we

must hurry.'

Jack pecked Anne on the cheek. 'Good luck.'

*

As Anne stepped over the threshold of the servants' entrance for the first time a cold chill met her causing her nerves to dance unpleasantly. The reality hit her as she entered the long, narrow, flag-stoned corridor, the cold exacerbated by the dark green tiles that reached half way up the walls. Joyce, a robust, well-built girl with an elegance that belied her size, took her along the corridor at a fast pace, her footsteps echoing. Anne glanced to her right into what was obviously the kitchen before finding herself in front of a door on the left-hand side of the passage.

'This is where the housekeeper has her rooms,' Joyce said. 'You don't go in here unless you knock and are invited in by Mrs Harley. And you never knock unless it is so urgent she needs to be disturbed – on pain of death,' she added with raised eyebrows as she knocked on the large, polished oak door.

Anne nodded and swallowed hard as a voice from within called, 'Enter.'

Joyce went in first and announced, 'Anne Dresser to see you, Mrs Harley.' Anne's stomach lurched as she entered, unsure what to expect after her parents' assessment of the housekeeper. As Joyce left and clicked the door softly behind her, Anne stomach rose into her throat. Mrs Harley looked up from her sizeable desk and moved some papers she was working on into a neat pile and put them on the edge of her desk where they joined several similar piles. Anne had time to take in the large room and the quality furnishings, including a deep blue velvet armchair and sofa and Anne almost laughed as she thought she would disappear if she sat there as her dress was the same shade, but she kept her face neutral as her eye swept over the marble fireplace with the fire laid but not lit, and a mahogany bookcase full of books. This last item filled her with envy as she loved to read and had often 'borrowed' a book from her previous employer's library, returning it surreptitiously. She'd never been caught, but doubted she'd get away with it with Mrs Harley.

She wondered at the opulence of the room, so different to the housekeeper's at her previous house.

'Ah, yes, Anne Dresser,' Mrs Harley said. 'Come in, child. Come in.' Her voice was deep for a woman's and full of confidence. Anne wondered about her background.

'Good day, Mrs Harley,' Anne replied as she moved further into the room and dropped a curtsy and felt her knees wobble.

The housekeeper stood up. She was a tall woman in her thirties whose strong, intense features were highlighted by the lightness of her hair pulled into a no-nonsense bun at the back of her head. 'Welcome to Oatlands,' she said in a voice full of authority. 'We need to go over a few things.' She looked closely at Anne. 'You are aware that you are very lucky to be a servant here. The duke values his servants and treats them well.'

'Yes, Mrs Harley.'

She looked searchingly into Anne's eyes. 'He expects total loyalty from you in return. You look after the duke's best interests and he will look after yours – within our stations in life, of course, you understand.'

'Yes, Mrs Harley.' Anne controlled her nerves.

'Your father is well respected by the staff and I hope it will be the same with you, Anne Dresser.'

'Yes, I hope so too. I will do my best.'

'Please make sure that you do. Now, you understand that when the duke is in residence, as he is now, the staff are very busy. People from high society accompany him and there are many parties. The duke's brother, the Prince of Wales, will be here from time to time. It is my job to train you to serve such distinguished people as our future king and his companions.' She paused, as if expecting an answer.

'Yes, Mrs Harley,' Anne said quickly.

The housekeeper looked down at a letter on her desk. 'You have an excellent recommendation from your previous employer, who especially praises your needlework skills. Exceptional, it says here.' She looked up and her gaze was penetrating. Anne shuffled slightly uncomfortable with the intensity of the gaze. I wouldn't like to cross you, she thought.

The housekeeper tapped the letter thoughtfully with her index finger. 'You will be in high demand if you are as skilled as is implied here,' but said no more on the subject. 'Now,' the word came out like an order, 'you are used to high society, but not as high as this.'

'No, Mrs Harley.' Anne tried to swallow but her mouth was too dry.

'As you will be a maid working above stairs, I expect a high level of competence and behaviour from you. Do the work as I have instructed. Remember, I will be checking it.'

Anne's hackles bristled. She objected to being treated like a novice. She was an experienced housemaid and had given good service to Sir Arthur for the past seven years. She'd never had any complaints. Royal dust and mess was the same as anybody else's. She tried to curb her thoughts, realising they wouldn't do her any good here. She mustn't get above herself even if she felt it was justified. I'm too touchy; it's just nerves she thought as Mrs Harley misconstrued.

'Don't look so worried. You won't get into trouble, not as long as you do your best and learn.'

Anne chastised herself for allowing her thoughts to show on her face, but then relaxed a little. Was there a hint of kindness in the housekeeper? Had she misjudged her?

'Thank you, Mrs Harley.'

'Now, Oatlands is a small house for someone of such high status as the duke, but it is still a large house to look after. It has twelve bedrooms as well as the servants' quarters. The main rooms include, the ballroom which is used for many kinds of events, the green room is used for the duke's comfort and casual entertaining of his close friends, the study and the duke's office, the withdrawing room, the dining room and adjoining card room, the library and, the duke's pride and joy, the armoury. But you won't be involved with the armoury and just as well as it's not a relaxing place with all those implements of war and torture. But we won't say anything more about that,' she said dismissively. 'There's over 3,000 acres of land, mostly woodland and some common land. This area is not good for farming and has been used for hunting mostly through the ages.' She looked down and smiled slightly, showing, Anne thought, a lighter side. 'Queen Elizabeth used to love to hunt here, you know, and her father, Henry Vlll.' Mrs Harley gave a slight sigh as if coming back into reality. 'But enough of that, the duke is the person who matters to us and he too, loves to hunt here. No doubt there will be many a hunting party for us to look forward to.' Anne thought Mrs Harley looked as if a hunting party was the last thing she looked forward to. 'There are two kitchens, one for preparing the servants' food and the other for the duke's food. You do not enter the duke's kitchen,' she looked up, 'is that clear?'

'Yes, Mrs Harley.'

'You will share a room with Joyce in the attic. She's senior upstairs maid. You will both keep it clean at all times. Your uniform will always be spotless and freshly ironed. You'll have a spare uniform and make sure that the dirty one is immediately sent to the laundry maids as soon as you change into your clean one.'

'Yes, Mrs Harley.'

'Mr Tucker is our steward and in charge of everything to do with the house and the estate. You have already met him together with the duke. But you have not yet met our butler, Mr Sweetman. Mr Sweetman and I work under Mr Tucker, but I want to make it very clear that if you have any problems, you come to *me* first. I will decide who needs to be informed after that. Is that clear?'

'Yes, Mrs Harley.'

'Do you have any questions?'

Anne had many but Mrs Harley scared her so she didn't want to linger.

'No, Mrs Harley,' she said, hoping that Joyce would help her get familiar with the way things were done.

'Then that will be all for now. Go to the servants'

kitchen and see Joyce. She will take you to your room and give you your uniform. She will arrange for your boxes to be taken up. You will start work tomorrow morning at five sharp. I will meet you at that time in the kitchen to take you through your duties. That is all.'

'Yes, Mrs Harley.' Anne bobbed a curtsey and left the room with relief.

As Anne entered the large servants' kitchen she first noticed the long wooden table which dominated the room and the shiny glare of the copper pots and pans neatly stored on the shelves around the walls. Joyce was sitting at the table drinking tea. 'She didn't eat you, did she?' She winked at a dark, swarthy young man who was stirring a big caldron of broth on the range with an oversized wooden spoon. 'This is Anne Dresser, Mr Pierre. Anne, this is the duke's assistant cook, Mr Pierre Pierre.'

'Pierre Pierre, at your service,' he said in a strong French accent, bowing extravagantly as he waved the spoon around in an arc.

'Careful of him,' laughed Joyce. 'He thinks he can charm the birds out of the trees and you'll join a long list of heartaches.'

A strong-looking middle aged man in a spotless white apron came in from an adjoining room. 'Less of this nonsense. Get on with your work, Pierre.'

'This is Mr Lange, the duke's cook,' Joyce said quickly, standing up and looking chastised. 'Mr Lange, this is the new housemaid, Anne Dresser.'

'Pleased to make your acquaintance, young Anne, but I warn you, stay out of my way while I am creating and you and I will get along.' His half-smile took the edge off his words but Anne could tell he was not someone she wanted to upset.

'Yes, Mr Lange. I'll do my best.'

'Mr Lange likes order in his kitchen,' Joyce said. 'He is the duke's special cook and he and Mr Pierre go with the duke from his London house to here and back again. Mr Lange has his own kitchen,' she nodded her head in the direction he had appeared from. She whispered, 'Better keep out of his way.' Out loud she added, 'We have a woman from the village who cooks for the staff in this kitchen, but Mr Pierre helps her sometimes. Staff eat breakfast in the servants' hall, she pointed to a room off the kitchen, at eight and dinner at midday. Tea is at four and supper time changes depending on what is happening with the duke but is usually about nine and is always cold. Better make sure you're not late. Mr Sweetman gets angry if we delay mealtimes. Whatever you're doing make sure you finish it by those times.'

'Mr Lange,' Pierre said, giving Anne a lingering look, smiling and expanding his right arm in a circle, still clutching his wooden spoon, 'is the creator of magic; the wizard extraordinaire; the envy of other cooks.'

Joyce and Pierre laughed, so Anne took her cue from them and laughed too. Maybe Mr Lange would not be such an ogre, she thought, for he smiled.

'I'll take you to our room,' Joyce said. 'I'll introduce you to the rest of the staff at teatime.'

Anne followed as they went up the stairs. 'Mr Lange is a renowned cook,' Joyce said. 'He's sought after by many and chosen by the duke, so he has high status. Never forget that.' She stopped and turned to Anne, whispering, 'And be careful around him as he is friendly towards the girls but can be very harsh with the male staff. He can turn a little nasty when under pressure and be very demanding, so you have been warned. But Mr Pierre is sweet, although he is a terrible flirt, just like a Frenchman! But he's harmless.'

'I hope so,' Anne responded with feeling.

Joyce looked at her curiously but didn't say anything. She continued climbing, saying, 'Remember this way as the staff will be too busy to show you if you get lost and there are a lot of stairs. Now here, at the top of the first flight is the door to the corridor that takes you into the main part of the house. You will use this entrance when you do your work. The duke is in residence until the end of the week so make sure you never meet him. If you see him, or any of his guests, you get out of the way fast. They do not want to see housemaids.'

'I am used to this kind of work,' Anne said, irritated. 'It was the same system in my old house.' She calmed herself. Joyce was only trying to be helpful. She mustn't get off on the wrong foot. 'How long have you been here?' she asked.

'A few months. I worked in a good house in London, but I really fancied coming to the clean air of the country.' She turned to Anne and lowered her voice again. 'The status of working for royalty was also something I really fancied and my employer is a friend of the duke's and he recommended me. I think you'll be all right here, Anne, it's a good place to work,' she added, continuing the climb.

'Did anyone else come from London?'

'Mr Sweetman did. He was under butler at the same household as me but is now our butler. He's a good one as far as I'm concerned. Don't upset him and you'll be all right.' She paused as they reached the top. 'This door leads to the bedrooms and the same rules apply as to the rooms downstairs. No guests ever use these back stairs and you never use the front stairs of the house as they are for guests only. Once you get to know your way around you can get to any part of the house without being seen unless you are very careless. And then, Mrs Harley will have your guts for garters.'

'Did Mrs Harley come from the duke's London house?'

'No, she worked for another large house as housekeeper but it was a big step up for her to work here. I'd keep out of her way as much as possible if I were you. She's got to prove her worth and is strict but she's fair as long as you do your work to her specifications. At least, that's what I think, but some of the other housemaids don't agree. They've got on the wrong side of her. She has her own ways of doing things and whatever you learned before try to forget it and do it her way and you'll be all right.'

'I'll stay out of her way as much as possible, then.'

'Now,' Joyce said as she glanced up at a narrower staircase leading up to the attics. 'These are the stairs up to the women servants' quarters. The footmen have quarters downstairs off the kitchens. They keep us separated, thank goodness.'

Yes, indeed, Anne thought to herself. She was immensely grateful to someone's thoughtfulness or foresight. It made for a much easier life.

Joyce raised her skirts up in an elegant manner and started up the stairs at a good speed which Anne had no trouble emulating. At the top, they walked down a long, uncarpeted corridor with rooms only on the left-hand side. She opened the door to the room at the end. 'You will share this room with me.'

It was small and bare, with whitewashed walls and a sloping roof. Two narrow beds sat close together, facing the door, each with a grey blanket and eiderdown over the top. The beds were divided by a low cabinet set against the wall.

'I consider myself lucky I was allocated this room. It is colder than the other rooms because it's on the end, but for me, the view is worth the cold,' she said, nodding to the solitary, small window in the end wall. 'I sit here sometimes in the early morning and watch the moon light up the lake. It's magic.'

'It is wonderful,' Anne said as she looked out over the gardens and the lake. In her mind, she could still see herself and her father standing under the tree, admiring the view. 'Yes, wonderful.' She sighed. 'Thank you so much for explaining things and, like you, I am very pleased to be in this room … a room with a view!'

Joyce smiled. 'Indeed. I'm glad you appreciate it, too.'

'I'm sure we shall get on,' Anne said, smiling back. She felt her spirits lift after her anxiety over her conversation with Mrs Harley.

'I'm sure we shall,' Joyce said kindly. 'Now, we have clean sheets every month. Your bed is the one furthest from the window. Keep your things in your chest on your side of the bed, please. Your two uniforms are there hanging on the hooks in the wall. Keep hold of your coat hangers as they tend to go missing for some strange reason and you need them to ensure your uniform is aired properly. Whoever is up first, washes first,' Joyce said with a grin.

'Then that'll be me, I think, as I always like to be

earlier rather than later.'

'Thank goodness for that,' Joyce laughed. 'I'm the opposite and have such trouble getting out of bed. By the way, I'm sure I don't need to tell you, but don't let any guests – especially the duke– see you looking out of the window.'

'No, indeed,' Anne chuckled. 'I'd be for the chop if they thought I was spying on them.'

'Well, thank goodness we don't behead anyone these days, but you've got the right idea.'

'I understand. And thank you for all you've told me. I do appreciate your trouble.'

'Well, we have to live together now,' Joyce said warmly, 'may as well make it as best we can for each other. I'll leave you now to have a rest and settle in. Come down to the servants' hall for tea at four and you can meet the rest of the staff. Oh, and don't forget to put your uniform on, it'll make you more one of us.'

Anne remembered some of the women servants at her old employers' house and realised what a breath of fresh air her new companion was.

*

Just before teatime, Anne made her way down to the servants' hall near the kitchens. Joyce had also explained to her that she should use the above-stairs servants' hall where they would have their meals and use it for relaxing whenever they got the time. The below-stairs staff shared a different servants' hall on the other side of the kitchens. Everyone, Joyce had warned her, is expected to respect the privacy of each. Do not go into theirs and they will not come into yours. Above stairs staff enjoy a higher level of prestige than below stairs staff. We want to keep it that way,' she'd added with a wink.

Joyce's words echoed in Anne's ears as she made sure she entered the right room. Her nerves were jangling as she hated meeting lots of new people at the same time and they increased as she heard the noisy chatter coming from the room. The door was open and, from a distance, she peered inside. Yes, right place, she could see Joyce. She paused by the side of the door to compose herself thinking, come on get it over with. She took a deep breath and walked through the doorway. A silence fell as the others scrutinised her. Taking another deep breath, she stood straighter and smiled as she looked around. Her mother had always told her to look confident even if she didn't feel it.

'Ah, Anne Dresser, I presume,' the butler said, 'come in. Everyone, this is Anne Dresser, our new housemaid. This is your assigned chair,' he said, pointing to a vacant chair at the end of the row. 'Please keep to it.'

Anne knew that she would be given the least important place at table as she was the newest member of staff. The other maids would come before her unless she got a promotion; therefore she sat furthest from the butler who sat at the head of the table. She noticed Mrs Harley sat next to Mr Sweetman on his right, and on his left, she assumed, was the under butler. The other four footmen sat opposite each other next to the under butler and Mrs Harley. The maids too sat opposite each other, the staff on the right of Mr Sweetman had precedence over staff on the left of him. Anne was on the left.

'Now, I will introduce you,' the butler continued and smiled at Anne kindly, 'but I don't expect you will remember all the names.'

'But we'll remember yours,' whispered one footman to another.

'No whispering, Charles,' the butler said in a no-nonsense tone.

Mmm, Anne thought, Charles. He must be the number one footman. My instincts tell me I need to keep clear of him as much as possible.

'No, sir, Mr Sweetman, sir,' Charles said with a straight face as he surreptitiously winked at Anne.

Oh, no, not again, Anne thought. She was determined that her beauty, which she regarded as a curse, would not determine her life this time. She'd had enough trouble in her previous place with the men on both sides of the social divide. She gave Charles the benefit of the disdainful look she'd perfected over the years and felt a glow inside when he looked shocked.

'Now everyone, let Anne settle in and eat her tea', the butler warned, 'she doesn't want all of you asking her questions all the time. You can chatter in your own time.'

Anne silently thanked him and gave him a grateful smile.

*

The next morning, Anne was in the kitchen at four fifty-five awaiting Mrs Harley. She'd made sure her uniform was perfect with her long white apron tied around the waist of her maroon dress with its wide skirt. Her uniform had been especially made for her in London and fitted perfectly. The bodice was not too tight and the waist had enough play to enable bending in comfort.

Mrs Harley appeared at five exactly. 'Good morning, Anne. Turn round for me please.' She examined Anne's appearance. 'Good. Now I want you to forget the way you did everything at your previous place and remember to do things the way I show you. Do you understand?'

'Yes, Mrs Harley.' Anne bobbed a curtsey.

'Now, your duties are above stairs, so your person will be clean and tidy at all times. You will do all your duties before the duke or his guests are up in the mornings. In the unlikely event you hear them coming when you are still about your duties, then you leave the room by another door. You do not come into contact with your betters, do you understand?'

'Yes, Mrs Harley,' Anne said as sweetly as could. She remembered Joyce's words and wanted to stay on the right side of the housekeeper.

Indicating with a sweeping arm, Mrs Harley continued, 'These are your brushes, pans and buckets. There are different kinds for different cleaning jobs. I will explain these as we go along. You will always take them with you when you clean. They are your re-sponsibility and for your sole use so keep them clean and in good condition or I'll know the reason why. This is my own rule here as I feel it gives maids a sense of pride,' she said rather pompously. She looked at Anne with a questioning look.

'Yes, indeed, so, Mrs Harley,' Anne said hurriedly.

This satisfied the housekeeper and she picked up a three-arm candle holder to light the way along the corridors and stairs. As they entered the spacious dining room the housekeeper used the candles to light the two large candelabras either end of the room and some of the wall lights, enough for them to see what work had to be done. 'The footmen will have already cleared the table the night before and taken the used candelabras to be cleaned and replaced them with clean ones for us to use.'

As the candles caught, the flickering light gave the dark room an eerie look with many pockets of shade dancing along the walls. Anne started slightly until she realised the looming shadows were nothing more frightening than furniture. The candlelight flickered and sparkled off the surface of the large mahogany table in the centre of the room and Anne's spirits fell when she saw it. All that polishing! As if Mrs Harley could read her mind, she said, 'You make sure this dining table is polished well. Do not miss any parts of it.'

'Yes, Mrs Harley.'

'Now, you can see that the walls here are painted in a very light shade of blue. You must check every morning that there have been no stains deposited,' she cleared her throat, 'accidentally or otherwise on the walls. You understand me?'

Anne's mind whirled with possible reasons for such action, none of them pleasant, and thought it was not like this at her last house. But all she said was, 'Yes, Mrs Harley,' and hoped for the best.

The housekeeper walked to the windows. 'The drapery here is magnificent, as you see.' She pulled aside the heavy, deep green curtains of one of the windows and tied them up neatly to the side. 'Take note of how I do this as I will expect the curtains to be drawn expertly and neatly every morning.'

'Yes, Mrs Harley.'

'When you've done that you open the shutters and secure them back and open the window to air the room. How far you open them depends on the weather.' She looked at Anne.

'Yes, Mrs Harley.' Anne tried to sound positive but it was getting harder. She knew all this, she wasn't a novice.

'You will be responsible for this room and the rooms either side of it. You will clean the fireplaces and lay the fires and light them in cold weather. Make sure you do not get the fireplace cleaning equipment mixed up with the other equipment.' The housekeeper gave Anne a glare.

'Yes, Mrs Harley.'

'You will dust the rooms and sweep the floors. As you can see this room is fully carpeted as all the major rooms here, make sure you get up all the detritus and pay particular attention to under the table and chairs. It can get messy after dinner parties and you have to leave it spotlessly clean. Fortunately, we have a Turkish rug under the table.' Anne thought Mrs Harley pronounced Turkish rug as if it was the most astonishing thing in the world. She swore she almost genuflected. Anne stifled a laugh and mentally shook herself. 'That is convenient,' Mrs Harley was droning on, 'for us as you can take it up with the help of the footmen to clean every week. But I'll advise you on that process later.

'I have allocated these rooms to you as I was given good reports from your previous house about your attention to detail.' She didn't pause for breath. 'You will put the chairs back neatly and dust all services in the manner I will show you.'

Doesn't this woman ever ease up?

'That's all the daily jobs gone through, we will do the special cleaning of drapery, carpets, paintings and the like another day. After you have finished here, breakfast will be at eight and then you will help the other housemaids with cleaning as instructed. Bedrooms are cleaned when the occupier is downstairs partaking of breakfast or otherwise when they are not in their rooms. There will be many rooms to clean when we have guests. You will make sure the rooms are aired properly, empty the chamber pots into the slop bucket, clean them and make the beds, dust and tidy, and all other cleaning duties. You will not handle the clothes of the guests, their valet or lady's maid will take care of those things. Make sure that they have gone in before you and taken care of the clothes.' She looked at Anne expectantly.

'Yes, Mrs Harvey, I understand,' Anne said quickly as she discovered a desire to throttle the woman.

'Good. After lunch we take care of sewing and lighter chores in the servants' hall as instructed. You will be on hand in the evenings to help in whatever way Mr Sweetman or myself require.' Mrs Harley nodded to herself as if well pleased with her delivery. 'I endeavour to give everyone an hour to themselves in the afternoons. You may retire to your room then to take a rest. If you have any problems you come to me. Not to Mr Sweetman or to any of the other staff. You come to *me,* is that understood?'

'Yes, Mrs Harley,' Anne said with some relief.

'Good, then let's start in the dining room first.'

By the end of the morning, Anne knew her duties and how to perform them to Mrs Harley's satisfaction. As she carried them out in front of the housekeeper's keen eye she had fought not to show her irritation and tumbling thoughts at being retrained to do menial tasks she had been doing for years. Lighting fires and cleaning rooms after other people's excesses were not her ideal way to spend her life. If she *had* to be in service, she would have chosen to be a footman serving at dinner, then she could listen to the conversations and understand how the other half lives and thinks but it was the thinking that really interested her. She had a very good idea of how they lived, and even how they loved, as you get to see many things as a servant of a great house. She had learned to swallow down her disgust at the waste of life and money and privileges most of her 'betters' displayed. She knew she had a mind equal – if not superior – to most of the men she encountered, whatever their social status. She had to swallow the bitter fact that being a woman, especially a woman of her low class, deprived her of any true worth. She didn't want to be angry, but it was hard sometimes. Her beauty didn't help and it was early in her life that she began to regard it a curse because it attracted men who relished pushing themselves and their stupid opinions onto her, regardless of her feelings, which were irrelevant to them. She was ambitious and wanted so much more from life than a man and marriage although she had learned to her cost to keep those kinds of thoughts to herself. But she was at Oatlands now, and would do her very best to make her life as successful as she could.

CHAPTER THREE

A few days later, during Anne's afternoon leisure time, Jack arranged to meet her just outside the lodge. He called out, 'Over here, Anne.'

She rushed over to her father and couldn't take the worry from her voice. 'Are you sure it's all right to do this? I don't want to get dismissed before I've even started.'

'Don't worry the duke is not in residence so no one will know.'

'Well, if you're sure, I only have an hour's leisure time you know. I have to be back by then.'

'Well, stop talking and take my arm. The sooner we get there the sooner we'll be back.'

With misgivings, Anne did as she was bid and they made their way over the undulating grassland. 'You'll love this place. It's magical. I guarantee you've never seen anything like it.'

'You certainly like it, Papa. I'm full of curiosity even though I'm not sure of the wisdom going there just now.'

Jack ignored her doubts. 'Look, there it is,' he pointed, 'the grotto. Won't be long now,' he hurried her along. 'It took eleven years to build. Eleven years! And cost £24,000!' He shook his head in disbelief.

'That's more than you could earn in twenty-four

lifetimes.'

Jack grinned at her. 'That's my girl. You always were excellent at mental arithmetic. You haven't lost your touch.'

She smiled with fondness at her father. 'I was taught well, as you well know. But you seem to know a lot about the grotto.'

'I do. I fell under its charms instantly and I was talking to Mr Tucker about it. He said the previous owner built the grotto and his steward kept an account book with all the details of the building works entered into it. As steward to the duke, Mr Tucker has inherited the book and we went through it together as he is as keen as me on the grotto.' They emerged from the trees into a tiny clearing. 'Here we are, look, it's on two floors and has three rooms downstairs and a large round room upstairs.'

Anne stopped to take in the strange appearance of the place. 'It looks like the house that Jack built,' she said. 'What on earth is it made of? I've never seen such a material before.'

'It's meant to look like a cave on a seashore and is built in brick but covered in a knobbly limestone to look like a cave. Look there,' he pointed, 'you can see large fossils, ammonites I think they're called, and sea urchins imbedded into it.'

Anne's eyes were wide. 'I've never heard of those things or seen anything like them before. How extraordinary. They're like something not of this world.'

'Wait till you see the inside. Come on let's go in,' Jack said getting more enthusiastic. 'You'll never believe it. Come on.'

Anne couldn't help laughing at her father's

enthusiasm; he was like a little boy with a new toy although she didn't dare say so. But she was curious, very much so.

'Now, Anne,' Jack said standing at the entrance, 'there are two entrances, one either end. But we'll start here at this entrance. Follow me,' he said disappearing around a corner.

Anne took a few steps inside and waited until her eyes adjusted to the gloom. She put her hand out to steady herself, 'Ouch!' she shouted as she quickly took her hand off the wall. Her father appeared from the shadows with two lit candles, one in each hand making him look like an apparition. Anne jumped. 'You frightened me, Papa, appearing like that,' she said as she licked a graze on her hand.

'Sorry, I didn't mean to frighten you. I suppose I'm so used to this place I forget it can be disconcerting on a first visit. And as you have found out, don't touch the walls they are very rough with all kinds of shells and things.' He gave her a candle. 'But don't worry, there are no ghosts or spirits here, I guarantee it.' He smiled and kissed her cheek and Anne gave him a look that said she didn't quite believe him.

'Look at the walls here, use your candle, yes, see they are inlaid with semi-precious stones. This one here,' he held his candle close to the wall and its flickering light illuminated the colour of the stone, 'is blue-john, it's luminous blue and purple with bands of amber and is the rarest mineral in this country, and this one here,' he lifted his candle a little, 'is spar, there are lots of colours, pink, yellow, green, deep blue and amber.' Jack moved his candle around finding other stones, his excitement increasing. 'And this, look, look,' his candle was flailing around in his excitement, 'this is feldspar and, oh, goodness knows what else, I forget now.'

The laugh in Anne's voice was gentle. 'Well, maybe it's a good job you've forgotten the rest, this is enough information for now. But it is beautiful as you say.'

'You've seen nothing yet, come on, follow me.' He led her around a corner and into a rounded chamber. He lifted up his candle to increase the light.

Anne's eyes open wide in astonishment.

'It's supposed to resemble a subterranean cave dripping with stalactites. Look, here are the red and blue stones again and … and horses' teeth—'

'Horses' teeth?'

'Yes, but without the horses,' Jack laughed, 'and inverted shells and fossils and—'

'What are stalactites?'

'These.' Jack indicated with his free hand at the imitation stalactites that hung in profusion from the ceilings. 'They are strange things that grow deep in caves from minerals or such like brought through from above with dripping water. They take forever to grow this size, so I understand. They have covered these with glistening spar to make them look wet as if underground in their natural state.'

'I'm astounded. I've never seen anything like this … the room is just covered in shells and stones and fossils and,' she twirled around looking at the encrusted walls and ceiling, her candle held aloft, its light highlighting the different colours and textures. 'It's … I don't know … strange and mystical and mysterious and extraordinary! And the colours shine so even in this dimness.'

'That's because of the little windows here with

the stained glass, look, see,' he pointed at several small windows overlooking the pond outside. 'They catch the light and transform it into the mystical and mysterious place you so rightly described.'

Anne looked at her father. 'You are very knowledgeable, Papa. I had no idea just how much you know about the place.'

'I've been here with Mr Tucker on several occasions. As I said, we share a passion for this place and it's all recorded in the book he inherited.'

'I see, well, I'm certainly getting the benefit of your knowledge. Is the rest of it like this?' Anne wasn't sure she liked it but dare not say. She didn't want to spoil it for her father.

'Come and see, let's go to the next room, it's down this winding corridor, stay close to me. The corridors are supposed to confuse you and give a sense of adventure as to where you are going, as if this is being discovered deep underground for the first time and you are the person discovering it. The ceilings are covered in patterns created by selenite, red calcite and … um… wait a minute, I'll remember soon … I know, vitreous blue material. There! I knew I'd remember.'

Anne didn't care if he remembered or not, she was totally overwhelmed as he was talking of things she had never heard of. She clutched her candle tightly, afraid she may drop it and it go out. She didn't admit, even to herself, that she was a little afraid. It was dark in the corridor and she made sure she didn't touch the walls. As she turned the last corner she gasped. Her father was again standing in the middle of a small circular room, holding his candle aloft and grinning from ear to ear.

'This is the duke's gaming room,' he said with pride.

'Gaming room? What do you mean?' She couldn't imagine what on earth would be played here.

'Cards, gambling, you know, things men do.'

'Here? In this tiny little room,' she looked around, 'with walls covered in … in shells and yet more shells and giant shells and …'

'Horses' teeth,' Jack offered.

'But why horses' teeth?'

Jack shrugged. 'Now that is something I don't know.'

'And yet more of those,' she waved above her head, 'those sta … oh, for goodness sake.'

'Stalactites,' Jack said, smiling fondly.

'Yes, those things,' Anne said a little crossly and then laughed at the absurdity of it all.

'But nice, don't you think? Lying here on these large cushions with the fire burning high in the grate and the candles flickering light over the gemstones and the dripping water the only sound apart from your own breathing as you bet a small fortune on the turn of a card.'

'That's a matter of opinion. It wouldn't appeal to me,' she said rather primly.

'Ah, but you are not a man.'

Anne kept her own counsel. She sneezed. 'Good gracious, it is so damp in here it's making me sneeze. It smells of damp and rot and goodness knows what else.'

'But that's the attraction for a man like the duke, roughing it like he was on army manoeuvres again. He's used to this kind of tough living and the comradeship of his fellow soldiers; the drinking, the gambling, the smell of nature.'

Anne couldn't help smiling. 'You seem to want to join in, Papa?'

He smiled and nodded. 'And never will be accepted, and never expect to be either. But as an old army man myself, I can see the nostalgia of it.' He sighed. 'Well, come on let's see the last room. Follow me back down the corridor.' And with that he disappeared and Anne scuttled after him afraid of being left in this strange world that existed in the normality of Oatlands' parkland.

Jack was stood in the middle of a similar size room holding his candle aloft. She was determined not to gasp this time and be prepared for anything. But as the gasp slipped out regardless she realised she was not prepared for this. The temperature in this room was noticeably colder, even though the rest of the grotto was as cold as a mid-winter snowstorm. The room, like the others, had walls covered in shells and the ceiling in stalactites but what she hadn't expected was the giant bath set into the floor. 'I'm sorry, Papa, I seem to be repeating myself, but I have never seen anything like this before. That bath! It's so big, and so deep,' she said as she gingerly walked around it to stand next to her father.

'And it's constantly filled with ice-cold water from the spring. That's why it's tiled, so that no water can seep out into the surrounds.'

She peered into the water. 'It so deep. I should drown for sure if I went in there.'

'Well it's five feet deep so you might just keep your nose above it. It's five feet wide and just under eleven feet long. You can get a fair few people in there at once.'

'All together?' Anne shook her head. 'And ice cold? But why?'

'Good question. I've never understood this fashion for cold water bathing myself. But for the aristocracy it is fashionable and considered very healthy as it is supposed to strengthen the constitution and guarantee good health.' He shivered.

Anne laughed. 'You jest, Papa.'

'No, I'm serious. This is for when the duke and his cronies finish cards and no telling how many bottles of wine and they can strip off and jump in for a frolic in the water. Then out again, dress and run through the parkland to the house and bed.'

Anne bent down carefully and put her hand into the water and drew it out instantly. 'It's freezing.'

'That's what ice-cold means.' Jack smiled at the look on her face.

'All right. I asked for that.' Anne gave her father a kiss on the cheek. 'This statue, is it marble?' she asked nodding in the direction of a statue of a naked woman.

'As far as I know it is. It's Venus.'

'She's mightily big.'

'She is, and stands guard over the bath and every man has to look up to her. It would take several men to move her, I think.'

'Mmm,' Anne said thoughtfully, looking up at Venus's beautiful face and untroubled expression, her smooth, white and unblemished body, a goddess indeed. She wondered why men always had to have a statue of a naked woman around. But all she said was, 'And the walls in here are faced entirely with shells. Tiny ones and slightly bigger ones and then enormous ones, all mixed up.'

73

'Indeed, supposed to represent being tumbled around in the sea, I suppose. And the beauty of it is that the water dripping down from the pipes above mean they never need cleaning. The water does it all.'

Anne shivered.

'You're cold.' Jack put his arm around her shoulder. 'You don't want to catch a cold.'

'It's not only that, if I'm honest,' she hesitated but had to tell him, 'this place is disconcerting. Can we leave now?'

'Really? You do not like it?'

She pondered for a moment. 'I'm not saying that exactly, but it is all very strange, I'll need to get used to it.'

'Well,' Jack said, recovering his enthusiasm, 'let's look at the salon upstairs before we go. If that doesn't make you love the grotto then nothing will. Come, follow me, we need to go up the steps outside.'

As they made their way up, Jack said, 'Be careful, the steps are a bit dangerous and in need of some repair. There's no handrail but as they are only used by servants no one bothers.'

Anne looked up the stone steps attached to the side of the grotto. 'They are dangerous,' she said, carefully making her way up, lifting her skirts to see the crumbling steps more clearly and making sure she kept her balance and not topple off the side. 'But wouldn't the duke repair them if asked? He's not uncaring as we know. At least a handrail would be beneficial.'

'Yes,' Jack answered standing at the top, looking down on Anne. 'But it won't come from me who is not supposed to be here anyway, and I learned to keep a low profile in the army, it is the best way for a peaceful and enjoyable life.' He gave Anne his hand to support her up the last step. 'There is a proper entrance around the back which is used by the duke and guests. But we are not encouraged to use that except when setting up a party and we have lots of things to bring in. This is suitable for access but not when carrying trays etc. Follow me.' He turned and disappeared into a passageway well lighted by circular windows in the ceiling, his excitement lingering in the air behind him.

Anne felt sure she'd seen it all and couldn't be surprised anymore so, as she followed her father, she was determined not to react to whatever lay in store, and especially not to say, oh. She made her way around yet another winding passageway and found herself in the upper chamber. She didn't say anything, of which she was proud, but inside she couldn't stop her brain exclaiming, oh! oh! oh!

It was like coming out of the dark and forbidding caves below and stepping into the lightness of a sweet dream. The shells and jewels and fossils and stalactites and yes, horses' teeth were all here too but also imbedded into the walls were pieces of marble, great chunks of coral branch sticking out at intervals and inset here and there were tiny convex mirrors which gleamed with reflected light and played games with your eyesight. But the room was spacious and round and large enough not to be overpowered by them. You could breathe up here and the air was fresh. The illumination from the large, rounded and coloured leaded light windows in the ceiling coupled with the similar, but long, windows in the outer wall gave the whole room a magical feel. The light focused different colours in different areas from dark purple to blues to pinks and reds which moved around with the passage of the sun. Anne felt uplifted in a strange way, as if she could do anything here. She laughed delightedly.

'Sit down,' Jack encouraged.

'What?' Anne was pulled out of her reverie.

'The chairs,' Jack said, sitting in one of them, 'are made by Chippendale, the sofas too, all gold and fancy and as uncomfortable as hell. But never mind.' He stretched out his legs. 'They are meant to resemble open oysters, so what can you expect. Hard and knobbly oysters are.' He laughed quietly to himself.

'You sit in them?' Anne was amazed at his daring.

'Indeed. Mr Tucker and I have sat here many a time and taken in the atmosphere. It is truly lovely, don't you think?'

'Well, if you and Mr Tucker have sat here I think I can risk it.' But even as she said this she looked around to see if anyone was looking. She sat down opposite her father and fidgeted around. 'I see what you mean, they are truly uncomfortable.'

'Indeed they are, but don't they look wonderful,' he didn't stop for breath, 'and the little tables here made to look like giant inverted shells, all golden and inviting, just waiting for sweetmeats or tiny glasses of port.'

'You have a good imagination, Papa. But yes, I do see what you mean.'

'Your eyes are sparkling, Anne. I can see you have succumbed to the power of the grotto,' he said with satisfaction.

She laughed and the very act of laughing made her feel light and worry free.

'You have won me over, Papa. It *is* a magical and mysterious place and one I could never have believed possible. But it is here, the upper chamber that I love.'

'Well, if you are careful, you can come up here when the duke is not in residence and make sure no one sees you. It will be our little secret. Use the side stairs.'

'But I couldn't. I just couldn't. It wouldn't be right.'

'Come on, Anne, you are too serious sometimes. I would have lost my sanity many a time if I hadn't taken a light-hearted look at some things and this is light-hearted, is it not?'

'It is.'

'Well then.' He looked at his fob watch. 'I think it's time for you to go. You need to be back.'

Anne jumped up, and kissed her father. 'Thank you, Papa, thank you for bringing me here and showing me so well.' She left him there, sprawled in one of the Chippendale chairs, looking well pleased with himself.

CHAPTER FOUR

As Anne was settling in and the December chill winds were flexing their muscles, the Prince of Wales was expected later that day and the household had been in a frenzy of activity preparing everything for days. It was his first visit to Oatlands and Mr Sweetman and Mrs Harley were anxious to impress.

Anne and another maid, Emma, had just finished lighting the fire and completing their chores in the final bedroom they were responsible for when a thunderous sound of horses' hooves clattered and slithered outside. A deep voice shouted, 'Whoa, boys. Whoa, now.'

Anne and Emma rushed to the window to see a lone figure jumping from a high phaeton. The two horses stood with their chests heaving and spittle dripping from their mouths, their eyes wild.

'Oh,' Anne said, 'who would treat horses in such a cruel way? They've been run into the ground. What a horrible man.'

'Be careful what you say. That's the Prince of Wales.'

'What? But it can't be, he's not due until later today and surely he would arrive in a large coach, with footmen and everything? Why would he be arriving like this?'

As they looked down, the prince brushed dust off his clothes and smoothed down his jacket. He put his hands on his hips as he examined the house. Suddenly, he looked upwards and they jumped back from the window. 'Our next king thinks he can do whatever he wants,' Emma said, 'and do you know what?'

Anne shook her head.

'He can!'

'Do you know him?' Anne asked, shocked.

Emma laughed. 'No, of course not, but I've seen him before, and,' she looked at Anne with a knowing look.

'And . . . what?'

'I've heard the stories about him. He's a rake: a scoundrel, as far as women are concerned. He likes women too much – you know – in that way.'

Anne frowned. 'I've heard the stories, of course, and seen his image in cartoons. But well, he's far more good-looking and distinguished than I had expected.'

Emma laughed again. 'You can't rely on cartoons. Their job is to ridicule for the entertainment of their readers.' She looked puzzled. 'You already falling for him?'

Anne bristled. Annoyed her curiosity should be misconstrued. 'Indeed not! Don't say such a thing. It's just that – well, you do not often get the chance to see the future king in person – and so close.'

A door slammed and a loud voice echoed around the house, 'Frederick? Where the hell are you? God damn you. Not still abed, I hope.'

'We'd better get back to the servants' hall,' Emma said. 'Mr Sweetman will be having kittens. The prince wasn't expected so soon.'

As they rushed into the servants' hall everything

was busy but calm. Mrs Harley and Mr Sweetman were deep in conversation and Anne heard him say, 'This is our first big test, Mrs Harley. We must cope. Take care of your responsibilities and I will take care of the rest.'

'Agreed, Mr Sweetman. Let's get on with it, then.'

*

By late afternoon, the servants were exhausted. Twelve of the prince's friends had arrived soon after him, their own horses in a similar state of collapse. Men, horses and phaetons had all been accommodated and the wine had started flowing from the minute of the men's arrival. The cooks quickly laid out the pre-prepared cold meat, pies, cheeses, salads and a plethora of desserts for the guests but the staff were too busy to stop for their own dinner at midday. Cold food had been laid out on the dresser of the servants' hall for anyone who was able to get enough time to eat some at whatever time they could. It was seven in the evening before the servants could find time for their dinner. But nobody minded as instead of their usual food provided by the staff cook, they enjoyed the leftovers from the prince's earlier meal as everyone in the kitchen was too busy involved in producing the food for the duke's dinner party that evening to prepare food for the staff.

'This is good,' Charles, the dark haired, over-confident, footman said. 'I wish we could eat the food from upstairs every day.' He pushed some more cold beef into his mouth.

'Don't speak with your mouth full,' Mr Sweetman chastised him.

Charles swallowed hard. 'Sorry, Mr Sweetman, sir,' but at the same time he winked in an exaggerated manner at Edward, the under butler, knowing it would embarrass him in front of the butler. Charles always dared to do things to belittle others.

Edward was strong, well-built and like all the footmen was of exceptional good looks. But even though he was under butler and superior to Charles he did not have the same cocky confidence of Charles and he admired him for it. They were friends but this time he ignored him. Edward had a nasty side which he mostly kept hidden, especially from Mr Sweetman, but everyone was wary of him as they didn't want to be on the receiving end of his often poisonous jibes. If he took against you, watch out. Thomas, the footman with the pretty, feminine face and Henry, with the whitest and straightest teeth which he always displayed with his ready smiles, looked at each other, worried that Charles would start on them.

Charles turned his attention to Anne and winked at her across the table. She bristled and gave him one of the glares she had perfected for over-familiar men but he just smiled and kept his head down not to attract the attention of the butler or housekeeper.

'You don't want Charles' attention, Anne,' Emma whispered next to her. 'I think he's getting too interested in you. He's a bad lot. I don't know how he got this job. I wouldn't trust him at all.'

'I'm trying to avoid him, but it's difficult at mealtimes. The more I disdain him the more he persists. I'm giving him no encouragement you can be sure.'

'Well, be careful.'

'The Prince of Wales is a fine man,' James said.

'I heard them talking upstairs, and the friends of the prince said he won the race from London fair and square. They didn't let him win.'

'James is nice,' whispered Emma. 'I'd give anything for that glowing skin he has. It's wasted on a man.'

Anne was getting agitated. Doesn't this woman think of anything but men? To Emma she said, rather too primly, 'I am not interested. Now let's just eat, please.'

Emma gave her a look. 'Come on, you must be interested in these footmen. They're the handsomest and tallest of men - only the best for royalty. I wouldn't mind—'

'Please,' Anne hissed, trying to keep her temper. She never had understood women who thought of little but men.

'I'm sure they would have let him win regardless,' Charles answered James, his mouth still overfull. 'You don't want to be known for beating your future king. In fact, you wouldn't be allowed to stay around for long if you did.' He guffawed and stuffed some stray food back into his mouth.

Frowning at him, James added, 'That's true but he is known for loving speed and being reckless with no heed to danger.'

'Not a good idea for a future—'

'Enough!' Mr Sweetman ordered. 'I'll not have this kind of talk. We don't gossip about our betters. And,' he glared at James, 'we do not repeat what we hear upstairs. Is that clear?'

James looked down at the table. 'Yes, sir, sorry, Mr Sweetman, sir,' he replied showing his annoyance that he had got the rebuke when Charles was always the worst offender.

'We're all new here, finding our way,' the butler said more softly, 'but I will have an orderly house, one the duke can be proud of, and gossiping will not be tolerated on pain of dismissal.' He looked around at all of them, one by one. 'Do I make myself clear?'

'Yes, sir, Mr Sweetman, sir,' they all answered with serious faces.

Mrs Harley whispered to Mr Sweetman, 'Mr Lange says, we need extra kitchen staff. They are almost overwhelmed with work and are grumpy because of it.' She looked down the table. 'And, I would venture, the above-stairs staff are overstretched too. This won't do for future events. Mr Lange is beside himself as he cannot get enough support for the preparation of the food and Mr Pierre has lost his temper several times and you know how easy going he usually is. And we need more maids too for big events like this.'

'I agree,' he whispered back.

'But when the duke is not in residence we would then have too many staff,' Mrs Harley added.

'It's a difficult problem.'

'We should arrange some extra help from the village, people chosen with care, of course. But we could train them in what we require and ensure they know it is not permanent. As long as the pay is good we can secure their loyalty for when we need it. The women especially can help us if grandparents or older children can look after their younger ones. It could be done.'

'Indeed, Mrs Harley, let's talk of this tomorrow when we are ourselves less busy and can give it our full attention.'

Mr Sweetman clapped his hands together and

everyone looked up startled. 'Now,' he said in a calm and reassuring voice, 'we are all to be finished eating in ten minutes and then we are to be at our posts within the half hour after that. We put on fresh uniforms and make sure they are pristine.' He looked around the table and a few of the maids quailed a little. 'This is our big test. Our first vitally important dinner party for the duke and we will not let him down.' He continued to look around the table. 'Will we?'

'No, sir, Mr Sweetman, sir,' everyone answered nervously, except Charles who smirked.

'Including you, Charles. Now, keep your concentration, never lose your temper or panic, if you get flummoxed or overwhelmed then speak to another footman or maid and ask for help or come to me or Mrs Harley if we are to hand.' He smiled kindly. 'Now, put your training into practice over the next few hours and let us all look forward to a job well done.'

'Yes, sir, Mr Sweetman, sir,' everyone said, especially Anne who felt a great relief that Charles would be too busy to bother her.

*

All the footmen were in position standing in the dining room and opposite the door to the ante-room where the food would be placed when brought up from the kitchen. Their dark red tailcoats and breeches were emblazoned with gold braid and buttons; their waistcoats, striped in white and gold, were cut tight to enhance their strong physiques. The lace frills at their necks were snowy white, as were their gloves and stockings. Their buckled black shoes sparkled.

Edward, the under butler, came into the room just in front of Mr Sweetman who took a last look at them and walked up to Charles and adjusted his wig. 'Off centre wigs will not be tolerated,' he hissed at him.

'Sorry, Mr Sweetman, sir. I must have scratched my head,' Charles answered, keeping his face expressionless.

The butler glared at him and then addressed them all. 'We are ready to serve the Prince of Wales for the first time. Make sure you don't put a foot wrong or you will have me to deal with.' He looked along the line. 'Is that clear?'

'Yes sir, Mr Sweetman, sir,' they all answered.

'Now, to remind you, we will serve tonight's dinner, *a la francaise.*' He paused. 'And for those of you who are confused,' he gave them all a shrivelling look, 'it is the serving of all the dishes at once which are laid out on the table before the guests arrive and the guests help themselves. The only thing to be served is wine or other drinks, and I will serve those together with Edward. But, you must be on your toes and watching for any guest who needs anything for whatever reason. Is that clear?'

'Yes, sir, Mr Sweetman, sir,' they all answered

The dining table could accommodate thirty guests with ease, but there would only be the duke and prince with his twelve friends. The duke would sit in the middle with the Prince of Wales opposite. The other gentlemen would sit in order of precedence. Even with so few diners the whole table was covered in pristine white tablecloths.

Mr Sweetman made a last-minute check of the best French silverware already laid out on the table. It gleamed and sparkled in the flickering candlelight which gave it a mysteriousness not seen in daytime. He made sure the elegant condiment containers were in the exact same position in front of each diner, the cutlery, plates and numerous flower vases and candelabras were also in the exact positions demanded by protocol. The merely decorative silverware was displayed solely to express the owner's wealth and the duke was more than happy to display his.

'The table looks magnificent this evening,' he said as he finished his inspection. 'Well done everyone, the silver is polished to perfection. Now, we have many dishes so we need to place them quickly so they do not to get cold before the guests arrive.' He walked up and down the line of footmen. 'I have arranged with Mrs Harley that the maids and cooks and anyone else available will bring up the food quickly from the kitchen to the ante-room. I will supervise where each dish goes so do not put anything down until I have sanctioned it. *And do not spill anything on pain of dismissal!* Now, let's get started as I see the soup has just arrived. There are three tureens of soup. Charles, follow me with the first one and Edward and James bring the others. Now, put yours here, Charles, between the duke and the prince's places.' Charles put down the tureen with more than necessary elaborate care and Mr Sweetman raised an eyebrow but didn't say anything. 'Now, Edward and James, you put your tureens here and here,' he indicated the precise locations in the area where the guests would sit. 'We don't want anyone to have to lean too far to extract the soup. That would never do. We don't want a mess of dripped soup debris on the table.'

'Yes, sir, Mr Sweetman, sir.'

They spent the next few minutes laying everything

on the table as they were brought up from the kitchens with not a drop spilt and the tablecloths still in pristine condition.

Mr Lange, the cook, and Mr Pierre Pierre appeared in the ante-room carrying a large and elaborate pastry concoction over twelve inches high. Birds had been sculptured out of pastry, succulently filled with meat and fruit.

'Right,' Mr Sweetman said, 'the centrepiece has just arrived. I want no mistakes with this.'

'Mr Sweetman,' Mr Lange said, 'Mr Pierre and I will place this if you don't mind. I am mindful of its delicacy if jiggled about too much.'

'I agree, please follow me and we will put it in front of the Prince of Wales' chair.' The two cooks put down the large dish with relief.

'I didn't want to trust this heavy dish to the maids,' Mr Lange said. 'We should have more male assistants for this kind of thing. It is not the cook's job to carry.'

'Indeed not, Mr Lange. I agree and something will be done about it for future occasions. Thank you for your help,' Mr Sweetman added softly, mindful of Mr Lange's occasional eruptions.

The centrepiece was surrounded by dishes of whole pigeons and capons in sauces, sides of venison and beef decorated with exotic fruit, complete salmon and trout arranged as if swimming upstream with rocks and pebbles made of marzipan and icing sugar and secret ingredients of Mr Lange, all with champagne poured over them as the river itself did in life, plus elaborate sweet and savoury pastries and plates of vegetables. The butler made sure that the best of the dishes were laid in front of the duke and the prince. Vegetables, salads and desserts were arranged towards the edges with the exception of an exquisitely presented bowl of trifle, the prince's favourite, placed near the centrepiece.

Mr Sweetman stood back and examined everything. 'Excellent,' was his only comment as he went into the hallway and rang the bell for dinner and within minutes everyone was seated. The princes' friends were his usual coterie of aristocratic sons who enjoyed the same entertainments as the prince; young men's games, frivolities, women, gambling and drinking. Responsibilities were cast aside for later years and a light-hearted devotion to pleasure prevailed and kept them together. They were a raucous lot who didn't know the discipline of restraint.

The duke tapped his knife on the side of his wine glass to obtain quiet and got an immediate result as the young men, although full of their own importance, knew not to try and usurp the prince or his brother or lose their place in the most exalted society in the land. 'George,' the duke said smiling across at his brother, 'you start serving yourself and we will follow on.'

'No, no, brother, this is your house you should be the one to start.'

'I insist,' the duke said, brokering no nonsense.

'Indeed. In that case, I will start with the soup. It smells delicious.' The prince helped himself and spilt some on the tablecloth. 'Damn fine soup, brother,' he said slurping quickly but it caught in his throat and he started to cough. 'Well, brother,' he said, recovering himself, 'maybe I need not worry about a regency and be carried off by your soup, instead.' He coughed again. 'You would become regent then.' He grinned.

'Don't you dare, the last thing I want to be is king.'

'Ha! You'd make a better king than me, Frederick.

And you know it. It would please our father, too. He always preferred you to me. You're his favourite.'

'Look, let's not talk like this. You will be king whether you like it or not.'

'Oh, I like it well enough, but that fool Fox has not been prudent. He's turned Parliament against me by asserting that the position of Prince of Wales entitles me to exercise sovereignty during the king's incapacity.'

'I see. And Pitt doesn't agree?'

'Of course he doesn't,' the prince said bad-temperedly as he turned his attention to the centrepiece. 'Well, Frederick, you told me you had employed an extraordinary cook. This looks exquisite and by God, it smells good. It is making my mouth water.'

Mr Sweetman noticed the prince's attention was now on the centrepiece and changed the wine to a robust burgundy which he served with aplomb.

'Well, delve in, George,' the duke said with fondness. 'Give us your verdict on my new cook.'

The prince picked up a large knife and sliced into the pastry, cutting a substantial portion. It held together as he placed it on his plate. He smacked his lips as he tasted it. 'Superb! I want this cook.' the duke cut a slice and tasted it. 'You will have him over my dead body, brother. This is superb, as you say.'

The brothers laughed as the other men took their cue and joined in, all stuffing their mouths full of pie or fish or whatever was near them and exclaiming, 'Superb!' The jollity increased as Mr Sweetman kept topping up the wine.

As he chewed on his second piece of pie, ignoring the platters of vegetables and the other guests, the prince said to the duke, 'That fool of a prime minister, that turgid man, Pitt, argued that, as there is no law to the contrary, the right to choose a regent belongs to Parliament. The bastard had the audacity to say,' the prince banged his knife up and down on the table in emphasis, '"that without parliamentary authority the Prince of Wales had no more right to assume the government than any other subject of this country".'

He swallowed hard, his face showing his displeasure. 'Can you *believe* that? Comparing *me* to any pock-marked, diseased profligate … beggar or . . . or even any old doxy!' Bits of pie splattered from his mouth. 'The *disrespect!* The man's an *imbecile.'*

The duke laughed. 'Come on, George, Pitt was not comparing you to beggars and prostitutes. He worries that if you have sovereignty you will dismiss him.'

'And so I would!'

'So, he's watching his back. This was the first thing I was taught as a young soldier. It's vital to always watch your back. You too, brother, should watch yours.'

'What do you mean by *that!'*

'Just that you need to handle this carefully. You don't want to antagonise Parliament.'

'I'm their future king, for God's sake!'

'Yes, and if you're not careful, you'll end up like Charles the First and have Parliament turn against you and chop off your head.'

The prince stopped eating and stared with disbelief at his brother, as did the rest of the guests who were looking decidedly uncomfortable. The pause grew, gaining momentum. And then the prince burst out laughing, 'You and your jokes.'

The duke leaned towards him and said slowly and firmly, 'I am not joking.'

The prince stared again. 'No, you are not. I can see that. What do you suggest?'

The duke was thoughtful. 'I will speak for you in the House of Lords as soon as I can. I will declare that you would not attempt to exercise any power whatsoever without obtaining the previous consent of Parliament. That should help, I think.'

'I agree,' the prince said readily, his relief showing. 'That would help. God, what a mess. Trust Father to go mad. I always said he wasn't right in the head. Too strict, too frugal, too pious, too loyal to our mother and the numerous offspring he has inflicted upon her. He needs to experience more of the world outside the home. Enjoy the things life has to offer. That would soon dispel his malaise. He spends too much time indoors reading dusty political stuff.' He took a long draft of his wine and looked at his plate. 'More pie, by God, I love this pie.'

The duke sat back in his chair and observed his brother. 'You eat too much.'

'Yes, and drink too much. More wine,' he ordered and laughed.

Mr Sweetman replenished the prince's wine and as he turned he saw Charles smiling to himself at the conversation going on around them. He glared at Charles for his lack of decorum and stood, hard, on his foot as he walked past him. The footman paled considerably but made no noise and tried not to hobble about for the rest of the evening.

'You need to modify your views,' the duke said. 'Fox has done you no favours by taking such a superior stance. You need to rein him in.'

'Mmmm!'

'Look, I know Fox is a friend of yours.'

'A good friend.'

'That's as maybe, but you cannot lend Fox your full support on this. You have to step back. Let him ruin himself if he so desires, but don't let him take you with him. He has not been prudent in this matter.'

The prince's attention wandered. 'Trifle!' he shouted loudly. 'That's what we need, trifle. Splendid,' he laughed as he took several spoonfuls. 'We'll talk again tomorrow, brother. Let's give our full attention to what is really important in life – trifle!' He laughed again as the duke studied him from behind his wine glass.

'Indeed. Enough for tonight,' the duke agreed as he downed his wine in one.

CHAPTER FIVE

The next morning, Anne was up at five as usual and as she went into the dining room wondered what had happened after she and the other maids were sent to bed at midnight leaving the footmen, the butler and the housekeeper to cope. The air was stale so she opened the shutters and threw several of the windows open. The cold December wind nipped at the room and she shivered as she surveyed things. The footmen had made a good job of superficial cleaning; the candlesticks were in the ante-room ready for cleaning and polishing, the napkins had been cleared as had all the crockery and tablecloths. But the floor was a mess of dropped food and debris she couldn't, and didn't want, to identify. But then something sparkled in the light. She crawled under the table to retrieve it and gasped as she picked up a ring full of brilliants. This must be worth a fortune, she thought, as she clutched it in her palm. Without hesitation, she rushed to Mrs Harley's room and knocked. As she expected, Mrs Harley was at her desk albeit with dark circles around her eyes, surrounded by invoices and ledgers. The housekeeper looked up in annoyance. 'What is it?'

'Sorry to trouble you, Mrs Harley, but I thought I ought to show you this. I found it under the dining room table,' she said as she came in and opened her palm.

'Goodness!' Mrs Harley sat back in shock. 'Let me see.' She took the ring and examined it. 'It's a huge diamond surrounded by rubies,' she said as she recovered herself. 'Find Mr Sweetman at once and send him to me. And Anne—'

'Yes, Mrs Harley.'

'Well done for spotting it. It could have caused a great deal of upset if it went missing. And you did well to come straight to me. Now, go along with your work and if anything else is found, bring it to me instantly.'

'Yes, thank you.' Anne bobbed a curtsey.

She went back to the dining room and carefully swept up making sure there was nothing more valuable dropped from the night before. Eventually, everything was tidy and clean and ready for another day. She closed the windows and opened the door leading into the adjoining gaming room. It was a small room used for card playing and she choked as she breathed in the stale smoke still permeating the air. She threw open the windows and took a deep breath of fresh air and then looked around at the mess of card tables and chairs abandoned by their late-night users in an unholy mess. Good grief, she thought, what a way to behave. She knew the duke was well known for his love of card playing, high stakes or low, he relished it all. He would play until he was the last man sitting and everyone else was only fit for their bed.

She decided it was better not to think about it too hard and took her bucket with the lid and emptied several overflowing ashtrays of cigars and their ash. She put the lid on and moved the bucket as far away from her as she could. The smell made her nauseous and she was glad she hadn't had breakfast yet.

'It must have been a very drunken night,' she told Joyce in the servants' hall later. 'There were cards everywhere and the tables were covered in cigar ash and had rings from the port and brandy glasses. There are some tables that need more attention than I am capable of and the rings are still visible.'

'Have you told Mrs Harley?'

'Yes. And she told me to get my breakfast before I faded away as we had so much more to do than usual. I had no idea it would be this hard. I'm exhausted. My previous house was quiet compared to this.'

'The duke is a young man and so is his brother. They have no care for the likes of us, only for their own enjoyment. You'll get used to it. You're better off here working for the duke than for the prince. He has no care for servants so I've heard, but I speak out of turn. We must be careful of what we say. Walls have ears. We don't want to lose our positions.'

'No. Indeed not, but I don't think I talk out of turn to say that I found a very valuable ring on the floor of the dining room.'

'Oh? What kind of ring?'

'Full of brilliants. A huge diamond surrounded by rubies, according to Mrs Harley. I have to say it was thrilling to hold something so beautiful.'

'Be careful, Anne, you don't want people to think you covet such things. That could be dangerous for you if anything went missing.'

'Mmm. Good advice, thank you.'

'Come now you two,' Mr Sweetman said as he walked into the room. 'Less talking and more eating. You are wanted upstairs as soon as possible. We have to get used to this kind of thing when the duke is in residence. I expect this is the first of many unexpected party nights. As I understand it, the Prince of Wales doesn't always let people know in advance that he is coming. He often arrives before his messenger so I've been told. And Anne,' he said sitting down and smiling kindly, 'well done in finding the ring. I will hold you up as a good example to the other servants. This is the kind of thing we all must do if we find something valuable gone astray. The integrity of the house depends on it.'

*

Hannah had been worrying about Mrs White since they'd arrived at Oatlands. She knew she was suffering at the hands of her husband. It was so obvious to her but with Jack's warning her off interfering, saying it was, 'none of their business and you cannot come between a man and his wife,' ringing in her ears she knew it was now or never. Jack and Mr White had been summoned to Mr Tucker's office for a meeting so it was a rare opportunity to talk to Mrs White without the interference of either husband. She wondered at the wisdom of it but decided she had to do something. Her instincts told her Mrs White needed help.

Hannah looked out of her window plucking up the courage to go and knock on her neighbour's door when, to her surprise, Mrs White came out of her lodge. Hannah took the opportunity and opened her door with a big smile. 'Hello, Mrs White, what a lovely day.'

The other woman started a little but smiled shyly. 'Yes, indeed, Mrs Dresser, it is a fine day. The children are taking their afternoon nap and that is a miracle in itself that they do so all together.'

Hannah laughed. 'Yes, a miracle as you say.'

This brought a genuine smile to Mrs White's face and Hannah noticed that when she smiled her eyes lit up and her face relaxed and Hannah could see she had been a beautiful woman when younger. She would be now if she wasn't always looking so worried and furtive but right now her eyes were gentle with long lashes that Hannah envied. Her skin was clear, beautiful in fact, but premature wrinkles had marked it giving her an aged look much more than her actual years, Hannah guessed. She searched her brain for something unthreatening to say. 'Are you a local woman, Mrs White? I'm from London and find the Surrey countryside a treasure after the frightful smells of London.'

Mrs White smiled. 'I am a Londoner too, so I know what you mean. I too find the air here delightful. It is so good for the children.'

'It is indeed.' Hannah was impatient to know Mrs White's history but had to tread carefully. She tried for nonchalance. 'My father sold vegetables at the local market, were your family in trade too?'

Mrs White stared into space and eventually said, 'We were a family of blacksmiths but my father and brother were killed in an accident with the forge. There were no other men in the family so we hit hard times … I have to admit that it was very difficult and then we all went into service.'

'I'm so sorry to hear that. Did you meet your husband through your household?' Hannah risked asking but saw Mrs White's face fall and cursed herself for being too direct. But the other woman surprised her by laughing under her breath as if she had a secret she didn't want to share.

'In a way, Mrs Dresser ... in a way.'

Hannah waited patiently as she really wanted to know how this soft, genteel young woman had met and married such a brute of a man. Mrs White walked slowly away from her lodge as if she didn't want the children to hear. She looked up at the sky and to the tops of the trees as if deciding something. Hannah kept her silence, giving the other woman time.

Eventually, Mrs White said, 'We met in a strange way, I suppose. I was shopping for the household I worked for as we had a special dinner that evening and I was sent out for a last-minute item we needed. I was the youngest you see so I could be spared. I was only sixteen and was so happy to be out on my own and was not paying attention and stupidly walked in front of a coach and horses and when the driver yelled at me to get out of the way I froze. I thought I had met my end but I felt someone grab me from behind and pull me to safety. It was a near thing.'

'And was that person Mr White?' Hannah asked.

She sighed deeply. 'Indeed it was. So you see ...' her voice was so low Hannah only just heard, 'I owe him my life and one thing led to another and a short time later we were married ... and here I am.'

So, that was it. That was why this woman was with this man. 'It was a lucky day for you when he saved you,' Hannah said because what do you say after someone tells you something like that?

Mrs White didn't seem to hear and just stared into the distance with troubled eyes. They worried Hannah, her troubled eyes. She tried to bring her back to the present. 'I know your husband was an army man like my Jack, but I think he was in a different regiment as Jack hadn't met him before.'

'He was,' she answered so quietly it was almost a whisper. 'He was a sergeant and had been in the army for many years. He was a good-looking man in his uniform and was a different man then. Rough, you know, but fair … mostly. That was before he broke his leg and was invalided out … the pain you know.' Hannah could see she was lost in her own world so held her tongue, hoping for more. Eventually, Mrs White said, 'The pain changed everything. It didn't heal properly you see.' There was such sorrow and anguish in her eyes Hannah wanted to take her in her arms and give her comfort and support, take her away from the brute, but she daren't. 'He cannot bear it sometimes. It drives him ...' a cloud came over Mrs White's face. She hugged herself and gave a shiver. 'It's chilly now, I must go in. It's been nice to talk to you, Mrs Dresser, another time maybe.' And with that she had gone into her lodge and shut the door firmly.

Damn, Hannah thought. I was doing well there and then pushed that bit too far. But at least I know what is going on there. She wondered how much to tell Jack or whether to at all.

*

A few days after finding the ring Anne was summoned to the green room at four that afternoon. 'The gentleman who lost the ring wants to thank you,' Mr Sweetman told her. 'His name is The Honourable Anthony Belknap but you just call him sir. If you should see the duke, you call him Your Grace. Along you go now, you'll be all right.'

Anne's knees felt weak as she knocked on the

door. She had never been in the green room before and for some reason that made her more nervous. 'Come in,' a strong voice called out. She entered and bobbed a curtsy as a tall man about the duke's age stood facing her, his back to the roaring log fire and his muscular body oozing arrogance.

Time slowed for Anne as, unbidden, her maid's mind took in the large square room with its pastel green walls, long windows, extravagant decoration, silk-covered sofas and chairs in soft pink and cream and a marble fireplace so large it made Anne's heart sink as she thought of cleaning it.

'Ah, you must be Anne, the maid who found my ring.'

She curtsied again. 'Yes, sir.'

'Come here, girl,' he commanded.

Reluctantly, she went deeper into the room.

'I want to thank you properly for finding it. It's valuable, you know.'

'Yes, sir.'

'Come closer. Here, let me look at you. What a pretty one you are.' He stroked her cheek.

Anne jumped back in alarm. No, not again, please no, her mind screamed.

'Come and let me show you my gratitude. Come, just a kiss of gratitude,' he said, his voice false and condescending. He made a grab for her and she pushed him away as hard as she could.

'Don't you dare put a finger on me,' he hissed as he snatched the back of her neck and pulled her to him, kissing her mouth. A hard, mean, distasteful kiss.

'No!' She gasped as he released her, the air shocked out of her lungs. She was not going to put up with this nonsense even if it meant dismissal. She turned her back on him and started to walk quickly towards the door. He grabbed her.

'NO!' she shouted as she struggled free. 'Leave me alone. I'm not that sort.' Her heart was pounding as he made to grab her again, more roughly this time.

'What's this, Belknap?' the duke had entered the room and in a few strides he was standing in front of them. 'Do you take liberty with my servants, man?' His tone was fierce.

'She's only a maid, Frederick. See sense. It is just sport. She found my ring and gave it up rather than put it in her pocket. I just wanted to thank her.'

'I am pleased to hear my servants are honest, and also to hear that she is not that kind of girl. Now, sir, take your hands off her and if you so much as touch one of my servants again, you will be the worse for it.'

The duke turned to Anne. 'What's your name?' he asked kindly.

'Anne Dresser, Your Grace.'

'Dresser … ah, yes, I remember now, Anne Dresser, daughter of our porter. Well, please go back to your duties. We will keep this our little secret,' he smiled. 'I think that would be best, don't you?' He added quietly, 'For all of us.'

She blinked at the injustice of it, but realising her position and that the duke, as kind as he was, would always stand up for his own kind.

'Yes, Your Grace. Thank you,' she said as she curtsied.

Anne left the room and stood outside it for a few seconds, her whole body shaking. Her powerlessness was yet again reinforced and her anger mounted. Her father had said what a fine man the duke was, how he cared for his servants and treated them with respect and she had hoped things would be different here. But now she knew that even here she was not safe. She had fought off men all her life. She didn't want them, hated them pawing her and wished she'd been born plain. Her beauty was her curse. Men desired her and women hated her for it.

She was determined not to let this pull her down. She decided she would never be alone in a room with a man if she could help it, unless he was her father or her brother, William. They were the only men she could trust completely. Oh, William, she thought, please, please come and work at Oatlands. He could protect her, surely. If he didn't come she wasn't sure how she would cope.

CHAPTER SIX

'Brrrr, it's the coldest February I've ever known,' Mr Sweetman said, putting his newspaper under his arm, rubbing his hands together and shivering as he entered the servants' hall. He warmed himself by the log fire which was burning high. The other servants were sat around the table waiting for him to arrive before starting their breakfasts.

'Rose, did you make sure my washing water was hot before you brought it to my room earlier?'

Rose was the youngest and least confident of the housemaids and looked stricken. 'Yes sir, Mr Sweetman, sir. It was *very* hot. I had to heat it up for ages as it was frozen.'

'Well, it was freezing over again by the time it got to me. I've never known such cold weather.'

'Well,' Charles whispered to Edward, 'the water in *my* washing jug was frozen *solid*. I wish we had the luxury of hot water in the mornings.'

'You'll just have to work up to be butler one day,' he replied as even he, as under-butler, didn't get hot water brought to him.

Mr Sweetman continued, ignoring the whispering of Charles and Edward, 'It's not your fault, Rose, don't worry. 'There's nothing we can do about the weather, so let's just try and keep warm and not get ill. Now, how is the oatmeal – hot?' he asked the kitchen maid who had just appeared carrying a large pot putting it down in the middle of the table.

'Yes, Mr Sweetman, sir. It's very hot. I made sure it was.'

'Good, well then, let's not take long to eat this up before it too ends up frozen.'

He lowered his head and the others followed suit. 'For all we are about to receive may the Lord make us truly thankful. Amen.'

'Amen.'

Everyone helped themselves to the loaves of sourdough bread already broken into sections. As they were finishing the steward's room boy came in with a large bowl of sausages and bacon. 'Ah!' said Mr Sweetman. 'A special treat. We have sausages *and* bacon today. Help yourselves. You'll need the food to keep warm.'

Everyone tucked-in with great enthusiasm until Mr Sweetman said loudly, 'Now,' he paused, swallowing a sausage in two bites and glancing down the table at each of them in turn in that disconcerting way he had. 'I have some news for you that concerns all of us. It is reported here,' he tapped his folded newspaper next to his plate, 'that the king, God bless him, has miraculously recovered from his illness and the prospect of the Prince of Wales becoming regent has now been abandoned.'

There was a lot of murmuring and someone said, 'God save the King. That is good news, indeed.'

Everyone agreed and said with great enthusiasm, 'God save the King.'

'As I reported to you before,' the butler said, ponderously, 'the duke spoke in the House of Lords

104

recently in support of the Prince of Wales and the position the prince had been forced to take because of the king's ...' he hesitated and cleared his throat. 'Ah ... indisposition,' he said dragging the word out. 'It was a speech well respected by many.' He nodded and raised his eyebrows, still looking briefly at each of them in turn. 'That is no more than we would expect from the duke, I'm sure you will agree.'

Everyone nodded, saying, 'Yes, sir. Mr Sweetman, sir.'

He opened his newspaper and peered at the small print with a little difficulty. 'It is reported here,' he tapped the newspaper again, 'that despite disagreement, Parliament was opened on 3rd February, 1789 for business even though Edmond Burke and the duke himself denounced the way it was achieved as illegal and unconstitutional as it was done without the consent of the king.'

'But the king was mad. He couldn't consent,' James said through a mouthful. 'Could he?' he asked, looking around, unsure.

The butler frowned at James. 'That is crudely put but in essence, correct.' A bad situation all round. But God moves in mysterious ways and the king miraculously recovered just days before the regency bill could be passed, and now, of course, it is no longer needed. So, we will go back to normal life I'm very pleased to say. The duke has advised me he will be in residence here again come the spring.'

Everyone started talking at once. Mr Sweetman stood up. "It's an extremely cold winter, so Mrs Harley and I have decided that we will start our spring clean now to keep everyone warm.'

Charles groaned.

'Enough of that, Charles, if you please. As the duke won't be returning until the spring we will all remain on board wages. And be thankful that the duke has seen fit to keep us housed, fed – and on half wages – during his absences. So, I want no complaining.'

'Yes, sir. Mr Sweetman, sir,' they all said, chastised.

He turned to the housekeeper and smiled. 'Mrs Harley, will you address the staff please.'

'Yes, Mr Sweetman,' she said standing up.

'Now, pay attention, everyone,' she said in her strong, well-modulated voice. 'As we've just heard, the duke will be in London for the winter so I want you all to use this time to make sure everything – and I do mean *everything* – is cleaned and polished to the highest degree. We will use the duke's absence to improve the house to the best of our ability. Every crevice, from the skirting boards up to the ceiling decorations must be dusted and washed if necessary. All furniture will be polished to the highest degree. Mats and carpets will be taken outside and beaten, floors polished, grates blackened, marble cleaned and polished. Fires will be lit in the main rooms every day to keep the rooms damp free. Dust sheets will be laid over the furniture. Uniforms will be cleaned and ironed. You will be responsible for mending your own uniforms as and when necessary.

'And,' she looked at Mr Sweetman, 'now is the best time we have for finding and training some extra staff to help when we have large parties. Mr Sweetman and myself, together with the cooks will conduct the initial training and do some trials to see how the temporary staff cope.

Now,' she said with finality, 'that should keep us

all busy. Let's begin as we mean to go on.'

*

The next day, Anne came into the kitchen to find Mr Sweetman and Mrs Harley busy with tasks. Charles and Edward were cleaning the silver in the pantry and chatting amongst themselves.

'Less chattering and more cleaning, Charles,' Mr Sweetman said as he crossed the kitchen and looked into the pantry with a frown.

'I was just saying, Mr Sweetman, someone in the Old Ship Inn recently asked me to check on a sum for him and we disagreed on the answer. He said he'd been cheated by the corn merchant. I checked the sum and said the corn merchant was correct but this man disagreed.'

'What was the sum?' asked Mr Sweetman, proud of his arithmetic and unable to resist a chance to show off.

'Seven pounds, thirteen shillings and five pence halfpenny, less five pounds, nine shillings and four pence farthing, which he already had in credit.'

'Let me write it down,' Mr Sweetman said, looking for some paper.

'Two pounds four shillings and a penny farthing,' Anne said instantly, and then froze as the others looked at her in amazement.

'Sorry,' she said.

Mr Sweetman wrote down the figures. 'Goodness me, she's right. That is the answer.'

'You did this in your head … and so fast!' Mrs Harley exclaimed.

'I'm sorry, it just came out.' Anne cursed herself

107

for her lapse but then felt she had to explain now she'd put herself in this difficult position. 'I've always been good at mental arithmetic … I used to do it with my brother as a sort of game.'

'I see. I didn't know you were educated to such a high standard.' Mr Sweetman's voice held a note of hostility.

Anne tried to keep her temper. Now she would have to explain further. She decided that the expedited version would be best in the circumstances knowing people didn't understand why her father, influenced by her mother, was keen to educate all his children, the girls as well as the boys. She knew he put great store on education for advancement for boys and enrichment for girls. 'Why should the girls be left in ignorance,' he'd say, 'when education feeds the mind and makes everyone a better person. I've seen the result of ignorance and it was always to the detriment of the person, man or woman. My children, the girls as well as the boys, will thrive one way or another.'

She'd learned how unusual this was and how most people were shocked by it and didn't approve. So she said, 'My father was keen on learning for my brother. He always said that was very important for a boy's future. So he arranged for a retired teacher to give lessons to my brother and told him he would give him a higher fee if he included me in the lessons.'

'Well, I'll be.' Mr Sweetman said. 'Mrs Harley, we have a genius amongst us.'

The sarcastic tone was not lost on Anne. She didn't want people to know how well educated she was and how easy she found arithmetic. It was not seemly for a woman and she always paid the price when men, rich or poor, found out she was better than they were at a lot of things. The hostility was cruel and relentless and her life was made miserable. Even upper-class women kept the extent of their learning hidden when around their men-folk. And she was a servant and servants, male or female, were not wanted if they had too much learning. It caused discontent. That was the way it was and she had enough trouble with men already and didn't want more because of her intelligence.

She noticed Charles staring at her with cold eyes. She glanced at Mrs Harley who was looking at her in a puzzled way and Anne wasn't sure if that was a good thing or not.

*

The next morning Anne finished making up the fires she was responsible for and went down to the kitchen to wash her hands and get rid of the dirty water in her bucket. She was surprised there was no one else there and then remembered she had arisen much earlier than usual unable to sleep with the events of the evening before racing around her mind.

The kitchen was equipped with two large sinks; the 'dirty' sink was used to empty used liquid as it flowed directly into a drain outside, the other was kept for cleaner things like washing food. She emptied her coal-black water down the dirty sink and swilled it out with clean water from a pitcher, then poured water into a bowl to wash her hands and get the coal dust out of her fingernails. As she was finishing someone grabbed her so forcefully from behind she thought her ribs would crack. Her head swirled as she was spun around and caught sight of Charles' face as he held her tight, his face bruising hers as he tried to kiss her. She threw her head from side to side in an effort to stop him and gasped as he grabbed her breast in a vice-like grip.

'Don't you dare try to resist me, you trumped-up little bitch,' he hissed. 'Think you are better than all of us, do you? Think you are better than me because you can count? I've seen you look at me in that superior way you have, looking down at me. I've seen it. I'll show you what's what in this world.'

He threw her against a wall and forced his hands up her skirts. Anne couldn't get her breath as her heart beat so fast she thought she'd faint. She screamed in desperation and he slapped her face and clamped his hand over her mouth. Panicking, she tried to kick him but he was too quick and forced her legs apart with his own. He used his superior height and strength to pin her against the wall until she thought her bones would crush. He struggled in vain to undo his breeches and had to pull away from her slightly.

This is my chance, she thought as without hesitation she screamed as loud as she could. It came out like an animal in distress, a roar of pain and disbelief. No man before had got this far and she realised how lucky she'd been. How easy it was.

A ringing blow across her face made her reel and she almost lost consciousness but was shocked into awareness when his hand found her most personal place and his fingers started to burrow into her. A place no one else had ever touched but herself.

Outrage flooded her as she struggled to stop him but she was no match for Charles' superior build and power and felt her own strength deserting her. She cursed God for making women weaker than men.

Charles can do what he likes with me … what use are your brains now, she screamed to herself. And then he moved his hand from under her skirts and clenched the sides of her face, kissing her deeply, forcing his tongue into her mouth and choking her. She tried to get her breath but couldn't. Her panic increased as she struggled but he was relentless. Her head began to throb from lack of air. Her lungs pumped harder until they hurt. She would die if he didn't stop soon.

'What's going on here?' Mrs Harley shouted as she stormed across the kitchen.

Charles spun round and released his grip on Anne and she panted painful air into her lungs. Mrs Harley slapped his face so hard he staggered. Recovering quickly he grabbed her, snarling, 'You want it too, do you, you bitch?' He held her in a vice-like hold and kissed her deeply as she struggled in vain to free herself.

'What the hell is going on here?' Mr Sweetman's loud, authoritarian voice echoed around the kitchen.

Charles swung round and pushing Mrs Harley aside threw a punch at the butler's chin. Mr Sweetman fell backwards onto the kitchen table, stunned. Charles lifted his arm to hit him again but Mrs Harley grabbed a rolling pin and smashed it against the back of Charles' head. He went down like a rag doll.

She rushed to Mr Sweetman, who was just pushing himself off the table and finding his feet. 'Let me help you,' she said. 'He's out cold so take your time.'

The butler stood for a moment, breathing hard, and smoothed down his waistcoat and jacket, using the time to recover himself. He looked down at Charles and then at Anne who was ashen and shaking, not taking her eyes off Charles, as if he would jump up and attack her again.

'I found Charles attacking Anne. A vicious, uncontrolled attack. He was like an animal, Mr Sweetman.' Mrs Harley made an effort to control her shaking voice. 'An animal.'

The butler looked between Anne and Mrs Harley as if trying to decide what he should do. He kept his distance from Anne, his face going from fury to compassion.

'Did he … did Charles …' He cleared his throat, obviously uncomfortable. He kept his voice soft. 'I have to know, I'm so sorry, but did he,' he paused again, 'despoil you?' It was all too much for Anne who only managed to shake her head before bursting into gulping sobs.

'I'll take her to my room,' Mrs Harley said. 'I'll look after her.'

The butler nodded at Charles. 'I'll take care of him. Don't worry, I'll tie him up and then get Mr Tucker to help me decide what to do with him.'

'Get rid of him,' Mrs Harley hissed. 'If I see him again I'll not be responsible for my actions. He's always been trouble.'

Mr Sweetman nodded. 'But I must confer with Mr Tucker, he's the steward and in charge of everything while the duke is away. We must keep this to ourselves. We don't want scandal. After all, the duke did employ him.'

'I wonder why?' Mrs Harley spat.

'He was well recommended, I fear. But the details are not for us to know. I will make it my business to steer the duke away from Charles' set.'

'Indeed.' She turned to Anne. 'Come,' she said as if speaking to a child. 'You're shaking from head to foot. Come to my room and rest. You need peace and quiet to recover.' She put her arm around Anne's shoulders and guided her out of the kitchen, across the passageway and into her rooms and helped her lie down on the sofa. 'I'll get you a blanket and a pillow. Lie still now,' she said, patting Anne's hand.

She made Anne comfortable covering her with the blanket and went over to the sideboard pouring them each a generous measure of brandy. 'Here you are. Can you sit up and take a few sips? It will do you good.' She put her arm around Anne's shoulders and lifted her up to drink the brandy. Anne let out a cry of pain and clutched at her ribs.

Mrs Harley helped her to lie back down on the sofa. 'I am so sorry, Anne, I fear you have some broken ribs. That Charles ought to be shot!'

Anne knew she would be blamed for what happened. People would say she'd encouraged him. Women always got the blame. She was shaking with fury as well as shock. 'I'm sorry, Mrs Harley.' Her voice sounded so weak, but she had to make herself clear. She ignored the pain and whispered, 'I didn't mean to cause trouble like this.' She tried to stop her voice shaking. 'I didn't lead him on, I swear.'

'Please be assured, it's not your fault, child. I've been watching Charles for some time. You never gave him encouragement, unlike that silly girl, Emma, twittering around him all the time. But he only had eyes for you. I could see that, but while he did nothing untoward, there was nothing I could do.'

'I'm so angry.' Her breathlessness made her pant.

'Take your time.' Mrs Harley advised. 'Breathe slowly and speak softly. I am afraid your ribs will cause you a great deal of pain for several weeks.'

Anne nodded. 'I'm so angry I let myself be caught by him like that,' she paused to get her breath, 'but he came at me from behind. I didn't know he was there, I swear.' She started to well up again.

'I believe you. Don't worry. We'll keep it quiet, that's the best way to resolve this.'

'But he'll get away with it. That's not fair.' She knew she was sounding petulant but she didn't care. If you couldn't be petulant after such an ordeal when could you?

'It's not fair, Anne, as you rightly say. But what is the alternative? The duke won't thank us to make it public. No, there are better ways. Charles will never get a reference, you can be sure of that. Mr Sweetman and Mr Tucker will take care of things.'

'Men always take care of men … *that* you can be sure of,' Anne hissed and the venom in her voice shocked her.

Mrs Harley looked at Anne for a few seconds, as if deciding whether to speak. 'That is true. But we women can take care of women. Is that not also the case?'

Their eyes met and there was a look in Mrs Harley's eyes which Anne couldn't quite identify. The housekeeper's normal aloof and superior manner had softened and Anne was sure she could see pain written in her eyes. She looked human. Anne couldn't help wondering if she'd suffered a similar fate at some time. And then Mrs Harley's eyes filled with tears which she blinked back. She stood up abruptly. 'I'll get some water and wash the blood from your face. I need to see how badly you have been hurt.'

As she disappeared into her bedroom Anne took the opportunity to ponder on Mrs Harley. She was a strange woman, lonely she felt sure, abrupt, too intent on work, but in reality not much different to other housekeepers. They have to keep a strict house otherwise advantages are taken by the staff … and yet?

Mrs Harley came back quickly with a bowl of water and a clean cloth. She sat down gingerly on the sofa and gently wiped away the blood. 'You have a cut over your eye but it is more blood than cut. It will be tender for a while but will heal well, I think.' She hesitated and then said softly, 'You told Mr Sweetman that Charles didn't … despoil you. Is that true?'

Anne breathed steadily through her pain looking down at her hands; it seemed important somehow that this woman understood. 'He … well, he …' she took a small breath and it shuddered, like hiccups making her ribs hurt even more. 'He touched me', she whispered, 'where no one else has ever touched me.' Racking sobs overtook her again and she cried out as the pain in her ribs stabbed at her like hammers.

A perfunctory knock on the door startled them both. Mrs Harley went to the door and opened it a crack. 'Oh, Mr Sweetman, it's you.' The competent housekeeper in Mrs Harley had returned. 'Come in, please.'

His face was full of concern as he walked over to Anne. 'Are you all right?'

Anne made an effort to stay composed. 'Thank you, Mr Sweetman. I am recovering,' she whispered.

'Are you sure, you don't look all right. You're very flushed.'

'She is as well as can be expected,' Mrs Harley offered. 'I fear she has some broken ribs, that … Charles,' she spat out his name, 'crushed her so.'

She inhaled deeply. 'I'm sorry, Mr Sweetman, I am angry that this should happen here, at Oatlands, in my kitchen. I am responsible for this.'

The butler looked at her with compassion. 'Indeed, you are not, dear lady. No one is responsible except Charles himself. I do not want blame apportioned, that will not do and will get us nowhere.'

Mrs Harley closed her eyes for a few seconds and composed herself. 'Thank you, Mr Sweetman, you are sensible and you are right, of course. I fear it will take some time for Anne to recover from this. I suggest she takes a few weeks off physical labour as she is certainly in no condition to fulfil her duties. I will give her some light duties when she is able. Maybe some sewing.' She glanced at Anne. 'Some embroidery perhaps? Something light, cushions, yes, I have several cushions for the main rooms that need embroidering.' She smiled kindly and Anne nodded and tried a smile of her own.

'Thank you, Mrs Harley, that would suit me well.'

'Agreed then,' Mr Sweetman said kindly. 'Now, let us concoct a story between us.' He looked at Anne. 'I think you have had a nasty fall, down some stairs maybe. Yes, a tumble down the stairs would do the trick. Mrs Harley can be the one to have found you and I, myself, was second on the scene.' He nodded to himself. 'Yes, that should do it. We will warn everyone to be careful on the stairs and to use the handrails.'

He looked at both women who nodded their agreement. 'Mr Tucker,' he continued, finding his authoritarian voice again, 'and I have already dispatched Charles from the house with his box of belongings. He has been told never to come near anyone of this house or any other house belonging to the duke. If he does, he will be prosecuted without mercy. He understands this. Mr Tucker is taking him to the village at this very moment to get the coach to London and will put him on it. Mr Tucker and I put the fear of God into him. He won't trouble us again.'

'You don't blame me, do you?' Anne despised her neediness but couldn't stop herself. She had always thought of herself as a strong woman emotionally and she so wanted to succeed here. It was vital to her self-esteem that people didn't falsely judge her. 'It wasn't my fault, Mr Sweetman.' She held on to her composure with difficulty. 'I did nothing to encourage him.'

'Don't you worry, young Anne, I know you are a good girl,' he said condescendingly, but Anne was glad all the same.

'She is,' Mrs Harley interrupted. 'I can vouch for her, Mr Sweetman. Charles has been making eyes at her for a long time, but she gave him no encouragement. I have been watching Charles for some time.'

'Me too, but was unable to catch him at anything improper but now he has cooked his goose, and do you know what? I'm glad.' He rocked back on his heels, hands behind his back, like the way he often stood. 'Yes, I am glad. We have enough work here without having to deal with men like him in the servants' quarters causing upset and assaults.' He cleared his throat. 'But I'm being insensitive, forgive me. Forget I said that,' he blustered.

Anne thought at that moment that Mr Sweetman looked human and more than a little vulnerable. She liked him all the more for it.

'Do not worry, Mr Sweetman,' the housekeeper soothed, 'what has gone on today stays between us.'

'And thank you,' Anne said, looking from one to the other, 'for everything. I will never forget your kindness and you can be assured I will never betray your trust.'

'Indeed,' Mr Sweetman said as he rocked back on his heels again. 'We are now fellow conspirators whether we like it or not.'

*

Mr Sweetman concocted a story of Charles caught stealing and was dismissed on the spot. The staff had been warned not to try to contact him on pain of dismissal as he was an unsavoury character all round.

Anne told no one of her ordeal, not even her parents and never would. Her father would kill Charles. It was as simple as that. And then he would hang for it and then where would that leave them. No, she had to keep this to herself. She was also ashamed, feeling guilty that she had somehow brought it upon herself. She so wanted someone to talk to, but it was out of the question.

Joyce had asked a few questions but Anne just said she felt so foolish about not taking enough care and falling that she would rather not talk about it. Joyce was becoming a good friend and didn't pursue it.

Mrs Harley kept her distance and was even more aloof than before.

*

Anne spent a lot of her recovery time with her parents

during the first two weeks, Hannah fussing over her and making everything so much better. Anne had started the embroidery of the cushions Mrs Harley had picked out for her. It was a saving grace as it occupied her mind and concentration and required no effort of movement except for the needle as her mother helped her with anything she couldn't cope with.

It was the bitterest winter anyone could remember and one day, when Anne was comfortable in front of their fire, the London coach pulled up outside and it was not long before her father came rushing in casting the other post aside. 'It's from William. Look, I recognise his hand.'

'Quickly, open it,' his wife encouraged.

Jack opened the letter and took it to the window to get the light.

Dear Mama and Papa

I have had a meeting with Mr Tucker and the duke in London and Mr Tucker has given me permission to write to tell you that I have been appointed new footman at Oatlands. The duke seemed to like me and I surely did like him. He's such an impressive soldier. I admire him greatly.

I write to confirm I will be arriving mid March on 15th. I will catch the early morning coach from London and be with you about noon all being well. I look forward to seeing you soon as it has been a long time since we last saw each other.

Your loving son,
William

'Yes, yes, yes,' Jack shouted out, waving the letter in the air as Hannah jumped up and hugged her husband.

'At last. It's happened at last. Oh, Jack,' she cried out, wiping away some tears. 'I can't believe it, both Anne and Will with us at Oatlands.'

Anne noticed the look of love they exchanged but it was more than that, a look of intimacy, of shared secrets becoming a reality moved between them which made Anne surprised at the feeling of envy building inside her. It was something she could never share with them, and, she thought, she could never share with anyone. It wasn't something she could open herself up to with another person. Still a little shocked at such intimacy, but not wanting to spoil the joy they were all feeling she jumped up and rushed to them, regretting it instantly.

'Oh, my ribs,' she cried out, clutching her side. 'I forgot about my ribs I am so excited to see Will again.'

Her mother took hold of her arm. 'Anne, dear, please come, sit down. We are all excited but don't forget about your ribs.'

Anne couldn't stop her smile spreading and ignoring the pain she kissed her mother's cheek as she helped Anne onto a chair.

'You always think of others, Mama. It's been a year since I last saw him and I am excited to see him again.' She didn't add that she was so looking forward to him coming as a protection for her as well as the joy of them being together again as a family. Surely, no one would dare to do anything similar to Charles, not with Will here. Then she realised she was being selfish. He was not here to protect her but to have a great chance in life. She shook herself mentally and chastised herself for her selfishness but knew she had changed since Charles' attack. She had to make sure that it didn't make her too bitter. She hadn't liked men much before, now she was finding she was anxious and even more hostile towards them. Will was her brother, not anything like Charles. And neither were the other footmen at Oatlands, not really, not if she was honest. She needed to keep a close rein on her emotions and feelings, throw Charles out and recover her life. It would take some effort, she was beginning to realise.

Her father interrupted her thoughts. 'A brief and to the point letter. Will was never a one for writing, unlike our Anne, here,' Jack said with a proud smile. 'You should have been a boy, Anne.'

How I would rejoice if that were the case, she thought, but just smiled.

CHAPTER SEVEN

Anne hurried from the house to the lodge, trying not to slip on the icy pathway, being careful of her almost healed ribs. The cut over her eye had healed well as had her bruises. She drew her cloak tighter around her as the bitter wind tried to whisk it away. William had arrived a couple of hours ago but this was the first chance she'd had to go to the lodge and see him. Her heart swelled at the prospect of her brother being at Oatlands. But as she approached the lodge she stopped abruptly, listening with mounting dismay to the shouting coming from inside. She knocked loudly on the door and opened it decisively, finding her father and William standing either side of the table both looking furious.

*

When William saw Anne a wave of relief went through him and he rushed to her, hugging her gently. 'Anne, how are you after your fall? I've just heard all about it. Are you recovering?'

She smiled and touched his cheek, affectionately. 'Don't worry, I'm all right. I'm healing well, it was just a silly fall, but don't squeeze my ribs mind!'

'I'm relieved.' He kissed her cheek. 'But let me

look at you. You look beautiful.'

'Ah! Always the flatterer,' she said with good humour. 'But you,' she stepped back looking at him closely, 'you *have* changed. I do believe you've grown taller and filled out. You've turned into a man.' She went on tip-toe and kissed his cheek and then looked from him to her parents. 'Mama? You look distressed, and you, Papa, you look so angry. I have never seen that look before on you.' She looked between them again.

'He says he wants to join the army and not work here,' Jack spat.

'What!' She looked at Will and then at her parents. 'I don't understand.'

Will took her hands in his. 'You know I've always wanted to be a soldier like Papa. You *know* that,' he pleaded.

'Yes, but you were a boy then. Now you are grown into a man I thought you'd realise that a soldiers' life is not so attractive.'

'It is to me.' Not you too, he thought, bitterness growing inside him as he tried to control his anger. It had all gone so terribly wrong. He couldn't understand the problem everyone had with his joining the army.

'You are not thinking this through,' Jack exploded. 'I'm not having any son of mine become a common soldier.' Hannah put a restraining hand on his arm but he shook her off, not taking his eyes off his son. 'Leave me, please, Hannah. This is between me and Will.' He took a deep breath. 'It is not a life to live unless you have *no* other prospects. Do you hear me? *No* other prospects. Or you are a *certain type* of man. And we have brought you up to be *better* than that.'

'I can do what I like when I'm twenty-one.'

123

'*You* are only nineteen—'

'*Stop!*' Hannah shouted. 'Stop,' she said more gently. 'Let's talk this over like civilised people with no shouting or petulance.'

'Who's petulant?' Will shouted.

Hannah gave him the look she used when he was little. It always stopped him as he knew not to push her with that look on her face, it would be worse for him and it had the same effect now. 'Let's sit down and talk like civilised adults,' she said. 'And I will remind you that baby Simon is asleep upstairs. So, keep your voices down, please.'

With some kerfuffle from the men they sat themselves around the table. Will next to his mother and opposite his father and Anne. 'Now,' Hannah said in a soothing voice, 'when you were a little boy you wanted to be a soldier like your father, it's what little boys do, emulate their fathers,' she smiled at Will. 'But you have not talked of it for years. So why do you now want to join the army and not come to work here in a job most people like us would sell their soul for?'

Will shuffled in his chair fighting his building frustration. They're treating me like a child. I'll show them I'm a grown man with my own needs and ideas but then he realised he *was* being childish and he felt ashamed. But he couldn't let it go; he had to help them see it from his point of view. If he was such an adult he could do that couldn't he? But how? He usually had a silver tongue which got him out of quite a lot of trouble, but this, this was too important for that – it meant too much to him.

He cleared his throat, still searching for a way and then realised the truth was his only option. He pulled himself up straight and made his voice as confident and loud as he could. 'I'm grateful, truly I am, for you finding me the place at Sir Arthur's house. Over the years, as a servant there, I've learned a lot and one of the things I learned is that being in service is … well …' he hesitated because he knew he was criticising his family and he didn't want to do that but he had no choice. He finally said, as gently as he could, 'It's boring! It's the same thing day in and day out.' He knew he sounded childish; he wasn't doing this well.

No one spoke but all eyes were fixed on him. He tried to gather his thoughts, desperate not to hurt them. 'I want … I'm sorry, there's no other way to say this.' He took a deep breath to steady himself. 'I want excitement and adventure. I can get all of that from the army. And I'll get paid for it. And I like the idea of the army.' He looked at his father, 'You spent most of your life in the army. If it's good enough for you then why is it not good enough for me?'

'Being a servant is safe, the army is not,' his father retorted.

Will's frustration overflowed. 'I don't want *safe*. *Safe* is for cowards.'

'How dare—'

'Stop it! Remember we're civilised people,' Hannah burst out as she looked at both men, brokering no nonsense. Jack glowered at her, but said nothing. 'That's better. Now, carry on, Will.'

He looked down at the table and Anne took hold of his hand, encouraging him. He had no idea this would be so difficult. It all seemed so simple back in London. He breathed in deeply again. 'I want to travel the world and see places other than England.'

'Stop mumbling,' his father complained.

He gave his father a challenging look. He'd had enough of this. He stood, looking at Jack. 'Look where you have been, Papa. You've served all over the world, even the Americas. I … I want to live before I die … and …' He rubbed his hands over his face deciding whether he should be brutally honest. He had no choice now he had come this far. 'There is nothing here. Oatlands will be like a living death.' There. He'd said it!

Hannah held up her hand to Jack and Anne who both looked fit to burst and, perceptively, she asked, 'Do any of your friends in London want to join the army, too?'

Will looked at her gratefully. 'My two best friends have already joined up but I wanted to talk with you before I did because, well, that's how our family is. That's how you brought me up and I thought it only fair. But then Mr Tucker came to see me and before I knew what was happening I was being seen by the duke and arrangements were being made for me to come and work here. It all happened so fast and they took it for granted I would be grateful and accept and I didn't know what to do.' He looked down at the table again. 'And here I am … at Oatlands … with a job I don't want, in a place I don't want to be.' His mother gasped and his father's face turned thunderous and as he opened his mouth to speak Will held up his hand to stall them. He took a deep breath and let it out slowly. 'I realise now that I'm here,' his face looked anguished, 'I just cannot do this ... this isolation ... this ... separateness from the world.' He ran his hand over his face and his voice dropped to a whisper. 'I'm sorry, but it will be like a living death for me.'

'*William, how dare you—*' Jack shouted but a

small shrill cry stopped him in mid flow.

Hannah glared at Will and Jack with a look that said this is all your fault. 'Now you have woken Simon up.' She didn't try to hide her frustration. 'I'll try and get him settled again. Please wait until I come back down before you carry on.' She glared at each of them in turn. 'Use the time to think hard on what is going on here. How we can resolve it. I'm relying on you to be sensible.'

Silence ensued as Jack, Will and Anne examined their fingernails in great detail or found the fire a great attraction. Will didn't know how to extract himself from this and was beginning to be sorry he hadn't just joined up with his friends and to hell with his family. Then he felt awful. It wasn't his way. He loved them all and the last thing he wanted was to cause them pain.

'There,' Hannah said, coming down a while later, 'he is settled but do keep your voices down. We don't want to wake him up *again*, do we?' She looked at Jack and Will.

'No, we don't, that is for sure,' Jack said quietly. 'I've been thinking and I have something to say.' He stood and walked slowly up and down the room a few times. 'William,' he started in a conciliatory tone, 'you are a man now, I can see that. I have never spoken to you as a man, but the time has come. You are old enough to understand many things you couldn't before.'

Will remained silent wondering what was coming.

'Let me tell you a story. *My* story.' He stopped pacing and stood facing Will, the table a barrier between them. 'As you all know, our family originates from a small village in Derbyshire. Good, honest people who ran a tannery. I had no choice but to work there, and make no mistake, work is hard in a tannery. I hated every minute of it. It is dirty work and tanneries stink!' Jack shuddered. 'Really stink and I stank of the tannery as my friends always reminded me.

'We lived simple lives and I was bored – as you say you will be in Oatlands – I wanted excitement too and when the Coldstream Guards came to Chesterfield to enlist as many men and boys as were suitable I went with my friends and we joined up. Just like that. No aforethought of what it would actually mean to my life. The glamour of the uniform and the thought of excitement and adventure is attractive to boys. My parents had given their blessing before I applied as they knew how fractious I was, and quite frankly, there were too many children. They were glad to have one less.'

He was lost in thought for a minute and then gathered himself. 'I was so excited when we set off to march to London with the other recruits full of dreams of adventure and new things. And for a few years I lived wild, with little control. I did things you might find attractive but it pales quickly, believe me. I realised my quiet life in Derbyshire was not so bad after all.'

Jack ran his hand down his face, scratching at his stubble, thinking. 'The army was an undisciplined force at that time, before the duke was made head of the Coldstream. For him and the other officers their social position and money made life easier but for the foot soldier conditions were harsh, more than harsh if I'm honest. Only poor men without education and hope of betterment would consider being a foot soldier in the army, men whose abject poverty was worse than what the army offered. That or coarse, often violent, men were the kind of men the army attracted.

'We travelled in extreme discomfort, marched for weeks, months sometimes. We often had little to eat and what there was, was of poor quality, rotten often. There were no comforts. If you were injured there was no medical attention for you. I've seen many a brave man scream in agony after battles and no one attends them. They die in their own filth and the filth of their comrades and enemies. There's no glory there, Will. That's the lot of the common soldier. And all that makes men aggressive and insensitive. There were many fights amongst ourselves before we even met the enemy. You learned to be a hard man or you faltered.'

He put his hands on the table, leaning towards his son. 'In the army I was not the man you know, this *nice* man who looks after you and nurtures you. That was your mother's doing, she wouldn't accept me any other way and you know how I feel about your mother. But in the army,' he speared Will with his eyes, *'I* was that hard man.' He pointed aggressively at his own chest. *'I* lived and fought and loved women along the way. Aye, and your mother knows all about that.' He looked at Hannah and she nodded her encouragement. 'And,' he went on, 'you might find that attractive too, many young men do. But the true fact is that we men didn't *love* women along the way, we *had* women along the way. We all drank, the women too, until we were like base animals, rutting and drinking and merrymaking. But it wasn't merry, we only thought it was. And the women, oh, they encouraged us, those poor creatures, those camp followers, were the only kind of women we had and as long as we paid for their services in money or in kind then they were satisfied. For you see, those women had less than us. At least we had the army and wages, they had nothing except us. I thought I loved women, and I was too crude to know that I didn't know what love was.'

He walked to the window and looked out, motionless except for his hands which clasped and unclasped behind his back, his whole body tense.

'And then, I met your mother.' He turned back and looked lovingly at his wife. 'And my life changed. She changed it ... love changed it. I discovered what love was. And that little boy from Derbyshire reasserted himself back into my life.'

Hannah wiped away some tears.

Jack's face had lost its fury and his features softened as he gazed lovingly at his wife, then he looked back at Will and his eyes hardened like stone. 'You want to know about the army, I'll tell you about the army.' He kept his voice soft, which made what he said the more powerful. 'The army is hard, son. The ordinary soldiers are treated as beasts. Your life is not valued. No one cares about you except your friends and they get killed or injured so often you give up having friends who you value and care about. You cease to be the man you'd like to be ... but I didn't know that until I met your mother.'

He looked at his wife again. 'What fate of good fortune brought you into my life, my darling wife? I have never worked out why you took me on but I do know that it was the making of me. And look at me now, a family man with children to be proud of and a good job where I am not going to be killed for doing it.'

He closed his eyes momentarily and breathed deeply. 'Because, to be honest, I was a beast of a man like the other soldiers, Yes, I had adventure and travel and saw many things and places that I would never have experienced, but do you know what? I realised when I met your mother that none of that mattered. That the love of a good woman, a happy and contented home, was of far more importance than any adventure or travel can give you. I learned that people are the same all over, only the countries and language change. Human nature is the same.

'Your mother,' he looked at Hannah again, 'your mother made my life worth living. Because, really, truly … *really* … if I am brutally honest, the life I was living was no life at all.'

He paced the room again, deep in thought and the air hung heavy with emotion. 'The army, William,' he still paced, 'teaches men aggression, brutality.' He smashed one fist violently into the other, which made everyone jump. 'Thump before you think. That's what I learned in the army. And yes, I've done my share of shameful things. Every soldier has. But I try not to think about them. I'm two different men,' he held up the index finger of each hand, looking at his son. 'One, I'm Sergeant Dresser,' he emphasised with his left finger, 'the soldier who can command and fight with the best of them. And two,' he emphasised with his right finger, 'I am Jack Dresser, husband and father and the true me emerges … the me I like.

'But I had to keep being a soldier as it was the only way I had, the only skill I had, to keep your mother and you living a good, safe life. That was everything to me. I joined the army for adventure and it made me into a man who was fit for nothing else. A trap, William. A trap most men cannot get out of once ensnared.'

Jack paused at last and Will breathed out as he realised he had been holding his breath. He had never seen this side of his father before and it scared him. He didn't know this man. His heart was pounding. Where was this going? He jumped as his father's stern, too loud voice interrupted his thoughts.

'And what happens to old soldiers? If they are not killed they get injured or too old and decrepit to fight and then they are left to fend for themselves. They have no skills outside the army. No one wants them, no one will employ them. They are considered troublemakers, drunks. They live on the streets and in the ale houses, and are the scourge of every town. Do you want to be like that?' He stared at Will. 'Dead or useless? Because that will be your future and it might be your future sooner than you think. It all depends on your luck.'

Jack looked towards the window and gestured towards it. 'Don't use me as an example of an army man. Look at that bad-tempered, decrepit wretch, White, in the lodge opposite. He is your usual army man – not me.'

William closed his eyes tight, feeling bruised and battered. He'd been expecting disappointment but nothing like this tirade. His limbs started to shake in shock or anger, he wasn't sure which.

'And when I had to retire through bad health we were facing destitution. I do not exaggerate. And yes, I was lucky again. I was granted a pension, but the army pension is such a small one that it would not keep body and soul of my family together. And who would employ me, an ex-soldier with gout and now arthritis?' Jack rubbed his leg absent-mindedly as he had a habit of doing when his arthritis was painful.

'Your father never complains,' Hannah said softly, looking at Will. 'I know he is in pain most days, especially in winter, but never a word is said.'

'Well, that's the army's way. No one likes a complainer. And you, William, will have to learn to endure your pain too if you join up, for it is certain something will get you. I do my job here and I keep my job and I say nothing because your mother and me were desperate. And then, from out of nowhere, the duke came into our lives and we have this rare chance to live *good* lives. *Comfortable* lives. We have security and the knowledge that you will not be killed or injured in your job. That you will be kept warm, have good clothes, good food and plenty of it – the greatest luxuries for poor people like us.'

Will risked a look at his mother who was wiping away tears then at Anne, who looked as stricken as he felt and as immobile with shock as he was. He surmised that she had not seen this side of their father either. His father's voice was soft in the distance and he brought his attention back to him.

'If you work here you will know that when the time is right for you to start your own family you can give them security, a warm comfortable home and good food and clothes and even education. You can get those things by not risking your life in war and hardly seeing your children. You can get those things without having to kill other men to ensure your own survival. And believe me that's a thing that destroys your soul.' He left that sentence hanging as if he was fighting demons. Finally, he added, so softly

133

Will hardly heard him. 'Your children will be able to prosper and become better than you and certainly better than me.'

The silence was intense and Will dared not speak, unable to understand how all this was happening. He felt like a child again. God damn him, he is undermining me and what I want for my own life. He thinks that what happened to him will happen to me, well, I'll show him. He felt tears well up again. He never expected anything like this but again his father's voice intruded on his thoughts.

'If you want to throw all this away for an unrealistic dream of the romance of the soldier then I pity you. If you decide that is the way you want to take then please do not start work here tomorrow. I couldn't bear the shame if you started here and left soon after. Of facing the duke knowing that my son had taken his shilling but had turned tail and decided the king's shilling was preferable. I couldn't bear the disloyalty. It's bad enough you've come this far just to change your mind, but don't make it worse.'

Will said nothing, stiff with shock. What should he do or say? His father looked like a man defeated, not like a man who had just demolished his son and was proud of himself like so many fathers might be, but as a man who cares deeply and was full of sorrow.

William's mind was whirling with so many thoughts he didn't know which to listen to and he was only vaguely aware of his father walking slowly up and down the small room. Then from the far end of the room he heard his father's voice, soft and caressing this time. 'And also, realise this. Here, at Oatlands, will be very different from being in service at Sir Arthur's. The duke is a young man and there are many parties and famous visitors; I can guarantee you that it will not be boring. You'll get to see and hear extraordinary things and you will not be able to talk about it. Your loyalty must be absolute. I'm going to be brutally honest … the duke has given you this chance because of me. Because he knows he can trust me and I have vouched for you. If you let the duke down you let us all down.' Jack let that sentence hang in the air like an accusation.

'Are you man enough to stay?' he said very softly. 'Because, believe me, you will find lots of fights here. There will be backbiting, jealousies, pettiness, bad feelings and many will try to fault you; that is usual for servants in large houses. And the mark of a real man is someone who can still do his job well and ignore the rest and not reciprocate in kind. And that is not easy.

'Think about it. A good life here where you can have a wife and children who you can take care of and give the best start in life you can. Good housing, good food, good prospects for them as opposed to army brats with wives too worn down by poverty and struggle to bring up the children well. Most army brats die anyway. Do you want that for your life when you have this chance?'

Will realised to his dismay that his shaking was increasing. He'd never known his father to speak so long and so earnestly. He had no idea he felt that way about the army.

'So,' Jack said decisively, 'decide now. Are you for Oatlands or the army?'

Three pairs of eyes looked at him. His father's bored into him and his mother's and sister's pleaded. The silence became a weight dragging at him. A weight he didn't want nor expected.

'I love you all very much,' was the only thing he could think to say, and he meant it.

His mother took both his hands in hers. 'Then show us that love and stay here. Your father knows what he's talking about. You have the benefit of his wisdom. Do you have the wisdom to let him guide you?'

Will looked from one to the other, not knowing what to answer. Were they right and he wrong? Had he been so mistaken? He'd been dreaming of the army for so long. None of this was supposed to happen. He had imagined that they would be pleased he was going to fight for his country. His life had been ruled by a military background and no one had criticised it before. Had they sheltered him? They had to realise he was a man now. He stood up abruptly, his chair scraping against the floorboards. 'I'm sorry, I need a walk.'

Will let the door slam shut behind him and took a deep breath of fresh air that was so cold it hit him like a punch. He'd forgotten his greatcoat but didn't want anyone to follow him so he started walking briskly, unthinking, following the roadway. He tried to control his emotions as his body shook uncontrollably. No, he would not cry, although he felt the deepest need to. He turned left into the woods and walked through the trees, for how long he didn't know. His thoughts tumbled and bumped into each other until he was a mass of confusion. He stopped beside the lake, not seeing it, lost in his thoughts. He was too soft. He'd been told that often. He needed to toughen up. The army would do that. He was a man now — nineteen, for goodness' sake. He so craved respect but everyone treated him as a boy and not a man. Girls had told him they liked his wholesome good looks, they wanted to mother him, they'd said in a way that didn't make him think of his mother. There was no other way. It was the army for him regardless of his family's opposition.

He saw his mother's face just before he ran off, pleading and full of anguish. Anne's too. His father's pale and haggard; he'd aged in front of him. That was a responsibility he didn't want on his conscience, but he had to think of himself. He couldn't be dragged down into the mind-crippling boringness of living in such a place and yes, his father was probably right, there would be quarrels, back-biting and jealousies of boring people doing boring jobs with nowhere to go and nothing else to do. He'd be ground down before he knew it. No, he had to find a way to explain to his family what it was that drove him to be a soldier and make them understand there was no other way for him. He'd go back and face them.

Then he realised with shock that he was striding towards Oatlands house itself. He was stopped in his tracks by the unexpectedness of it. It's not grand, he realised. It looked like a rich person's house but not a royal house. It was big, but not too big and nothing as imposing as the palaces he'd seen in London. The duke is the king's second son, he pondered, and he'd become king if anything happened to his elder brother. So for someone so high up why had he decided to live in a house that didn't comply with his status? That said a lot about the duke. He thought back to his interview with him and realised that he had really liked him. Thought he was a man of substance, who cared about people. He'd been told he was a man of vision, character, backbone and fairness and Will believed it.

A weak sun appeared and he had to shield his eyes with his hand as he approached the front entrance, surprised by its simplicity. A few steps led to a large plain porch with a wide front door made of unembellished elm that was beautiful because of its starkness.

He imagined the people arriving for balls and parties; the Prince of Wales ... even King George and Queen Charlotte themselves. He was surprised by a shudder of excitement down his spine as he thought he could be part of all that.

The front door was snatched opened unexpectedly which made Will jump. Mr Sweetman strode out and confronted him. 'Tradesmen around the back,' he barked, nodding his head in that direction.

'Oh, ah, sorry, sir. I'm … I'm William Dresser, the, ah, the … new footman.' Will froze, horrified. Why had he said that? Confused, he realised he was making a fool of himself by dithering.

'Well, the famous William Dresser, no less,' the butler said. 'You're a day early,' he snapped. He looked him up and down. 'And, you're not as impressive as your father made you out to be. Stand up straight, boy! You're in a royal household now, not some new money tradesman's house. We do things properly here.'

Boy! How dare he call him that but to his surprise Will stood to attention as if he were in the army and realised then what his father meant by surviving and succeeding in such a household. He hadn't expected animosity as Anne had spoken of the butler with fondness. The challenges would be considerable. And this man was only the butler. What would it be like with a house full of royal people? Was he up to the challenge? Did he want it?

'You may think you warrant visitor status, young William, but I have news for you, no one else thinks so. Do not use this entrance again unless you are on duty. You use the servants' entrance. Is that clear?'

'I was on my way to the servants' entrance, sir,' Will replied, trying to control his temper as the unfairness of the criticism, 'when you opened the door.' Again, he thought, why did I say that? Fool! He tried to keep his face passive, tried not to show the thunderous thoughts going on behind it.

The butler looked down on Will. 'Well, as you're here, I'll take you myself to the servants' quarter through the main house as the duke is not in residence. You may as well get the lie of the land as soon as possible.'

And like an obedient dog, Will followed the butler into the house surprised at his acquiescence, his mind reeling like a fish being jerked out of the water into a world where he couldn't breathe, knowing a slow and painful death awaited him. He didn't know what to do and it would soon be too late. He must decide.

Like a man being dragged to the scaffold he saw every detail as if it were the last time he would look upon life. Time slowed as the air inside the large hallway chilled his skin, colder than outside and exacerbated by many white marble pillars that disappeared into the distance. The sun that had blinded him outside did the same inside as he walked further into the hall. He stood in a beam of sunlight and looked up to see a vaulted ceiling as high as the house and instead of a roof a huge elegant circular window giving views of the sky and on sunny days the rays of the sun would shine down as it did right now. He felt he'd been caught in the sun's beams like a chosen person, a religious experience, and then chided himself for being silly. But then thought again how that feeling would wrap itself around other people and if it made them feel as special as he felt at that moment, well, then that would be a magical thing to have in a house.

'Come,' the butler said irritated at Will's tardiness as he made his fast way through the hallway. Without thinking, Will spurred himself to follow the butler more closely. His footsteps echoed on the black and white floor tiles until he noticed that the butler's footsteps were almost silent which made Will moderate his gait somewhat. There was a light perfume in the air caused, he thought, by the polish used on the grand elm staircase which branched off to the right. He noticed the imposing elm doors, thick, wide and tall, which led to rooms he couldn't see into, and he wondered what secrets they would unfold to him. How they were used and who used them would be discovered another day. He didn't know whether he was more intrigued or anxious, but a tingle of excitement tickled his back bone as he followed the butler. He liked that feeling.

Mr Sweetman walked so fast William had trouble keeping up with him. He marvelled at the big man's ability to move so well. He must be at least forty. He couldn't imagine himself ever being so old.

They went down stairs and along corridors, passed the kitchens until they were in the far end of the basement. The butler stopped and opened a door. 'You will share this room with James, another footman,' he said as he went inside. William followed him and looked around the small white painted room and thought it a tight squeeze for two big men. The beds were squashed in so close they could almost be a double. Mmm, he had better accommodation at Sir Arthur's. He assumed James would be as tall as he was as all the best footmen were tall. And royalty would have the best, he knew that and it gave him a thrill to know he'd been chosen. He recognised he was seeing everything from a different angle and a shock went through him as he realised he'd made his decision. He was here. He hadn't baulked or run. He'd followed the butler like a dog on a lead and he was filled with a sense of his own importance. Yes, royalty would have the best footmen and he was the best. He decided to keep that boast to himself.

He felt a glow of superiority ripple down his body. Yes, he had made the right decision. Better a footman at a royal household than a base foot soldier. His father's words echoed around his head. His excitement increased as to what awaited him but deep inside he also wondered if he was giving in too easily. But he pushed his doubts aside and concentrated on the moment.

'So, you are the son of Jack Dresser and brother to Anne.' The butler interrupted Will's thoughts of grandeur and looked him up and down. 'You've got all your family around you, Dresser, a proper little home from home. I don't want you getting too comfortable. We've heard a lot about you from your family and you have a lot to live up to, young William. I do not envy you that. I will be keeping a hawk's eye on you.' He walked around William in the tight space which made Will uncomfortable. And what did he mean, 'A lot to live up to'? But he knew better than to ask and Anne had warned him that the butler's bark was worse than his bite so his natural buoyancy was not dented.

'We do things differently at Oatlands,' Mr Sweetman said, importantly. 'The staff are close-knit as we spend a lot of time together and for a lot of that time we are on board-wages. The duke is not here that often and he deems it advisable to keep us all on staff so that things will run smoothly and with commitment and loyalty when he is here. Therefore, we are more affable to each other than a normal household, a little more relaxed. But,' he said loudly, 'don't think that gives you room to be lax. You do your job well, not just as well as you can, but even better than you can and you will survive. That applies to jobs done on board-wages as well as when the duke is in residence. Is that clear?'

'I sincerely hope I can live up to expectations, Mr Sweetman, sir,' Will said with the cheeky grin that had got him out of a lot of trouble but had the opposite effect on the butler.

'Indeed.' Mr Sweetman said as he rose up on the balls of his feet and gave Will a harsh look. 'We shall see. And the standard mode of address here is, 'Yes, sir. Mr Sweetman, sir.'

'Yes, sir. Mr Sweetman, sir.' Will repeated.

'Where is your box?'

'It's at the lodge, Mr Sweetman, sir.'

'Well go and get it and bring it here. I'll send James to see you to explain everything but he'll be at least an hour yet. Make sure you and your box are back here before then.'

'Yes, sir. Mr Sweetman, sir.'

'These are your uniforms.' The butler pointed to two footmen's uniforms hanging from hangers on pegs knocked into the wall. 'They should fit like a glove as they have been made for your measurements. Look after them as if you damage them you will be charged for the replacements.'

Will had never seen anything so grand. He had no idea when he was being measured for it that it would make him look like royalty itself. 'Yes, sir, Mr Sweetman, sir,' Will said as the butler raised an ironic eyebrow, as if he could read his mind. He left the room, leaving the door open. Will closed it softly and looked at his uniform and whistled low and long. He couldn't resist running his hand over the rich, dark red velvet of the jacket which changed hue as his hand caressed it. Mmm, nice. He buried his face in the softness of it all and smelt the scent of fresh wash and good air. He had to smile at the profusion of gold braiding that adorned the jacket and matching waistcoat and nodded his approval. The breeches were in the same opulent red as the jacket and he noticed the gold buttons at the sides of the knees matched the buttons on the jacket. The soft silk of the white stockings pleased him and made him glad he was, 'good of leg', as he had been told by more than one admiring woman in the past. Finally, he couldn't resist trying on the white powdered wig with its queue. As he looked in the mirror of the small dresser he couldn't stop his smile, until he noticed he was looking decidedly smug. Pull yourself together, he said under his breath. It's obvious from the butler's attitude that I am going to have to earn this uniform. He used the trick he'd been told about from the butler in his previous household. A footman always looks earnest and capable, he could hear the old butler saying. When in doubt, but make sure you are unobserved, move your hand slowly down the front of your face and adjust your features into the 'footman's look'. William tried it and checked the mirror. A calm, pleasant face full of earnest intentions and total sincerity looked back at him, a face that didn't cause concern to the employer. Then he spoilt it all by laughing. I'm going to have to practise this more, he thought as he realised he should run to the lodge, get his box and tell his family of his decision.

*

He'd just returned to his room when James came thundering along the corridor with noisy footsteps and threw open the door. The two looked at each other appraisingly.

'You must be William.'

'And you must be James.' Mmm, I could take him in a fight, so nothing to worry about there. But he's hostile to me. It's to be expected I suppose he was probably a friend of the sacked footman. Only one way to deal with this. He gave James one of his brilliant smiles and approached him, holding out his hand. 'Glad to meet you, James. I'm sure we will get on well. You are above me in this household and I will respect that. You're the boss in this room.'

'And don't you forget it,' James said.

Will could tell by his tone that he was softening a little so he rummaged in his bag and pulled out a very clean cloth, untied it and exposed a most exquisite fruit cake his mother had given him. The mouth-watering aroma of freshly baked fruit and spices filled the room.

James' eyebrows shot up.

'Like a slice?'

'Indeed so. Your mother's?'

Will nodded as he pulled out a ready cut slice and gave it to James.

'She is famous here for her fruit cakes.'

'Is she now?' Will felt pride as he bit into his slice and decided not to ask James anything about working at Oatlands in case he resented it, in case he thought Will wanted it easy. They ate in silence.

Swallowing his last mouthful James said, 'Delicious. However, Mr Sweetman asked me to show you around the house so come on, let's get started. He will go through your duties with you tomorrow.'

Will followed him, feeling he'd got on the right side of James but his nerves fluttered in his stomach nonetheless. He couldn't let his parents down now, but he wasn't sure he could live up to their expectations.

*

The first few weeks went by quickly for Will. He had little time to see his parents and only saw Anne during meals, but he was getting to know the house and his fellow servants. He defended himself when other staff commented he was young to be a footman, saying he gained good experience as a steward's room boy with Sir Arthur and a footman was the usual promotion after that. He'd got his position on merit, he insisted. He wasn't going to let people push him around. He didn't mention anything about his misgivings on being there; he wasn't a fool. As the duke was now in London, the staff were on board wages and the housekeeper and butler made up a roster of jobs for all the indoor staff under their control to follow. Will was given menial tasks to do which he felt were below him, such as helping the maids scrub every inch of below stairs. This included furniture, pots, pans, crockery, floors and even ceilings and staircases. But he made sure never to complain to anyone less it got back to his superiors. He was last in so bottom of the heap. He had to prove himself. His time would come. Although the other footmen working above stairs didn't fare much better, being engaged in taking down floor to ceiling drapes, taking up rugs and carpets and beating them outside – and then putting them all back again once they were clean.

One morning, Will was instructed to help the maids upstairs to clean all the bedrooms. He and James moved aside huge mahogany beds while the maids cleaned under and around them. He helped James take down the drapes and take up the rugs and beat them outside, heavy, dirty work. 'Don't worry,' James had said over a rug they were both beating. 'I know we do maids' work sometimes but we all muck in here. Help each other, you know. The maids help us when we are overwhelmed with work when the duke is here. We are an unusual household in that way.'

'Indeed you are. But thank you, James, I was feeling rather puzzled and wondered if I was being tested but now you have explained I am looking forward to a time when I need help from a maid!'

James looked at him, unsure. Then Will burst out laughing and James relaxed. They were getting to know one another.

It also gave Will the opportunity to see the rooms the duke and his guests used. They were sumptuous and more richly furnished than at Sir Arthur's house. Will deduced the furniture of royalty was far superior to anything he had seen before. Quality, his father had said, the duke much values quality both in things and in people. Don't let him down.

Some of the younger maids had made eyes at Will and he was tempted but knew he should establish himself first. And then his mind was filled with other things as Mr Sweetman came downstairs one morning where the staff were waiting for him to give permission to start their breakfasts. He settled himself in his chair at the head of the table and looked around at the eager faces.

'Well, good morning, Mrs Harley,' he nodded to the housekeeper, 'and everyone. I have an announcement. It gives me great pleasure to inform you that the duke will arrive here next week. He will be bringing about twelve friends and he expects to have several parties where other overnight guests may be invited.'

Will glanced at Anne and smiled but the frown on her face worried him. She was not joining in the murmur of excitement bubbling up as the butler added, 'Mrs Harley, let's meet in my office this afternoon to discuss this.'

The housekeeper bowed her head graciously. 'Will three of the clock suit, Mr Sweetman?'

'Very well,' he nodded back.

The butler looked at Will. 'This is your chance, young William. We will be so busy you won't know if you're coming or going. It will be vastly different to anything you have known before. We have all been through this and know what to expect. You are the virgin amongst us so be guided by us.'

Will's eyes widened in consternation as he swallowed down a mounting embarrassment. Was he being played with?

'I don't think Will is a virgin, Mr Sweetman,' one of the footman guffawed.

'Oh, for goodness sake,' Anne said, exasperated.

Will looked at her with gratitude.

Mr Sweetman stood on his dignity. 'I use the term advisedly, as experiencing a week of partying with the duke and his friends is tantamount to starting in a state of innocence and coming out the other end in a state of worldly experience.'

They all laughed, even Anne. Will looked around and felt he *was* being played with so he laughed along with them. And he recognised the butler was right, he was a virgin as far as royal entertainment went. He would indeed have to depend upon his peers.

*

The week of the duke's visit went so fast and was so busy that when it ended, Will felt like a deflated ball that had been hit too hard. He'd never known such unending activity, from early morning, helping with the cleaning up and preparations for the day, to the end of it, which was often almost at the start of the next day for the servants. It was exhausting but so, so exciting.

It had been a week of all-night parties with heavy drinking and gambling interspersed with some energetic bedroom activity many of the guests indulged in, including the duke. Several women came and went through the week, some staying days and others just overnight. Will had no idea who these women were but knew they were most definitely of a superior class to him and the other servants. He served them with as much reverence as he would have served the duke. It wasn't for him to judge, although he couldn't help a feeling of envy for the men but squashed it down instantly. That was no way forward for his new career. He knew he had to learn to accept a different lifestyle, one he could never attain, and to let it all wash over him.

He'd found the duke to be friendly and easy going to his servants as long as they did their jobs well. His standards were high and everyone tried their best to please him. He was that sort of a man, no one wanted to disappoint him. However, some of his friends were of a different order. Full of their own importance and on occasion, uncivil to the servants. He remembered one party in particular. The duke reprimanded one of his guests who spoke sharply to Mr Sweetman. 'My butler is spoken to with respect, Belknap,' he said. 'I do not expect to have to remind you again.'

Will filled with pleasure at the rebuff, making sure he did not show his feelings. The butler kept his dignity and merely bowed briefly to the room and disappeared through the tall double doors and reappeared shortly with several more decanters of wine. That particular night Will had kept a count of the bottles of wine decanted and consumed over dinner and twenty people had consumed 36 bottles and Will wasn't sure if he felt envious or disgusted at the excess.

After dinner the port and brandy came out as the party decamped to the adjoining room which was laid out for card playing. The duke's passion was playing cards but unfortunately he often lost heavily. Will noticed the man who had been rebuked by the duke had beaten him several times, pocketing huge amounts of money. 'God damn you, Belknap,' the duke bellowed as he threw down his cards. 'Will you take the clothes off my back too? You'll give me recourse tomorrow night, sir.'

And with that the duke had stormed off for bed discreetly followed by one of the women of the party. An extremely charismatic woman, Will thought. A woman full of personality and hidden depths he felt sure, discreet on the outside and full of passion on the inside. He realised he was attracted to women like that but shook himself mentally as women like that were not for lowly footmen. That much he did know.

As he helped to clear up he put the woman out of his mind but the man named Belknap went round and round in his head. He determined to tread carefully when he was nearby. He had a bad feeling about him.

*

The morning the duke and his cronies left Oatlands was one of brilliant sunshine which warmed the chilled air. The silence left hanging by their departure hung heavy in the servants' hall with everyone eating a much-needed dinner and all concentrating on eating rather than talking.

'The duke certainly likes his gambling,' Will said, into the void. 'He lost huge amounts of money some nights and won a little bit of it back the next. You'd certainly have to be rich to be a friend of his.'

'Well that lets you out,' James said, with a grin.

'I wouldn't want to gamble like that,' Will replied. 'It made my eyes water to watch it – so much money on the table. More than anyone can earn in a lifetime.'

'Our lifetime - not the toffs' lifetime,' Edward whispered to Will as he walked by his chair. 'They were born with money spewing out of their screaming mouths.'

Will was glad Mr Sweetman had not heard him. He didn't want to get into trouble because of Edward's indiscretions. He'd have to watch him. He wasn't sure if Edward really believed what he said or was just trying to force an indiscretion from him. He'd noticed an animosity towards him from the first.

'I don't know how they do it?' Will added quickly to cover for Edward's whispering. 'Partying all night every night for a week. I'm exhausted.'

'Well, they don't have to get up in the mornings to clear up their mess after serving them all night,' Henry, ventured, smiling, showing off his beautiful teeth as was his habit. Nothing kept Henry's good nature down for long.

'Hear, hear,' agreed Thomas, who was getting over his shyness.

'And what a mess they left behind,' Joyce added.

'Now, now,' Mr Sweetman warned. 'We'll have none of that, thank you. Respect your betters and most importantly, respect your employer. I know it's hard, but that's why you've been chosen to serve the duke. You can cope with it. He treats us all well and he expects to be treated well in return. And you are paid much more than in a normal household so if you don't like it there are many would be delighted to take your place. There would be a queue at the door and they'd knock you aside to get your job. Think on it.' He looked at them in turn, his mouth turned down and his eyes like icy pebbles. Everyone looked chastised. *'And* it's not as if it happens continuously. He is only here from time to time. We have an easy time of it when he is not here. So I want no more talk like that.

151

Do I make myself clear?'

A subdued, 'Yes, sir, Mr Sweetman, sir,' went around the table.

'I can't hear you,' he whispered.

'Yes, sir, Mr Sweetman, sir,' they all answered loudly, looking shamefaced.

The meal continued in silence until Mr Sweetman finished his and patted his stomach like an old friend. He looked around the room, smiling. 'I have more to say ... something nice this time. Well done, everyone. It's been a hard week, we're all agreed. But we were up to the task. Everyone performed well and in harmony,' he glanced around at each of them, 'and harmony is *very* important.'

'Indeed, very important,' Mrs Harley confirmed.

'And you, William,' he turned his head to look at Will, who froze, expecting some kind of rebuke as everyone looked at him. He hated being picked out and the butler seemed to sense this and did it all the more. At least, that's how it felt to Will but the butler surprised him. 'You did well. You didn't *drop* anything.' Everyone laughed. 'You didn't *spill* anything on anybody.' They laughed louder. 'And ... nobody *noticed* you. That is the mark of a good footman. You do not want to be noticed by the guests. You supply the service required while keeping yourself invisible.'

'Thank you, Mr Sweetman, sir,' Will said with relief, laughing with the rest of them. A feeling of pride rose up in him, he couldn't help it and the butler noticed. 'But don't get big headed, William because we all did well. Every last one of us did our job well.'

'Thank you, Mr Sweetman, sir,' they said in unison, this time with smiles. Will made a great effort to suppress his excitement, exhaustion, elation and anticipation for the next time the duke visited.

*

Will felt a lot more confident in his position now he'd survived a week of the duke's partying without incidence. He'd hidden his nerves from the others worrying whether he'd cope, whether he could prove himself worthy of his place as footman. He knew some of the staff had wanted him to fail and make an idiot of himself, especially Edward. He knew he was the particular friend of Charles, the footman who was sacked and whose place Will had taken and assumed that was the cause of it. Anne had told him how close Edward was to Charles and he was very upset when Charles was discharged, but to hell with him, and everyone else. He was ready to devote some time to his love life.

He'd always been popular with girls and considered himself a bit of a ladies' man. Alice, one of the upstairs maids, had been making eyes at him for a while. So Will asked her if she would take a walk with him and she'd readily agreed. He missed female company. He liked women and they liked him. He knew he was good looking and he felt confident his personality matched his looks.

He listened to women more than most men did. Maybe it was because he'd been brought up by his mother with a sister and an absent father. He loved his father, of course, but it was his mother and sister who he kept in his heart. He felt comfortable around women, especially when they put their arms around him and responded to his touch. He loved the weight of a girls' body against his own.

But as time went by his worst fears were being realised. Life in Oatlands was dull compared to London. He felt hemmed in, constrained mentally as well as physically. He couldn't be himself. That was the hardest part of it for him and he felt beholden to behave in a most proper manner towards Alice for everyone was watching and talking about them. He didn't want to misbehave or do anything Alice was not willing to do, but he wanted a bit more passion than a few chaste kisses snatched whenever they thought no one was watching. To have some fun together and get to know each other seemed an insurmountable task as he was always looking over his shoulder no matter where they went there was usually someone watching. Mostly Edward, who watched him like a beady-eyed carrion crow, just waiting for something to pin on him. Alice felt it too and they both agreed life was easier before they got involved and their budding romance died like rosebuds in frost.

But Will was the type of man who needed a woman, wanted a woman. He wasn't ready for marriage but he felt incomplete without the adventure of romance and the satisfaction being in a young woman's company gave him. It wasn't long before he asked a shop assistant from the village to join him in a walk, hoping he would be able to relax more outside of Oatlands. But her father was never far away and the romance faded. Over time, he invited others from the village to walk out with him but things didn't improve. Now he felt as if the whole village was watching him. Could the good-looking new footman be trusted? The family of the last young woman he went out with, after a few visits, invited him to share their pew in church. That made Will run like the devil into the welcoming arms of barmaids. The village of Weybridge was blessed, some would say cursed, by seven inns, a vast amount for such a small village. But they were on the coaching route to London and the Navigation canal ran alongside the village, carrying traffic to the corn and iron mills in the area, resulting in a plethora of customers for each establishment. Consequently, there were many hearty, obliging barmaids who didn't expect anything but a good time and amongst other things Will was always ready for a good time. He gave himself over to them and their administrations and didn't worry about anything else. He was young, he wanted adventure. Well, if he couldn't have the army he'd have some adventure, even it was only the female sort. And he was popular with the barmaids and even got into some fights with the other men who were jealous of his success. He was getting a reputation. And he enjoyed his notoriety. But deep inside him there was something he couldn't quite pin down. It rankled. And as successful as he was with the easier women of the village, he had the feeling he was missing out. That there was something he didn't have the nous to understand; something that caused him dissatisfaction, and even if he couldn't understand it, he was becoming more aware of it. More convinced that he had chosen the wrong path that maybe the army was really the right way for him.

CHAPTER EIGHT

A year had passed and Anne and Mrs Harley had got into the habit of taking walks together from time to time since the 'Charles incidence' as it had become known between them. They walked slowly through the dense woodland surrounding the house. It was a mild day of dull skies and grey clouds, weather to depress rather than uplift. Even the trees looked sad as they hung motionless in the murk. The duke was away and the staff were looking forward to his return, whenever that may be. Each day was merging into another until the months became a glut of indecipherable time rather than the interesting times the staff enjoyed when the duke was in residence. And each and every one of them loved the interesting times, even Mrs Harley, who, of course, kept herself aloof from all that or at least, gave the impression of it.

Walking together had put their relationship on a different footing from maid and housekeeper. They recognised each other's loneliness and apartness from others. On these outings Mrs Harley was as aloof and distant as usual but that suited Anne as she didn't want to talk, preferring to listen to the birds and watch the squirrels and foxes. She felt safer with someone else with her and she supposed the housekeeper felt the same.

But in a rare moment of intimacy Mrs Harley asked, 'How are you, Anne? How are you *really*?' She hesitated, 'I mean, after the "Charles incidence". We don't talk about it and it's been over a year now. You know you can rely on my discretion. I just want to help, to make sure you're bearing up.'

Anne suppressed her surprise and gave a fleeting sideways look at Mrs Harley, who looked uncomfortable. It wasn't like her. They just didn't talk about anything personal. What could she say? That she was always on a knife edge of breaking down into sobs; that her nerves were shattered; that she had never felt so alone in her life; that it was taking over and ruining her equilibrium, her relationships with the other staff and her family. No! Her internal voice shouted. Keep up the pretence. It's the only way you can survive. You cannot let it out or you'll crumble.

Anne looked around at the multitude of trees surrounding them and took pleasure in their grandeur; they calmed her inner turmoil. Then she put her mind to the ugliness of what her life had become. 'I'm coping, thank you, Mrs Harley,' she said, but her voice quavered and the housekeeper glanced at her quizzically. They continued to walk slowly and silently for a while and Anne hoped that was the end of it.

Mrs Harley cleared her throat. 'Do excuse me, Anne, for pursuing this, but I have noticed that you are more distant than you were before, and I say that advisedly as I know you were distant with the staff prior to the events with Charles, but you seem more so, worryingly so. Do you need someone to talk to?' Mrs Harley stopped walking and looked directly at Anne. 'If I may venture to say so, I know how it is to be locked into your distress, to be unable to talk about it because you dare not.'

Anne's surprise at the conversation turned to astonishment and a feeling of unease crept up her backbone; she was not used to such intimacy. And was that pain she saw in the other woman's eyes? What could she mean? She didn't know how to respond so kicked at some of the fallen leaves in a desultory way, playing for time.

'My father,' Mrs Harley continued in a soft voice, 'was a country vicar and we were used to people coming to us for help. Women who had been abused by husbands or fathers, people starving, husbands and wives in despair after the death of yet another baby. I learned to listen and offer practical help. I worry that you need some help to get over this. I know you are not at liberty to speak to anyone but myself or Mr Sweetman or Mr Tucker, as we are the only ones who know about it, but I would not recommend confiding in them. They are men after all and not suited to this kind of confidence.' She cleared her throat again and hesitated before saying even more quietly, 'Women need women for women's matters.'

Anne remembered Mrs Harley saying something similar just after the attack. Something like, women can help women. Again she wondered what had happened to the housekeeper. Had she faced a similar situation? Had someone helped her?

Without realising she was speaking her thoughts out loud Anne said, 'I worry that it will happen again. I have had,' she took a ragged breath, 'in the past I had several attacks of this nature but none as serious as this one, none that invaded—' Anne gulped down a sob.

'I know. I know,' Mrs Harley said quickly, looking more uncomfortable. 'You are a beautiful woman, Anne, and beautiful women sometimes get more attention than they desire. It depends on what kind of woman you are. And you … well, you are not the type to desire it, I venture.'

Anne shook her head, fighting mounting tears. I must not cry, she said to herself. *I must not.* Did the housekeeper understand her feelings, really understand? Could she tell her about her inner feelings? Her thoughts reeled. It had been so easy for Charles to breach her defences and physically touch her most personal place. He had been ruthless and insensible to her wishes and she realised afterwards that, for him, she was just something to have power over as if she were an animal he had to control and dominate … but she would never treat an animal as he had treated her. Stop it, she cried to herself, she had to stop thinking like this. Her anger was getting the better of her, so she resorted to her childhood trick. She imagined a rod of iron which she picked up from the floor and plunged, rather savagely, down the back of her clothing. This held her up straight and instilled unyielding courage into her. Silly, she knew, but it worked for her. Part of her defence was also clenching her stomach until it hurt. This concentration of pain and unbending posture usually worked to get her through unpleasant or emotional things, as it did today.

She gazed into the distance and kept her voice low as if afraid the wildlife would hear and tell tales on her to her peers. 'I'm sorry, Mrs Harley, I have to make sure this never happens again. I really,' she paused for a long moment, deciding what to say, but in the end it just came out unbidden, as natural as could be. 'I couldn't bear it, not again. Not now when I am so lucky to be here, with my family around me. So I have to defend myself against the men. And you are right I am not that kind of woman. I like being alone. I am not cut out to share myself with anyone except my family. I do not like intimacy.' She risked a look at Mrs Harley who was nodding agreement almost imperceptibly. 'The only way I know to do this is to keep myself distant from the men here, hope they'll get bored and start to dislike me … and I cannot be friendly to the women and unfriendly to the men as it will cause caustic comment. So I have to keep myself apart from both. They have got used to it now. They say, *oh, that's just Anne being Anne …* and I know that behind my back they add, *and her parents and brother are so friendly, why isn't she?* But it does the trick, they leave me alone and that's what I want.'

To herself Anne added that every night she prayed to God to help her and ask, why did you make me so attractive to men and give me a nature that abhorred any relationship with them in that way, and not only with men, but women too. She knew there were women who loved only women, but she also knew with certainty that she didn't want that either. She just didn't want intimacy, with anyone, not that kind of intimacy. It put her at odds with the God who had created her. She was afraid she was losing her faith and her faith was very important to her. She went to church every Sunday as expected but now it just left her empty whereas before the services had fulfilled a need in her. And this loss made her so angry; and God remained silent.

They walked on without speaking for a long time

and Anne was grateful as she felt close to breaking down. She had gained her equilibrium by the time they returned to the lake.

They paused on the bank, looking down into the water. 'The lake is so calming, I find,' Mrs Harley said. 'It gives me such pleasure after a hard day. I often come out at night and just stand and look at it.'

Anne hid her surprise that the housekeeper would do such a thing, and not only that, but confide it to her. She didn't want any more confidences so tried for joviality to break the mood.

'Mind you don't fall in.'

'Indeed,' Mrs Harley responded. 'That would never do. And Anne, I do understand what you are going though and understand your thinking. More than you can guess, I venture. But there, let's leave it at that and suffice it to say that you can approach me anytime you feel the need to.'

Gratefully, Anne said, 'Thank you, Mrs Harley. I will never forget it. If I need to, be assured I will. Please do not worry about me.'

'Good, we understand each other. We'd better get back,' and with that she turned and walked briskly away towards the house, leaving Anne looking at her reflection in the lake which rippled when a heron landed on it, breaking her image into pieces. Just like I feel, she said to herself as she looked deep into the lake, wondering where her life was taking her. She liked more cerebral things than the other servants and so did Mrs Harley. They both liked to read and were exceptionally skilled at needlework; they didn't like tittle-tattle and gossiping over the table. Is that why the housekeeper offered her the hand of friendship? It was a lonely life for any housekeeper of a large, important house. They devoted themselves to the family they served and didn't allow any distractions such as husbands and a family of their own. Or if they did, they left their employ. A housekeeper was always given the title Mrs but it was just a courtesy.

Anne didn't want to be a maid all her life but as she did not want to marry then she would have to support herself by staying a maid. There were no other options for her except, if she was very lucky, to become a housekeeper herself, but not many women made it to housekeeper. She knew as time went by and she aged she would find being a maid more and more difficult physically. But, she was being morbid, she was young and fit and now Will was here. She was counting on Will. He would look after her if she got ill or injured or too old to work. She could help with looking after his children, help his wife. Oh, God! How depressing it all was. She didn't want that either. She cursed God again for making her a woman and dependent. She felt overwhelmed by melancholy thoughts and a rage rose within her. She picked up a large stone nearby and threw it with all her might into the lake. It landed with a great splash and as she watched the tumultuous ripples she was surprised at how it calmed her. As she walked away she decided to seek out her brother. He always put her in a better mood and she was determined not to let things drag her down.

*

Will had taken to going outside the house for some fresh air whenever he could get away and as they were on board wages it was easier for him to

162

disappear for a while. It calmed his mind and spirit. He leaned against the back wall of the kitchen and looked out into the woods surrounding the house. The great trees which crowded the scenery calmed him with the noble oaks, tall ash and majestic elms vying with each other for space. A light March wind had come up and moved the bare branches gently this way and that with the light catching them at various angles. It's beautiful here that's for sure, he thought, but beauty is not excitement. Damn! There I go again. I must stop thinking like this. I'm so lucky to be here. I know this. And yet …

Anne crept up to him and shouted, 'Boo.'

He jumped. 'Damn it, Anne. Don't do that,' he snapped.

'You're only annoyed I crept up without you knowing. You always hated that from the time we were little.'

He nodded and then smiled. 'We had some good times, didn't we?'

'We did, but if you don't mind me saying so you've looked a bit morose of late.' Anne let the concern in her voice show. 'I'm beginning to worry about you. Is there anything wrong?'

He studied her for a moment. 'Well, I could say the same for you and you've looked more than morose if *I* may say so, my dear sister.'

She nodded and sighed. 'A little, maybe, but that is just women's troubles, nothing to concern you, but you, you have been even more morose than me if *I* may say so, my dear brother.'

He smiled to acknowledge her joke as he peered at her from under his eyebrows. 'You were always able to know my feelings better than me; it is disconcerting.'

'Come on. Tell me what's wrong,' she cajoled, putting her hand over his and looking up into his face. 'You've been here a year now. You should be feeling happier or more relaxed, at least.'

'Nothing is wrong,' he said mildly. 'I have a bit of a melancholy on me, that's all.'

'You're spending too much time in the village messing with the trollops there.' She softened her voice. 'That would give anybody the melancholy.'

He chuckled as he looked out over the woodland and slowly shook his head. 'Nothing escapes your notice. You know me so well. You are right. Maybe I am too adventurous in my romantic escapades.'

She kept her voice soft. 'There are many nice girls in the village. Why don't you try walking out with them? It would be better for you, you know'

He looked at his sister and spoke wearily. 'Oh, Anne, please don't patronise me. I don't want pleasant. I don't want nice. I don't want pretty. I don't want suitable.'

'Then what *do* you want?'

He sighed deeply. 'What I want …' he tailed off trying to be honest with Anne and himself. He pushed around a few small stones with the toe of his shoe, buying time and as his gaze settled in the distance, said again, 'What I want my dear sister is … exciting … unpredictable … fun!' He worried the stones some more and gazed up at the sky. 'I want a woman not afraid of herself or of others, who is full of ideas, thoughts, and is not afraid to express them … at least to me. A woman whose personality is too big for here … has experience of what life has to offer and wants more than Oatlands, or Weybridge come to that. A woman who will take me to places I have never been to before.'

Anne smiled an indulgent smile. 'You don't want much, do you?' She let her fingers caress his cheek and then stopped abruptly. 'But wait a minute, you don't mean you want to leave Oatlands, do you?'

'No!' he said too quickly, shocked at his sister's perception. 'Oh, I don't know …' He didn't want to admit his doubts to Anne. Admit that he worried he'd chosen the wrong path, that he was having doubts. 'No,' he said slowly at last, 'I don't think so but I want to have some excitement, can't you understand that? The only excitement we get is when the duke is in residence and he is away more than he is here. Oh, God, Anne, I am bored. Bored. Bored. Bored. I am bored with board wages. There, I can't even laugh at my own joke.'

'Well, it's not very original.'

'No, I suppose not, but truly, Anne, I am able to cope when the duke is here but when he's not then I get the melancholy after a while. There is nothing interesting to do. Nothing to stimulate me. We can only do so much cleaning and maintenance and although we have more free time Weybridge is so small … I am not used to the confines of village life. How everyone else knows all your business, knows your feelings before you know them yourself half the time.'

And then he knew he had to tell Anne about his doubts. She was his friend as well as his sister, the person he loved most in the world apart from his parents. He owed it to her. If the worst came to the worst he couldn't let it come as a great surprise to her. But he was nervous. 'You know, we've always got on well. You've been there all through my life and talking to you has always been good for me. Helped me to see what I really thought, wanted, what was best. You always knew better than me.'

'I always let you make your own decisions, you know that. I wouldn't dare try and persuade you to do something that is guaranteed to make you do the opposite.'

Will smiled. 'Well, that well may be true, but talking to you has always been good for me. Helped me to see what I really thought, wanted, what was best. And it's no different now. I have to be totally honest with you.' He breathed in deeply. 'I am unsure whether I have taken the right path. Whether I should have joined the army as I'd wanted to or whether I was weak and let others persuade me as to what I wanted.'

Anne gasped. 'Don't mention this to our parents. It would kill them.'

'Oh, thanks. That really makes me feel better.'

'I mean it.' Anne walked away from him a little, deep in thought and then returned and put her hand on his arm, looking up into his face. 'I cannot deny that I'm shocked. But please, please, rethink this. I'm sure you will feel differently if you only give it a good chance. Everything is still new.'

'I've been here a year Anne, *a whole year!* I think I've given it long enough.'

'I disagree. One year is nothing. You are still maturing. You are such a boy sometimes … I'm sorry I don't mean that like it sounds. You have many qualities and I think those qualities can give you a good life here. It's only the fact that you don't have any excitement that is giving you these feelings. And yes, village life is constraining. And Oatlands itself is like a very small village, a hamlet within a village, if you like. Which means, when you leave the hamlet you only have the village to visit and three hundred people are not a great many when we are used to the population of London and the excitement of the place. Three hundred people can live in one street in London. But, Will, how many of those people in London do you actually know?' She gave him a quizzical look. 'Not many, I hazard a guess. But you know many people here and they know you too. If you think about it, the number of people you actually knew in London was less than it is here.'

'But I could get away from them. If I didn't like them I could just find other people to associate with. I cannot do that here.'

Anne sighed. 'That's true, but is that not just running away? Not sticking by your friends through good times and bad, making life easier for you by not getting too involved.' She frowned. 'Will, I have to be brutally honest. You are not a child anymore. You must act like a man now. You owe it to our parents who brought you this great chance to be working here and more importantly, you owe it to yourself. You need to challenge yourself and mature and gain wisdom. You cannot run away from people you don't like forever.'

'For goodness sake, stop treating me like a child. I'm not a child.'

'Then behave like an adult. You cannot run away from boredom forever. Most of life is boredom if you examine it closely. We cannot always live in a frenzy of excitement and activity. We couldn't cope with it. We need some quiet time in our lives. You just haven't seen the value of it yet.'

He was shocked. Anne had never been so blunt before. She had changed a lot recently, had become more distant and, if he was honest, a little crabby. But he brought his mind back to himself, which was Will's way. Was he really so childish? So immature? He didn't think so. 'You don't understand. You don't understand how men think. How we need more than a woman to keep us occupied.'

'Oh, really!' Her tone was mocking. 'Is that so!' She let that sink in. 'Come on, you know that's not true. You have a mother who is a strong woman, a sister, me, who knows you well enough. You know it has been our mother who has kept this family together. Who rules the house and yes, who rules her husband, but she is too clever for you or him to see it. Maybe that's what you need, Will, a strong woman to rule you. To excite you. To make you realise that joining the army and killing and violence are not the answer. That there is enough excitement in a marriage to an exciting woman to keep any strong man in his place.'

'How can you say such a thing?' He tried to control his rising temper. 'What nonsense you speak.' And to himself said, and I'll never let a woman rule me. If you and Mama have in fact ruled me, which I doubt, then I will never let it happen again.

'Seriously, Will, I'll make a pact with you. Give Oatlands another year. If by that time you still feel the same way, well, I for one won't stand in your way and will take your side when you talk to our parents. But please, just give it one more year. Two years in a place is not asking too much in the grand scheme of life.'

He tried to hide his irritation, pushing the stones again with his shoe for some time before sighing deeply, coming to a decision. 'All right, Anne, my dear sister, my strong and wilful sister. I will do as you say if you will promise absolutely that you will take my side if I decide in one year's time to join the army.'

Anne rose on her toes and kissed him lightly on his cheek. 'I promise you. And you know I always keep my promises.'

'I know that. That's why I am willing to do as you say. I will try my best but I cannot guarantee the outcome you want.'

'Thank you, Will. I'll take my chances on that.'

CHAPTER NINE

Since his conversation with Anne, Will had spent the following year trying to look forward rather than back. He had settled into a routine at Oatlands and was given more responsibility, which he relished. The duke had been in residence on several occasions with his cronies, which Will loved, but as soon as they left life became dull again. He still longed for more excitement but kept swallowing it down for the sake of Anne and his parents. Anne in particular sought out his company and seemed to rely on him for companionship whenever they had some free time and he relished her company too. Neither of them had referred to their agreement that if he wanted to quit she would support him and he was sure that she realised the one year deadline had passed. Something inside him kept him tied to Oatlands, but he wasn't sure what it was. He was popular with the other staff and had had a relationship with one of the shop girls from the village, which he knew pleased Anne, but it didn't please him so much and he very gently broke it off as she was getting far too serious. He still craved that excitement he imagined for himself.

He was mulling all this over as he sat with the others at the breakfast table waiting for Mr Sweetman to arrive when he received his first shock. The butler arrived slightly out of breath. It was a hot day and he dabbed his reddening face with his handkerchief. He cleared his throat, always a sign he was going to say something important.

'I have a very important announcement to make. I have this morning received a letter from the duke.' His eyes swept around everyone, enjoying the tension. 'The duke has informed me that he intends to be married shortly and he will be bringing his new bride here to Oatlands.'

Everyone started talking at once.

'Who is it?' 'I wonder what she's like.' 'Has anyone heard any rumours?'

'Enough! Thank you.' Mr Sweetman said looking down at the letter. 'He will be marrying Her Royal Highness the Princess Frederica Charlotte Ulrika Catherina, who is the eldest daughter of King Frederick William ll of Prussia and the niece of Frederick the Great.'

'What a mouthful,' someone whispered, which caused the butler to look up sharply and his eye settled on Will. He tried to look innocent, as he in fact was, but it had the opposite effect. Mr Sweetman's glare cut off the giggles of the other staff. 'They will marry at the end of September this year in Berlin,' he paused as he looked around the table, 'and again at the end of November at Buckingham House.'

'A marriage for each country,' Mrs Harley commented.

'And a marriage of all the Fredericks, male and female,' James said with a laugh.

'Indeed,' the butler cut in, 'your comments are an accurate assessment but not for us to pontificate about. But it does mean we have good notice to prepare ourselves and our arrangements. The duke wants everything here to be perfect for her stay and he wants Oatlands itself to be looking perfect. He wants his bride to like it here. He is proud of Oatlands, it means a lot to him. So we cannot let him down.'

'No, sir, Mr Sweetman, sir,' they all said, enthusiastically.

At last, Will thought, at long last some excitement. But a bride! Who would ever have thought of that? That'll curtail his night-time adventures. I wonder how much of a difference this will make. Maybe it will all be happy married couples, which is nice for them but so boring for the rest of us! Damn. He wasn't sure he liked this idea as he loved to see the machinations of the duke's guests vying for the duke's attention and approval in whatever outlandish or boorish way fitted at the time. To see the rich and powerful struggling for influence and power with the duke in a similar way as the servants behaved in their own small power struggles was so satisfying. The only difference was in the scale of success. But he couldn't speak his thoughts aloud as everyone else seemed to be enchanted.

*

At last, the big day arrived. The duke was bringing his bride to Oatlands for the first time. Christmas was only two weeks away but they'd been told the duke and duchess would travel back to London for the celebrations. They would stay in Oatlands for a week.

Everyone was in a state of great excitement. No one knew what to expect except that it would be different from the Oatlands they had known.

'What would she be like?' 'Would they like her?' 'Would she be superior and unapproachable? She was a foreign princess after all.' 'Would she speak English?' 'Would she like Oatlands?' 'Would she like the staff?' 'What would happen if she didn't?'

The stress was taking its toll on everyone. For the butler and the housekeeper everything had been about making things as perfect as possible, and now the house was as clean and polished as it could be. Exquisite and elaborate flower displays decorated every room created by a specialist sent from London by the duke.

Mr Lange, the chef, and Mr Pierre Pierre, his assistant, had been busy in the kitchen for the past week making jellies, pastries and cakes, knowing the duchess had a sweet tooth. Great displays of swan and game birds were being created for later today and Mr Pierre Pierre was looking harassed and had become volatile and French while Mr Lang had stayed very British and kept a strong back and stoical attitude.

*

The loud scrunch of gravel announced the imminent arrival of the royal coach and its six magnificent black horses as it approached the entrance. It was early afternoon, the air was fresh and clean, and the weak sunlight caught the gold fittings of the coach making them sparkle. The servants were lined up outside the house in the cold, without cloaks and trying to look like it didn't bother them. Everyone was looking pristine with fresh uniforms and perfect hair. Thank goodness it was not windy, one of the maids muttered, putting a stray lock of hair back under her cap.

The horses came to an orderly stop and the four footmen, in full royal red livery, jumped down from the rear of the coach. One opened the door nearest to the house and another put up the steps while the other two lined up either side of the door. The duke got out dressed exquisitely in a purple silk tailcoat with matching waistcoat, white shirt and breeches. He held out his hand for the duchess. The first anyone saw of her was her small hand resting on the duke's large one. The smallness of hers made the duke's look even larger as she carefully descended from the coach.

'My, she's tiny!' William whispered.

'Oh, so she is,' one of the maids exclaimed.

'Shhh,' hissed Mr Sweetman.

The duchess looked around at the staff before her and smiled the sweetest of smiles to each and every one of them. She was so petite she only came up to the duke's chest and was less than half his girth, even though he was considered slim. She was wearing a silk dress of the most striking fresh lilac with a low neck and her bare skin was covered in a necklace of rubies and diamonds. Her plum-coloured cloak swept around her like a protective shell. She was the most exquisite little woman any of them had ever seen.

The duke took her towards the servants and introduced the staff to her, starting with Mr Tucker, then Mr Sweetman, Mrs Harley, the footmen and maids. She made a point of shaking hands with all of them, smiling and greeting each one in excellent English and repeating their names. Everyone was enchanted. When it came to Will's turn to be introduced he bowed as low as he dared without striking the duchess full on the top of her head and smiled his most winning smile. He was so pleased to be there, so pleased with the duchess, so pleased about his life, and glowed with pride that he was here, being introduced to royalty. The duchess caught his enthusiasm and asked his name again and Will felt as proud as a peacock.

Anne was much more discreet and decorous but gave the duchess a perfect curtsey of elegance and grace. The duchess looked her up and down and nodded her head, looking Anne directly in the eye as if she was looking for something.

As the duke and duchess entered the house, the staff got back to the kitchen as quickly as possible to make the coffee and bring up the savouries and cakes which had been prepared beforehand. An excited babble of voices accelerated through the room.

'She's lovely.' 'She's so kind.' 'She's not stuck-up.' 'I like her enormously.' 'Oh, what a lovely lady.' 'I am so relieved.' 'But she's not pretty.' 'Beauty is in the eye of the beholder.' 'She's so tiny.' 'Did you see her small hands?' 'Exquisite hands, I wish I had hands like hers.' 'And her feet! They are even smaller! How can she walk on such tiny feet?'

The duchess had specifically said that she wanted to get to know the staff at Oatlands so had only brought a lady-in-waiting with her; a German aristocrat who was just a head taller than the duchess but did not possess her good nature. The duchess had asked that a member of Oatlands staff be assigned to her as her personal housemaid and Anne had been appointed.

She was nervous but had been reassured somewhat by the duchess' greeting to her. She obviously knew

Anne had been given to her. There had been a certain amount of jealousy among the other maids on Anne's appointment but most thought it was fair. Anne was a good maid and she was most certainly the best looking of them. And that counted for a lot in royal circles. Everyone knew that and accepted it even if they didn't like it.

'Rather you than me,' one of the maids said to Anne. 'Her lady-in-waiting looks as ferocious as a hound in pain.'

'I expect she's only being protective. She will have responsibility for the duchess' health and well-being.'

'Mmm,' the maid frowned. 'I hope you're right.'

Dinner was to be at eight and the pressure on the cooks to produce something 'perfect for my bride,' as the duke had requested, had grown through the day and there was non-stop activity amongst the servants. Mr Pierre Pierre had several outbursts which upset the kitchen staff and startled William so much at one stage he dropped a crystal glass. As it smashed loudly onto the stone floor it silenced everyone momentarily until Mr Sweetman took up a pan and brush and swept up the glass while Will was still frozen, rigid with shock and shame. The butler made a big production of emptying the glass into a rubbish container and gave Mr Pierre Pierre one of his extra powerful disapproving looks which shut him up and he got on with his work in silence thereafter.

It was just after this that the butler was summoned to the green room by the duke. As the butler arrived at the door he brushed down his clothing with his hands as if to eradicate all previous trouble, knocked on the door and entered.

'Ah, Sweetman, it's good to be back. The house is

looking splendid.'

'Thank you, Your Grace.' The butler bowed his head at the compliment.

The duke strode around the room looking pleased and seemingly without purpose. 'You know, Sweetman, I have known my wife for many years and always been enamoured with her. I am the happiest man alive.' He stopped and stared up into the ceiling, lost in thought. 'She has the most wondrous disposition; she is an angel, the best girl that ever existed.' He sighed deeply and long. 'Yes, the best girl that ever lived,' he repeated, sighing again.

'Yes, Your Grace. I can see that she is.' Mr Sweetman smiled with genuine warmth and the duke noticed. Their eyes locked momentarily in a look of mutual pleasure.

'Yes, Sweetman, you will all love her I am sure ...' he suddenly seemed to come back into himself as if he had realised he was talking to his butler and not to one of his friends. 'Well, enough of all that,' he said almost to himself, 'I want to talk about the arrangements for this evening. I want it all to be perfect.'

'Yes, Your Grace.' Mr Sweetman was still smiling. 'I will make sure it is.'

*

Everything went off well. Will helped to bring the dishes into the dining room and lay them out on the table under Mr Sweetman's supervision. There were only the duke and duchess and her lady-in-waiting for dinner but that made the pressure worse for the cooks. You could hide imperfections on a busy table but not on one for three, but the duchess had said how wonderful the dinner had been. There would be a ball for many guests in two days' time to give the duchess time to explore the estate beforehand and get to know the house.

In the servants' hall later, as they all had their last cup of tea and bread and butter before retiring, Will said. 'I think the duchess is lovely. So down to earth and she laughed a lot at dinner. The duke is certainly deeply in love with her.'

'You think so?' asked Edward.

'I certainly do.'

'How would you know, William Dresser, you've never been in love,' Edward snapped.

'It's obvious,' Will shot back, knowing full well that it was true, he had never been in love but he knew enough about it to recognise it. He wanted to fall in love, he had tried to fall in love but it had never happened. He'd had women he liked very much. Women he admired in one way or another, but love? It had eluded him and he felt a little envious of the duke. But he'd never admit that to Edward.

'And what's the matter with you, anyway?' Will added. 'What's it got to do with you?'

'Now, now. We're all tired. Let this rest now and let us all retire to our beds.' Mr Sweetman cooed. 'We have another busy day tomorrow.'

*

The tray of coffee and breakfast for the duchess wobbled alarmingly in Anne's hands as she made her way to the duchess's rooms at nine the next morning. The silver sugar bowl clinked against the matching milk jug and the bone-china cup rattled in its saucer.

178

The large silver dome which covered the food rattled on the plate. She had to do better than this. She'd been delighted with her promotion but this was the first time and first times were always nerve racking, at least, Anne had found them so. This meant so much to her and the extra responsibility and importance it had given her within the house had delighted her. It set her apart somewhat, which suited her.

She wanted everything to be just right that morning and had spent hours polishing the breakfast silver until they shone like brilliant stars. As she approached the bedroom she put the tray down on the side table by the door and knocked, not too loudly but loud enough to be heard, as she had been taught. She'd been careful to ensure that the duke had left the duchess' room prior to her arrival. She knew he'd be served in his own room by his male staff. It would not do for a maid to serve the duke in bed.

'Come in,' the duchess' lady-in-waiting called. Anne opened the door and picked up the tray. She took a deep breath and entered. The duchess was sitting up in bed looking radiant with her light blue silk bed jacket over her shoulders, her hair a little untidy. She smiled so sweetly at Anne that she couldn't help but return an equally radiant smile, which made her a little flustered as she knew it was not her place to smile in such a way at a guest, especially not her employer and a duchess. But the duchess didn't seem to notice.

'Put the tray here,' the lady-in-waiting ordered indicating a side table and her tone was so clipped Anne almost dropped the tray in alarm. She put the tray down and as she turned to leave the duchess cleared her throat.

'Good morning,' she said in her slightly high but

cultured foreign voice with only a trace of accent. It sounded soft and sweet to Anne like soft cream over sponge.

'Good morning, Your Royal Highness,' Anne said, curtseying, thankful her voice had stayed steady.

'It is Anne, is it not?'

'Yes, Your Royal Highness,' Anne replied, as she curtsied again.

'Please, just call me Your Grace. It is much quicker and easier, don't you think?'

'Yes, thank you, Your Grace,' Anne managed to get out without displaying her mounting panic. She hadn't expected the duchess to be friendly. She didn't know how to react.

The lady-in-waiting bustled around Anne carrying the tray to the bed and spoke softly to the duchess in rapid German as she placed the legs of the tray over the duchess' knees and poured the coffee.

The duchess nodded her thanks and turned her attention back to Anne, much to the other woman's annoyance, Anne could tell.

'Tell me about yourself. I like to know my servants.'

Anne froze. What to say? Her mind was as blank as the outside of the coffee pot she stared at hoping for inspiration. She felt stupid and at a loss. 'Oh, I … um …' she stammered, feeling shy. She made a great effort to pull herself together and did what she usually did, spoke the truth. 'To be perfectly honest, Your Grace, I am an ordinary woman from an ordinary family. I am no one special.'

'Oh, really? I am disappointed to be served by someone so ordinary,' the duchess said, smiling as she took a sip of her coffee and looked over the rim of her cup at Anne. The duchess continued to smile and raised a quizzical eyebrow until Anne smiled, unsure of her ground. Then the duchess laughed so delightfully that Anne relaxed and laughed too. The duchess laughed even more becoming in danger of spilling her coffee.

'Oh, Anne, you and I shall get along well. I can tell. The duke, I understand, runs his households in a relaxed manner as long as everyone does their job well.'

'Yes, Your Grace, that it true.'

'I shall do the same. I like that way of living. The court I was brought up in was very strict and it is so nice to relax more.' She glanced at her lady-in-waiting with a challenging look. 'Let us both do our jobs well, Anne, and keep up our standards at all times. But we will have fun at the same time.'

Anne was so astonished she stammered. 'Y- yes. Yes, indeed, Your Grace. That would be very nice. Thank you, Your Grace.'

The duchess held Anne's gaze as she sipped her coffee again. 'This is delicious coffee and I am looking forward to the breakfast,' she said lifting the lid. 'Ah, good, one boiled egg and two rounds of toast, just as I ordered it. Thank you, Anne.' She nodded her dismissal.

Anne curtsied feeling very pleased and at the door, curtsied again and left, breathing a sigh of relief. It was over, her first meeting with the duchess.

*

The night of the ball arrived. The duke and duchess had decided that this first ball should be relaxed and only for the people of Weybridge who did business with Oatlands or were neighbours. The duchess wanted to get to know them. Therefore, the vicar, the doctor, the baker, the butcher, the several cobblers of the village and even the inn keepers of the seven inns plus others were invited with their wives – around sixty people. A formal dinner had been decided against as it would make things too awkward for all but a ball with music, a buffet and plenty of wine would do nicely.

The evening was cold but fine as the guests started arriving at eight. The duke and duchess would appear at nine and the dancing would commence. There was a tension in the air to start with as people explored the room, eager to see who else had been invited. Most of them had never entered Oatlands before except by the tradesman's entrance. They were keen to look around the ballroom with its circular frontage enhanced with many long and imposing windows overlooking the lake. In daytime it gave the most glorious views but tonight the darkness beyond enabled the glass to reflect the hundreds of candles around the room giving a magical glow to the evening. The high ceiling was extravagantly decorated in plasterwork and painted in the lightest and most delicate blue. The walls were painted a slightly deeper blue and all with the decorative plaster reliefs painted the softest cream. The hardwood of the highly polished floor had been brought from the other side of the world and shone in deepest bronze. It was a light and airy room purposely made for dancing and socialising. Many buffet sideboards had been laid out in a line on the left-hand side of the room and were filled with plates of various meats, cheeses, pies and cakes and their accoutrements. The musicians, a string quintet, sat on a raised platform unobtrusively in the corner of the room. The whole effect was enchantment itself.

As people relaxed and settled in their voices rose above the excellent music and they confided in each other that although they were eager and excited to meet the duchess they were concerned that a Prussian princess would be stern and aloof, even though they had heard through gossip that the duchess was delightful.

At nine exactly, the orchestra went silent but it took a few moments for the guests to realise that this was because the duke and duchess were about to be announced. The noise levels decreased in a hesitant way at first with people looking around, unsure, but was then quickly replaced by a mounting excitement as they realised the time they had been waiting for had come. Everyone turned towards the double doors being opened. Into the complete silence Mr Sweetman appeared in the doorway dressed in his usual black gentleman's suit with white cravat and waistcoat. He looked straight ahead.

'Ladies and Gentlemen, I give you the Duke and Duchess of York.'

He moved aside with a bow and the duke and duchess walked through the doorway, paused and looked around, smiling. The duchess held the duke's arm and looked like a child playing grown-ups until you noticed her knowing eyes taking in every detail and the confident maturity that exuded around her. Her eyes were dancing with smiles as they swept the room and there was not a person there who didn't feel special when they alighted on them.

The duke looked regal in a suit of turquoise velvet with the only relief being his white stockings and cravat. The extravagant gold braiding on the coat, waistcoat and breeches could only be worn with such aplomb by someone of the duke's bearing and poise. The duchess wore a matching dress in the same colours as if they wanted to emphasis their union and she too impressed with her bearing and manner. Her necklace and tiara were a gift from the queen and their brilliants sparkled and shone, awing the guests.

Mr Tucker made his way to the duke and duchess and bowed deeply, saying, 'Allow me, Your Royal Highnesses to introduce you.' He led the couple to the vicar and some of the dignitaries of the village who happened to be stood nearest. It was a casual affair and people were introduced not by status but by who was next on the meander around the ballroom.

The royal couple continued to walk arm in arm addressing and greeting everyone with great bonhomie. After all the introductions had been accomplished the music started again. The duke led the duchess onto the dance floor for the first dance, a gavotte. They were both accomplished dancers and under the duke's expert direction they danced effortlessly around the dance floor obviously in great enjoyment. Several of the braver guests joined in the dance. But many were satisfied with just looking at this breath of fresh air that had come to live amongst them.

Will and the other footmen were serving wine from silver trays and crystal glasses and he was enjoying himself enormously. This is more like it, he thought. He'd been enchanted by it all and especially by the duchess. He tried not to show it but he couldn't help but feel himself to be superior to the guests. He knew many of them from his forays into the village. He was used to the royal presence while most of the guests had only seen the duke striding through the village or at church and didn't know how they should act.

Will felt people were treating him with a new respect at how well he was doing his job and how he knew just what to do in every circumstance. He saved some embarrassing moments with a whispered few words of advice to a few guests who were floundering somewhat over the correct way to behave. He wondered if the duke's London house was as exciting as this on a regular basis. He felt sure it was. But this was fine too. Maybe, at last, he would find the satisfaction and interest he so craved. He knew now that he couldn't leave Oatlands, leave his family, that had become very clear to him, but there was a hole still there inside him and he just wanted to fill it. Happy as he was that evening, that hole just got a little bigger.

CHAPTER TEN

'This overnight snow is serious, Jack,' Hannah said as she cleared the breakfast things away and looked out of the window. 'It's so deep, must be well over one's ankles if one was foolish enough to go out in it, and it's drifted in places too. It's too bad it's snowed for the duchess' first visit to Oatlands. The poor thing must be freezing.'

'Don't forget she comes from a colder country than ours, she'll be fine. Don't worry.'

'Well, you know about these things more than I do but I'm not sure about letting the little ones play outside.'

'Please, please, mamma,' the children yelled. 'Please, please, please…'

Jack laughed at their disappointed faces. 'Don't be down on them love, come on, we don't get a lot of snow; you can't possibly keep them in.'

'Hurray,' they all shouted as Jack got up and gathered their cloaks and scarves. 'Come on, put on your togs and out you go but stay close to the house mind. Don't wander or the snow will kill you and the snow devil will eat you all up for his dinner.'

Little Simon started to cry.

'Oh, Jack, don't make things worse,' Hannah said bad-temperedly.

'You can't keep them in, come on, Hannah, they're only young once.'

'Well, you go out with them and keep an eye on them, then,' she said with finality.

'I will,' Jack bellowed, encouraging the children. 'Come on, let's make a snowman.'

'What's a snowman?' Simon asked.

'I'll show you,' Jack said putting on his great coat and gloves. He shivered as he wrapped his scarf around his neck. 'I'm glad my gout is in remission, Hannah love. I'd hate to have the gout in this cold.'

'Well, Mr White is on daytime duty at the moment so you don't need to worry about it.'

'It was a fair old storm last night, that's for sure. It kept me awake worrying about trees blowing down but you slept like a baby, Hannah, my lovely.' Jack caught her around the waist and tickled her. Laughing, he said, 'You can sleep through anything; even a storm.'

'That's as maybe. I thank the Lord for small mercies as I see no profit in lying awake all night worrying about things I cannot control. But I am worried about the White children. They've been crying on and off since daybreak. I think I ought to just knock on their door and check everything is all right.'

'I've told you before, we must not interfere. It's White's place to take care of his family, it is not ours. If there was a confrontation the duke may take White's side and go against us. We need to protect our own place here.'

'But Jack …'

A loud knock on the door made them both jump. 'Who on earth is that in all this snow?' Hannah said rushing to the door. 'Maybe it's Mrs White.'

But it was one of the lads from the stables. 'I have a message for Mr Dresser, please.'

'Come in. You look frozen. Quick now, so I can shut the door.'

He stepped inside and twirled his cap in his hands, looking shy. 'Mr Tucker has asked for your help in the stables, if you don't mind, Mr Dresser. Some of the horses have got spooked by the storm and he says you have a way with horses. One of the lads has fallen over and hurt himself. They need another pair of hands.'

'Of course.' Jack turned to Hannah. 'I'm sorry, I'll have to go. You'll have to take care of the children. But you will let them out, won't you? Please? They're only small and need this playtime. They'll be all right, you'll see.' He gave her a kiss on the cheek. 'You worry too much. Let them play in the snow.'

'But they might fall and—'

'So let them fall. You cannot protect them from danger, Hannah my love.'

She smiled. 'I know when I'm beaten.' She whispered in his ear, 'But if we have children with broken legs and arms then I will blame you and you can look after them.'

Jack laughed and kissed her again. 'Indeed. I will indeed.' But both he and Hannah knew that was about as likely as a heatwave following the snowstorm. He turned to the children. 'Go out and play now and do as your mother tells you. Don't go too far and be careful playing. Right, off you go.' He opened the door and the children ran out with cries of joy with little Simon following on and falling on his face in the snow. He got up and laughed, ran on and fell again. Hannah made to go out and help him but Jack stopped her by gently holding her arm. Simon got himself up again and looked around and got a snowball in his face. He laughed gleefully and made his own snowball. 'He's a bright lad, that Simon,' Jack said, amused. 'We don't need to worry about any of them.'

'You're right. As usual you're right, I give up,' Hannah said, with a sigh.

*

By early afternoon, the children had worn themselves out playing in the snow. They'd eaten their dinner and were sleeping peacefully in their beds for their afternoon nap. The White children had continued to cry intermittently all morning but there was no sign of Mr or Mrs White. Hannah couldn't bear it any longer, she was sure there was something wrong. She put on her cloak and boots, thinking to hell with Jack's concerns about interfering someone has to see what's wrong as there certainly is something. She could feel it.

It was only a few yards away but she almost slipped as she crossed the compacted snow the children had created. She gave a tentative knock on the Whites' door. 'Mrs White, is everything all right?' She knocked harder. 'Is anything wrong, Mrs White?' Putting her ear to the door she heard nothing. At least my knocking has finally stopped the children's screaming and crying, she thought, but then felt frightened, as if the hand of foreboding had skimmed down her backbone. Her hand shook as she reached for the door latch and slowly pushed the door open. 'Mrs White? Are you there?' The darkness within clouded her eyes after the brightness of the snow and she could see nothing. She stepped over the threshold and a movement made her jump, causing her heartbeat to pummel in her ears.

'What do you want, woman?' She recognised Mr White's voice slurring his words. He'd been drinking again, she realised.

'I'm—' the word came out as a squeak so she cleared her throat. 'I'm sorry, Mr White, but the children have been crying … screaming, for hours and I was worried something was wrong.'

Hannah's vision cleared and she saw Mr White sitting in his chair next to the cold fireplace. 'Stay out of our business, woman,' he said as he pulled himself out of his chair. He lunged towards her, unsteady on his feet and Hannah shrank back into the doorway. She looked about frantically to see it she could see Mrs White but as her eyes continued to adjust she could only see the children. Elizabeth, the eldest, was sitting next to the fireplace with the others gathered around her. All were shivering under their outdoor cloaks, their eyes like saucers, faces drawn like a child's should never be.

The hand of foreboding increased its pressure.

'My *wife*,' White spat the word out like a poison, 'is not here as you can see.'

'N… not here?' Hannah repeated. 'W… where,' she tried to pull herself together, knowing you don't show weakness to this man. She gathered her courage. 'Where is she, Mr White?'

'Don't know and don't care,' he slurred as the baby started screaming again. Hannah noticed that Elizabeth didn't stir, as if she was in a trance. Something was very wrong. Keep calm. Use your brain. He's dangerous. Don't let him near you. The fear growing inside her gripped like a vice.

She stepped back onto to the snow and felt safer. She shouted through the open door, 'When did you last see her?'

Mr White swayed and then his knees crumpled. He hit the wooden floor hard and fell on his face but made no sound or movement.

Elizabeth said, hoarsely, 'Mama ran out of the house last night in tears … without her cloak.'

'Last night?' Hannah said, confused. 'But it was snowing and we had a storm last night.' And then the children started to scream, setting each other off, as they picked up Hannah's panic.

'Stay here, children. Elizabeth, I'll be back as soon as I can. Look after the little ones and just wait here,' Hannah instructed them, trying not to show her fear. She went back to her own house and checked on the children, who were still fast asleep. She made sure her own front door was closed securely and made her way to the main house as fast as she dared, slipping and sliding and cursing the snow. She couldn't get out of her mind that child's voice saying her Mama went out last night, without her cloak.

She got to the side of the house just as Mr Tucker was coming out of his office, bundled up against the weather. 'Mr Tucker,' she called. 'Wait, please, something terrible has happened.'

He rushed towards her. 'Mrs Dresser, please calm down. What has happened?'

Hannah took a few gulps of air into her near exploding lungs. 'Mrs White ran out of her house last night without her cloak and hasn't come back. It seems to me she was running away. The children have been crying and screaming all morning, which isn't unusual but never for so long. In the end I went to enquire at their lodge and Mr White is passed out drunk and the children look terrified and are cold and hungry. Something is very wrong, Mr Tucker. Mrs White is missing … and in this weather.'

'Come into the house,' he said, taking her elbow and guiding her into the warm kitchen. 'Sit there while I get help.' He disappeared shouting, 'Mr Sweetman, Mrs Harley, anyone?'

Hannah saw Mr Sweetman come out of the servants' hall and talk to Mr Tucker. Mrs Harley rushed into the kitchen from her own rooms looking startled, and did a double take at seeing Hannah sitting there. 'Mrs White is missing since last night,' Hannah told her and explained what had happened.

'Mrs Harley,' Mr Sweetman called as he strode over to them, 'we have a bit of an emergency it seems. We need to gather a search party.'

'And we need to get those children out of there if the man is drunk,' Mrs Harley added. 'Mrs Dresser has told me they are in a bad way.' She turned to Hannah. 'Mrs Dresser, can we put the children with you to look after while the search party is organised?'

'Of course,' Hannah said, trying to copy Mrs Harley's calm composure. She didn't want her to see how upset she had become. It seemed a matter of principle. 'But I'll need some assistance. All the children will need considerable attention and, of course, there are my own children too.'

'Indeed. We are stretched here with the duke being in residence so I think Anne would be the best under the circumstances. I'll send her to you at once. Please wait here,' she added as she strode towards the stairs, moving swiftly and elegantly.

'Mr Sweetman,' Hannah called as he was hurrying to the door, 'I don't think the children have eaten since their mother left. They'll need food.'

'Indeed.' He thought for a moment. 'You gather as much food as you think you'll need, there are baskets over there. Take whatever you think is appropriate from this kitchen. But please do not take anything from the main kitchen next door as that is reserved for the duke.'

Hannah picked up two baskets and started to fill them with bread, cold meat, cheese, milk and cake as Anne rushed in to help her. 'Mama, oh, this is awful. Are you all right?'

'Yes, yes, child, I'm all right. It's Mrs White I'm worried about.'

'Mrs Harley said we should stay here until Mr Tucker can organise a couple of the men to escort us back to the Whites' place. It's too dangerous for us if Mr White has regained consciousness.'

It wasn't long before two men from the gardening staff joined them and they hurried back to the lodges, Hannah explaining things as they went.

One of the men said, 'Mr Tucker told us to get the children safely out and into your lodge and we are to stay with Mr White to stop him leaving. I'm not looking forward to this, I can tell you.'

As they arrived at the Whites' lodge the door stood open and they could see him still unconscious on the floor. 'Thank goodness for that,' said the same man.

Elizabeth came to the doorway with fearful eyes, shivering. Hannah put her arm around the child's shoulders and hurried her across to her own lodge. She went back for the others and found Anne and the men already carrying them across. Hannah had had a fire burning all morning and set to building it up with logs as the last of the children were carried in. 'There children, gather around the fire and eat some food,' she said, handing out bread and milk to the ones able to eat on their own and Anne took the two youngest onto her lap and soaked the bread in the milk. 'I'll warm some milk on the fire in a moment but eat this first. You need nourishment now,' she said to them.

'Mama,' a small voice called from the stairs, 'what's happening?'

Hannah rushed towards Sarah and said quietly, 'We have to help Mrs White's children, my darling. Can you help me by keeping your brothers upstairs for a while? Just until we get organised.'

Sarah's eyes were wide with disbelief and then fear at the chaos below her.

'It's all right, my lovely, don't worry, things are a little strange at the moment but we need to give the children some food and warmth. It's nothing to worry your little head about but it would help so much if you could just keep your brothers upstairs until I say so.'

Sarah nodded and gave her mother a wan smile. 'Yes, Mama.'

Loud voices came from outside. 'Mrs Dresser,' someone shouted followed by a sharp knock on the door. Hannah rushed to answer it and was faced by Mr Tucker and a party of some ten men with Jack and Will among them, everyone carrying a long stick.

'Mrs Dresser, do you have any idea where Mrs White is likely to have gone? Did she have any special places?'

Hannah braved the cold and went outside and shut the door behind her. 'I don't want to upset the children anymore than they are already, Mr Tucker. I've been thinking about where she may go but unfortunately, I don't know of any such place, she was a secretive woman. It's obvious she didn't go to the main house, or knock on our door, so I'm assuming she was running blindly away from her husband.' She couldn't resist adding, 'He's a cruel man.'

Jack glared at her.

'If she was in terror,' Hannah continued, ignoring Jack, 'I think she would have blindly run straight ahead from her door without any clear thought. That's what tends to happen when you are in a panic you look for the path of least resistance.'

'That makes sense,' Mr Tucker said. He looked around. 'She'd probably follow the track behind your house which leads through the woods into to the village.'

'Yes, probably. She must have been in a terrible state, poor woman, else why run away in such weather? It was treacherous.'

'Anyone else got any other ideas?' Mr Tucker asked, looking around at the men.

'No, Mr Tucker,' they murmured.

'Right then, let's spread out and follow the track as best we can in this weather. Keep your eyes and ears open. Call out her name as you walk.'

As the men turned away, Jack and Will hurried to the door. 'Are you all right?' Jack asked.

'Yes, we're fine,' Hannah answered. 'Now, go, or you will get into trouble as laggards.'

As they disappeared around the back of the house, rushing to catch up with the others, Hannah went back inside and looked at the children with a heavy heart. Elizabeth met her eyes and burst into racking sobs as Anne, busy with the little ones, looked helplessly at her mother. Hannah sat next to Elizabeth and drew her into an embrace, stroking her hair. 'What happened, child, can you tell me?' she asked gently as Elizabeth clung to her. 'There, there, you're safe now. Nothing will harm you. I've got you safe.'

Eventually, Elizabeth gulped, 'Mama had been very quiet for a long time, she had stopped eating … and … and … papa hit her a lot.' Hannah soothed her tears. 'Last night,' she whispered, 'Papa had been drinking as usual and told her to get upstairs as he … he … wanted ...' another sob broke from the depths of her body. Hannah stroked her hair again, doing her best to calm her.

'Is that when your mother left the house?' Hannah asked gently and the girl nodded. 'Mama moaned like an animal in pain and ran for the door just as she was. I shouted, "Mama, Mama, don't go", but she ignored me.' The sobs started again. Hannah had no words for her as she hugged her closer.

*

The men scrunched their way through the virgin snow, trying to avoid the snowdrifts.

'She would have left footprints if she'd come this way,' someone shouted out.

'Not necessarily, it snowed hard all night.'

'Dear God!' Mr Tucker cried out. 'She cannot live through this.'

'If you'll forgive me, Mr Tucker,' Jack called out, leaning heavily on his stick, 'we should be more organised with our search.'

'Indeed, Jack, you are the old soldier here with plenty of experience of this kind of thing. Guide us, please.'

'Well, if you'll allow me. We work in a straight line, each man ten feet away from the next and move as one, keeping our eyes peeled for anything unusual. A mound, an unusual shape, anything that attracts your attention. She'll likely be covered in snow if she fell to the ground. Gently explore each suspicion, including snowdrifts with your sticks. If you have any doubt call out and we all stop immediately, keeping our place, until it has been investigated. Then we move on again as one.'

It was cold, arduous work which stiffened the limbs but sharpened the brain and the men stayed focused. There was no sound except the crunching of boots on snow, or other movement as the animals hid themselves away in their lairs or nests. It was an eerie silence which made Will shiver, not necessarily from the cold.

The men stopped several times to investigate something, each man keeping to his allotted place until given the clear to go ahead. Then Will saw something in the distance. He stopped and used his good eyesight until he was almost sure. 'Look,' he cried out, 'there's something, I think she may be over there,' he pointed ahead, 'lying there between the trees.'

He ran with ungainly steps through the snow but stopped several feet away. 'Oh, dear Lord,' he cried as he took off his hat, staring at the figure on the ground. A shiver that was more than just cold seared itself up his spine and he felt his knees go weak.

Jack had quickly followed him and uttered an oath even he felt he should apologise to the Lord for.

Mrs White lay on her back as if sleeping with her

hands neatly crossed over her chest. She was resting on top of a mound above the snow line. Her body, partly covered in snow, was unclothed and her skin looked as white, pure and untouched as the snow. Her head lay to one side and her face was serenely peaceful.

'She looks like a marble statue,' Will whispered, 'smooth, shiny and very, very cold … and' – his breath stopped in his chest – 'pregnant?' He couldn't take his eyes off her swollen stomach as he felt bile rise up in his own.

'Aye, looks like it to me,' Jack answered. 'Poor, poor woman.' He wiped some tears away. 'She's found peace at last.'

As the other men gradually gathered around, each one took off his hat and the silence was spine-chilling as they waited for Mr Tucker to reach them. Will tried to speak but the words wouldn't come. Mr Tucker looked down on the body for a long time, his face creased with distress. 'She looks like an angel, a fallen angel. I've never seen anything like it.'

'It's the snow and the strange light we have today, it can play tricks with the eyesight,' Jack said.

'Where are her clothes? Has she been attacked?'

Jack bent down and brushed off some of the snow on a small mound next to the body. 'They're here,' he said, brushing more snow away. 'She's laid them out carefully, as if she was just going to take a nap and put them on again. I don't think she was attacked. I think she just wanted to die and took her clothes off to accelerate the dying.'

'Dear God,' Mr Tucker said as he looked upon the dress arranged on the snow and smoothed neatly and then the petticoats equally neat and finally her stockings lying carefully along the top weighed down with her shoes.

Mr Tucker took one of the blankets they were carrying and laid it over the body. 'Take it in turns men, to carry her back.'

'I'll carry her, sir,' Will said, desperate to do something for her. 'I'm strong.'

'This snow will defeat you, strong as you are, William,' Mr Tucker said. 'Follow me back all of you. Someone pick up her clothes and you, William, shout out when you need relieving of your burden. Don't be a hero and hurt yourself, we need you for the duke's parties this week.'

'Yes, sir,' Will replied as he bent over the body and moved her onto her front to gather the blanket around her. 'My God,' William shouted in shock. 'Look, look here.'

The men quickly gathered around the body again and several gasped as they saw the black and yellow bruises covering her back.

'Poor woman,' someone said. 'There's not a space between them.'

'And look at those welts on the back of her legs,' someone else said, not bothering to hide his distress. 'She must have been caned continuously to get welts like that.'

Mr Tucker breathed in harshly. 'This woman has been beaten … and beaten harshly over a long period.'

'Good God,' Jack said as he staggered backwards slightly, his eyes showing his distress. 'It's my fault … *my* fault.'

'What do you mean?' Will looked up at the anguish on his father's face.

Jack shook his head as if he couldn't believe it.

'I knew … *I knew* … White was a cruel man but I – I didn't know he beat her like this. It's *my* fault. Hannah warned me but I wouldn't listen.'

'Come now man,' Mr Tucker said in a practical tone. 'How can it be your fault? No, it is no one's fault except White's. I must take this matter to the duke. I have no choice now. He must know and deal with White in his own way. William, carry her carefully, we can respect her in death if we were lax in that direction in life.'

Will tucked the blanket around her and as he lifted her he exclaimed, 'But she's no weight at all. Like a feather; poor woman.'

Will had no trouble carrying her back to the servants' entrance where Mr Tucker and James were waiting for him outside the nearby stables. Mr Tucker called out to him. 'Over here, William, we can put her in the tack room.' To James he said, 'I can cope here, you go and get the doctor, speedy now. We don't want this hanging around. We need her to be examined to know what happened to her.'

As James ran off as fast as the snow would allow Will asked, 'You think it might have been foul play, Mr Tucker?'

'I really don't know but we don't want any rumours starting. I really need the doctor here fast but goodness knows how long it will take him in this weather. I need to know whether it was foul play or suicide before I tell the duke. He would not thank me to worry him too soon.' He paced up and down, thinking.

'I need all the footmen to help with the arrangement of things for this evening's party. I cannot spare you either, William. Damn, what a time for this to happen.

Mrs Harley is needed in the house too.' He paced some more. 'It will have to be one of the maids. Yes, one of the maids. Go fetch Joyce, she'll be the best.'

'I'm sorry, Mr Tucker,' William said, unsure, 'but why I am fetching Joyce?'

Mr Tucker looked at him as if he was stupid. 'Well, to watch over the body, of course. We don't want anyone to interfere, or God forbid steal the body, now do we?'

'Interfere? Steal?' Will repeated almost to himself, feeling that maybe he was stupid.

'The world's a wicked place,' Mr Tucker said, irritated. 'Think. If she was murdered, the murder may take the body to get rid of the evidence ... or some perverted person may think it's a joke to mess with her.'

Will thought this was ridiculous but knew better than to say so. But on his way out of the tack room door he turned, unsure if he should say anymore but feeling that he had to. 'But Mr Tucker, sir, wouldn't it be dangerous for just a maid to be guarding the body? If someone was intent on mischief, then she could be easily overpowered ... or even worse.'

The steward stared at him for a few seconds, which seemed endless to Will and he thought he'd gone too far this time. But in all honesty, he didn't think Mr Tucker was handling this well.

'The devil have it, you are right. There's no choice. You can handle yourself well, William, and beat off any attacker. It will have to be you and Joyce, you to ward off any attacker and Joyce to vouch for you that you did not touch the body.'

Me! Touch the body? William's mind cried out. He was incredulous. He couldn't think of anything worse. Did the man think he was a monster? He looked at Mr Tucker's hard face and realised he was in great seriousness. He decided the less said the better. 'Yes, sir, I'll fetch Joyce and return as soon as possible.'

'See that you do. I'll wait here until then. I've much to do, so don't be long.'

'Yes, sir,' William threw over his shoulder as he made his way back to the house as fast as the snow would allow. It had been cleared somewhat, but that only made it more slippery.

Will and Joyce arrived at the tack room at the same time as the doctor rode up on his horse.

'Am I glad to see you, doctor,' Mr Tucker said. 'You have arrived much quicker than I could imagine.'

'As it happens I was enjoying a slow ride through the snow, I love it so, and was just passing Oatlands when your man stopped me. It was pure good fortune.'

'William, Joyce,' Mr Tucker turned to them, 'go back to the house and get on with your duties. I must stay here with the doctor.'

*

The duke came into the reception room, frowning. 'Tucker, what is amiss? I assume it's important to summon me when we have so many guests.'

The steward explained what had happened as succinctly as he could.

'Good God, Tucker! Are telling me that White mistreated his wife? Well, I'm telling you that it is a man's right to do as he pleases with his own wife. We cannot interfere in a man's own business.'

'Indeed, Your Grace, but the doctor says she has been roughly treated many times recently beyond the acceptable. Looking at the condition of the body he thinks this has gone on for a very long time. The doctor confirms she was with child again. It looks like the melancholy had set in on her and this can make women do extreme things. Something happened last night for her to decide to end it all.'

'Damn! You are telling me the woman killed herself because of White's treatment of her?'

'I am afraid I am. And she has left behind six young children in the charge of a man who is quite obviously a drunkard. It is my duty to inform Your Grace that I think the man incapable of doing his job let alone look after his children.'

The duke shook his head and paced a while. 'This is a bad case; a very bad case.'

'According to Dresser's wife, Your Grace, she says that she has been concerned for a long time that White was mistreating his wife and children but Mrs White would never say a word against her husband. The children were so terrified of him that they would not speak of their father to anyone. Therefore, she and her husband took the view that they should not interfere in the White's business unless the wife asked them for help.'

'Which she did not?'

'No, sir.'

'I see.' He paced some more, his face concentrated into a deep frown. 'This is indeed, a very bad business.'

'Indeed. A bad example to the staff, if I may say, Your Grace.'

'And where is Dresser Senior?'

'I sent him back to the lodges to keep an eye on White with orders to restrain him forcibly if necessary.'

'Right!' the duke boomed. 'I need to warn my wife that something is amiss and to entertain everyone on her own. Damn it. I'm sorry for the woman and what she's apparently suffered but her timing is abysmal.' The duke thought for a moment. 'Wait here, Tucker while I speak to my wife and then come with me to White's lodge.'

It wasn't long before the duke, forgetful of his cloak, strode in great anger to White's door. 'Stand aside, Dresser, I'll take care of this. *White,'* he bellowed as he stood on the threshold.

White had regained consciousness and was sitting on his wooden chair looking towards the open doorway. He struggled to his feet, a half empty bottle of whiskey on the floor beside him and a glass in his hand. 'Your Royal Highness! Sir.' White slurred as he offered a shaky salute.

The duke didn't return it. 'What is the meaning of all this? Your wife is dead in the snow. Killed herself by the look of it. And, she has been ill-treated by you for a long time it seems. The doctor says her body has been abused atrociously.' The duke tried to control his anger. 'It is obvious that you are incapable of looking after your children and now *I,'* he emphasised the word I as he pointed aggressively to his own chest, '*I* will have the trouble of seeing that they are looked after. *And, I* have to bury your wife. *And, I* have to explain to my guests *and* my new wife what has happened. I do not take kindly to this kind of thing happening on my property by my staff. *Do I make myself clear?'*

White staggered back. 'Yes, Your ... Your Grace ... Royal Highness ... Grace... sir. Indeed, Your ... Your...'

'Stop blubbering man. What do you have to say for yourself?'

The silence hung heavy until White stammered, 'I-I apologise, s-sir. It will n-not happen a-again.'

'*Not happen again! Are you serious man?*' The duke's face reddened and the veins in his neck stood out.

'Y-Yes, yes, sir, I am serious.' White's body was shaking uncontrollably and his voice trembled and pleaded like a child's. 'It will never h-happen again. I will make it up to you, sir, Your Royal Highness, sir. Please b-believe me.'

'Good God man,' he roared. 'Your wife is *dead!* Died running away from *you!* Your children are now motherless and you abandoned your children's welfare. Most certainly it will not happen again. Not here.' He paused, breathing deeply to calm his anger. 'Look, White, I gave you a job here because you saved my life in battle and put your own in great danger to do so. I would not be standing here today if it hadn't been for your bravery. But I am sorry to say that you have abused my trust. I have no alternative but to discharge you immediately.' He turned to the steward. 'I take it the coaches to London are not running in all this snow?'

'No, sir. But I'm sure they will be as soon as the snow permits it.'

'Very well.' He turned back to White. 'I want you out of here and on the coach to London as soon as possible. Until the coaches start I will arrange for you to stay at one of the inns in the village. I will put a man with you to ensure you do not leave the inn for any reason. *Any reason.* I never want to see or hear from you again.' The duke stared hard. 'I will make arrangements for the wellbeing of your children. They are innocents in this and should not be punished for such a father as you have proved to be. I am a patient man, I reward good service and look after my staff but if I am crossed then I am merciless. You have crossed me. You are lucky to get away with just banishment. I will get my steward here to pay you the wages you are owed. Do you understand me, White? Never let me see or hear from you again.'

He turned to Jack. 'I want to check with you that you can cope with manning the gates without help until I can find a replacement for White. It would oblige me a great deal.'

'You can rely on me, Your Grace. I can cope well enough. I do not see lots of people coming and going in all this snow but even if there were, I would do my duty, sir.'

'Good man, Dresser. Do not leave the gates unattended even if you are asked to help elsewhere.' He turned to the steward. 'You got that, Tucker? Dresser is to stay on lodge duty permanently until we get a replacement.'

'Yes, sir.'

'And Dresser, stay with White until someone comes with his wages and to accompany him to the village. Don't let him leave. Keep control of him even if you have to knock him out. Understood?'

'Understood, sir.' Jack almost saluted feeling he was back in the army.

'I'll speak to Mrs Dresser, now.' He walked over to the front door and knocked quietly. It was opened immediately by a curtsying Hannah, looking apprehensive.

'Good day, Mrs Dresser,' he said entering. 'I am

sorry about all this. I have discharged White and he will be leaving shortly under escort. He will be put on the coach to London as soon as they start running.' He looked at the snivelling children gathered around the fire, fear showing in their eyes. 'You are overrun with children, Mrs Dresser. I will arrange for them to be looked after by someone in the village as soon as possible. Please bear with me. Can you look after them until I can arrange it?'

'Of course, Your Grace. I will do my best for them. They will be well looked after.'

'I don't doubt it, Mrs Dresser. You have my thanks.'

Hannah curtsied again as the duke left.

*

The next day, four men and two women arrived at the gates in two sledges. 'Good morning, Mrs Dresser. We have come for the children,' one of the women said.

'Where are you taking them?' Hannah asked.

'We have a small orphanage in the village as you know, Mrs Dresser. I have been able to squeeze the little ones in there and the older ones will be housed with families who are willing to keep them for a fee.'

'They'll be broken up?'

'Unfortunately, that is the only way we can do it. But children are resilient and the families chosen are well respected. They will be treated well.'

'I'm sure they will be treated much better than they are used to,' Hannah said. She looked at them all. 'Come now, children, put on your cloaks and go with these good people. They have brought sledges for you to travel in. It will be an adventure.'

The younger ones started to cry. 'Now, now, that is not the way,' Hannah coaxed them. 'Be brave. I will come and see you all next week when you have had time to settle in.'

She turned to Elizabeth. 'Don't worry, my lovely. The duke will make sure you are well looked after. Things will be much better for you now. You just wait and see. Be brave, it will be all right. We can meet in the village from time to time. If you have any problems you know you can come to me. My husband and I will help you and your siblings any way we can. You've had a bad start to life but that doesn't mean it will continue bad.'

Elizabeth hugged Hannah tightly, trying to hide her tears. Before Elizabeth could object, Hannah helped the child into her cloak, scarf and gloves and walked outside with her. If she kept the child with her any longer, Hannah knew she would relent and keep Elizabeth with her but also knew that it was not possible to have yet another child in their small house. It was crowded enough and Jack wouldn't put up with it. It was better this way. She helped her and the other children into the sledges and the women took up a convenient place among the children. Two men took up the reins of each sledge and started to pull. They glided easily on the still solid snow.

'Don't worry, Mrs Dresser,' one of the women said. 'We will play a game with them as we go along. We will keep them entertained. We have sweetmeats for them and that always puts a smile on the little ones' faces.'

'Thank you.' Hannah wiped some tears away from her cheeks. 'What a terrible business this has been.'

Pulling herself together she smiled and waved as the sledges slowly pulled away and stayed watching until they disappeared from sight.

CHAPTER ELEVEN

Just after Christmas, with the staff yet again on board wages, and Will fretting about his future, Mr Sweetman and Mrs Harley gathered them all together in the servants' hall. He looked gravely at each of them in turn. 'Oh, Lord,' Edward whispered, 'looks like we're in trouble.'

'I've had some correspondence with the duke recently and this letter has arrived today.' He looked at Mrs Harley, who smiled. 'Ah, Mrs Harley, you give the game away,' he smiled. 'It is good news. The duchess has said how much she liked Oatlands and would like to spend some more time here.' Everyone hung on his words as he paused dramatically. 'The duke informs Mr Tucker, Mrs Harley and myself and I am now informing you, that the duke intends to transfer one of his senior housemaids from his London house to Oatlands. You will need the extra help of a good housemaid with the duchess being here. Everything will be run as usual with the new maid helping out as necessary. She is not, and I emphasise this, *not* above any of you senior maids but she will, of course, be above you younger ones.' He looked at each of the housemaids and seemed satisfied. 'Now,' he said rather too loudly, 'Mrs Harley will fill in the details.' Her turned to her and smiled.

'Thank you, Mr Sweetman. Her name is Mercy Batchelor and she has worked for the duke at his London home as a senior maid but I reiterate, she will be joining us not as a senior maid as we need a general purpose maid. She has agreed to serve in that capacity as we do not want to upset the good working structure we have strived hard for here at Oatlands.' Mrs Harley glanced around the room and gave a small smile. 'I am sure that we will all do our best to make her welcome and to help her settle in. I am told that the duchess has expressed a desire to continue to have Anne as housemaid to her apartments.' Anne felt a surge of excitement run through her body but when several of the female staff turned to look at her, a blush started to creep up and build. She was annoyed with herself for being embarrassed but also relieved that she had done a good job when the duchess was here. She was aware that this appointment would set her even further apart from the others, that they would now be more circumspect in her company, which pleased her. She just hoped that she would be just as pleased with Mercy Batchelor.

Will, meanwhile, was trying to take all this in. What did it mean? Would the duke spend more time here? Would there be more parties? Excitement? His heart beat harder. Would it mean less time on board wages? He felt sure that the maid from London, being senior, would be older and probably a curse to work with; bossy and superior. Damn. He could do without all that.

*

Will had been chopping wood all afternoon and was

211

sorry when the last of the blocks had been split small enough to fit the kitchen fires. They just eat wood, he said to himself as he stacked the last few neatly onto one of the sheltered wood piles. The wood had been drying out for over a year and would be dry enough to burn without smoking the house out by next winter. The site was on the other side of the stables where the steward had decided there would be least disturbance to the house. Will liked using his strength for a job well done. He enjoyed it so much he wished he didn't have to share it with the other footmen.

He was hot, even though the weather was bitterly cold. He went to wipe the sweat from his face but then thought better of it. He'd have a laugh with the kitchen maids about doing real work because he knew they would be complaining of the cold even in the kitchen.

As he approached the kitchen door a laugh coming from inside stopped him in mid stride. It was joyous, confident; musical even. It couldn't be the new housemaid, could it? He knew she was due sometime today. There it was again, louder this time and yes, definitely musical. No new housemaid just arrived would be confident enough to laugh like that, surely? He brushed off some errant dust from his jacket and, as an afterthought, wiped the sweat off his face with his handkerchief and entered the kitchen, full of curiosity.

Some of the maids were sitting at the table and in the middle of them was a stranger. She turned to face him as he entered and gave him a look of frank appraisal which left him feeling stripped raw, as if she could see into his secret desires and thoughts and left him feeling ashamed of them. Her laughing eyes, the bluest he'd ever seen, focused on him as she pushed a strand of her thick, auburn hair back into the loose bun on top of her head. Her hair was unruly in an animal kind of way and several wisps of it had escaped the bun and caressed her face. Her back was straight, accentuating the perfect form of her body. A womanly woman, he thought, but more than that, much more. Was this Mercy Batchelor – the housemaid being transferred from London? He'd thought she'd be a bit of a battleaxe as much had been made of her age being three and twenty, much older than the other maids and one year older than him. Yet, he'd never seen such an imposing and beautiful woman. She was an angel, not a battleaxe. Then he thought, no, I don't want her to be an angel, no sir, no way did he want that as he imagined himself taking her into his arms. What was he thinking? His mind whirled in so many scenarios and he hadn't even spoken to her yet. He felt he'd lost control of his mental capacity. What was happening to him?

He smiled but felt it came out more as a grimace as he tried to say something confident and clever, like, nice to meet you. But something stopped his lungs from working and made his heart pound, while his stomach turned like a clown doing summersaults. He felt weak and stupid as he became aware of staring at her like some sort of an idiot, in way over his depth.

'Ah, William,' Emma, his ex-girlfriend said but she sounded a long distance away and it was only when she continued that Will became aware of what she was saying. 'This is our new housemaid, Mercy Batchelor. William is our number five footman.' She put the emphasis on the number five.

Mercy stood up, still with that enigmatic smile of

hers, and bobbed him a curtsey in a manner which was not as respectful as he felt it should have been. He bristled despite his admiration of her. What was it about this woman who was causing him so much discomfort?

'Pleased to meet you, William,' she said, her eyes twinkling amusement.

'Pleased …' he cleared his throat, furious that he had sounded like a toad with a cold, 'pleased to meet you, Mercy Batchelor,' he said as he sat down opposite her before his legs gave out.

'My, my,' Helen, the loudest of the housemaids mocked. 'I do believe our William has met his match.'

Mercy laughed her joyous laugh again as Will glared at Helen. 'I've been told,' Mercy nodded at the other housemaids, 'that I should be wary of Mr William Dresser, the handsome footman whose intentions are not always honourable.' The soft brogue of her voice soothed him like the best brandy administered after an injury; a voice well modulated, firm but with an underlying softness of honey and deep burgundy wine. An unusual voice for a maid. A temptresses' voice … was that a lilt? An Irish lilt? But more importantly, was she mocking him?

Her amused eyes continued to search his in question and he felt stupid. He had to do something, but felt as if he had been hit by a cannon ball and somehow survived but not necessarily in one piece and the pieces left were jumbled up and struggling to sort themselves out. The world had stopped for him but he had to recover his male authority, somehow. He felt like a fool. He was furious. He hated Mercy Batchelor.

Much to Will's chagrin, he didn't hate her. As the weeks went by his feelings increased and deepened. In his eyes she was everything he'd ever wanted even if he didn't know it before he met her. He stopped going to the village inns, it seemed pointless now. He had lost the enjoyment he used to get from it and realised one day that he never really had much enjoyment from it. It was just something to do. Now, all he wanted was to spend time with Mercy. But she showed little interest in him. He tried to make her laugh and succeeded a lot of the time, but she still kept him at a distance. He was beginning to think he was trying too hard. It was so unlike him he didn't recognise himself as frustration oozed from him and made him miserable and he didn't know what to do about it.

He went outside for some fresh air and looked up at a sky full of stars. It made him feel so small and insignificant and then, he thought, what did it matter? What did anything matter? Was God looking down on him as he was looking up? Was he testing him? Was he, William Dresser, in love? If he was, he'd had no idea before how painful it was. Had other people ever felt as deeply as he was feeling about Mercy? And then he remembered his father's words when he told him how much he loved Will's mother. How he would do anything to keep her and their children safe and happy. Even stay a soldier when he hated it as he had no skills for anything else. He began to understand his father's meaning.

But whatever Will tried to do to impress Mercy it didn't make much difference. She was always friendly and polite but never responded to his advances, or indeed to any other man's advances. Several of the other men at Oatlands were enamoured of her too which made Will far too jealous for his own good. He was at a loss of what to do. He had always had great success with women. He had a way with them but in retrospect he realised that the women he had usually associated with were not, and never would be, like Mercy. She was special, more than special. He had to accept he was deeply in love and it was agony. He couldn't sleep and thought of her incessantly, he couldn't take his eyes off her when they were in the same room. He tried to please her, do things for her but still she hardly noticed him. His job was suffering because of it and then the other footmen started passing comments and making fun of him. He was mortified as he realised he was making a fool of himself. He cut himself off from her then, went to the other extreme and ignored her. He got depressed and bad tempered. He didn't know how to cope, didn't know he was capable of such feelings.

*

One afternoon, Anne saw him making his way towards the woodpile with the axe over his shoulder. She'd been worried about him and decided it was time to have another chat with her brother. When she got there he was furiously chopping wood.

'Will, stop, please. I can't talk to you with wood chips flying.' He ignored her. 'Will,' she shouted. 'Please stop.'

He looked at her with his axe raised above his head and let it drop behind him. 'I'm sorry, Anne. I

216

should not take things out on you. It is bad of me.'

'You can say that again. You've been impossible of late. Mama is really worried about you and Papa says he will come down and knock some sense into you.'

'Oh, God, Anne. I don't know what to do.'

'You have got it bad. I've never been in love and I am glad of it if it gives one so much pain. It is not like you. I don't recognise you, my darling brother. What can I do? I must do something, I think. You cannot go on like this.'

'I'll leave Oatlands. That'll be for the best. I should have gone a long time ago. This proves I'm not fit for this place. My future doesn't lie here. I'll be better off in London.'

These were the words Anne was dreading. He couldn't go, she wouldn't let him. 'Is it the army again?'

'No,' he said sharply looking down at his feet. 'No,' he said more moderately, 'I don't think so. It is too late for that now. I'm of a different mind. I feel ... well ... I seem to have lost my drive, my ambition ... a poor specimen of a man who cannot win the woman he loves.'

Anne felt his pain but was not good at this kind of thing. 'I want to help you ... I really do. I'm not sure how, but please don't leave Oatlands right now. Maybe ... let me try and talk to Mercy. Find out what she feels.'

'Good God. No!' Will exploded. His face full of fury. 'How could you suggest such a thing? I could never live down the shame of my sister recommending me to the woman who spurns me at every turn.' His anger dissipated as quickly as it had begun. 'Anne,

217

please,' he pleaded, 'I have my pride.'

Anne took his arm and squeezed it reassuringly. She could see the hurt in his eyes. 'Do you know what I think?'

He looked at her and shook his head in a wearisome way.

'I think you are not your usual self around Mercy. You've become tongue-tied, shy, and if I am allowed to say so, a little bit boring. No, that's a lie, you've become very boring! You're like a puppy dog pining for his master and who will not have anything to do with anyone else. You need to calm down. Realise that Mercy is only a woman – a nice woman – a feisty woman – a woman who will lead you a dance, I suspect, but a good woman, nonetheless. Treat her normally. Treat her as a woman and not this goddess you have made her out to be. A goddess you want to worship. Worship her if you must, but do it as a man paying court to a woman, not a goddess. You will be calmer and Mercy will see the real you. The Will I know and love, not the Will who has got himself lost in a sea of feelings.'

He stared into space, thinking. 'That's fine for you to say, but tell me, how do I *do* that? I start to shake whenever I see her. My insides turn to jelly and my heart beats so fast it feels like it wants to run from my body.' He turned his back on his sister and looked up at the sky as if the answer were there. 'Truth is, I don't know how to treat her as an ordinary woman. I have fallen to pieces over a woman. *Me!* I cannot believe it.' He started to pace. 'Women always fell for me. I was always in control of them … but now! Now, I just don't know what to do, how to get back to my old self. I can only do that by starting afresh somewhere else. It's the only way I can see.'

'That is so typical of you!' Anne tried to calm her frustration. 'I'm sorry, but you need speaking to severely. You are running away – *again*!'

'What do you mean, *again*? When have I run away?'

'Oh, Will. You wanted to run away to the army. Run from here.'

'I object. I was not *running away* to the army.'

'You were running away from boredom and letting your dreams get in the way of real life.' Anne softened her voice. 'You're a dreamer, Will,' she smiled, 'but a nice dreamer. You have a lovely personality. Inside you can be as soft as anything and I think you are afraid of showing your softness. Afraid you'll be teased by other men. But women! Women love a man who can show softness.'

'No they do not,' retorted Will, un-mollified. 'A woman, in my experience, loves a hard man … a man who will fight other men for her honour and protect her against the hardships of life.'

'But that's not all a woman wants. Yes, she wants her man to protect her and her family but she also values a man who can be sensitive and loving and silly in love.'

'And you would know all this would you?' He spat, his temper spiralling. 'You who are not too enamoured of men! You would know what a woman like Mercy would like in a man?' He saw his sister's face fall, the hurt in her eyes. 'Oh, Anne, Anne, forgive me. I'm not myself. I didn't mean that.'

Silence reigned between them for a while. 'You're right,' Anne said at last. 'I am not experienced with men – or at least – I have been bothered by them, but I've not loved a man. However, I do take notice of other women. I listen to them talk about men and I've realised that what women want in a man is not necessarily what a man is capable of giving.'

'What do you mean?'

'Well, I haven't spoken about this before but I've noticed that men like to impress other men? That they are more concerned about what their men friends think of them than what their women folk think of them.'

'Oh, come now, Anne, that's the most ridiculous thing I've heard.'

'Take notice of things around you and you'll see that once the blush of love has worn off for the husband then the woman goes down in her husband's priorities and estimation.'

Will laughed. 'Oh, Anne, we are going off the subject of Mercy and becoming very serious about men and women. Whether you are right or not, how can any of this help me now? I do not care about other men and their wives. I only care about me and what Mercy thinks of me.'

'Are you sure that's true? You are not thinking what your male friends and colleagues think of you rather than Mercy? You are not thinking you are diminished in your male friends' eyes because you cannot get the woman you have set your heart on?'

'That is enough!' Will face flared with anger. 'You do not know what you are talking about. I disagree. I totally, totally disagree.' He started pacing again.

Anne sighed; worried she'd gone too far. She knew she had views not shared by many and she had learned to keep them to herself. But this was her brother and she loved him very much, but maybe she'd made things worse.

'Oh, Will, I'm trying to help you, please believe me, really I am. I agree that I'm different to you … different to most people, I suppose. My feeling is you want love and a family … at least … you want love. But you know very well that I am not enamoured of men. I'm happy as I am and I do not want my life to change to become a man's chattel and breeding machine to perpetuate his line.'

Will took hold of his sister's hands and looked into her eyes. 'You have a very jaundiced view of love, my darling Anne. Where did you get such ideas from? Our parents are very happy in their marriage and are good examples to both of us. Why do you have to be like this?'

Anne clutched Will's hands harder, trying not to let her frustration show. 'You know my history well. How many times have you rescued me from men being pests to me? You know I don't like it. Don't like to be bothered by some man who thinks all he has to do is smile in my direction and I'll fall for him and think he is Prince Charming? You know all that.'

He caressed her face with his finger, looking into her eyes as if he had just understood her. 'And I had not realised before just how against men you are. I thought it was just one or two pests, but I am seeing now that it is men themselves you do not like.'

'I like you,' she said, gently. 'I like Papa. But you don't want anything else from me but my pure love and that I am very willing to give you.' Much to her annoyance, Anne began to cry. 'I just want to be left alone to live my life as I want to.'

Will took her in his arms and hugged her close. 'I'm so sorry, we both want things we cannot have and they are at different extremes.'

Anne allowed herself to be hugged, enjoyed it in fact. Will was a nice man and she wanted to help him regardless of her own situation. She sighed and pulled away, and took his hands. 'What would our parents think of us? Everything is so simple for them. But think about what we have talked about, don't dismiss things out of hand.' She went on tip-toe and kissed her brother gently on his cheek. 'I love you, Will Dresser.'

'And I love you, too, Anne, far more than you may realise,' he said gently, kissing her back.

CHAPTER TWELVE

'They're coming, Hannah,' Jack shouted. 'Look lively.'

Hannah quickly put on her cloak, scarf and gloves and hurried out. Although rain had taken the snow away it had replaced it with ice but transport was almost back to normal. The coach from London was pulling up outside the gates as Jack opened them to the new porter and his family. He walked forward and opened the door to the coach and a man in his mid-thirties stepped down as the driver clambered onto the roof to bring down their boxes. 'Ben Moat, I assume,' Jack said with a smile. 'Welcome to Oatlands. I am Jack Dresser, porter, and this is my wife, Hannah.'

Ben Moat stepped forward and bowed low to Hannah and shook hands with Jack. 'Glad to meet you, sir.' Ben smiled, showing strong, white teeth a little too large for his mouth. He was in his early thirties, tall, a little too thin but sturdy enough. He turned and went back to the coach to help down his wife.

'She's pretty.' Hannah whispered to Jack as she stepped forward to welcome her. 'Welcome to Oatlands, Mrs Moat, you must be tired after your journey.'

'Thank you,' she said. 'I am fair worn out. It has been a long and uncomfortable journey.'

'It is that, especially with the road so frozen. And you must be frozen too. Come, I have lit the fire in your lodge and laid out some cake and there's a cask of small beer.'

'You must be Mrs Dresser,' the young woman said, pushing back a long brown curl that had escaped from her bonnet. She was short with a pretty, pert face.

'Oh, do forgive me. Yes, I am Hannah Dresser and that is my husband, Jack.' As they moved forwards Hannah heard cries of 'Mama, Mama, don't go.' They turned to see Ben Moat lifting down his children one by one. A boy of about six, who had called out, and two girls aged about four and two. They all rushed to their mother and held on to her skirts, looking terrified.

'They're frightened of the countryside,' Mrs Moat said. 'They have never seen it before and the little one screamed when she saw the large black gates here.' She laughed and hugged the child to her. 'I must get Ben to stop making up those frightening fairy stories full of witches and demons.'

Hannah smiled in understanding and took charge. 'Come, children, come inside and have some cake.'

They looked at her shyly but followed Hannah and their mother inside their new home.

'I have been informed about you,' Jack said to Ben Moat. 'I will be happy to show you how we do things here and my wife and I will help you get settled in.'

'Yes, sir,' Moat said, saluting Jack.

Jack smiled warmly. 'We are not in the army any more. We're just ordinary people now so no formality or saluting or anything like that.'

Ben smiled back. 'Forgive me, habit I'm afraid. I'm not used to not being in the army. I got my discharge papers just as this post became vacant and I was lucky enough to obtain the position. It was all a bit of a rush.'

Jack was curious about the new porter and had been told that he had been discharged because he was 'worn out'. Army speak for soldiers who had had too many injuries to keep up with the other men. He was no longer any use to the army, hard as that was for many a man to accept. But as long as the man had a good conduct record they were given a pension by the Chelsea Hospital but it was never enough to live on for a family man.

'You served under the duke?' Jack asked.

'I did, Mr Dresser. He's a fine man.'

'Indeed, I cannot fault him. And you, Ben Moat are a lucky man as we have a most generous employer. Do your best here and the duke will look after you.' Jack took him aside as the coach pulled away. He lowered his voice. 'You do know the history of what happened to the family you are replacing?'

'I do, sir. I was saddened to hear of it. But it is one person's bad luck and another's good luck. I cannot dwell upon it.'

'Good. That's the way,' Jack replied. 'This is a great chance for you. My wife has cleaned your lodge from top to bottom and it sparkles like a new pin. So you do not need to worry about anything unsavoury being left behind. You and your wife can put your stamp on it.'

'You are too kind, sir. I am most grateful for your generosity.'

'It is our pleasure you help you. We have to work

and live here in close contact, and cooperation and pleasantness makes such a difference. Unfortunately, we did not have that with the previous family, but I feel that you'll fit in very well. Mr Tucker, the steward, will see you in his office at eight tomorrow morning. I'll show you around the estate after you have refreshed yourself.'

'Thank you, sir.'

'Oh, and please make that the last time you call me sir. We are equals here now. Let's not stand on ceremony, Mr Moat.'

'Thank you, Mr Dresser.'

CHAPTER THIRTEEN

As Mercy sat down in the servants' hall she knew she was a little early for the afternoon break but her back was aching. Oh, lord, I overdid the carpet cleaning this morning, she thought. That'll teach me not to show off to the others.

There'd been some rivalry between Mercy and the other maids who felt a little threatened that Mercy had been lauded as such a good maid and they should all learn from her. Mrs Harley is a good housekeeper, Mercy acknowledged to herself, but she didn't do me any favours by saying that kind of thing about me. It's too much pressure. Her thoughts were interrupted when Anne, looking weary herself, came into the room and smiled at Mercy sitting at the table with a cup of tea in front of her.

'Gracious, how unusual,' Anne said. 'We have the place to ourselves. Where is everyone?'

'Not sure, we're early, I think. I've only been here a few weeks but I know when to enjoy some time alone, let's make the most of it while we can,' Mercy answered with a welcoming smile.

'I agree, let's make the most of it,' Anne repeated, walking over to the large oak dresser where the tea things were laid out. 'I look forward to afternoon rest time because we can have tea. I have to admit to loving tea. I am not a great lover of the small beer or ale we mostly drink.'

'I don't mind the beer but I just love the tea,' Mercy said, raising the cup to her face and inhaling the scent. 'Mmm, we're so lucky to have it even though it's rationed out. I've just made a pot for myself and there's enough for you too.'

Anne smiled. 'Thank you, Mercy, we haven't had a chance to relax and chat together since you arrived.'

'Well, let's put that to rights. We'll be two ladies getting to know each other over tea.'

Anne laughed. 'I'm not sure about the "ladies", but yes, that would be nice, let's get to know each other a little better.' Anne poured some tea into one of the bone china cups and saucers which had been set out. 'You know, although I've been here quite some time now, I still marvel at the duke's generosity. But he's a cultured man as well as a kind one. He realises that if you are going to drink tea it must be from a bone china cup and saucer to bring out the delicate flavours.' She took her time pouring the tea, savouring the aroma. 'We are lucky to have such luxury.'

'We are indeed.' Mercy sipped her tea. 'When he started his household in London we were all surprised at his largesse but one gets used to it and you are right, we should never take it for granted. It could so easily be taken from us.'

Anne nodded as she sat down opposite Mercy. 'That's so true.' She picked up her cup and offered it as a toast. 'Here's to the duke.'

'To the duke,' Mercy toasted.

Taking her first sip Anne sighed, 'Ah, nectar.'

'You might like to know that the housekeeper asked me how I was faring and then asked how I thought you were doing?' Mercy raised an eyebrow, teasing her. 'I said you were doing very well and she was pleased. I think she likes you.'

Anne took another sip of her tea and smiled at Mercy. 'I'm grateful, thank you for speaking well of me.'

'No need, because it's true. I speak as I find. I don't put a gloss on things. I find that works better in the long run.'

'But you have a way of saying quite harsh things sometimes and doing it in such a way that people don't take offence. I wish I had that skill. I'm often a bit sharp, I fear. I upset more than I attract.'

Mercy laughed. 'Oh, Anne, you are so serious sometimes, but it's true, you are a little brusque, too much maybe, unlike that brother of yours who can charm the birds out of the trees if he'd a mind to.'

Anne sighed deeply. 'Ah, yes, my brother.'

'You seem to want to say something, Anne. Come on, out with it.'

'It's not my place, but you're right, I do have something on my mind. And yes, it's about Will … you know he's in love with you, don't you?'

'*In love!* That's a bold statement.' This was the last thing Mercy wanted to hear but it was out now, it had been said and she had to respond. 'I think you're right. He has fallen for me. He moons around and tries so hard to impress me he achieves the opposite. I'm feeling a little sorry for him. But love? I'm not sure you would call that love. You have to have a relationship with someone to have love.'

'And … you do not feel inclined to encourage him?'

Mercy sipped her tea, pondering. 'If I'm truthful,

229

no, I don't think so. It would make it all worse.' Mercy lowered her voice. 'You see, Anne, I'm not ready for romance.'

'Really? But you are not so yo—' Anne's hand shot over her mouth. 'How rude of me, please forgive me. I meant nothing by it.'

Mercy smiled. 'You were going to say, not so young anymore?'

'No, no, sorry.'

'Don't look so mortified. I'm not offended. You just speak the truth.' Could she confide in this woman? This woman she liked and trusted. This woman she would like to have as a friend. But at the same time, this woman whose brother was in love with her and this woman so obviously cared deeply for her brother. Make up your mind, Mercy, there will probably be no better time. She made a snap decision and leaned towards Anne and lowered her voice. 'I trust you, Anne. I feel I can say things to you that I would not say to others. Am I mistaken about your confidences?'

Anne leaned towards Mercy. 'I thank you for your confidence in me. You can indeed rely on my confidences one hundred percent.'

'Thank you.' She rubbed her hand over her mouth and closed her eyes for a moment. 'This is difficult to say – for me to admit ...' she looked down at the table, unable to make eye contact with Anne, 'the ... humiliation ... heartbreak … and to be brutally honest while I was not exactly jilted at the altar it was not far off it.' Mercy cursed as a sob broke out unbidden; she didn't want Anne to think her a sop but at the same time she couldn't disguise the heartbreak inside her now she had said it.

Anne put her hand over Mercy's. 'How awful. I'm

so, so sorry.'

'Well, it was a while ago now and I should be over it,' she looked up at Anne and frowned. 'But it stings, you know? Hurts like I swallowed a giant wasp and it just keeps right on stinging my heart whenever I think of it. It's made me wary of men, especially men who are good looking and have a way with women … just like he was.' She wiped away a few unwanted tears, annoyed they had taken on a life of their own. She had to decide whether she should tell Anne all or keep her dignity but when she saw the concern in Anne's eyes she knew she could tell her all.

'Truth be told, I'm frightened of Will.'

Anne started, surprised.

'Oh, I know it sounds silly but I'm afraid he'll do the same thing to me. So, the best thing I can do it to keep the boys at bay and become a spinster. A housekeeper in the making – dedicated to the family who employ me.' What the hell am I saying, Mercy thought, I'm making light, giving the wrong impression. That is so typical of me. Pull yourself together. Her breath shuddered. 'I'm sorry.' She looked down at the table again. 'Now I'm being frivolous, but you see, my heart is still breaking. I'm raw. My heart cannot take any bruising from an amorous footman.'

Anne tightened her grip on Mercy's hand. 'I'm so sorry. I see how you suffer. I'm feeling your pain, please believe me.' Their eyes met and held. A bond came between them in that moment, a rare, intimate bond between two women who understood each other.

'He's young, your Will.'

'He's two and twenty, but alas, he acts much younger. He is a late developer, I fear.'

'And quite honestly, I cannot see him maturing

231

any time soon. He is in puppy love. I understand he has got a reputation in the village as a lover of women. They fall at his feet, I was told.'

'It is true. I cannot deny it.' Anne lowered her voice. 'You have confided in me, in return, I'll speak honestly of Will. He does have such a reputation. But I know him. He's but a boy still, immature, and has lost his way somewhat. But I cannot tell you what he does want for I'm not sure he knows himself. He's floundered since coming here and been dissatisfied. He feels he was brought here and persuaded to stay by family ties when he really wanted to do something else. This has embittered him.'

'What did he want to do?'

'He wanted, and still wants, I think, to join the army. He wanted adventure - and he got Oatlands!'

Mercy couldn't help herself and laughed. 'I would take Oatlands any time over the army.'

'So would most people, but Will, well, he has some notion about adventure and excitement and that only the army can give him that. And it is true, we did persuade him to stay and I have been persuading him on and off ever since. He's almost quitted his post several times.'

'What made him stay?'

'I'm not sure … maybe loyalty? A realisation, deep down, that he knows the truth of what we are saying. He's young and maybe he fights with himself knowing he's so very lucky to work here but at the same time, he wants to see life before he settles. Oatlands is a bit sedate for him, or at least he thinks it is. He's a dreamer, Mercy, and that can be nice in a man as long as he realises they are just that, dreams.'

'But it has all changed now the duke has married,'

Mercy said. 'We have had nothing but socialising, parties, get-togethers. The highest of the land come here, the Prince of Wales himself and his entourage, the *ton* fight to be invited here. It could not be more exciting and Will, as a footman, sees so much more than we do. He's like a fly on the wall as no one ever notices a footman. So ubiquitous to the rich they cease to see them. I would give anything, Anne, to be a footman rather than a maid. Will is lucky to be a man with a man's opportunities.'

'I agree, that could be me talking, I'd love to be a footman too. But we women, well, we clean up after other people. That's our lot.'

'That or marriage. And maybe they are the same, cleaning up after someone else.'

Anne shared out the rest of the tea with Mercy which they sipped in companionable silence until Anne put her cup down and said, tentatively, 'I feel you are a bit like me, Mercy, attractive to men because you are pretty.'

'Oh, I am not pretty but nice of you to say so.'

'You are a very attractive woman, Mercy. You cannot deny it.'

'Not like you, Anne.' Mercy's thoughts were getting in the way of her tongue. Can I take more liberties with this new friend of mine? Do I risk offending her? 'You are exceptionally attractive, but … well, if I speak too freely please forgive me … but I get the impression you do not favour men much?' Mercy held Anne's eyes with her own.

Anne smiled a small smile. 'You are astute,' she said slowly, thinking as she fiddled with the spoon in her saucer. 'The fact is, I am happier in my own company. I do not want children and to me it's the only reason to wed. Judging on my own observations, as a general rule, men do not value women, I fear.'

'You are right there, I have found it so too. I do understand your point of view. Some women are better off on their own. I can see clearly that you are one of them. You know your own mind and are willing to stand by your convictions, not so easy to do. I admire your convictions.'

'Thank you, so many people do not understand, it's nice to meet someone who does, more than nice if I'm honest.'

They looked at each other and burst out laughing at the same time. 'Goodness, it's a good job no one else is listening to this,' Mercy guffawed.

'Indeed, so,' said Anne, gaining control of herself, 'but if I may be bold in my turn, how do you feel about, not now of course, but later, about marriage and children?'

Mercy reflected for a while. 'I like men well enough, fool that I am. I would like to marry and have children. You see, Anne, my own mother died when I was ten.'

'I'm so sorry,' Anne said, gently.

'Well, it was all a long time ago. My father was an English soldier based in Ireland and married a local girl. My mother died when I was ten and he left the army soon after and took me to London. He died when I was thirteen and I went into service.' This was all coming out in a tremendous rush but she couldn't get it out any other way, it was still raw deep inside of her. 'I have no brothers or sisters or relatives to speak of so I am alone. I think that's why I would like to be a mother of a large brood. You could say I've been unlucky what with my parents dying so young and me being useless at choosing the right man. In fact, I have a knack of choosing the wrong sort although I have not seen it for myself until it all went sour.'

Mercy fought her emotions and took refuge in tracing the wood grain of the table with her finger, anything to not look at Anne and see the sympathy she knew would be there. That would finish her off. She'd shared too much. She was angry with herself.

'Thank you for telling me about that,' Anne said quietly. 'I can see how much it means to you and I can see how you are so protective of yourself after your experiences. I feel we are both protective of ourselves but for different reasons. But I wonder ...'

Mercy encouraged her. 'Go on; please tell me what you were going to say.'

'Oh, dear, me and my big mouth ... I'm not sure it's wise to pursue this now.'

'I would like to though, if you don't mind. I trust you and value your viewpoint.'

'All right, Mercy, if you want, but remember I'm not as good at saying things as you are.'

'Don't concern yourself, I would welcome it, please Anne.'

'Well, as I said, you are a very attractive woman and ... well, maybe you attract the wrong sort of man?'

'How do you mean?'

Anne hesitated.

Mercy kept her voice gentle. 'Come on, you've started now. You cannot stop. I am interested in what you see in me that I have not seen in myself.'

Anne smiled. 'If you'll forgive me, you are lively and funny - and fun to be with. Maybe the men think that they need not be serious about you and they take advantage of that. Then, when they want to settle down or are pressured to by their families to do so they look elsewhere for a staid and reliable wife, even if she is not pretty like you.'

'Mmm,' Mercy said, frowning, feeling like she had been hit by something of some force. Could it be true? Was it all her fault? She'd have to think seriously about this.

'I'm sorry, I've been rude,' Anne said. 'I was only trying to help. Sometimes a person coming in new to a situation can see what is happening better than the people living it. Do forgive my impertinence.'

Still frowning, Mercy took a sip of tea to cover her confusion, her mind busy with the ins and outs of what Anne had implied. Maybe she was right. 'I see,' she said slowly. 'I wonder?' She took another sip of tea, not noticing her cup was now empty. 'It would explain a lot. Maybe you are right but,' she paused, 'I cannot change my personality to suit a man. It would lead to disaster in a marriage. And anyway, I like being lively, funny and fun to be with.' She stood up. 'Back to work for me, I'm afraid.' She put her hands on the table and leaned towards Anne. 'You may have something there, Anne. I am not offended. I want to choose a husband wisely. I do not want to dally with a scoundrel or someone not serious about a family and all that entails. I want someone who knows his own mind.'

'You want a loyal man. And that brings us back to Will. I cannot answer for him for I do not know what is deep in his heart. He's certainly well enamoured by you but how deep it goes I cannot say. He's never been serious about a woman before. But I can say he is not himself. He has changed, I think.'

'Indeed. I have a lot to think about. You will be a good friend, I think. Thank you.'

Anne smiled and on impulse held her hand out to Mercy who without hesitation shook it firmly.

*

The next time Mercy saw Will they passed each other on the staircase leading to the main house. He stood aside for her to pass. 'Thank you, Will,' she said, giving him a genuine smile. He looked shocked and blushed.

'Mmm,' Mercy said to herself as she strode into the kitchen.

When she saw him next at the dinner table she smiled at him again and to her astonishment, he blushed again. From the corner of her eye she noticed Edward looking at her and because she was staring at Will, he looked at him too. Will went even redder and then got up and strode out of the room.

'I've never seen Will blush before,' Edward said, grinning. A look of malevolence passed over him.

'You leave him alone,' she hissed, and to her surprise, she discovered she wanted to protect Will. I feel like his mother, she thought and then, no … not that. I feel more like I want to be on his side. She glared at Edward, who smirked.

Will did not reappear for his meal and Mr Sweetman sent one of the footmen to look for him. He came back and said Will was in his room with a headache and begged to be excused.

'James, you make sure he is all right when we retire for the night. Take him a plate of some leftovers just in case he feels like it. It is unusual for William to be off his food. I hope he is not sickening for anything. I cannot afford to have him ill, when we have a big party this weekend.'

Mercy was thoughtful throughout the meal and came to the conclusion that because she had changed her attitude to Will and smiled and was nice to him it had produced a reaction she had not expected. He was not cocky nor had he taken advantage of her, instead it had had the reverse effect. She couldn't help thinking that maybe he was serious about her.

*

The next morning, Will was up and about as usual.

'You look very pale this morning,' Edward said to him over breakfast. 'Did you eat your leftovers like a good boy?'

'Enough of that,' Mr Sweetman said, mildly. 'Edward, if you've finished your breakfast please go and get on with your duties.'

'But I've only just started my breakfast, Mr Sweetman, sir.'

'In that case keep your opinions to yourself and get on with eating it.'

Mercy noticed Will blush again. He glanced in her direction and their eyes met and he quickly looked away but he couldn't disguise the look of love in his eyes.

CHAPTER FOURTEEN

Mercy was aware that Will had been avoiding her as much as possible over the past few weeks and she was relieved as it gave them both some time to think about things. The other servants had been teasing him and she knew this upset him and that made her more interested in him as it showed his sensitivity. She was finding sensitivity in a man more attractive since her traumatic experiences with the kind of men she had chosen in the past.

It was a sunny spring morning when she was cleaning in one of the main rooms and thinking about Will when the sound of horses' hooves scattering the gravel made her glance outside as visitors were not expected. She saw the lone figure of the Duchess of York riding fast up to the house.

'That's the duchess,' she said to the junior maid she was working with. 'Looks like something's wrong.'

She saw Will and Edward run out of the house and stand to attention at the open front door ready to be of service. The duchess pulled the horse up too hard when she reached the front of the house and he reared up and whinnied loudly, shaking his head violently with the duchess only just hanging on. He reared again and she wrapped her arms around the horse's neck in even greater danger of falling off and being trampled. Will ran to the horse as it reared again and made a grab for the bridle. He missed and the horse's legs almost knocked him down but he held his ground even as a hoof caught him just above the knee and blood started to ooze onto his white stocking. As the horse started to rear again he made another grab for the bridle, jumping up with the horse putting himself in great danger. He caught hold of one side of the bridle and was able to pull the horse's head downwards. The horse reacted by kicking up his back legs with the duchess being thrown around like a rag doll. The horse tried to rear up again but by this time, Will had grabbed hold of the bridle on the opposite side of the horse's head and as the horse went up so did Will. But he was too heavy for the horse and after a half-hearted attempt at another rear kick he calmed as Will spoke to him softly, over and over, 'There, there, lad, all over now. Calm down, you're fine. Calm down.'

Edward had been watching this from the safety of the doorway, and then rushed forwards to help the duchess slide down from the horse. She collapsed against him as he helped her into the house. Mercy and the junior maid had witnessed the whole thing from the window and they now rushed to the duchess and took over administrations from Edward. They helped her into the drawing room and laid her on one of the sofas. 'Go quickly and tell the ladies-in-waiting they are needed and ask them to bring a blanket,' she instructed the maid.

Mercy loosened the clothing of the duchess who was struggling to breathe. Eventually she got all the buttons undone on her jacket and bodice as Mrs

Harley and Mr Sweetman rushed into the room and Mercy covered the duchess' loose clothing with a cushion for modesty. Mrs Harley was carrying a glass of water and said, 'Here, Your Grace, drink this, it will help,' and as she offered it she added in surprise, 'oh, I seem to have lost most of it in my rush to get here. I'm sorry, Your Grace.'

'No, no, thank you, Mrs Harley, that was thoughtful,' she said as she took the glass and sipped some water choking on it slightly. 'I'm all right … I think. Mein Gott, I am lucky to be alive.' She took another sip of water. 'And who was that brave footman? He saved my life.'

'That was William, Your Grace, our number five footman.'

'Well, he saved my life, Mr Sweetman. Please send him to me.'

The ladies-in-waiting, Lady Susan and Lady Elizabeth, rushed in at that moment and said in unison, 'Duchess, are you all right?'

'I will survive, although I am greatly shaken.' Lady Susan laid the blanket over the duchess as Mercy removed the cushion. 'You warned me not to go out riding alone but I knew best. Well, I have paid the price for my over confidence. He's a magnificent horse but too boisterous for me to handle. I have learned my lesson.' She smoothed down the blanket, deep in thought. 'It was all my own fault, I admit. And I put my staff in danger. I will not be so stupid again.'

'We must take you upstairs.' said Lady Elizabeth. 'You need to rest and recover in bed. Has the doctor been called?'

'Yes, Lady Elizabeth,' Mr Sweetman answered.

'A footman is already on his way to fetch him.'

'Yes, that is just as well,' said the duchess, 'but in the meantime I need to thank the man who saved my life. I must do that now. Send him in. I do not think it seemly to see him in my bedchamber, Elizabeth dear.'

'Indeed not, Duchess.' She looked at Mr Sweetman who called out to Edward. 'Fetch William straight away, please Edward.'

Will walked into the room unaided, his leg sporting a makeshift bandage. He bowed deeply. 'You wanted to see me, Your Grace.'

'I did, William. You saved my life. I want to thank you most sincerely. And I am sure the duke will want to as soon as he knows what has happened.'

'Thank you, Your Grace, but I am sure I did no more than anyone else would have done.'

The duchess stared at him for a moment. 'But I did not see anyone else there but you, William. So I think not. You are a very brave young man. You put yourself in great danger for me. I will not forget it. Please accept my thanks.' She frowned. 'I can see you have been injured.'

'It's nothing, Your Grace. I assure you.'

'Well, if you are sure. I am feeling unwell and I must go to my bed now. Shock, I think, is setting in. And you too, you must be feeling just as shocked. You must take the rest of the day off.'

Will looked up at Mr Sweetman, who nodded. 'Thank you, Your Grace. It was my pleasure to help you.'

As he turned away the duchess called out, 'Wait, what is that on your stocking? Fresh blood? Mein Gott, you are injured more than you say.'

Will looked down at his now profusely bleeding

leg and turned pale. He staggered a little putting his hand to his forehead.

'Get this man to his bed please, Mr Sweetman, and get the doctor to him before he sees me. I do not want to be responsible for killing the man who saved me.'

She smiled at Will. 'William, please take as much time as the doctor tells you and, Mr Sweetman, do make sure the doctor sees to him first.'

'Indeed, Your Grace.' Mr Sweetman bowed, helping Will out.

'Well done, William,' he whispered. 'I am proud of what you did.'

Mercy followed them out and as they walked unsteadily down the grand hall she asked, 'Are you all right, Will?'

'No, it's nothing … really.' And with that, Will wobbled and was caught by Mr Sweetman and Mercy.

'Mr Sweetman, shall I help you downstairs with Will?' Mercy asked. 'He needs to lie down quickly I fear.' Mr Sweetman nodded and Will was too woozy to stand on his pride and refuse. Mercy help the butler lay Will down on his bed.

'He looks very pale, Mr Sweetman.'

'Indeed. But I think you had better wait outside while I cut off Will's breeches.'

'Oh, y y yes ... ' Mercy said, flustered, annoyed with herself that she had not seen the impropriety of it herself. As she waited outside her pulse raced uncomfortably as she realised she was more affected by Will being in danger than she would have thought.

James arrived at a run and asked breathlessly, 'How is he?'

'I don't know,' Mercy said. 'I think it might be

243

worse than we at first thought.'

James nodded and opened the door disappearing into the room without giving Mercy a chance to catch a glimpse of Will. After a while, James opened the door and peered out. 'Mercy, thank goodness you're still here,' he said in some panic. 'Will's injury is nasty. Can you bring up a clean bowl of water and some clean cloths. As soon as possible please, he's bleeding a lot.'

Mercy caught James' panic and fought down her own. 'Right away,' she said as she ran towards the kitchen. On her return she was accompanied by Mrs Harley who knocked on the door. Mr Sweetman took the bowl and cloths from them and glared at Mrs Harley as she offered to help. 'I think this is my place to minister to him', he said. 'William is not properly attired for visits by the opposite sex.' He emphasised opposite in a way that brokered no discussion.

'Are you good with injuries, Mr Sweetman?' Mrs Harley asked unperturbed.

'Not really, I have to admit. I can but try to clean out the wound.'

'And there is a great danger you will make it much worse, I fear if you do not know what you are doing. I have had experience of wounds when ministering to my father's parishioners who were always injuring themselves. I have gained some skill in the matter.'

Mr Sweetman cleared his throat, unsure.

'You go and prepare him, keeping the covers over him and just expose the injury. That should solve his blushes.'

A weak voice sounded from inside the room. 'Not Mercy, please Mr Sweetman, just Mrs Harley.'

'Very well. I will inform you when he is ready and

244

you come in alone, Mrs Harley.'

Mercy looked crestfallen.

'I am beginning to think you have a soft spot for William, Mercy,' Mrs Harley said, raising her eyebrows and looking questioningly at her.

Mercy sighed. 'I don't know. I confess I'm confused by my own feelings.' She sighed again to fill the silence as it become obvious that Mrs Harley was still waiting for Mercy to expand on her statement. 'But,' she finally added, 'I am relieved in a way not to have to administer to his injury, it might prove awkward.'

'Indeed. You are so much younger than me. No one can talk about impropriety with young William and myself.' She smiled at Mercy.

Mercy smiled back, but it was strained.

The door opened and the butler said, formally, 'The patient is awaiting your administrations, Mrs Harley.'

She entered the room and smiled at Will who was prone on his bed looking pale and drawn. The sheet had been pulled up and a blanket covered his modesty.

She examined the injury without touching it. 'It's not such a bad injury,' she lied to him. 'It will hurt a bit but you are up to it, I'm sure.' To Mr Sweetman she whispered, 'We must stop the bleeding soon. His is losing a lot of blood.' She washed the wound carefully and thoroughly while Will groaned and gritted his teeth. Mr Sweetman kept wiping the sweat off Will's brow and gave him a small wooden ruler he always kept in his pocket to bite down on.

The housekeeper put a clean dressing on the wound binding it up well. 'I've stopped the bleeding, thank goodness. I think Will deserves a brandy, Mr

Sweetman.' She patted Will's hand. 'You were very brave. I'm proud of you.' Will tried to smile but couldn't quite manage it.

A sharp knock on the door announced the doctor arriving.

'Ah, doctor,' Mr Sweetman said unable to disguise the relief in his voice. 'Mrs Harley has cleaned the wound and managed to stop the bleeding.'

The doctor looked at her and said curtly, 'Has she now?' He unwound the dressing. 'Mmm.' He looked at Mrs Harley and took a closer look at the wound. He prodded around it, opened it up a little causing it to bleed again and closed it over quickly. 'Good work, Mrs Harley. It has been cleaned well and you have closed the wound. I will put a few stitches in it and apply my ointment. That should do the trick but we need to be careful as infection can take over very quickly. Now, William, he said as he took out a large needle and thick thread from his bag, 'I want you to be very brave,' he said looking at Will. But Will had passed out.

*

Later, Mrs Harley escorted the doctor to the duchess's bedchamber and knocked. Lady Elizabeth answered. 'Do come in, doctor.'

The duchess was lying in bed in her nightclothes. 'How are you feeling, Your Grace?' the doctor asked.

'Shaky, but I think I am all right. But how is the footman?'

'He has a nasty injury to his leg but it has been cleaned well by your housekeeper, and I have stitched and salved the wound. He needs to rest for several weeks otherwise it will not heal. I believe he will be all right as long as there is no infection. I will visit him again tomorrow with your permission, Your Grace.'

'Whatever you feel is necessary. The man saved my life.'

'So I have heard: a brave fellow indeed. Now, please allow me to examine you for broken bones and general health.'

'Go ahead, doctor,' the duchess said throwing her arms outside the bedding like a sacrifice. She laughed. 'Elizabeth, dear, please help the doctor by removing the bedding off me.'

The doctor examined her solicitously, over her clothing. 'You have been very lucky, Your Grace. You have no broken bones or other injuries that I can detect. But shock is a very dangerous thing and can come on after the event. So I suggest you stay in bed for the next few days and rest. I will come to see you tomorrow. Oh, and no alcohol. I have always found alcohol very bad for shock.'

'Oh, really,' replied the duchess. 'I have always found it most advantageous. With thanks, and good day, doctor. I will see you tomorrow.'

CHAPTER FIFTEEN

Will was off work for four weeks as the wound healed. He'd been bruised and battered by the horse's antics and tried to ignore the pain throbbing through his body incessantly. The doctor had advised plenty of rest and Will was glad of it as he wasn't sure how much more he could take. Isolation and rest felt like heaven to him. During the first week, when he was not quite himself, the duke visited him. Will thanked his lucky stars he had been given no warning of the visit as he found his heart beating wildly. This was most irregular and he felt embarrassed. He knew he looked a sight.

'I'm sorry, Your Grace, I cannot rise,' he stammered.

The duke stood at ease by the side of the bed. 'No need, William. I wanted to thank you personally for saving the life of my wife. You were, by all accounts, very brave and I am in your debt. And I will not forget that I am in your debt. I feel myself to be a very lucky man to still have my wife under the circumstances. So thank you, William.'

The duke astounded Will by bowing his head to him. Unheard of! My God, he thought, the Duke of York has honoured me. He felt ridiculously satisfied by it but tried not to show it.

'No, no, Your Grace, please, it was my pleasure to assist the duchess, I assure you.'

The duke smiled. 'Is there anything that you need? If so, just ask Mrs Harley or Mr Sweetman, they have instructions to look after you very well.'

'Thank you, Your Grace,' Will managed to say before feeling a little woozy. It had all been too much for him as he felt himself start to shake. This was almost more of a shock than saving the duchess.

A short time later his parents came to visit him. One or the other of them had been popping in daily and keeping him company. Will told them about the duke's visit.

'Well you deserved it, deserved to be thanked by the duke. I am proud of you,' Jack said.

'We both are,' Hannah added, 'you know we are. But that was a great honour the duke paid you. That is good news indeed.'

'And what's your news?' Will asked with a smile, knowing that they usually didn't have anything much to report. He liked to tease them about it.

Hannah smiled. 'Well, we do have some good news as a matter of fact. Mrs Moat is with child and it should be born in August. They are very pleased.'

'I'm pleased for them obviously,' Will said. 'I wish them well.'

'I will pass on your good wishes. You know you are thought of as a hero now so it will please them mightily. Who knows,' Hannah winked at Jack, 'they may even name their child after you if it's a boy!'

Will cringed and then felt pleased. 'Oh?' he said with as much nonchalance as he could manage. Deep down, he felt proud.

'Now don't get a big head,' his mother said. 'I

249

know you, you settle down now, it might be a girl, anyway.'

Again, Will disguised his irritation. Still treating me as a child, he thought.

*

Mercy, in the meantime was fantasising about Will. Was he genuinely in love with her? Was she in love with him? She had certainly felt more affection for him over the weeks he had been recuperating. Absence makes the heart grow fonder kept going through her mind. She had never been in such a quandary about a man before. At night, trying to get to sleep, she kept counting his attributes. Good looking with a fine figure? Without doubt. But more importantly, was he kind? He was kind to animals, but to people? Yes, she seen him on several occasions giving help and advice to the temporary staff brought in to help during the many parties Oatlands had hosted since the duke's marriage while some of the other footmen had turned their noses up at them. Generous? She thought so. He was certainly generous with his time and always willing to help anyone in difficulty. Honest? She assumed so. She knew Anne was and their parents. Yes, she felt sure he was honest. Gambler? No, she'd never seen him gamble but that didn't mean anything really as she didn't follow him around. Drinker? He did drink, but not to excess, at least she had never seen him do so. And so the thoughts went round and round her mind until she had to admit that she didn't really know him at all. This had to change. One of them had to take control and if he wouldn't, she had to decide if she would.

*

It became clear that Will had no infection and as his aches and pains diminished he became bored lying in bed alone all day week after week. He fantasised about Mercy until it was like an obsession and finally decided it was sending him mad. He had to do something about it.

On the third week of his recovery he came into to the servants' hall for the first time. As he limped in leaning heavily on a stick, a spontaneous round of applause went round the room. 'Welcome back,' the other servants called out. 'Here comes the hero,' someone called. Mr Sweetman, smiling broadly, got up and helped Will to his chair, taking his stick and leaning it up against the wall behind him. People chatted and welcomed him until Mr Sweetman said, 'Enough noise for now. We are all pleased to see William back with us and we welcome his continued recovery. Now, let us eat our breakfasts.' He clasped his hands together and lowered his head and started his usual prayer, 'For all we are about the receive make us truly thankful,' and added, 'thank you, Lord, for delivering our duchess safely and also our colleague, William, who by his brave actions has changed the course of history, or at least, stopped the course of history from changing as the duchess was in mortal danger.'

'Amen,' everyone said enthusiastically and someone shouted. 'Three cheers for Will.' Everyone joined in with three hurray's, all except Edward, Will noticed. His face was like a lemon being squashed between the strong fingers of Mr Lange. Will was beaming and accepting all the accolades when he looked over at Mercy and their eyes met. He expected her to look away but she held his gaze.

Something passed between them in that moment of noise, merriment and congratulations and Will's heart raced.

Will took succour from the look Mercy had given him. He knew this was the time to make things change one way or another. He had to take charge. Be more like his old self, so as everyone was rushing off after breakfast to their allotted jobs Will gently put his hand on her arm as she passed him and said quietly, 'May I speak with you, please?'

She hesitated, taken by surprise. 'Yes … yes, of course.'

'It's rather private. Would you please come outside with me? The weather's not too chilly.'

He led her to a secluded area where no one could overhear them. He was careful not to stand too close and make her nervous as he balanced himself on his stick. To his relief he felt reassuringly calm. In his mind he had been over this moment many times but had been unsure if he could keep his nerves under control.

'I have something to say to you,' he said, looking directly at her. 'I'll say this straight out. I can say it no other way. I hope you do not find me rude; it is not my intention I can assure you.' He cleared his throat. 'I remember when you first came and I saw you in the kitchen. You fired my heart … it was like a lightning bolt hitting me. I had never seen anyone like you ... anyone I desired so much. I couldn't understand what was happening to me. I was confused.' He shook his head as he relived it. 'And you! You were so confident ... you ... well, you frightened me.'

Mercy looked puzzled. 'Frightened you?' She laughed nervously. 'How on earth could I do that?'

'You think I'm joking, well, I'm not,' he said more sharply than he intended. He had to make her understand, he couldn't lose her now, through his own incompetence. Stay calm, he repeated to himself. He closed his eyes and took a deep breath, keeping his voice as even as he could. 'Yes, I do mean that you frightened me because … because I didn't know what was happening to me. I was feeling emotions I had never known before, that I didn't know I was capable of feeling.' He paused, leaning more heavily on his stick. 'I'd heard of love at first sight, of course, but I never believed it. I was confused and to be truthful, I felt it couldn't be happening to me.' He paused again, unsure, and then decided he had to tell her all. He took a deep breath and let it out slowly. 'Before, and again I will be truthful, not boastful, you understand, just truthful, it was always me who had an effect on women. I never thought it could be the other way around. And again, truthfully, I didn't like it. I decided there and then that I would hate you.'

'Wait a minute. What are you saying to me?' Her voice was harsh. 'First you say you loved me at first sight? Now you're saying you hated me?'

He closed his eyes momentarily trying to think how he could explain. He looked down at his feet, embarrassed. 'I'm sorry. I'm making a mess of this.' He cursed himself as his thoughts tumbled. Call yourself soldier material? Ha! He couldn't even tell a girl he loved her. Be a man! Take control, you can do it. He looked into her eyes, come on, you can do it. 'What I'm … what I'm trying to say is that as time went by I realised that my feelings were …

were turning into love … and those feelings grew. It didn't matter what I did or thought, I had no control over them. I just fell more and more in love with you. I realised for the first time how it felt to be out of control of yourself.'

Mercy was staring at him intently. He could see she was unsure and he felt the silence between them like a physical force. He had to do something drastic and knew it was now or never. He had to just say it as it was and it all tumbled out. 'I am declaring myself, Mercy Batchelor. I am declaring my love for you which has grown and grown. It left me weak and powerless at first, I didn't want it. I didn't want you to have this power over me. But I soon realised I was helpless to stop it. I didn't know what to do. You were not interested in me, you made that very clear.'

Mercy put her hand on Will's arm. 'Will, I'm—'

'No. Please, let me speak. I must say everything to you and then you can say whatever you want.'

She took her hand away and nodded.

'My feelings for you became more intense. I tried to act naturally around you, to make you like me but you didn't seem to have any special feelings for me at all until it was almost unbearable to be in the same room as you, especially when you were laughing and joking with the others. I didn't know what to do and I knew I was making a fool of myself but I couldn't do anything about it … I lost my confidence.' He took a deep breath to steady himself. 'That had never happened to me before and I didn't know what to do … then it became so important that you liked me that I couldn't function at all. It was like being in a haze, a fever maybe, where things are seen through a foggy mist and your brain doesn't function properly and your limbs don't work and you struggle to be your normal self but the fever just becomes more intense and you lose sight of reality.' He stopped abruptly. 'I'm sorry, it's all pouring out in a rush. You look confused, unsure whether I've gone mad.' He rubbed his fingers across his forehead and dug them in, as if that would help. 'Well, maybe I was mad … but what I do know is that I have had plenty of time to think about things over the past three weeks and I have become calmer and can see things more clearly. I know that I cannot go on like this. It must be resolved one way or another so I must find out how you feel about me. I'm not asking for a declaration, just some encouragement or discouragement. Because, Mercy Batchelor, I love you. I love you with all my heart and soul. And if you don't want this from me then I will leave Oatlands. It is impossible for me to stay here in this half-life. I know that now after what happened with the duchess. Life is so fragile and I could have died that day. I have nothing to lose now as I feel I'm on a second chance at life. I'm taking that chance right now. And I want a life with you. I am offering myself, my love and my future. Do what you will with it. I can do no more.'

He turned away awkwardly on his stick, unable to bear Mercy's look of pity and incredulity. He didn't want her to see the tears of emotion which were rising up inside him. He wanted her to see a strong man. Only a weak man sheds tears.

Mercy put her hand on his arm as she said gently, 'I don't know what to say.' It was then that the tears Will was so afraid of shedding made their own decision and cascaded down his cheeks. He couldn't stop them.

*

Mercy's heart was beating hard. She was shocked: shocked at his eloquence, his honesty, the depth of his feelings. No man had ever talked to her like that. She hadn't even realised a man was capable of speaking to a woman in such a deep and personal way. Her heart went out to him but confusion was building inside her. She believed that he loved her but wasn't sure of her own feelings.

And did she want the kind of love Will was offering her? She didn't want a husband who put her on a pedestal and worshiped her like a goddess. That was destined for disaster. She couldn't act like a goddess. She was a real woman with a woman's wants and desires ... and foibles and failings. Did he understand that? She couldn't live up to his image of her. She needed some time to think but knew she had to speak now. What could she say to such a declaration? But whatever happened, he deserved honesty, she knew that much.

'Will,' she said, hesitant as he still had his back to her, trying to hide his tears. She stood in front of him and put her hand on his arm, her heart going out to him. I have to confess I am not sure what to say. I wasn't expecting such a confession, or that you feel so deeply about me. It has come as a shock. But it also makes me realise that I have been unfair to you. I want to put that right now.'

'What do you mean?'

'I think that maybe you see me as you want me to be rather than who I am. I think you have put me on a pedestal, made me out to be better than I am.'

'You're wonderful.' His voice trembled.

'Please … that's what I mean. I am *not* wonderful. I am plain, ordinary, Mercy Batchelor, housemaid to the Duke of York. I am *not* anything special.'

'That's where you are wrong—'

'Please, let me finish. Do me the courtesy of listening to me as I did with you. Do not interrupt, please.'

He nodded.

'You talk about when we first met and your feelings. I admit I also felt an attraction towards you and it frightened me too, because you see, I didn't want to feel love for a man again.' She hesitated and the silence grew but the compassion and obvious love in Will's eyes encouraged her to be brutally honest. 'I had been let down very badly by a man and I didn't want to have to go through it again. My heart was … and is … broken.' She looked down at the ground, fighting her emotions and took a deep and shuddering breath. 'So … I pushed you aside, maybe clumsily, but I didn't know what to do. It was all still raw, it still is raw. And you, you had a reputation with women and not a desirable one either. I didn't want to make another mistake over a man.'

'What happened?' he asked, and the gentleness in his voice touched her.

'If I tell you,' her voice shook and she silently cursed the trembling that was taking her over. She closed her eyes and took another deep breath. 'I need you to promise me that you will keep this to yourself. I have told no one of this except for Anne. I confided in her … but I couldn't bear the humiliation if you spoke of it to the others here.'

'Please, Mercy,' Will's voice broke in his distress. 'Of course I will not breathe any word of this conversation to anyone … I am not disloyal – whatever you think of me, I am not that.'

'I'm sorry. I didn't mean that. Let me just tell you straight out, as you told me.' She gathering her thoughts. 'I was happily engaged to be married to a man I loved and who had good prospects. The day we were to publish our banns I was full of excitement, as you can imagine, but that was the day he chose to tell me he was breaking off our engagement. He had found someone else and he was sorry and all that but that is how it was.'

'What? Just like that?'

'Yes. Just like that. I had no idea he felt that way. No idea he had met someone else. And he just walked away ... left me to tell everyone that I was jilted. I fell to pieces. That's how I ended up here at Oatlands. I needed to get away to somewhere I wasn't known, where my history wasn't known. Fortunately, this position became available and I asked if I could be transferred from the duke's London house to here and, God bless him, the duke agreed.'

'Oh, Mercy, I'm so sorry.' He balanced himself and put his free hand very gently on her shoulder and gave it a gentle squeeze. 'What a stupid man to give *you* up.' He shook his head. 'I cannot understand it, but thank goodness he did because it brought you here to Oatlands. I would marry you tomorrow, now, anytime.

'No, please, don't. I must keep control of myself. Tell you all.' She walked away from him and paced as she talked. 'I have been unlucky in love all my life. I don't know … maybe …maybe I attract the wrong sort of man. Or maybe I've always chosen unwisely. So even though I felt attracted to you, I was not going to let myself fall in love again. Especially to a young, handsome footman who liked his chances with women. That is not what I want from life.' She hesitated again.

'Tell me all … please,' he pleaded so softly, she hardly heard it.

'Yes, you deserve the full story. Please bear with me, I will just have to say this all straight out before I falter. You see, Will, I have no family, my mother died when I was ten. We lived in Ireland where my father was an English soldier but he lost heart after her death and left the army. He returned to London taking me with him. He inherited a small legacy just after that and used some of the money to engage a tutor for me. He had hopes of a good marriage for me, to a man of learning rather than a man of poverty, and he felt this was the best way to achieve that. He owed it to my mother's memory, he said, to get the best he could for me. She was always keen on learning but it was impossible in Ireland. Girls like me were just not educated. I was grateful, and, truth be told, I was a good student and studied hard for my parents' sake. I became literate, lost my Irish accent, which my father didn't like as it reminded him of my mother. I did everything he wanted. I loved him dearly and he was all I had but as I grew older I realised he had a secret. He was a man of drink … and that the drink …' she wiped some tears aggressively away, as if they were irritating flies rather than her own emotions, 'I realised the drink was taking him away from me.' Her voice faltered and she swallowed hard. 'He died when I was thirteen. There was no money left as he'd drunk it all away. I was told I was a pauper. I had no choice and it was going into service for me or something much,

much worse.

'I did my growing up scrubbing other people's floors, washing their dirty clothes and cleaning up after them. I had no value, just someone to order to do things. I'd look at the family I worked for and my heart ached for a family of my own, people who cared for me above all others. But, you know, time heals and I grew up but those feelings never left me.'

'Mercy,' Will's voice was soft and low. 'I'm so sorry.'

'No, I don't want your sympathy, I want your understanding.' It was as if Will's sympathy had given her courage. 'Now,' she said with authority, 'I'll tell you what I want from *my* life.'

She locked eyes with him.

'I want a loving husband who will stay faithful and I can trust to have my children with. Who will look after me and my children whatever passes between us. Forever, Will. Forever. And I didn't think you were that man. Now, I'm not so sure. But what I am sure of is that I am not the woman you think I am. I am just an ordinary woman, not the woman you have put on a pedestal to worship.'

After a pause, he said, 'I think I understand what you are saying.' He briefly and gently caressed the side of her face with his finger, his eyes full of love. He looked down at the ground, thinking. 'I'm so sorry your experience of family was so different to mine. I'm beginning to understand how important having a good family is and how stupid I was to not value it before in my own family. I'll never forget it ever again.' He took a few awkward steps away from her and was silent for a while. He turned back to her making eye contact. 'You talk of putting a person on a pedestal. But doesn't love put the other person on a pedestal? Don't you worship the other person? Doesn't love make the other person seem like a god or goddess? How can you love deeply and not feel like that about the person you love? That's what it's all about, isn't it? My father still worships my mother. It's what I was brought up with … to believe my mother was the most wonderful woman on earth and I really believed it until … until now. I feel my mother is the second most wonderful woman on earth.'

He put his arm on her shoulder again but this time gently pulled her to him. 'Let me heal you, Mercy.' He stroked her hair. 'Listen, can you hear my heart? It's beating wildly, surely you can hear it. Surely they can hear it in the house, all over the neighbourhood?' He hugged her tighter. 'Mercy, do me the honour of believing that I know my own mind. I know how I feel. I am not a child. Yes, I'm younger than you, and yes, I have never had my heart broken, and do you know what? I intend never to get my heart broken. Because I mean to marry you, Mercy Batchelor. If not straight away, then when you are ready. I do not intend to let you go. I realise I am more like my father than I thought. He is a one-woman man and I know now that I am too. There is nothing you can say or do which will change my mind. And if you don't like it, then, I will never give up. I will win you round. I am determined.'

She stepped away from him, wiping away some tears and held up her hand to silence him. 'Let's wait and see what happens,' she said very softly, 'see how things develop. We need to take things slowly.' She kissed his cheek. 'There is no great rush. I need time.'

'All the time in the world, my lovely. You have

made me the happiest of men. Thank you. You have given me hope.' He took her hand and kissed the back of it. He held her hand to his face and closed his eyes for a moment. When he opened them he was smiling. 'You see this happy face? It's the face of a man who feels he is the cat that got the cream.'

She laughed, as he had hoped she would. He bent forwards and kissed her lips so gently she hardly felt it, like silkworms making silk.

CHAPTER SIXTEEN

The fifteenth of August 1792 was a date no one at Oatlands would forget. It had been a hot summer and that day was no exception as the staff gathered in the servants' hall for their mid-day dinner. As they waited for everyone to arrive, Anne entered and took her allotted chair which was, thankfully, next to Mercy's. 'Goodness, it's hot today. I do believe I'm melting,' she said as she mopped her face and neck with her handkerchief. 'I feel like I should wring this out it's so sodden.'

Mercy mopped her own face. 'It's certainly hard to work in this weather. Still, on the whole, I have to say I prefer the hot weather to the cold.'

Anne whispered so that no one else could hear. 'And a little bird told me that things are hot elsewhere?'

'I'm sure I don't know what you mean,' Mercy whispered back, keeping a straight face.

'You and Will are getting very serious I feel. And I'm glad.'

Mercy made sure no one was listening. 'Is it so obvious?'

'Well, it is to me, but then, I have a special interest.'

'You're right, Anne, we are getting serious. I'm seeing a different Will to the one I knew before. But I'll just warn you that I am not rushing into anything.

I need time to adjust, so please do not say anything to the other staff. We are trying to be discreet.'

'Don't worry, I wouldn't dream of speaking to anyone, but I just wanted to say I'm feeling very pleased about the whole thing.'

Mr Sweetman strode purposefully into the room and everyone stood up. He was looking serious and had a newspaper under his arm, always a sign he was about to impart some news. He slapped it down in front of him as he sat down.

'Attention everyone, please.' He looked around the table with a frown as everyone sat back down. Anne knew something awful had happened as she'd never seen him look so serious and worried. Her heart fluttered uncomfortably and the unexpected news rocked her to her toes.

'Listen to me, carefully,' he said in his loud, calm voice. 'I have very, *very,* bad news.' The silence was palpable and Anne felt everyone stiffen. 'The latest news from France is devastating. It is my sad duty to inform you all that the King and Queen of France have been arrested by the mob and put in prison.'

No one moved a muscle as their eyes, glued to Mr Sweetman's, registered shock and then everyone started talking at the same time.

'What?' 'No! Surely not!' 'Impossible!' 'This cannot be true!'

Anne's throat constricted and left her speechless. She had never imagined the French would go this far.

'Settle down, everyone,' Mr Sweetman said in a soothing voice. 'I think it safe to say we all know what implications this has for our own royal family. We are in a very serious situation and we must all give our support to our royal family, especially here to the duke and duchess.'

'Yes, indeed,' everyone echoed each other.

'I cannot believe it,' Mrs Harley exclaimed. 'Has the world gone mad? Arrested the King and Queen of France and put them in prison. I am speechless.'

'I agree, Mrs Harley, the world has gone mad.' He addressed the rest of the staff. 'Now, I rely on all of you to do your jobs extra well and not cause the duke or duchess any extra stress. This is a blow of mammoth proportions.'

'But didn't we kill our own king last century, Mr Sweetman, sir?'

Mr Sweetman glared daggers at James. 'Indeed we did. And a very sorry day that was too. I never thought our king could be threatened again.'

'It all ended badly though,' Mrs Harley added. 'We now have our royal family back and I for one am mightily grateful to have them. Order is kept with a royal family. Chaos reigns without them. Forward thinkers are nothing but trouble. The rabble should never be listened to.'

'And rabble they are in France, Mrs Harley. Rabble indeed.' Mr Sweetman added, 'Now everyone, settle down and eat your meal. We have to digest much more than just our food today. I will keep you informed as I receive any news. I would expect the duke to be leaving for London soon as he will be much involved in dealing with this crisis. The duchess has informed me she will stay here unless called for by the duke. Now, she will need support and I intend that she shall receive it.' He tried to glare at everyone but Anne felt he had physically diminished over the last few minutes. She left sorry for him. He was so loyal.

265

'Mr Sweetman,' Mrs Harley said, 'do you think it a good idea for Anne to speak to the duchess on our behalf?'

Anne started. She looked between Mrs Harley and Mr Sweetman, wondering what was coming next and by the look on the butler's face, he did too.

'I mean,' Mrs Harley continued, 'Anne has access to the duchess as she is her housemaid, an access which we do not have as a normal every day event. I was thinking that maybe she could reassure the duchess that we are all supporting her and will protect her to the very best of our abilities.' The silence in the room grew as she looked at Mr Sweetman, until she shrugged her shoulders in a gesture that she would comply with his decision.

He nodded a few times. 'A very good idea, Mrs Harley … mmm … yes, a very good idea.' He tapped the tabletop with his finger, thinking. 'Anne, would you be so kind as to speak to the duchess on our behalf and say how distressed we all are at the news from France and that we will support her and the duke and protect them to the best of our abilities, as Mrs Harley suggests.'

This was serious and Anne felt a flutter of nerves but swallowed them down. 'I would be honoured to represent everyone.'

'Anyone disagree?' His looked brokered no dissent from the likes of footmen and maids. Everyone readily agreed.

'Good. As soon as you get the opportunity, Anne, and let me know when you have spoken to her.'

'I will, Mr Sweetman, sir.'

*

Jack had been keeping Ben Moat company manning the gates. It was Ben's duty week for the day shift but he was in no condition to do his job properly.

'It will be all right, you'll see, Ben. She'll be fine. The baby will come soon.'

'But it's been days now and it still hasn't come. And her screams. I can't bear it.'

'If she can bear it so can you,' Jack answered.

'It's been quiet for a while now. I'm frightened. I've never been so frightened even in fiercest fighting. I don't know what to do. I feel so helpless. It's never been this bad before.'

'Come, let's knock on the door and see how things are. My Hannah will be able to tell us. The woman from the village is good with births but my Hannah is just as good.'

As Jack raised his hand to knock the door opened and Hannah appeared. The look in her eyes and her tears said all that was needed.

'I'm so sorry,' she said as Jack put his arm around her. 'She's dead, Jack,' she whispered, 'and the baby. We couldn't save them. I can't tell him. I just can't, will you—'

'Of course, go back to our place, my love. I'll see to everything here.' He made sure Hannah was inside with the door closed and then put his arm around Ben's shoulders.

'You don't have to say anything,' Ben's voice cracked. 'I know by Hannah's face and the silence that screams as loudly as my wife has been doing for days.' He ran his hands over his face roughly and said, 'May the Lord give her peace now.' He went into his lodge and shut the door on Jack.

Jack didn't know what to do. The woman from the

village came out after a while and shut the door behind her. 'Leave him alone with his grief, Mr Dresser. It's best. Mrs Moat is clean and tidy and the baby is too. He's wrapped in a beautiful shawl, he looks lovely. Mr Moat needs time to grieve. Just keep an eye on the door in case he appears but don't check up on him until tomorrow.'

Hannah appeared. 'Thank you so much. It's a sad day. We did our best.'

'We did. Not even the doctor could have helped. The baby born dead and the days of agony she suffered was too much for her, sapped her strength. I've seen it all too often, I'm sorry to say. I'll go now, Mrs Dresser, there is nothing more I can do. I'll make sure my sister keeps the Moat children with her for a while more. Please let me know when he is ready to have them back. But don't worry, we are used to this happening and have worked a system out between us to help stricken families.'

'Maybe you could help us a little more,' Hannah asked. 'When the children come back, Mr Moat will need help with them and I cannot give him all that needs as I have three of my own to take care of.'

'Don't worry, Mrs Dresser, I know of a young woman in the village who is looking for work and she is good with children. I'll ask her if she would like to work for him. But it would be daytime only, you understand … for proprieties sake.'

'Of course. That will be most suitable. Thank you, again.'

'It's a bad business,' Jack said to Hannah as he closed their door. 'I am so grateful that our children were born easily.'

Hannah gave him a look. 'Really? Easily? I

268

sometimes wonder about your thinking, Jack Dresser.'

*

The next morning Anne took her time in the duchess'
apartments, hoping to delay things so that she saw her
after her morning walk. The duchess bustled in with
fresh, ruddy cheeks surrounded by six small, yapping
dogs. She looked surprised when she saw Anne still
in her rooms. 'Oh, Anne, you are running late today?
I hope everything is as it should be?'

'Yes, Your Grace.' Anne hesitated. 'May I speak
to you a moment, please?'

'Of course.' She smiled. 'Let's go into my sitting
room.' She sat down on one of the plush armchairs
and two dogs jumped into her lap and the smallest
settled himself over her tiny feet while the others
started playing together, throwing themselves across
the room. The duchess stroked her lapdogs absent-
mindedly, her attention all on Anne.

Anne was nervous. She didn't know how the
duchess was feeling about the news from France but
assumed she was upset. 'Your Grace, I would like to
speak to you on behalf of all the indoor household
staff.' Anne hesitated and the duchess inclined her
head in acquiescence. 'We are desperately upset at the
news of the imprisonment of the King and Queen of
France. We have all agreed that we want you to know
this and to reassure you that we are all in support of
you, the duke and the whole royal family. We will
protect you here at Oatlands to our utmost ability.'

The duchess looked at Anne with a surprised look.
'What a wonderful thing to say.' She stroked the dogs
for several seconds. 'I am most grateful. It is a great

comfort to me. Please, thank them all and tell them I am deeply touched.' She took a measured look at Anne. 'You know, I am more reassured by your message than you may imagine.'

'You are, Your Grace?'

'I have read my history books and know that your country went so far as to behead your king last century. King Charles the First.'

Anne flushed a deep crimson. 'Oh, Your Grace, please … please do not think we are like that now. It was a very long time ago.' She felt lost but decided she must speak. 'You are correct, of course, we did do that to our king but we soon found out that the alternative was just as bad, if not worse. The country was in turmoil and most people just wanted things to get back to normal. Cromwell was a disaster as far as I am concerned … and as the country took our king's son back to be our monarch, I think most other people felt the same.'

The duchess nodded as she continued to caress the dogs. 'That was the conclusion I came to as well when I thought it through. Your confirmation and the support of the staff has touched me greatly.'

Anne breathed a sigh of relief.

'You know I have become very fond of English people. They have been so kind to me. I was educated in English and loved English literature and developed a love of England through that. Then of course, I met the duke and started to think more seriously about England although I didn't know what to expect when I came as the duke's wife. How would England respond to me?' She smiled to herself. The duke told me everyone would love me here but I was not sure … and do you know … he was right. However, it was still hard to come to a strange country with other customs to the ones I have been used to.' She seemed lost in thought for a while. 'I have had nothing but kindness from everyone from the king down to the people in the village here.' The duchess' smile grew as she looked down at her dogs. 'When people knew I loved dogs they brought me presents of puppies from the most expensive lap-dogs from the rich right down to the goodness knows what mixture from the villagers here. And I love them all, Anne.'

'Yes, Your Grace, I understand how much you love them.'

'Do you mind, Anne … cleaning up after them? They can be a little naughty during the night. The duke throws them all out when he comes but after he has left I let them all back in again.' She laughed lightly and Anne risked joining in. She couldn't help it as the duchess had such an infectious laugh.

'I don't mind. They amuse me with their antics. If you don't mind me saying so, I also love dogs … maybe more than people,' Anne confided.

The duchess laughed heartily. 'Me too sometimes.' She was thoughtful. 'But now, to more serious business, the duke leaves for London tomorrow. As you can imagine, he will be very busy with the king and his advisers over this matter but I will stay on here at Oatlands. I will make sure the duke tells the rest of his family of the wonderful support we have received from the staff here. They will be most gratified, I am sure. Please express my gratitude and that of the duke to all the staff.'

'Thank you, Your Grace, I will tell them.' She left the room and curtsied in the doorway before taking her leave, feeling relieved it had all gone so well.

271

The duchess was as equally good an employer as the duke. She felt very lucky to be working at Oatlands and didn't want anything to spoil it. And she knew the largesse of the duke and duchess could only be stretched so far.

CHAPTER SEVENTEEN

Jack came into the lodge and called for Hannah. 'I'm upstairs making the beds.'

'Were the children well enough for school this morning?' Jack called back.

'Yes,' Hannah answered as she came down the stairs. 'This autumn weather attracts colds like wasps over a pot of jam. They were keen to get back. You've been so busy this morning all I saw of you was your back disappearing through the door at daybreak.'

'There's been nothing but deliveries. At one stage I had them queuing up outside the gates as there were so many carts down at the house we couldn't fit any more in. Mr Tucker sent word to restrict the number coming in. Use a one out and one in policy. The drivers were none too pleased I can tell you but the duke and his guests have been partying that hard over the past week we're having trouble replenishing stock. The duchess told Mrs Harley and Mr Sweetman not to skimp on anything.'

'Well, it's nice to have the duke back at Oatlands. He's been through a terrible strain up in London what with the King and Queen of France and all the rest of it. Anne's told me he's been in the middle of all the discussions and decisions of how to protect our own royal family in case dissent broke out over here. The duchess says that the duke needs a rest as he's been working too hard.'

'Anne's not supposed to gossip about the family. She knows that.'

'Come on, Jack. She's only telling me and I'm only telling you.'

'Well …' Jack prevaricated. 'I suppose so, but she needs to be careful. And I don't doubt the duke has been working hard; he's a conscientious man and a good leader of men. I envy his energy.'

'That's because you're getting older,' Hannah chided with a smile.

'Oh, to be young again,' he sang out, trying to catch Hannah for a hug.

Hannah moved out of his way. 'Serious now, Jack.' She looked out of the window. 'Looks like some of the drivers are getting impatient.'

Jack looked out and sighed. 'They have all descended on us at the same time.' He shook his head. 'We have never had so much delivered by so many and it was my misfortune to be on duty today. Young Moat there has slept through it all, no doubt!'

'Come on now, Jack. Don't be unfair. He does his bit. He's a good worker. It was his turn to work nights this week so his good fortune and he needs some good fortune since his wife died.' She shook her head. 'Childbirth, it is so precarious … I feel so sorry for him and his children.'

Jack sighed. 'You're right. I'm sorry I'm a bit bad tempered. He has had a rough time of it. Maybe I'm getting too old for this job. I get too tired.'

Hannah rubbed Jack's back and massaged his shoulders as he sat at the table. 'Don't worry you're up to the job. You just need a rest, that's all.'

'Fine chance of that. Well, I admire the duke's energy as I said. He can host a dinner party and gamble and drink all night and still be up early and ride out for a canter in the woods.'

'He is extraordinary and you're right he never seems to be the worse for wear, unlike some of his guests. Anne tells me some of them don't get up until the afternoon and then they play and whatever else they get up to all night again. Playing cards and drinking and goodness knows what else.'

'Best not to ask,' Jack moaned and then laughed. 'Oh, Hannah, we sound like two old people ready for our rocking chairs.'

'Never!' Hannah said as a loud knock on the door interrupted them.

'Now, who's that,' Jack said. 'It had better not be impatient drivers.'

Hannah opened the door. 'Why, Ben! We didn't expect to see you so early. Couldn't you sleep? Are the children all right?'

'Oh, yes, I'm sorry, Mrs Dresser, they're fine. The girl from the village has come up to look after them as usual. But it's about the children that I wanted to talk to you. May I come in for a moment?'

'Of course,' Hannah said.

'What can we do for you?' Jack said kindly, standing up.

Ben Moat stood in the middle of the room turning his hat around in his hands, looking at the floor.

'Don't be nervous, out with it,' Jack encouraged him.

'Yes, thank you. Ah … well … since my wife died …' he wiped some tears away and sniffed. 'Sorry,' he mumbled.

'It's only been two months since she died, Ben,' Hannah said gently. 'And your baby son too, it's bound to be hard to talk about.' She put her arm around his shoulders and asked, 'Is the girl we found for you looking after the children properly?'

He pulled himself up straight. 'Oh, yes, Mrs Dresser. She is doing her best. I have no complaints, but that is why I have come to see you. I loved my wife and we were happy together but I must do what is right for my children and they need a mother not a minder.' He looked from one to the other. 'I have decided, for my children's sake, I must find myself another wife as soon as possible.'

'But Ben, it's too soon,' Jack soothed.

'With respect, I know what is best for my family and … well, that's why I have come to see you.'

Puzzled, Hannah said, 'Let's sit down at the table and tell us what you have in mind.'

'Yes, thank you,' he said sitting down and shuffling in his chair as Hannah and Jack waited patiently, giving him time. 'As I have already said,' his voice was low, unsure, 'I am truly grateful for your help and for arranging for the village girl to come and look after the children and for you arranging everything when … when … well, when I was in no condition to do anything.' He swallowed several times. 'And, you're right,' he cleared his throat, 'it is too soon for me but my children,' he stopped and breathed deeply a few times. 'I see them suffering every day and they are upset when the village girl leaves them with me. I think they do not think me a good replacement. I'm a soldier and not good with children. I struggle … and well, I think this is the best option.'

Jack and Hannah looked at him with compassion

and Hannah put her hand on Ben's, reassuringly, as he cleared his throat again. 'But, well, I was wondering if you would have any objections to me asking Anne to walk out with me?'

'Anne!' Hannah exploded, as she shot up, unable to control her surprise and her hand flew from his as if she'd been burned.

Jack frowned. 'Maybe our Anne is not the best option for you. She is not keen on marriage she has told us.'

'Yes, many times,' Hannah confirmed. 'I have tried on various occasions to encourage her to marry but she is happy working for the duchess and wants to continue doing so.'

'Well, the thing is, Mrs Dresser, I am … well, I am very keen on Anne.'

'But she may not be so keen on your offer,' Jack said, gently.

'But I cannot ask another until I have heard from Anne herself.' He sighed. 'That's how it is, I'm afraid.'

'Are you sure?' Hannah asked with compassion.

He nodded. 'I loved my wife and miss her dreadfully but I must do what is best for my children and, as I said, they need a mother not a minder. I must do this now. I must.' He wiped away a tear and Hannah put her arm around his shoulder and patted him. She looked at Jack questioningly. He nodded, understanding her.

'I tell you what,' Hannah said, 'why don't you go and talk to Anne, see what she has to say and then we will know what is possible and what is not. If you are determined to ask her, then do so. Jack and I have no objections to you as a son-in-law. You are a good man. And you were a good husband.'

'Indeed so,' Jack confirmed as he exchanged a look of resignation with his wife.

*

It was Anne's half day and she had decided to go into the village. She wore her best clothes and bonnet, making sure her dress didn't catch on any undergrowth as she walked along the woodland pathway. She heard a crack of wood behind her and turned sharply.

Ben Moat was rushing along the pathway to catch her up. Her heart sank. The last thing she needed was Ben Moat.

'Good afternoon, Anne.' He lifted his hat politely and made a bow. Anne nodded her head towards him briefly, hoping to discourage him as she turned to walk on.

'A moment, Anne,' he said putting his hand out and touching her arm.

She looked down at his arm and then up to his face and despaired to see him looking so earnest.

'I must speak to you. Please.'

'I'm sorry, but I have no time now. Forgive me.' She made to go but he kept his hand on her arm.

'Let me go,' she snapped.

'Please, just a moment. I must speak.'

It was obvious to Anne that he would follow her until he had spoken so she decided it was best to get it over with. 'Well, I'd be grateful if you'd make it quick. As I said, I am busy.'

He looked into her eyes, his own pleading. 'In that case I will make it brief. Would you do me the honour of walking out with me?'

'*What!*' She spat out, staring at him in disbelief.

'Man, your wife has only just gone to her Maker. You cannot be serious.'

He reared back at her venom and she could see he was trying to keep his dignity. 'My children need a mother. I have always been enamoured with you and thought you the most beautiful and lovely of women. I would be most honoured if you would consider me favourably.'

Good God! Not again, she said to herself. I can't bear it. Why can't men leave me alone? But this? So soon! Shock rippled through her. Was the man mad? She had given him no reason to approach her, of that she was sure. She had behaved coolly to him, always. Letting her fury show, she hissed, 'I see I must speak frankly. I am not a slave, and to me marriage is slavery and certainly your kind of marriage is. I will never marry you Ben Moat, now leave me alone and look for someone more suitable.'

'Anne … Anne, please. I have eyes only for you.' He put his hand on her arm again and she shook it off.

'I told you, NO! Please respect that.' She was losing her composure.

He let go of her arm. 'Think about it then.'

Her temper snapped. 'Have you not listened to me? I have already told you *NO*. Please do me the courtesy of believing me. Believing I know my own mind. There is nothing to discuss. If you persist I will speak to my father. Now, I am due elsewhere. Good day to you.' She turned abruptly and walked away from him, not looking back, afraid he would take it as an encouragement. She walked fast, her heart thumping hard as her anger built even more until she was full of fury. How dare he? It was happening again, why oh why couldn't I have been born plain?

God help me, am I to get no peace?

She had enough sense to realise she couldn't go to the village in the state she was in. People would notice and ask her what was wrong. She needed some time alone, to recover her equilibrium. She turned in a large circle, making sure Ben Moat was not behind her but it was all clear. She saw the grotto in the distance perched on its man-made crag surrounded by the artificial lake. Since she'd first seen it with her father she'd visited the upper chamber alone several times, making sure no one knew where she was. For some reason, the ridiculousness of the room always soothed her. She knew she was not allowed inside when the duke was in residence but she reasoned it would be unlikely that anyone would be there now, as everyone was involved in the parties which went on all day. If the duke and duchess were not in the grotto then no one else would dare to be.

As she approached she looked around to make sure there was no one else about. The thick trees and bushes surrounding the grotto acted as a barrier between her and the more open space around it. She ran up the steps on the outside of the grotto looking forward to sitting in one of the strange chairs and admiring the views to the glorious North Downs. If that doesn't calm me then I don't know what will, she thought. She turned into the room and stopped dead in her tracks. Lounging on one of the chairs was Belknap, a supercilious smile on his face.

'Well, hello, it's the beautiful maid with the morals of a saint, if I'm not mistaken,' he drawled drunkenly. 'Didn't expect me, I don't suppose.' He nodded to the window. 'I saw you coming,' he took a large gulp of the port in his glass, 'and I've been thinking of the joys of your body which you hold so dear. You should really share them, you know.'

Anne's limbs froze as surely as if she had jumped into the bath of ice-cold water downstairs. In seconds her panic built until her heart thumped so hard she had difficulty breathing. This was as bad as it could get. She was trapped.

She tried to calm herself. 'Sir,' but to her vexation her voice quavered. She tried again this time with more success. 'Sir, please forgive me. I am on an errand for the duchess and am expected back instantly.' She hoped this would exert some pressure on him to let her go about her business.

'Not so fast,' he sneered, his eyes shining bright with excitement.

Anne, with great effort, kept hold of her composure. 'I'm sorry, sir. But the duchess is waiting.'

'Let her wait then. *You* have pressing business here, with *me*. We have unfinished business between us.' He sat up in his chair and held out his hand. 'The duke is not here to stop me. And you, little lady, cannot stop me, of that I am sure. Now why don't you just be a good girl and come here and let me touch your luxurious hair, and beautiful face, and smooth neck, and ...' He lunged and made a grab for her.

She jumped out of his way, knowing she had to run. It was her only chance. She turned so suddenly she almost tripped but saved herself and ran back along the passageway and down the steps as fast as she could. Belknap's loud footsteps behind her spurred her on but he was catching up. His long legs unencumbered by long skirts were working in his favour. Damn. Damn. Damn.

As she got to the bottom of the steps she made

to run straight ahead but he grabbed her from behind and dragged her around the corner into the bath room. He pinned her arms down by her side as she struggled but he was too powerful. He kissed her lips and she threw her head from side to side and her bonnet was knocked onto the floor. The smell of the alcohol and his stale breath turned her stomach. Her arms ached and throbbed from the strength of his grip. And then he let her go. He slapped her face hard and grabbed at her breasts trying to rip her dress. She cried out in pain as he pushed her against the statue of Venus and grappled with her skirts pulling them up. Blinding rage increased her strength and she lashed out violently at the same time letting out an almighty animal cry which startled him so much he slackened his hold on her. She pushed him with all her might and caught him off balance. He crashed backwards his head cracking with a sickening thud on the raised lip of the bath. He lay there, motionless.

Anne froze, unable to take her eyes off him. She knew she had to run. Take advantage of this. She made for the doorway but something made her turn back, a stillness about him which was not natural. He lay on his back where he had landed like a rag doll, his head and neck lolling over the edge of the pool, the ice-cold water rippling through his hair. Her thoughts tumbled into an incoherent mass of thoughts knowing instinctively he couldn't hold that pose if he was alive – could he?

Panic gripped her as she realised no one would believe her. He was a man of substance, a friend of the duke, part of the aristocracy. She struggled to keep control of herself, not let herself get emotional, that would make everything worse. She gulped for air, trying to breathe in deeply. Who knew she was here? No one, as long as Ben Moat hadn't followed her, and she felt certain he hadn't. Then was she safe? How could she be sure? What should she do? Should she go to the village, no, she was in an even worse condition than before. She had to act fast. Delay may mean the gallows if she was discovered.

Dear God! The gallows!

It would not only kill me but my parents too. They would die of shame. She needed an alibi. Who? Who could she trust? Who would want to help her?

Will? Of course he would help but she knew he was busy serving at the party. She'd never get access to him. Who else? Mercy? Would Mercy help her? Could she risk it? She knew Mercy was working alone in one of the outside buildings used for dirty jobs. She had no choice; she'd have to trust Mercy. As she left the grotto she looked around carefully and seeing no one walked quickly, keeping herself as hidden as she could in the trees and shrubs. She made her way around the back of the house, praying she did not meet anyone. She was lucky and saw no one.

As she reached the stone-built, single-storey outbuilding she opened the door quietly and slowly. Thank God, Mercy was there alone. She closed the door as quietly as she had opened it and called out, 'Mercy,' her voice coming out as a low hiss.

Mercy jumped and turned. 'Goodness, Anne, you did give me a—what's wrong?'

Anne legs went from her and she crumpled on the flagstone floor and sobbed. Mercy rushed to her and held her close. After a few minutes, Anne recovered enough to tell her what had happened.

'Good God, and may He have mercy upon us all.

This is a disaster.'

Anne tried to control the violent shaking of her body. 'I didn't intend to kill him, but I couldn't let him violate me … could I?'

'No! Of course not.' Mercy recovered her senses a little. 'It serves the bastard right. He was a vile man always after all the female servants. I don't know why the duke favoured him so.'

Anne had enough sense to say, 'Careful, Mercy, in what you say. Let's be circumspect or we'll find ourselves in more trouble.'

'True, it was the shock. But we must tell Will, don't you think? He'll know what to do.'

'But he's on duty at the party? And what can he do?'

'I don't know what he can do. But this is too big for us to deal with alone.'

'Yes, you're right. Of course, you're right.'

'I know Will's roster and with luck he may be taking his meal break about now. I'll sneak into the servants' hall and see if I can find him. You, Anne, can cover yourself by pretending to help me with the scrubbing of the rugs. Don't actually do any, you don't want to spoil your clothes, but have a brush and bottle in your hand just in case someone comes in. But I am not expecting anyone. No one likes this job and it was just my bad luck to get lumbered with it.'

'Or my good luck.'

'Indeed.' Mercy stroked Anne's cheek. 'Stay strong and wait here. Do not move.' she said as she made her way out of the door.

Anne felt her legs go again and sat down in front of one of the rugs trying her hardest to pull herself together. She thought the time would never end but finally, Mercy appeared with Will. He rushed over to Anne and took her in his arms and hugged her tight. 'Oh, Anne. I am so sorry. So very sorry. Mercy has told me.'

She cried into his shoulder for what seems like an age to her. Then, Mercy took her arm and gently led her to a bench and sat her down. 'We have been thinking hard.'

'On the walk over here I have come up with an idea,' Will said. He pulled up an old three-legged stool and sat on it in front of the women, taking care not to spoil his livery. He took one of Anne's hands in his and squeezed it reassuringly. 'Now, whatever happens it must be me who does it.'

'No, I'll help,' Mercy said.

'No, I will not have the women I love mixed up in this in any way. It must come from me. Now, listen. I've been on duty with the duke and his party all day. And I know that we haven't seen Belknap for hours. Someone is bound to ask where he is sooner or later and I will whisper to Mr Sweetman that I saw him going towards the grotto this afternoon. I'll volunteer to go and look for him and discover him and run back with the bad news. You will not be implicated at all because, why would you be? You were not supposed to be at the grotto ... were you?'

'No, not at all. I only went because of that Ben Moat upsetting me. I expected it to be empty.'

'Good, then no one will be any the wiser. But you must have an alibi. You must go down to the village now, hurry there as fast as you can. Make sure you go into lots of shops or chat to people and make them remember you were there. Tell them you have been in the church or went for a walk or something and have been in the village for ages.' He looked at her with tenderness.

'I can't.' She started to cry. 'I can't control my shaking.'

'Look, by the time you get to the village you will have recovered somewhat and your life depends on this. You *must* recover. Show your bravery, your solid heart. You're always telling me how strong you are. Now prove it.'

'I'll do my best.' It came out as a whisper.

'Do more than your best,' he said gently. 'And you, Mercy, you must have an alibi too. Make sure you go into the kitchen and talk to as many as you can. Get something to drink. Make a fuss; say you are starving … that you would like to see the back of those rugs. Make a thing of how tired you are. Anything to make people remember you and that you have been working hard all afternoon. I have my alibi as I have been on duty with Mr Sweetman all day and we have not been out of each others' sight for more than a short time.'

'Do you really think it could work, Will?' Anne pleaded.

'I certainly do. But you must play your part. Did anyone see you come from the grotto?'

'No, I'm pretty sure no one did.'

'Good, then go back out and make your way to the village. Try and make sure no one sees you. Don't forget, make out you have been in the village for hours. Can you do that?'

She nodded. She had never known Will so forceful but realised he was right. She had the power to save herself. She must do this. You can do it, she said to herself over and over. Stay calm. Do it for Will and

Mercy. You *can* do it. But as she thought this her insides were churning like a cork in a storm at sea. Keep a strong hold on yourself the mantra inside her head repeated as Will and Mercy fussed at her. And then the bolt of shock, like a crack of lightning hitting her full square.

Mercy's voice from a distance. 'Let me tidy your hair—Anne! Where's your bonnet?

'My bonnet?' Anne repeated, putting her hands up to her head in disbelief. Her eyes widened and a wave of fear made her shudder uncontrollably. 'I ... I ... remember ... vaguely ... it got knocked off in the struggle ... I remember thinking, it will get ruined. Stupid thing to think in the circumstances ... my God!' she rasped. 'It's still in the grotto!' A sob burst out of her and she struggled to breathe.

'Anne! Anne! Will grabbed her shoulders and shook her. 'Stop this. We do not have the luxury of losing control. It's not like you.'

'It's the shock,' Mercy advised him. 'She's in deep shock.'

'Well, she cannot afford to be in shock, deep or otherwise. Everything depends on us keeping our heads.' He shook her shoulders none too gently. 'Listen, Anne, breathe calmly. This is not the end. There is an answer to every problem. You have to go back to the grotto. Collect your bonnet and make your way to the village as we agreed.'

Anne struggled for air as her heart missed beats. 'I can't. I can't. He's there. Oh, Will, what am I to do.'

'You must. Don't you see? You must. Do it for our parents if not for yourself. It will kill them if their daughter is involved in such a scandal. And don't forget. It was not your fault. Don't ever forget that.'

287

'Yes. It will kill them,' she said slowly forcing herself to calm her breathing. 'I must do it for them,' she said more to herself than to Will.

'That's the way. Think of our parents. Do it for them. And remember, it was an accident. You are not responsible.'

'But I am. Don't you see? I'm only a servant and a lowly maid at that. They will crucify me. They won't believe me. You know they won't. He's an aristocrat and a friend of the duke's. They will back their own.'

'All the more reason to go back to the grotto and get your bonnet. Come on, Anne.'

She nodded, trying to calm herself.

Mercy kneeled in front of her. 'Come,' she said softly, 'let me wash your face and you dry your tears and let's have no more of them until this is all over. Can you do that?'

Anne nodded and let Mercy wipe her face with a clean wet rag and allowed her to tidy her hair. By the time Mercy was finished Anne had controlled herself enough to function.

'Right, you go first, Anne, then Mercy. I will go last. And remember, we must all play our parts to perfection or all is lost. Only think about getting that bonnet and then to the village and act normally and making people remember you.'

Tears welled up in Anne's eyes. Will opened the door a little and looked out. 'All clear,' and then shouted into Anne's ear, 'DO IT, ANNE! DO IT!' He steered her out the door and then shut it sharply.

'God, Mercy,' he wiped the sweat off his brow. 'I had to be firm. She must get control of herself. If I shout at her with luck she will do it to spite me.'

'I understand,' Mercy said. 'I think you did right.

It's all down to each of us now. Come on, let's do it. We can only worry about our parts and let Anne deal with hers.'

Anne walked briskly, keeping away from the main pathways and made her way to the grotto. She tried not to think of what was awaiting her. You can do it, she repeated over and over until the grotto loomed into sight. Don't stop, keep moving. Don't think. Just do it. She was inside and only hesitated as she approached the doorway to the bath room. What if he's not dead? What is he's sitting there? Oh, God help me, please. Her knees started to shake and she knew she was losing control. She stood tall, stretching her back and breathed in hard. To her astonishment her legs moved her forwards and she was at the doorway. Don't think. She peered around it. Keep breathing. There was Belknap where she had left him. She'd never forget it. Don't look. Get your bonnet. Again, she was astonished that her legs took her inside the room and she made her way round the wall furthest from the body until she saw the bonnet lying on the ground. She picked it up and ran so hard she almost fell over. Outside, she examined it. Apart from a brush down it was undamaged and she put it on as if it would bite her and stepped out making sure no one was about. She strode out as if in a dream and the next thing she knew she was in the village. She put everything out of her mind and like an actor playing a fictional character she knew was not her, she went to several shops and bought small items. She made sure everyone remember her ... she complained of a headache in one, in another telling them her bonnet blew off and got covered in dust and so on. It was exhausting. Drained and depressed she made her way back to Oatlands and no one said a word about her absence except to say she had missed the excitement of Mr Belknap's body being found. Mercy nodded to her and gave her a strained half-smile acknowledging things had gone well for her. Anne pleaded a headache and went to her bed.

*

In the meantime, Will hurried back to his post in the main rooms of the house, fighting down indigestion as he had gulped down his food as Mercy whispered what had happened and he realised the urgency of it all. Fortunately, he was the only one in the servants' hall at the time. Footmen were often on almost permanent duty when the duke came with his friends to stay but had leisure time when the duke was not in residence. No one minded. It was a good trade.

Will tried to hide his mounting excitement and swallow down an irritating surge of nerves as he entered the grand salon. He felt important and confident. Anne and Mercy were depending on him. He loved the responsibility of it.

After a while, the irritated voice of the duke rang out loudly. 'By God, where is that reprobate, Belknap? He should be here. I need him for cards.'

Mr Sweetman looked around for a footman and Will attracted his attention and walked quickly to the butler and whispered, 'I saw Mr Belknap going towards the grotto earlier on this afternoon, Mr Sweetman, sir. Shall I go and look for him?'

'Yes, go, quickly, now. I will explain to the duke. Don't dally.'

'No, sir, Mr Sweetman, sir,' Will said as he felt a

great release of tension ease from his body. So far so good, he thought as he rushed to the grotto. This may just work was one of the many thoughts that were echoing around his mind but what if Belknap was not there or still alive and waiting for him. He stopped in his tracks. Or waiting for Anne; she must have been and gone by now, surely. Maybe it would be Anne lying there injured ... or ... or ... he shook himself mentally, saying concentrate on what you're doing. You need all your gumption now.

Pausing at the entrance a wave of fear ran through him but also one of excitement, he just couldn't help it. What was waiting for him inside was unknown and dangerous. He knew where Belknap was, or was when Anne had last seen him. He couldn't know for sure if he was dead, Anne had been so upset she could have been mistaken. As he entered the grotto his fear increased to almost painful levels. He had never felt more alive.

He turned the corner to the entrance to the bath room and peered around it, ready to defend himself if necessary. But on the floor, just as Anne had described, lay Belknap. It was obvious he was dead but Will went over to him and forced himself to feel for a pulse in his neck, just in case. He was not only dead but very, very cold. Will shivered in the damp frigid air thinking the ice-cold water had had an effect on the body, making it colder than it should have been.

He looked around to see if there was anything to implicate Anne but found nothing. Thank God, he thought. Anne must have retrieved her bonnet. Every nerve in his body was on high alert and he saw everything in slow motion as he went into all the rooms to check there was nothing incriminating. In the upper chamber, he saw an almost empty bottle of port sitting on a table with a half-filled glass next to it. It looked as if Belknap had been there drinking for some time.

He kept a close look out as he descended the stairs to make sure Anne hadn't dropped anything or snagged her clothing on the walls, and ran back to the house. As he entered the grand salon he rushed to Mr Sweetman. 'Mr Belknap is in the grotto, Mr Sweetman, sir, but I am afraid he is dead.'

'Dead!' Mr Sweetman said rather too loudly in surprise.

'What's that?' the duke asked. 'Who is dead?'

Mr Sweetman looked uncomfortable as he approached the duke. 'I'm sorry to tell you, Your Grace, but William here has checked the grotto and informs me that Mr Belknap is indeed in the grotto, but,' he cleared his throat, 'but unfortunately, he is dead.'

The duke quickly rose from his chair and approached Will with all the authority of his position as a soldier and a duke. Will began to doubt his own judgement as he quailed somewhat in front of the duke's anger. He'd never seen him like this and he realised what an effective commander of men he was. He was a formidable man.

'William, what is this? Out with it, man.'

Will clenched his stomach in an effort to calm his nerves. 'I'm sorry to tell you, Your Grace, but it's true. I found him lying in the bath room. It looked like he missed his step and has fallen and hit his head on the side of the bath.' Will decided he should not be too sure about things so added, 'At least, that's what it looked like to me.'

'Good God!' the duke said, exchanging a look of alarm with his wife. The whole room had gone silent with everyone following the duke's and Will's exchange with concentration and suppressed excitement. 'You'd better stay here, Freddie,' he said to his wife. 'I'll go and see what has happened.'

'No, you won't leave me out of this. I'll come too,' she said as she rushed out of the room behind her husband's retreating back. The other guests in the room followed, including the women following the example of the duchess. Will and the butler brought up the rear with the other footmen tagging behind them. A score or more of people snaked behind the duke with the duchess leading them as they tried to keep up with the duke's long strides. Silence reigned except for the snapping of twigs trodden upon and the rustling of clothing. Wildlife scampered out of the way and birds flapped their wings vigorously in their effort to get out of their way.

The duke's long legs took him to the grotto well before his wife and he stopped in the doorway to wait for her to catch up. No one else would dare overtake her.

'Freddie, you stay here. It is not a place for a woman.'

'But, Frederick—'

'I know what I'm talking about, please.' His expression halted the duchess.

'Yes. You are right, I suppose.'

Everyone lined up behind the duchess, no one daring to speak.

'Where is William?'

'Here, Your Grace,' he called out as he raised his

arm, showing the duke he was at the back of the crowd.

'Let the man through,' instructed the duke as he waited for Will to make his way forward. 'Now, everyone, stay here. No one is to enter. The grotto is too small for all of us and this is not a sideshow. I will go inside with William.' the duke looked around. 'Am I understood?' he said with great authority.

'Yes, Duke,' murmured the guests, chastised and trying to hide their building excitement.

'Right.' He looked at his wife. 'Freddie, make sure no one comes in.'

Will thought it would be a brave man to disobey the duke and he was glad he was on his side.

The duke entered first and he turned into the bath room without hesitation. Will followed at a discreet distance. The duke halted in the doorway, his hands on his hips, his body language confident, as he surveyed the room.

'It's obvious he's dead,' he said walking up to the body in a couple of long strides. He did the same as William and put his hand on Belknap's neck. 'Yes, indeed.' He stood up and looked around. 'I see what you mean about him maybe slipping or catching his foot and falling. I'll bet the scoundrel was drunk again. I have warned him of his excessive drinking. Let's examine the rest of the grotto. If you see anything suspicious, don't touch, just let me know.'

'Yes, Your Grace.'

They made a good sweep of the rooms and then went up the outside steps to the upper chamber. the duke saw the bottle of port on the table and picked it up. 'Mmm, almost empty.' He sniffed the residue in the glass. 'It's port all right. Lethal stuff port. Looks like he was up here drinking alone as there is only one glass. Strange fellow that Belknap, but I liked him for goodness knows what reason.'

Will wondered why he was telling him this and realised that the duke was acting naturally in the face of death and disaster. He realised how much this kind of thing was a way of life for him. He probably did the same on the battlefield, chatting to his men.

'Well, we can't do anything more here. Let's leave the fellow as he is and call the doctor. He can confirm our findings – or not as the case may be.' They made their way silently back to the entrance. Standing tall and commanding the duke announced, 'It is as we feared. The Honourable Anthony Belknap is dead. It looks like he was drunk and slipped and hit his head on the bath. Now, I want everyone to go back to the house. Mr Sweetman,' he looked around, 'there you are, you send someone to get the doctor as soon as possible to come and look at the body.' He looked around again. 'Ah, Mr Tucker, good, you go to the other entrance of the grotto and lock the door so no one else can come in. William, you stay here at this entrance and make sure no one comes in until the doctor arrives. You do not allow anyone in, do you understand?'

A frisson of excitement shot up his backbone. 'Yes, Your Grace. No one will pass me,' he answered confidently. And then he was alone. He stood in the doorway trying not to think about the body lying in its absurd position. There is no dignity in death, he thought. He would be very familiar with death if he'd joined the army but he had realised just how cold and unpleasant death was. He didn't want to be responsible for bringing death to someone, even an enemy. The thought surprised him. He was changing, he'd felt it for a long time but was now realising by how much. He had time to ponder his position as he stood guard. He felt important. He had the duke's authority. He was doing a good job, an important job, the duke trusted him. For this death could be a great scandal if badly handled, that much he knew. The duke already owed Will for saving his wife's life and now he had trusted him with this. Where was all this going? How much more exciting than the army was this? For a man born into poverty he was living a life of great interest. He saw things that others would give almost anything to know about. But it was him, William Dresser, who was in this favoured position. He felt himself growing more confident and mature as he considered his life and what was to come. The thrill of excitement which had shot up his backbone moments before now surged throughout his body. And then he remembered Anne and felt ashamed he was thinking only of himself. But he was saving his sister's life and he reasoned the two were connected. He was also winning Mercy, he hoped. His parents were here too, what could be better? He began to understand just how lucky he was and what a fine fellow he was becoming and his head got bigger and bigger until he burst out laughing and couldn't stop. How ridiculous you are, he chastised himself. You're better than this. You need to be better than this. You are just a footman, but by goodness he'd made his mark as a footman. And that was good enough for him. He knew then he couldn't do better with his life. In a strange way he grew as a man during that wait for the doctor. Things slipped into place in his mind and a calmness came over him with a new confidence in himself and his abilities. He'd brought about a solution to this mess. It was his plan which would save Anne and also save the duke and duchess much embarrassment, for if ugly rumours started as to what kind of things were going on at Oatlands, the king would jump on that in a moment. He relied on Frederick to counter the profligate life of his elder brother, the Prince of Wales. Frederick must remain beyond censure in the king's eyes. Will knew this from reading newspapers. He'd discussed these things with Mercy and Anne from time to time in an effort to understand more the life that was going on around him. But he must not become overconfident. He needed to watch himself.

Finally, the doctor and the duke appeared, walking fast towards the grotto and Will stood to one side and to attention as they passed. It didn't take long for them to come out again.

'Thank you, William,' the duke said. 'Please stay here a little longer while I get someone to come for Belknap's body and arrange where to take it until his family can claim him. It would not be suitable to keep him here, under the circumstances.'

'I'll take him to my place,' the doctor said. 'He can be properly laid out and visitors are welcome if they would care to come.'

'Thank you, doctor, that is most helpful. And, we are agreed, he must have drunk too much, decided to cool down with a bath and somehow fell. Serves the fellow right, he was becoming a fool. We should hold the coroner's inquest as soon as possible. We'll need your testament, William. I will inform you when.'

Will froze. He hadn't thought he'd be needed at an inquest. To the duke he said, 'Yes, Your Grace. I am at your service.'

It wasn't long before the doctor and men from

the stables came with a horse pulling an enclosed carriage and laid the body into it and as they took it away a wave of relief swept over Will. He didn't need to stand at the grotto for any longer, but as he walked back to the house he felt his new confidence in himself and his abilities settle in and he felt comfortable with them. He was a different man to the one who had woken up this morning. It felt good.

'Ah, William,' Mr Sweetman called to him as he entered the great hall. 'The duke says you are excused duties this evening as you have taken a big toll today in your duties. Go now and well done.'

'Thank you, Mr Sweetman, sir,' he said with relief.

As Will entered the servants' hall he had hoped for some peace but to his dismay, he found everyone who was off duty gathered there. 'Will,' someone shouted, 'Will, come here, sit down and tell us all about what has happened. We are all eager for news.'

He looked around the room and saw Mercy, first. She looked anxious and then his eyes found Anne who looked stricken but trying to hide it. He knew his sister and could see how upset she was.

He went over to the sideboard to check the cold food waiting there. 'We left you some food,' someone called out.

'Good, I'm starving,' he said, helping himself to a selection of cold meat, a hunk of bread and a large pat of butter.

Mercy jumped up and rushed to Will's side. 'I'll pour you some ale, you go and sit down and eat.'

Everyone was eager for news. 'Let him eat, for goodness sake,' Anne pleaded. 'He needs sustenance.' She had put on the act of her life as she waited for news from the grotto. She and Mercy had agreed

298

that Anne must be there at the same time as the other servants as her absence would be suspicious in view of the excitement going around. The servants knew of Belknap's death but not the details.

People grumbled but complied.

'What do you think has happened, Anne?' Emma shouted out.

'Me!' she exclaimed. Her shock that someone should ask her made her voice too loud.

'Yes, you have been quite quiet all through this. Come on, you must have some thoughts.'

She gathered her strength. 'I am sure I have as much idea as you have—'

'Oh, for goodness sake,' Will cut in. 'I'll tell you all about it if you just give me a few minutes to eat. What can Anne know of things? Just wait, can't you?'

Anne gave Will a look of relief as Mercy sat down next to her. When people had started talking among themselves Anne whispered, 'You don't think anyone saw me do you? Oh, God, Mercy…' Anne's voice almost gave out on her.

'Keep yourself in check. It will be all right. No one saw you. It's just Emma making mischief again. You know what she's like. So smile, pretend I am telling you something really interesting, or funny or something. Come on, Anne. We can do this. Not much further to go now and then we can all go to bed.'

Anne looked over at Will who, munching with his cheeks full of food and puffed out like a greedy squirrel, winked at Anne. She laughed despite herself.

Will swallowed and took a long drink of his ale and someone filled up his glass again. He burped.

'Pardon, now, I am ready. How much do you know already?'

'Mr Belknap was found dead in the grotto,' someone said. 'And there has been lots of activity and people coming and going.'

'Well, I can tell you that Mr Belknap was indeed found dead in the grotto, in the bath room.'

'Had he fallen in the bath?'

'Well, it looked like he might have decided to bathe but somehow slipped and hit his head. He was dead when I found him.' Will paused and looked around the table, dragging out the suspense. 'But I must not say anything about how he died as that is the job of the coroner's inquest. It will be as soon as possible I was told. So we will all have to wait for that.' He looked around the room again unable to resist making himself sound important, 'And I shall be called as a witness.'

'Oooh!' Several of the maids uttered together like an out-of-tune chorus.

Will glared at them.

'But what did the doctor say?' someone else asked.

'I'm not at liberty to say. That is between the doctor and the duke,' Will said, keeping up his self-important stance.

'Oh, come on. You can tell us,' James said.

'What's going on here?' Mrs Harley said, coming into the room. They all rushed to stand up. 'Ah, William,' she said noticing him, 'you're back.'

'Yes, Mrs Harley. I've just been explaining that Mr Belknap was indeed found dead but that I am not at liberty to say anything more as it is for the coroner to decide how he died.'

'Indeed, William. That is correct. Now!' She

looked around the room exerting her authority. 'It's late. Let's all go to bed and get some rest. It will undoubtedly be a busy day tomorrow ... whatever it brings but for us it's normal duties.'

'Yes, Mrs Harley,' they all echoed.

CHAPTER EIGHTEEN

Anne tossed and turned that night in bed, unable to get the image of the dead man out of her mind. One moment he was alive with his sneer, arrogance, strength and odour and the next he was flailing backwards through the air and that sickening thud as his head hit the side of the bath and she could swear now she heard a snap of bone as it struck. His puppet-like body at cruel angles stayed in her brain no matter how much she tried to forget it. She didn't think she ever would; his final triumph over her.

She got up extra early, sickened by her jangling thoughts, and washed herself down in a strip wash in freezing water. She wanted to shock the images out of her mind, make herself think of other things, even if only of her freezing body. It was the only way. She must forget this now. She forced herself through her usual duties and tried to act normally. She mustn't do anything unusual. During breakfast a message was sent down to the servants' hall to ask Anne to report to Lady Elizabeth, one of the duchesses' ladies-in-waiting.

She made her way to the duchesses' apartments nervous and apprehensive. She composed herself before knocking on the door. Lady Elizabeth answered. 'Ah, Anne, come in. The duchess has had a misfortune with one of her dresses and it needs some special attention. It is far beyond my capabilities with the needle which is why I've sent for you. I know you are renowned for your needlework. I would ask you to take a look and see if you can repair the damage.'

Anne breathed a sigh of relief as she realised it was not about the affairs of yesterday. 'I'll help if I can, Lady Elizabeth,' Anne said as she looked at the dress. 'Oh, my goodness.' She looked at the other women in despair.

'I know it's almost beyond repair. One of the dogs got hold of it and chewed as well as ripped it, I fear.'

Anne examined it closely. 'I'm not sure but the only way to find out is to make a start. I'll do my best, but I may need some assistance.'

'I am at your service, Anne,' Lady Elizabeth said in her usual restrained and distant way. Anne knew she did not share the duke's and duchess' attitude to servants and treated them with disdain when the duchess was not around. They were employed in their task in the duchess' drawing room when Freddie came in.

'Ah, Anne. Just the person I wanted to see.'

Anne jumped up as did Lady Elizabeth.

'Elizabeth, my dear, would you mind leaving us a moment. I would like to talk to Anne.'

Lady Elizabeth curtsied. 'Of course, Duchess,' she said with a smile as she left the room, but Anne could see her expression change to one of disapproval as she closed the door.

'Put the dress on the chair,' the duchess said as she sat down.

Anne, rather awkwardly, put the dress on the chair she had just vacated and stood and clasped her hands in front of her.

'You are aware of our excitement yesterday and the tragic death of Mr Belknap?'

Anne's heart missed a beat. 'Indeed, Your Grace. I am most sorry. It is distressing news,' she said as confidently as she could.

'As you say …'

Freddie's hesitation made Anne's already pulsing heart rate turn chaotic. She tried to breathe normally.

'The duke,' Freddie finally continued, 'told me of Mr Belknap's bad behaviour towards you when you found his ring.'

The sentence was like a smack in the face and Anne's head started to swim. She must keep control. 'Yes, Your Grace,' Anne said as calmly as she could, 'there was some trouble but the duke came into the room and he put a stop to all that.'

'Yes, he told me. But the fact remains that Mr Belknap was not behaving in a way we expect of our guests. I don't know why the duke kept inviting him. I didn't like him at all. I, ah, I just wondered whether he ever bothered you after that?'

Anne tried not to gasp as her whole body stiffened. She mustn't let the duchess see her distress. 'No, Your Grace. I made sure if I saw him I went the other way.'

Freddie laughed. 'Good thinking. The man was a scoundrel … and I will say so if I am called at the inquest.'

This change of direction eased Anne's terror and she jumped on the chance to take the attention away from herself. 'Oh, but Your Grace, no one will call you, surely?'

'No, I expect not. But I am asking whether he bothered you, or any of the other female staff that you know about?'

Anne shook her head, trying to give the impression of thinking hard. She couldn't let on that the man was a menace it would cause too much trouble, better to let things die away now. She shook her head. 'No, I think that most maids kept out of his way as much as possible. I heard no more of … well … you know, that kind of thing.'

'That is good, I am pleased. The duke, you know, was obviously a bachelor before we married and he lived a full life but always with honour, you understand?'

'Yes, of course, Your Grace.'

'But some of the duke's friends are not to my liking and I will speak to the duke about who he invites here in future. There is one class of friend for men alone and another for wives and they should not mix. I tell you this because I want my staff to be happy. If there is anything troublesome going on with guests or any other thing, then I want to know about it. I feel I am the mistress of Oatlands, I feel it is my home, much more than the London house. I want to make my mark. Will you tell the other staff that? If there is anything untoward, I want to know about it. Please be my ambassador, Anne, keep me informed.'

Anne couldn't keep the surprised look off her face. 'Me!' slipped out before she could stop it. 'I mean, um, sorry Your Grace. I'm surprised … you want me to be your *spy*?'

The duchess laughed uproariously. 'A spy! Well, I hadn't thought of it like that. So, no, Anne, not a spy but a confidante, shall we say. A friend below stairs.'

Anne looked at her with relief. 'A confidante?'

'Yes, I am the kind of person who likes to know

305

what is happening under my roof, nothing sinister, you understand, just interest and understanding.'

Anne was thinking how pretty the duchess was. She was not conventionally beautiful, nothing like that, but she had an inner goodness, a glow, something inside that was much more than just a pretty face. You wanted to please and help her as much as you could. Anne smiled and nodded her head. 'Yes, Your Grace, I understand.'

'There will be no repercussions from Mr Belknap's death, I will see to that. Please tell the staff that this kind of thing will not happen again while I am mistress of Oatlands.'

'Yes, I understand and I thank you very sincerely and I am sure the rest of the staff will too.'

'I want a happy staff here. I could not bear to live with people unhappy in their positions. Life is too short.' She smiled at Anne and considered her a moment. 'Tell, me, are you happy here … or are you thinking of leaving?'

'Leaving?' Anne had trouble hiding her surprise.

'You know, getting married, maybe not right now, but later.'

Anne was flabbergasted.

The duchess laughed. 'Don't look so surprised, you are a very pretty young woman and pretty young women are in great demand with men. It is not natural you would want to marry and start your own family?'

Anne knew she had to tell her the truth. It was her chance to show her loyalty and her ambitions. But would the duchess recoil at her forwardness, her assumption that she thought she could rise further than a maid? A battle went on in her mind which lasted only seconds but seemed to Anne to be a lifetime. She looked down at her hands surprised they looked so relaxed. Concentrate, she told herself. Now is your chance, grasp it. 'I appreciate your concern, Your Grace, and I also appreciate that you are correct that most young women want marriage and a family … but,' she took a surreptitious deep breath to steady her nerves, 'but I am not of that mind. If I may be truthful,' she paused and looked at the duchess who nodded her assent, 'I have never felt the maternal instinct or the desire to have children and for me the only reason to get married would be to have children.'

'Would you not marry for love?'

'I do not wish to lose my independence. It means more to me that anything else, including love. I do not wish to be a slave to a man. I'm sorry, Your Grace, I'm being very frank …'

'No, please, go ahead. I am interested.'

Anne knew it was now or never so she gathered up her courage and looked everywhere but at the duchess. 'Well … as you know, when a woman marries she becomes the property of her husband ... but,' she risked a look at the duchess, 'well, maybe not so much for Your Grace, but for someone like me, a poor woman of no status marriage means I have no power over my life or my choices in life. I would be at the mercy of the good graces of my husband and I do not want that.'

'What you say is true. Women do become the property of their husbands,' she smiled, 'even duchesses, Anne. But it is the natural order of things. An aversion to it is an unusual viewpoint.' The duchess gave Anne a puzzled look. 'And what do you want from your life?'

Anne shuffled her feet, feeling a blush creep up

on her, but stiffened her back and forced herself to show confidence. 'I want to be independent. I want to rely on my own work and to be beholden to no one but my employer. I want to create my own life for myself. I am ... please forgive me ...' Her courage was failing but she knew she had to finish this, say what was in her heart. 'I am ambitious and deem myself very fortunate to be in your and the duke's employ. If I may say so, I never want to leave it and I will do my utmost to be a worthwhile employee for however long you need me. I want to stay here with you, I want to stay single and keep my independence.' Anne couldn't stop tears forming and running down her cheek. 'Is it so very bad and selfish of me?'

'Well,' the duchess dragged the word out, 'you surprise me.' She looked long at Anne. 'But having said that it is a delightful surprise. You have been honest with me so I will be honest with you. I like you, Anne. You give good service to me and we get on well together. I feel relaxed with you and believe me that is not always the case with servants. I am delighted to hear that you wish to stay in my employ and serve me. Do you want to rise in your job?'

'That is for you to say, Your Grace.'

The duchess pondered for a while and then said, out of the blue, 'This Belknap business ...'

Anne froze. Her heart almost jumped out of her body. What? What is she saying? Why has she brought this up again? She kept her face neutral, as she had trained herself to do hiding the panic going on inside her.

'I want you to put it behind you, Anne.'

Anne couldn't stop her eyes from blinking as she struggled to keep her composure. My God! She suspects. She must do.

'There will be no repercussions I guarantee that. Do your job well and we will leave this conversation here and know we have an understanding between us.' She smiled warmly.

Anne was so confused. Did the duchess know? Had she seen something? Maybe she'd seen her going into or coming out of the grotto? Had she given herself away somehow? She knew the duchess was an acute observer. She pulled herself together with a great effort. She mustn't give anything away. Must not show she was disconcerted or upset. With a great effort of mind over emotion, Anne returned the smile. 'Yes, Your Grace, thank you. I understand and would like to reassure you that I am most grateful and will always do my best for you and the duke.'

'That's settled then. Now, Anne, I will send Lady Elizabeth back in as I understand you are helping her in sewing. I have heard your work is outstanding.' She stood up and leaned over the dress Anne was repairing. 'Yes, outstanding needlework.' She looked at Anne. 'You are talented. I have seen the cushions you embroidered for the main rooms and they show exceptional needlework.' She smiled. 'Please continue here until Lady Elizabeth dismisses you. And thank you again for your honesty.'

'Thank you very much, Your Grace.' She curtsied low and the duchess acknowledged her with a nod and left the room.

The turmoil inside Anne threatened to overwhelm her. The duchess couldn't know, could she? She started to shake. She had to get control of herself. Whatever the duchess thought had happened or not she had made it clear it was not to be talked of again.

That it would remain between them. Anne's breath was coming in short bursts as Lady Elizabeth returned to the room. Anne made a supreme effort to throw all her emotions away for now. She had to act normally in front of Lady Elizabeth. She knew she would pick up on anything untoward. She curtsied, knowing that Lady Elizabeth would never ask what had passed between Anne and the duchess but she may try to wheedle it out of her in small ways. She knew she had to be on her guard for the rest of her life. If, in fact, the duchess had guessed, so could others.

CHAPTER NINETEEN

'Anne, for goodness sake, you're like a cat with new kittens being stalked by a fox,' Mercy said, not unkindly. 'If you're going to help me with polishing this fireplace, then please keep your mind on the job. Don't keep looking around and jumping at every noise.'

'I'm sorry.' Anne made an effort at buffing a bunch of grapes which were part of the decoration. She sighed. 'I'm sure you'd be nervous if you were me.'

'It's true. I'm sorry.' Mercy stopped polishing for a moment. 'I suppose I'm being influenced by Will who was like a cock in a hen house this morning, strutting around, full of his own importance.'

'Well, he is the main witness in the inquest this afternoon. I suppose he is enjoying the attention.'

'That may be so, but it's not becoming. Hopefully, he'll calm down later.'

'Sometimes with Will though, it's nerves that make him like that. He's probably nervous and trying to hide it.'

'You think so? Oh, I hope so.' She smiled and patted Anne's hand. 'You and Will were close when you were children, I feel.'

'We were, but we have grown apart somewhat. I

suppose that's what happens when you grow up and become your own person.' Anne tucked a stray lock of hair under her cap. 'Don't worry about him. He can take care of himself. He just likes to look stronger than he actually is. It's no great fault, in fact, it's rather nice, I think.'

Mercy took her time in replying. 'You're right. It is rather nice. I'd sooner have him like that than like some of the other footmen here.' She looked around furtively. 'But don't tell anyone I said so.' They both laughed.

'That's better, Anne. You worry too much.'

'I suppose so, but then, I have a lot to worry about.'

'In that case a vigorous polish of this fireplace will keep you occupied,' Mercy said, laughing.

'Don't worry, I'm going to keep myself busy all day and polish every damn thing that needs a polish and some more.'

Anne did her duties automatically and tried not to think what it would mean if they found that foul play had taken place. It had only been two days since the death of Belknap but it seemed like a lifetime – and this day, an eternity. It was early evening before Will returned from the inquest and everyone who could postpone their duties for a little while gathered in the servants' hall, waiting for him.

As he walked in Anne's heart missed a beat when she saw his serious face. It's bad news, she thought, and her breathing became ragged. With great effort she sat quietly, trying to not attract attention to herself, and avoided Will's eye.

He strode to the table self-importantly, sat down on his chair, took his handkerchief out and dabbed at his face. James put a tankard of ale in front of him, saying, 'Now, take a draft and tell us all.'

'Yes, tell us,' a chorus of excited voices rang out.

He held up a finger to pause everyone and drank down the ale in one. He wiped his mouth with the back of his hand and burped. 'Sorry,' he said, 'I needed that.' James refilled the tankard.

Mrs Harley came in then and it caused a clatter of chair scraping as each person stood up sharply and waited until she had seated herself before sitting back down themselves.

'William!' Her voice was stern. 'What was the result? We are all anxious to know.'

'Well, it was all fascinating,' Will started.

'Do not procrastinate,' Mrs Harley cut in but was interrupted as Mr Sweetman walked in. They all stood up again until he seated himself at the head of the table and then they sat down again.

'Now, William,' he said in his loud voice, 'what are the findings of the inquest?'

'Yes, sir, Mr Sweetman, sir. The result was …' he couldn't resist pausing momentarily, looking around the room, 'the finding of the inquest was accidental death probably due to the inebriation of the victim, The Honourable Anthony Belknap.'

A collective sigh of relief went around the room.

'Well, thank goodness for that,' Mrs Harley said. 'We did not want to have any other result. That would have been unthinkable.'

Anne sat silently, not quite believing it. She so wanted to ask Will to repeat it but dare not. She was holding herself so stiffly she started to ache. She risked a look at Mercy who smiled at her.

'That is very satisfactory. Yes, indeed,' Mr Sweetman said.

Then to her horror, Anne started to shake and the more she tried to control it the more it increased. She was losing control, but thankfully, Mercy noticed and stood up. 'Well, that's good, but Anne and I have a few more duties tonight so we will leave you to it. Come on, Anne, we must get on.' She took Anne's arm and guided her out of the room. But no one was taking any notice of them as all eyes were on Will who realised what was happening and began to talk about the inquest again to deflect everyone's attention.

'I gave my evidence first,' he said, addressing them as if he was the coroner himself. 'I told them I had seen Mr Belknap walking towards the grotto with a bottle in his hand earlier in the afternoon. I wasn't sure of the time but I definitely saw him. He was alone. I then told them of going to the grotto and finding the body and rushing back to the house with the news.

'One of the duke's guests, then gave evidence that he had been drinking with Mr Belknap earlier in the day where they both consumed a bottle of wine each.' Will took a long draft from his tankard and burped again. Mrs Harley gave him a look of censure and he put it down quickly.

'Then, the duke gave evidence of how he went back to the grotto with me and found the body and the almost empty bottle of port and the single glass, which were produced. He said he secured the area and left me on guard and sent for the doctor. He said there was no evidence that anyone else was involved as we had both looked around the grotto for any evidence of another person but found none.'

Will's hand went to his tankard but then he thought better of it. He cleared his throat. 'The coroner then said that he had also examined the body in his position as doctor and was sure Mr Belknap was drunk as he could smell the alcohol very strongly on the body. In his opinion, he said, the way the body had fallen indicated a drunken fall where the victim was unable to help himself … that's about it really.'

'Indeed,' Mr Sweetman said. 'That's it, then. 'Now, let us all get back to our duties – and don't gossip about this all around the place.'

'Some hope,' someone mumbled as they left.

*

Mercy escorted Anne to her room. When she closed the door behind them she leaned her back against it and breathed out deeply. Anne sat down on the side of her bed and burst into tears.

'I'm sorry, I didn't mean to cry. I think its relief,' she mumbled, trying to control herself. 'I feel …' she burst into tears again.

Mercy sat next to her and put her arm around her shoulders. 'I understand. You've been keeping a hold on your emotions and now it's all over it has released everything that's been building up. Have a good cry, because you cannot afford to do any more crying. I'm sorry, Anne, but Joyce will be curious if you cry in front of her. There is no privacy here, you know that.' She took Anne's hand and gave it a sympathetic squeeze. 'I tell you what; I'll stand by the window while you have a good cry and get it out of your system.' Mercy walked to the window and looked out with her back to Anne. Anne felt foolish for behaving in this way but she couldn't stop the tears and sobbed uncontrollably. Her talk with the

315

duchess yesterday and how that had shocked her and the strain of the inquest was only just hitting her. But she knew that she must keep the duchess' suspicions to herself; it would never do to worry Will and Mercy. She couldn't do that to them.

Mercy gave Anne a good ten minutes and then sat next to her again and gave her a clean handkerchief. 'That's better, there's nothing like a good cry when you need one. I think you should stay here and gather yourself until supper time. I can cover for you until then, but you must come down to supper as you will be very conspicuous by your absence. We don't want any odd instances to be associated with this.'

'I don't think I could eat anything.'

'That may be so, but you would be as eager as all of us to interrogate Will about the inquest. We are all curious. It's the most exciting thing that has happened here. People will be talking about it for a long time so be prepared. If you have to, say you have a stomach ache and not much of an appetite but don't want to miss out on any information – or something like that.'

'Thank you. I don't know what I would have done without you and Will. I'd be hanging from the scaffold by now if you hadn't covered for me.'

Mercy patted Anne's hand and whispered, her face very close to Anne's, 'That's enough of that.'

'But, Mercy, I killed a man; took his life from him. I'm a murderer. How can I live with that? He'd be living today if it hadn't been for me and what I did to him.'

'Enough, Anne,' Mercy said gently. 'It was his own fault. You did nothing to him, you just defended yourself any way you could. It's all his fault. His fault he was drunk, his fault he was such a rotten human being, his fault that he tried to ravage you, his fault that he thought he could do that to you without consequences. All of it was his fault. He had choices and his choices resulted in his own death. That was his decision, not yours.'

'But if I hadn't pushed him quite so hard.'

'Enough,' Mercy whispered more harshly. 'You did not push him too hard. You had to get him off you and did what you had to do to achieve that. Again, it was not your fault and I want you to remember that he brought it on himself and you are not to blame. You have to remember that or you will be lost. Your life will be ruined if you do not remember it. He will have won. He will have ruined your life and believe me, if he'd lived he would have no qualms in ruining your life and turning away and forgetting you ever existed. Now, you don't want him to win and ruin your life, do you? You are better than that, Anne. You really are a much better person than he was or ever could be. You must not let him win. Remember, you were just defending yourself. Everything else was down to him.'

'Oh, Mercy, do you really think so? I keep thinking I should have confessed straight away and not dragged you and Will into this. I panicked and now we're all paying the price.'

'Anne … Anne.' Mercy's voice was full of compassion as she took hold of Anne's hands and squeezed them gently. 'You're not thinking right. You are overwrought and everything seems too big to handle but just give yourself time and you'll realise you did the best thing because if you hadn't your parents would know about it and so would the rest of the world and your father would want revenge.

It would destroy them. And you know you'd never win, don't you? You know that women always get the blame and pay the price – you would have been hanged.' She paused to let that sink in. 'Because you know as well as I do that you cannot have servants of the Duke of York killing his guests. It's unthinkable. You did the right thing and you'll see the truth of that as you gain your equilibrium.'

Anne took several deep breaths. 'I don't deserve you; you're such a good friend to me.'

'Dear Anne, you would have done the same for me, I know that and so do you.' She kissed Anne on the cheek. 'Now, to practicalities. I never want this referred to again. Walls have ears and you never know who is lingering outside a door. You must resign yourself to this and let nature take its course, time will lessen the trauma of it all. Be kind to yourself as you would be kind to me if it happened to me. You would be saying the same things to me and you know the truth of that. You know, as I know, as Will knows, that it was not your fault.'

Anne sighed deeply and her breath shuddered in her chest.

'Now, I will tell Will too not to talk about it again – ever! We must be very, very careful. We were all complicit in this cover up and we got away with it and I want us to continue to get away with it and that means it is never talked about ever again.' She gently ran her finger down the side of Anne's cheek as she added, almost in a whisper, 'You have got that, Anne, haven't you?'

Anne hiccupped and sobbed at the same time. 'My mind agrees with you, I can see the sense in what you're saying but my feelings and emotions are

318

getting in the way of accepting it.'

'I understand. You need time, but unfortunately, time is something that is a luxury people like us do not have. You have to cope. Please, Anne. Please cope. You always said you were a strong woman now prove it to us.'

Anne's head dipped almost to her chest and Mercy took her chin and lifted it up a little. 'We're relying on you. You have to stay strong and become stronger if you have to. It's what women like us have to do in life. Come on, you can do it. Do it for yourself as well as for us. Do it for your parents.'

Anne nodded. 'I'll do my very, very best. I must find myself, my own self, again. I must find my courage.'

'And you will, you will. You wait and see. It will come. Just give it time. Every time you think of it throw it out like the rubbish it is. Don't let your mind dwell on it. Now, I have to go or I will be missed. You stay here until dinner time and remember all that we have said. I know you can do it.'

And with that, Mercy left Anne and closed the door quietly behind her.

Anne lay back on her bed and closed her eyes, fighting the urge to cry. No, she said to herself, I refuse to cry any more. Mercy is right. I must conquer this. She got up and walked up and down the little room breathing deeply, gathering her inner strength as best she could. Reinforcing as a mantra, I will not let this ruin my life or the lives of others. It was not my fault.

*

Mercy spent the next day doing her usual jobs but

she couldn't stop thinking of the events of the past week and how close she, Will and Anne, had come to the gallows. She never thought she would be caught up in such a conspiracy. She went over and over things. How it had happened, how she and Will had got involved and how their lives were changed by it. It was all Belknap's stupid fault. The fact that he was trying to rape Anne was neither here nor there as far as the high-ups were concerned. She and Will had done the right thing and protected Anne; it was all they could do. But it had changed everything. Mercy now saw Will in a different light. He had saved Anne almost single-handedly and risked everything to help her. He had gone up considerably in Mercy's estimation. Her whole view of him had changed. She'd been seeing a different side to him over the past few months but could never be sure he was truly committed to family life and all that entailed. She had been unsure of his maturity. Now, it was all different. She felt she had seen the real and true character of the man. So much so that by the end of the day she had made her decision.

That evening, when her jobs were finished for the day, she went to the servants' hall and was surprised to find Will lounging with his feet on the table, drinking some ale. 'You not working tonight?' she asked in surprise.

He took his feet off the table, smiling at Mercy. 'No, Mr Sweetman thought it best if I didn't show my face tonight and remind everyone of the inquest and everything.' He stood and reached for Mercy's hand. 'Suits me and luckily there's no one else here, give me a kiss sweet Mercy.' He smiled as he pulled her to him.

She felt warm inside and gave herself up to his embrace and kissed him with enthusiasm.

'Wow!' Will said as they finally parted.

'You complaining?'

'No! Not at all, in fact, let's do it again.'

Mercy took him in her arms and stood on tiptoe and kissed him again, thoroughly. She felt her passion rise to levels she had never felt before and knew then that her decision was the right one. She stroked his cheek with her finger. 'I've come to a decision.'

He looked at her quizzically. 'You look so serious. Is everything all right?'

'What do you think after kisses like that? Yes, you daft man. Everything is more than all right.' Will still looked puzzled and she realised he needed some guidance.

'Do you remember you said something to me a few months ago? Something you said you would never change your mind about?'

'Yes,' he said, tentatively.

'Well, if you should ask me again, I might give a different answer.'

His face lit up and he immediately dropped down on one knee, looking up at her, taking her hand in his. He cleared his throat. 'Mercy …' he cleared his throat again with exaggeration which made her laugh. 'Mercy Batchelor, would you do me the honour of becoming my wife?'

Mercy smiled down at him. 'William Dresser, it will be my great pleasure and honour to say yes!'

He stood and took her into his arms.

'Your face looks like sunshine,' Mercy said as she kissed him and they lost track of time. Footsteps brought them back to reality. 'Quickly, someone's coming. Let's go outside before they see us,' he said, as he took her hand and they rushed through the side door, laughing like children.

Mercy shivered. 'This cold ought to cool your ardour,' she said.

'Never!' He put his arm around her waist and pulled her to him. 'The cold air makes your breath look like a dragon's.' He roared as he thought a dragon would roar but it made him cough.

Mercy gave way to a fit of the giggles. 'I feel like a little girl. You know when you're a small child and are able to feel total happiness without a care in the world? That feeling doesn't last long but for a while it belongs to all children. You'll make a wonderful father.' She caressed his face. 'I do love you so.' She put her arms around his neck and kissed him passionately until she realised things were getting out of hand and she broke away. 'No, Will, not until we are married. I want to do this properly. I will be all yours on our wedding night.'

'When? Tomorrow?'

She couldn't stop the laugh bubbling up in her throat. 'No, not tomorrow but seriously, I've been thinking.' She stroked his cheek again, speaking softly. 'I want to marry in Weybridge, even though both of us have many friends in London but here feels like home now and your parents are here and Anne, of course. It grieves me not to have any family to share our special day so it would be wonderful to feel part of a family again.'

Will hugged her close. 'I understand, and yes, I would like that too.'

'And I would like to show off my new husband to the whole village of Weybridge.' She pulled him close and stroked his cheek, keeping her voice soft and seductive. 'My brave, handsome, charismatic, intelligent … and … gloriously desirable husband.'

Will looked into her eyes and kept his face stern. 'Well, I can't disagree with any of that.'

'Oh, you,' Mercy said, kissing him.

'And … I would like to show all of Weybridge that the most beautiful woman in the world is my wife. That her beauty surpasses all the goddess of old, leaves them lying behind her, floundering in the dust of her sparkling beauty.'

'Well,' Mercy said trying to keep a straight face, 'that's a lot to live up to. You do know don't you, that I will get old and wrinkled and arthritic?'

'And even more beautiful to me, I've never been so happy. I had no idea a woman could give a man such feelings. Oh, Mercy, let's get married soon. I'm bursting with love for you.'

She smiled and kissed the end of his nose. ''Ah, but a girl always wants a summer wedding when the weather is good so that she can show off her nice clothes and flowers. A day as different to her ordinary day as it can get. She doesn't want to shiver in winter. That would be too, too miserable.' She gave him another kiss, on his cheek this time. 'Let's make a plan for the summer. June is always a good time for a wedding.'

'June? Eight months. Oh, Mercy, can I wait that long?'

'Well, if we rush it people will think we *have* to get married.'

Will looked at her closely. 'Which, of course, we won't, will we?' He put all his longing and emphasise into the word 'won't'.

'No, Will, my darling, you know my feelings on that. We won't, indeed we won't.'

'Of course, anything you want. But, just one thing, let's not tell the staff until I have had a chance to tell my parents. I would not want them to think they are the last to find out. I should get some time to go to the lodge soon.'

'Of course, yes, of course, Will. There's no rush,' Mercy said, standing on tiptoe and kissing Will.

They stayed outside talking and kissing and making plans until the cold drove them back inside.

CHAPTER TWENTY

The next day, Will was still in a warm buzz from his engagement to Mercy and had trouble keeping his attention on his work. He and Edward were in the ballroom rearranging furniture when they heard the distinctive scrunch of horse shoes galloping on the gravel outside followed by the noisy sliding of wheels and the neighing of horses. 'It's nearly dark, who the hell can this be?' Will said as he rushed towards the front door closely followed by Edward. Mr Sweetman had already opened it. Within seconds the Prince of Wales stormed in.

'Ha! Sweetman. Where will I find my brother?'

'The duke is in his rooms, Your Royal Highness, I'll have him called.'

'Don't bother, I'll go straight up,' the Prince of Wales said as he bounded up the stairs two at a time.

Mr Sweetman looked at the startled Edward and Will. 'Well, this is unexpected.' He paused. 'Edward, you come upstairs with me to stand attendance and William, you go down to the kitchens and tell cook to prepare refreshments at once and bring it up as soon as it is ready. Cook knows what His Highness likes best.'

'Yes, sir,' Will said, running towards the stairs leading down to the kitchens.

A short time later he was carrying a large silver tray bedecked with a matching silver tea service and a plate of chicken legs, beef and a variety of cakes on porcelain plates. Will's strong arms had no trouble carrying the heavy tray upstairs and as he approached the duke's rooms Mr Sweetman checked the tray, nodded and knocked delicately on the door and entered.

As Will went in with the tray the prince was lounging on a chair with his feet on a sofa covered in pink silk. Will tried not to stare at the marks already left on the material by his dusty boots. Mercy will have to clean that off tomorrow, he thought with annoyance.

'Ah, tea, good,' the prince said. 'I need warming up. It's too cold for November. I'm frozen right through.'

'Well, you should know better than to ride down here in an open phaeton in November. What did you expect?' The duke answered a little sharply.

'Oh, well,' the prince waved his arm dismissively, 'I had to get out of London. A good ride down here was just what I needed.' He looked at the butler. 'Sweetman, please arrange quarters for my servants; they should be here soon, I left them somewhere on the road trying to keep up. There are only two and I will have my usual room.'

'Yes, Your Royal Highness.'

'There will be just the three of us for dinner tonight, Mr Sweetman,' the duke added.

'Tell cook to make one of those wonderful meat pies he makes so well,' the prince added, 'and ... trifle, yes, trifle for dessert.' He looked at his brother. 'All right with you, Frederick? Freddie is fond of those dishes too.'

'As you wish, brother,' he replied with resignation.

'Oh, and that wonderful French wine we had last time, Sweetman, if you please.'

'Yes, Your Royal Highness.' Mr Sweetman and Will bowed out of the room.

Outside, Edward was grinning.

'And who are you to grin like that, Edward!' Mr Sweetman said a little tetchily. 'You will be helping with dinner with,' the butler hesitated as he looked directly at Will, 'yes, William, I think. It's about time you took on more responsibility; the experience will do you good.'

'The other footmen won't like that, he's only number five foot—' Edward said but stopped suddenly as he saw Mr Sweetman's face.

'And who is in charge of this establishment, Edward? You, the other footmen, or me?'

Edward met the butler's determined gaze and answered, 'You, Mr Sweetman, sir.'

Will thought he could have done without all this.

'Indeed!' Mr Sweetman said with raised eyebrows. 'In that case I want you and William to make sure there are no mistakes this evening. The prince's visit is unexpected but I want to prove to him that we can cope with anything here at Oatlands just as his own servants undoubtedly can at his own establishments.'

'Yes, sir, Mr Sweetman, sir.'

*

The prince always made Will nervous and dinner that evening was no exception. He liked the duke and duchess but he didn't like the prince and that made

327

him feel guilty as he felt he should like the next king. He steadied himself as the dishes from the kitchen arrived in the outer room. The table had already been laid by the butler with the silverware shining in the candlelight from the candelabras and the fire burning well, giving the room an added glow of warmth. The duke had instructed the butler to lay the end of the table nearest the fire. He would sit at the head with Freddie and the prince either side of him. 'It will be cosier like that, it's just an informal dinner.'

Mr Sweetman supervised while Will acted as second servant to Edward. 'Let's make sure we don't drop this,' Edward said. 'On the count of three we'll pick it up between us and take it in first. It's the centrepiece.'

'It's a masterpiece,' Will added, as he lifted his end of the silver platter with the half life-size pie in the shape of a swan. It was heavier than he thought and he faltered a little.

'Careful,' Mr Sweetman warned.

Will gritted his teeth and got into step with Edward as they slowly made their way into the dining room holding the tray between them.

'Put it here, in the middle of the table settings, and put it down carefully.' Mr Sweetman's voice was soft and gentle as Will and Edward successfully put it down without any damage.

'Well done. Now, get the other dishes and put them around the swan but not too close.'

'Yes sir, Mr Sweetman, sir.' They arranged the dishes of beef, salmon and vegetables under the butler's guidance and then stood at attendance some distance from the table but near enough to be of assistance if needed.

It wasn't long before the duke and Freddie came into the dining room and took their places at the table. Freddie sat on the duke's left and made herself comfortable with her beloved pug, Augusta, on her lap, keeping control of her as her nose rose into the air sniffing the aromas and drooling. The dog struggled to get to the salmon and Freddie restrained her and wiped the drool from the dog's mouth with a special napkin used for the purpose. 'She loves salmon so much,' she said fondly.

'You indulge that dog far too much, Freddie,' the duke was saying as the prince bounced into the room. 'I'm starving, by God! Look at that,' he said as he took his place on the duke's right and admired the swan. 'It smells delicious and looks wonderful.' He picked up the long, sharp knife laid beside it and Will noticed a fleeting look of irritation from the duke but then he gave a smile of indulgence which he shared with the duchess. Will knew the duke to be casual and relaxed about his brother and his ways.

'What is in this, Sweetman?'

'If I may explain, Your Royal Highness,' Mr Sweetman said as he approached the table. 'Cook tells me that the pie is a mixture of the best meat of fowl including swan, chicken and duck in rich gravy. The neck and beak are made of pastry filled with bone marrow.'

'Excellent! Where now … where to cut it?' The prince pondered and suddenly cut the pie in half crossways and as he opened it up chunks of meat and thick gravy oozed out slowly emitting the most delicious aroma. 'Ah,' the prince exclaimed with pleasure as he scooped up some of the pie onto a plate. He added some of the pastry and gave the plate to the duchess.

'Here, Freddie. You take the first plate. Just like happy families.'

'Oh, not too much for me, George, remember I don't eat as much as you and Frederick.'

'Nonsense,' he answered, 'eat up and build your strength, give some to the dog.' He piled more pie onto a plate and gave it to the duke and then piled his own plate high with pie. He ignored the dishes of vegetables.

Later, the prince leaned back in his chair. 'Magnificent meal, Frederick, extraordinary cook you have. That trifle was incredible. Far better than my own cook can make.'

'I doubt that,' the duke said. 'I know you have one of the best cooks in England.'

'Well,' the prince said, pondering, 'maybe so, but I think your cook will be poached soon by some rascal sat nearby.'

'Don't you dare,' the duke threatened. 'You leave my cook where he is. Freddie would kill me if we lost him and I don't fancy being killed just yet.'

The duke and duchess laughed but the prince didn't join in. 'Ah! Yes, being killed. That brings me to the reason for my visit.' He looked around. 'Sweetman, take your two servants and attend at the end of the room. I need to speak in confidence.'

'And, Mr Sweetman,' Freddie said, 'please take Augusta and ask one of the footmen to take her outside for a while.'

'Yes, Your Grace.' The butler bowed as he took the dog gently from her and ushered the two footmen to the end of the room, giving Edward the honour of exercising the dog.

Freddie was feeling unsettled and had been asking herself why George was here so unexpectedly. She had never completely trusted him. He was too enamoured of pleasure in every way and too used to his own way. In Freddie's opinion he was as selfish as her husband was loyal and she knew her husband's loyalty to his country and crown and to his friends was absolute. She tried to put her concerns to one side.

'Frederick,' the prince said in a low voice. 'We haven't seen each other for a while, I've been busy and you too, but there is news. Maybe I should just say for Freddie's benefit,' he glanced at her, 'that since the King and Queen of France were imprisoned the so-called Republican government of France has been running the country.'

'I do know that, George,' the duchess snapped trying to control her irritation.

'Yes. Yes, of course.' He looked uncomfortable. 'But maybe you do not know that France has been fighting with Austria – and winning battles. They defeated the Prussian army at Valmy recently and,' he paused, 'this will be news to you, Frederick, we have just heard they have defeated the Austrian army at Jemappes, annexing most of the Low Countries.'

The duke sucked in his breath in alarm. 'That's bad news indeed.'

'And things are not good in London either,' the prince said quickly. 'The king is at his wits end. There's no consoling him as it just goes from bad to worse in France. It's total anarchy. Each report we receive is more horrendous than the last. Unrest is endemic there.' He sighed deeply. 'The king fears the same thing will happen to us.'

'Revolution? Here?' Freddie asked, horrified.

'Indeed,' the prince answered. 'It could happen, don't make the mistake of thinking otherwise. Thank the good lord, Frederick, that our country has not built up the army as we did the navy. A powerful national army would be a huge threat to us right now. Insurrection is contagious and men love to get the better of their superiors. And I for one do not want my head on a block.'

Freddie looked at her husband in dismay. 'Frederick?'

'He's right, Freddie.' The duke couldn't hide his worry. 'It could happen here given the right circumstances. We have been worrying about this for some time.'

'I wouldn't be surprised by anything or anybody right now,' the prince continued in a loud whisper, leaning towards his brother and Freddie. 'The world's gone mad. My spies tell me the mob in France is just that. A mob: a mob of ignorant, dirty, poor peasants glorifying in the power that has suddenly befallen them. And the women! The women are the worst, so I've been told. Never trust a woman!'

'Excuse me!' Freddie snapped indignantly.

'Sorry,' the prince sighed. 'Sorry, Freddie, nothing personal. 'But the king,' he paused, his face suddenly looking haggard, 'the king and – truth be told – the rest of us … me … need your steady hand and strong leadership, Frederick.'

'But, George, would a few days matter?' Freddie asked. 'Frederick has only been here a short while after months in London exerting his – how did you put it – steady hand and strong leadership. He needs to rest and recover his strength. Give him this time, for goodness' sake.'

'Mmm … yes, indeed, maybe a few days. Sorry, Freddie.' The prince looked even more haggard. 'But he's missed. The family flounders around in a tizzy without him.'

'Come now, George. That is an exaggeration. I am *not* indispensable.'

'But you are. To me you are,' the prince said earnestly as he leaned even more towards his brother. 'The damned politicians keep asking me questions and wanting me to help the king make decisions and the king won't listen to me. He has no respect for me as you well know.' He lowered his voice further. 'I am floundering too, I need you, Frederick.'

'Well, I still say a few days won't matter,' Freddie reiterated. 'He will be with you early next week as agreed. I will not allow him to leave any sooner. He's exhausted. Let's be honest here amongst ourselves, yes? No one is indispensable but I agree, the duke is *almost*,' she looked at her husband and smiled, 'indispensable. I also agree that the duke is needed in London,' she glared at the prince, *'after a rest!'* Her glare challenged the prince to disagree as she let the sentence hang in the air. George is a weak man, she thought, and like all weak men he panics when things get difficult. She glanced at her husband. Unlike Frederick, who is strong physically and mentally. He's man enough to be kind and caring and intelligent enough to learn from mistakes; his own or other peoples. I trust him … maybe not as a husband; she'd had suspicions of possible dalliances while he spent time away from her but that was to be expected of a prince, although it hurt her deeply that she had not been able to keep her hold on him even for this short a time. Thirteen months of marriage was still a honeymoon in her eyes.

But I trust him as a man of honour and influence. I must not fail him. I can do things for him that a mistress can never do. He needs me. I know he does. And I feel sure he is going to be very important in what happens. Freddie took a leisured look at the prince and then at her husband and made her decision. 'I have decided that I will go to London as well,' she announced in a strong voice and with finality. She held up her hands as both men opened their mouths to object. 'No, wait, let me finish.' She put her small hand over Frederick's much larger one leaning towards him, speaking quietly. 'I love you, Frederick.'

'As I do you,' he whispered back.

'I know,' she said softly, squeezing his hand. 'I feel I may have disappointed you in not liking London as much as you do … hiding myself away here at Oatlands as much as I do.'

The duke smiled at her. 'You could never disappoint me, Freddie.'

'That is noble of you, Frederick, but there must be honesty between us, especially now. We have feelings of loyalty and love and honour between us, but we are very different people. We have different needs. I will not get in your way … what I mean is …I will not interfere in your private affairs. What you do outside my company is up to you. I am aware of your preference for London life and all that entails. You are a royal prince and must have your own life but do not forget that I am your wife and your loyal servant and supporter.'

The duke nodded his head slightly, smiling in acknowledgement that she spoke the truth.

'During this difficult time,' she continued, 'you will need someone close to you who you can rely on totally, someone who will keep your innermost thoughts and reactions private, someone who cares more for you than for themselves. You will need someone to discuss ideas you are unsure of, discuss the ramifications of those ideas. And for that, one needs someone who will not judge but is open to discussions. I am that person for you. Sometimes you will need my counsel and other times you will not. I will not mind whichever it is. My only priority is to help you and to do that I have to be with you.'

'By God! That's a good idea, Frederick,' the prince whispered loudly. 'Freddie is so sensible. The most sensible woman I know. And totally trustworthy, I know that too.'

'It may be dangerous for you,' he said to his wife. 'We do not know what will happen.'

'Bah! Danger! I welcome the chance to help. I am a foreigner here, but I have grown to love this country and value it. I have made good friends here. I am suited to this country. I want to help it every way I can.'

The duke hesitated.

'Please, Frederick ... please.' The duchess' eyes filled with tears. 'Do not leave me here on my own not knowing what is befalling you and the country. That is the worst thing for me. I feel so useless. And yes, I know I am only a woman but I am an intelligent woman and understand your world. Never forget I am the daughter of a king as you are a son of a king.'

Frederick silently looked from his wife to his brother, a frown drawing down his face.

'Bah! Mein Gott,' she blurted furiously. 'It is so frustrating to be a woman!'

The prince laughed out loud and the duke joined in. He took her hand in his and his eyes shone with love for her. 'I understand. I would feel the same if I were you. So yes, dear Freddie, if you feel this way then please come, I would welcome it.'

Freddie beamed. 'Thank you,' she said, leaning over and kissing him on the cheek. 'Thank you for understanding.' Their eyes met and held.

'Excellent!' The prince interrupted, breaking their intimacy.

Frederick glanced at his brother and then looked back at Freddie. 'But I think George is right. We should go to London without delay. War waits for no man – or woman,' he added gently. 'We'll take more staff up to town with us than usual. I fear we will have many visitors coming and going, many unexpected things happening. Urgent messages being passed between interested parties, meetings and innumerable other things, I do not want to skimp on staff and I need staff I can rely on.'

Freddie frowned. 'I cannot decide who should come and who shouldn't instantly. I need to talk to Mr Tucker, Mr Sweetman and Mrs Harley. I cannot shut up the house in such a hurry. Mr Tucker will have a … a … what do you say?'

'A fit, I'll warrant,' the prince said.

'Ah, yes, that is it – a fit. Mr Tucker will have a fit if I tell him to reorganise the staff and stables within hours. It cannot be done. I am aware of the logistics of such a thing and I am telling you it cannot be done.'

The duke laughed. 'Oh, Freddie, dear Freddie, it's a good thing you are not in the army. You would never survive. You and Mr Tucker, you would be the stragglers left behind.'

'Well, that is the army and this is a royal household; different things.'

'You are right, Freddie,' the prince agreed, 'your household and especially your stables are the envy of many and needs careful thought.'

'Indeed, the stables are my pride and joy, but we also need to make careful choices of which servants we take with us.'

The duke got up and put his arms around Freddie's slight shoulders, kissing her on the cheek. 'You may be small, my dear Freddie, but you have a power inside that people often do not see. Courage, sensitivity, generosity and an ability to see people for how they are rather than who they are. I do admire you so.'

She looked up at her husband. 'Thank you, I am touched.'

He glanced at his brother. 'I suggest we go together tomorrow and Freddie stays here and gets everything organised and joins us within a few days.'

'Good. Wonderful,' the prince said, smiling as he shouted down the room. 'More wine, Sweetman, if you please. Let's drink a toast to the most wonderful woman I know.'

Freddie raised an eyebrow. 'I doubt that, George, but thank you for the sentiment.'

*

The servants' hall was buzzing with noise the next morning with everyone babbling excitedly.

'What's going on?' 'The house is in turmoil

337

upstairs.' 'Anyone know why?' 'Where's Mr Sweetman? Mrs Harley?' 'It's not like them to be late for meals?'

Mr Sweetman came bustling in followed by Mr Tucker and Mrs Harley. The butler clapped his hands and into the sudden silence said, 'Now everyone, listen carefully. the duke has decided to go earlier to his London house and the duchess is going with him. They will be there indefinitely.'

'The duchess is going too?' someone said in surprise. 'She hates London.'

'That is not for us to comment on,' Mr Sweetman said sharply. 'Now, the duke wants more staff than usual to go to his London house for the duration. The duke and the prince are leaving today and the duchess and staff will leave as soon as possible within the next few days.

'Of course, Mr Tucker, Mrs Harley and I will stay here to look after Oatlands and Edward, as under butler, will go to London, but that is all that has been decided so far. The rest of the staff who will accompany the duchess will be announced soon. Just to confirm that everyone staying here will be paid board wages for as long as the duke and duchess are away, so you don't need to worry about that.' He turned to the steward. 'Mr Tucker, you wanted to say a word, I understand.'

'Thank you, Mr Sweetman.' His clear, concise voice belied his small stature as it echoed around the room. 'The duke has asked me to make events clear to everyone.' He looked around the room. 'We are *royal* servants and you need to understand the seriousness of what is happening. As you know, the King and Queen of France were imprisoned some months ago and the

338

unrest in Paris, in France itself, is getting worse. It is a very serious situation and gets more so every day. The duke together with the king, the Prince of Wales and the government are all concerned with the security of our own country. Insurrection is an ugly word and an ugly deed. We must avoid it at all costs. We do not want the insurrection in France to spread over here.' Shocked faces looked back at him. 'We must take measures, but what those measures will be is not our concern. Our concern is to support our master,' he paused, making brief eye contact with everyone, 'and a very good master too, as I'm sure you are all aware. This will be a time of strife and trouble, I have no doubt.'

A silence descended as everyone absorbed this information. Some looked at their feet in studious contemplation while others looked about them with concern.

'Now, everyone,' Mr Sweetman said loudly, 'we all know where we stand and how serious this situation is. For those who go to London, you will be right in the middle of it. You will need to hold yourselves strong and ready to serve in whatever way is necessary. We cannot know what will enfold. I rely on you to do your best at all times whatever the situation.' He gave a short, sharp nod of his head to indicate he'd finished.

'Yes, sir, Mr Sweetman, sir,' everyone chorused.

Will looked over at Mercy, who had paled visibly. A melancholy descended on Will as he saw all his plans overrun by matters of state.

'So,' Mr Sweetman said in his confident voice, 'you all now understand the importance of what we are doing. You are taking part in affairs that most people can only imagine. You are in a privileged position and you need to show that you are up to the job. We do not know what will happen but in our positions we must be prepared for any eventuality and give the duke all our support whether in London or here at Oatlands.'

'Yes, sir, Mr Sweetman sir,' everyone answered emphatically.

'You can rely on us,' someone said.

'Hear, hear,' others added and then a cacophony of voices rose to the ceiling in confirming their loyalty.

Mr Sweetman's words had penetrated through to Will and his melancholy lifted as quickly as it had befallen him. His thoughts tumbled, his nerves tingled and his eyes sparkled with excitement. He suddenly heard himself shouting out, 'Three cheers for the duke.'

An immediate chorus of, 'Hear, hear, three cheers for the duke,' went up in unison and they shouted, 'Hip, hip hurray. Hip, hip hurray. Hip, hip hurray.'

Will sidled over to Mercy. 'I saw my parents yesterday and told them of our engagement, they were delighted, but frankly, we cannot announce it to everyone else, not now. It is completely the wrong time and atmosphere,' he whispered. 'I asked my parents not to say anything for the time being, so there is no problem there.'

Mercy tried to smile. 'I'm glad they are pleased, but I agree, this changes everything. Oh, Will, what's going to happen to us all?'

'It'll be all right as long as we can be together.'

'And how do we do that? We don't know who is going to London and who isn't.'

Will shrugged. 'We must hope for the best, I suppose,' he said taking her hand and giving is a gentle squeeze.

'We have to do more than hope for the best.'

'I know, but what?'

'Look, there's Anne just coming in. She may have seen the duchess.'

Anne rushed over to them. 'Have you heard the news about going to London?'

'Yes, Mr Sweetman's just told us,' Mercy said.

'The duchess spoke to me this morning and said she wanted me to go to London and continue as her housemaid and for you to come too, Mercy as you have experience of the London house. She wants to be surrounded by her familiars as she hasn't been up to London for such a long time.'

'What about Will? What will become of him? He's only number five footman so he'll probably stay here.'

'No,' Anne whispered quietly, 'he's coming too. The duchess asked for him especially. She said she would feel more confident if Will was around to protect her.' She looked at her brother, smiling. 'She thinks of you as a hero since you saved her life. A brave man, she said she has great confidence in you, therefore, you're coming too.'

'Hurray,' Will said quietly, catching hold of Mercy's and Anne's hands and giving them both a quick kiss on the cheek, whispering to Anne, 'I'll tell our parents as soon as I get the chance. I know you will be too busy.'

'What's going on here?' Mr Sweetman asked in a loud voice. 'I'll have nothing of that sort in the servants' hall.'

'No, sir, Mr Sweetman, sir,' the three of them said in unison trying to hide their smiles. Will winked and

341

followed Mr Sweetman out of the room. He turned in the doorway and blew each of them a kiss with an even bigger wink.

*

Will rushed to his parents lodge in his afternoon rest period. 'We've heard the news,' Jack said, as Will settled himself into a chair and his mother put a piece of her fruit cake in front of him. 'News travels fast here.'

'It'll be quiet here for you. Sure you'll be able to cope?' Will said with a teasing smile.

His mother gave him a playful swipe on his arm but couldn't help laughing. 'I think we will cope all right.'

'I could do with a nice rest,' Jack added, grinning. 'My aches and pains keep telling me I need to rest and now that Ben Moat's married again, well, he's got more time and is more relaxed now. He owes me a few days holiday.'

'I'm so glad he married the girl who came to look after his children, she's so suitable,' Will pontificated. 'She's a nice girl, good with the children, too. I've seen her out with them and they all looked happy.'

Hannah looked at Will suspiciously. 'You sound like an old married man already, and yes, she's very suitable but, more importantly, how do you know she's a nice girl? Come on, out with it. You knew her at the village didn't you?'

Will laughed. 'Don't look at me like that. I did know her slightly but only to know that she was a nice girl, very quiet and liked church a lot. I didn't have anything to do with her. Honestly, Mama, I didn't.'

'Well, that's good,' Jack added. 'Could be awkward if you had, Ben's the jealous type deep down.'

'Yes,' Hannah said. 'I'm glad to know you had no dealings with her. As you say, they are looking very happy together and the children too love her. She's so good with them.'

'Knowing Ben, she'll be having her own soon,' Will said matter of factly.

'Less of that, young man,' Hannah chastised him. 'See to your own business and don't get involved in anyone else's love life, that's the way to trouble.'

'But I only meant they are a nice couple and get on well. You can see that without even trying.'

'Well, yes, sorry, maybe I was a bit sharp,' Hannah admitted.

'Don't forget,' he said looking at his mother with love, 'I'm a respectable fiancé now. I don't talk of other women.' He raised his eyebrows questioningly. 'Really, I do mean that.'

'Yes, I can see you do, Will. Mercy has tamed you and that makes me very happy. And another thing that will make me happy is the extra time I'll have to go to the village daily to visit the White children.'

'How are they doing?'

'Very well. The little ones have never had it so good but the eldest, Elizabeth, I'm a little worried about her. She's taken it bad.'

'You couldn't have done more for her, Hannah,' Jack said. 'You've been to see her a lot.'

'I know, and she's settled in with the family but I just feel ... well, responsible, I suppose. I just want to make sure.'

'You just like to help people, my love.' Jack couldn't stop his smile. 'That's why I married you.'

She raised an eyebrow. 'Really? That's why was it?'

'No need for sarcasm,' Jack said.

She laughed. 'I'll talk to you later, husband dear, when our son has taken himself off.'

Will laughed. 'Oops,' he said through a mouthful of cake and almost choking. 'I think I'll just eat my cake and be off. Don't want to get in the middle of this.'

'Take your time, Will.' Jack said sitting down opposite him and picking up his own piece of cake. 'Ben Moat and I will sort out an agreeable timetable so we all have a good rest. But you, son, you'll be in the middle of everything. It'll be a good time for you. I envy you.'

'Thanks, Papa. I'm looking forward to it although it seems I shouldn't be thinking like that. The situation is so serious.' Will took another bit of cake and mumbled through it, 'I'll write and tell you how I'm getting on. Anne too. We'll write.'

'Of course you will, my darling son.' Hannah winked at Jack. 'But I won't hold my breath.'

Jack stifled a laugh. 'Just do your best, son. That's all we can ask. Don't worry about us, we'll be all right.'

344

CHAPTER TWENTY-ONE

The relocation of the servants from Oatlands to Albany House in Piccadilly, the duke's new London home, went smoothly thanks to the good organisation of the staff at both houses. The duke hadn't long owned the prestigious premises, the best in London many believed. It was built a few years before by the First Viscount Melbourne and originally called Melbourne House. It was so luxurious and extravagant and cost such a vast amount that it plunged the viscount into debt and he was forced to look for relief. The duke owned the lease on Dover House, some short distance away, and they came to an agreement to exchange Albany House for the lease on Dover House plus the duke paying the viscount the sum of £23,570. The duke was delighted with the deal as he now had much larger premises to impress and entertain in style.

Anne smoothed down her maids' uniform, tied on her white apron and adjusted her white cap in the small mirror on the wall. 'It was lucky we were put in the same room,' she said to Mercy. 'It's so much nicer to share with someone you like and know well.'

Mercy struggled to control her hair as she tried to push it under her own cap. 'Oh, Lord, my hair is such a trial sometimes. It just will not go where I want it too, but I agree. It has all been such a rush coming up from Oatlands and so busy here I'm not sure where I am half the time. There! At last!' she said pushing the final strands under her cap. 'I've hardly seen you or the duchess. Is she faring well?'

Anne smiled. 'She's extraordinary. Whenever I see her she seems to be in her element. She's excited, I think. She feels involved and because of that I too feel more involved than I would normally do. I know we servants are only on the edge of everything but it's exciting to be part of it, however small.'

'Well, the comings and goings never stop. I've never seen so much activity. The butler is constantly admitting visitors. Will helps out answering the door sometimes, he says he has a list of people he can admit and has to tactfully refuse admittance to those not on the list.'

'Tactful?' Anne queried. 'Will tactful! Well I never!'

Mercy laughed. 'We'll see what comes of it.'

'Now we are settled in here, are you going to announce your engagement?'

'We should do soon, I think, but it never seems to be the right time what with everyone so busy. And the atmosphere is so stressed and urgent and not conducive to a marriage, especially a marriage of servants.'

'Maybe it would be better to announce it sooner rather than later. We don't know if things will get worse, after all. There's no reason for secrecy, is there? And I've seen a few of the London maids giving Will the eye.'

Mercy frowned. 'Mmm, I've seen them too. I think you could be right, we should announce it soon. I'll talk to Will about it.'

'I'm curious,' Anne said, sitting on the side of her bed and watching Mercy make the final adjustments to her appearance. 'Was life this eventful when you worked for the duke before … at his other house? You know, was there excitement like here?'

'Mmm ... not like this. This is exceptional, I think. But we had our moments as the duke was single then and there were lots of parties and entertainments. But quite honestly, this house is much better than the other one. This is so luxurious I don't know where to put my bucket down sometimes for fear of damaging something.'

Anne laughed. 'Oh, Mercy, you are funny sometimes, but I know what you mean. The duchess' apartments are so magnificent I get the same feeling. The duchess has told me she prefers her Oatlands' apartments though. More informal, she says. And I have to agree with her. It's a lot quieter at Oatlands too. Sometimes I can't sleep for the racket of carriages passing down Piccadilly and horses clip clopping and doesn't anyone sleep around here? Passers-by go on noisily till the early hours. I'm losing my beauty sleep.'

'Be thankful for the large forecourt between us and Piccadilly which helps cut out the noise. In the old house we were right on the road. But you get used to it,' Mercy said, amused. 'After a while you don't notice it, but I'm surprised you don't just collapse with exhaustion every night. I know I do.'

Anne sighed. 'Busy and exhausted I may be but I am constantly awoken by the noises from outside. I look forward to not noticing it.'

'If you don't mind me saying so,' Mercy hesitated, 'well, you seem a lot more relaxed here. You know, able to laugh more and enjoy yourself.'

'Is it that obvious?'

'Well, maybe just to me.'

'You're right though. I do feel more relaxed and I am enjoying myself. It's an opportunity to forget what happened at Oatlands. Everything is so new and interesting here. I can forget about the past. I'm determined to forget about it. I don't want that man to take over my life.'

'I'm happy to hear that, dear Anne.' Mercy took her hand and smiled. 'Will and I have been worried about you. It's as though you lost your joy in life. You deserve some happiness after … well, you know, all that. Keep it up. Let life take its course.'

Anne gave Mercy a peck on the cheek. 'Thank you. I feel that a new life deserves new attitudes. I'm determined to enjoy my stay here. I feel so much … how can I say … lighter here, as if all the noise and bustle has lifted me up and improved my spirits, despite not being able to sleep!'

Mercy squeezed Anne's hand reassuringly. 'Keep it up, my dear Anne. You know Will and I are always here for you.' She noticed tears forming in Anne's eyes and determined to lighten the mood. 'And it's as noisy inside too, don't you think? People coming and going all the time and the mess they leave behind, some of them. It's a non-stop job to keep the place clean. And trying to clean and also be invisible is even more difficult. The amount of dirty footsteps in the hallway is never-ending in all this recent rain. I was on duty for hours yesterday rushing into the hallway and getting down on my hands and knees to rub off the imprints of boots from the tiled floor after people entered. What are they all doing here, that's what I'd like to know.'

Anne laughed.

'You're lucky being the duchess' housemaid.'

'I do my fair share don't forget that,' Anne said. 'I've taken on a few more jobs for the duchess recently and I've started to look after the duke's office during the day. And you're right the visitors do leave it in a state. Ashtrays full to brimming and ash all over the floor, glasses knocked over and left in a pool of alcohol and pieces of paper scrunched up all over the place including the floor. What do they do? Throw things at each other? Play soldiers with paper balls or—'

Mercy burst out laughing so hard she set Anne off. 'You are funny, Anne, I can just imagine all those important men throwing paper balls around and shouting, 'Take that, you, you, French cad, you!'

Anne tried to control herself. 'We mustn't laugh. What they are doing is really important. They're saving the country, or trying to,' and then she burst out laughing again.

A perfunctory knock on the door and the quick entry of the housekeeper stopped their merriment like a slap. The small attic room became even more claustrophobic as the tall, bosomy housekeeper entered. As usual she was immaculate even at five in the morning. Her maroon dress and matching short jacket were always freshly pressed and her ring of house keys attached to her waist sparkled so much they looked as if she polished them every week.

'I like to see my staff happy,' she said in her soft Scottish lilt, 'and I must say such merriment so early in the morning is a joy to the spirits.' She smiled her rather crooked smile and neither woman was certain whether she was being sarcastic or not.

'We're just getting ourselves ready for another day, Mrs Woodruff,' Anne said. 'Life is so serious at the moment we took some frivolous time out of the day.'

'Indeed. Well, frivolous or not, I need you, Anne, to go to the duke's office and start cleaning straight away and you go and help her, Mercy. The duke wants his office from seven this morning and it needs a good clean and airing. I have just been informed he has a very important meeting. See to it that several jugs of hot chocolate, coffee, toast and biscuits are on the tray in the office at six fifty-five on the dot. You know how punctual the duke is.'

'Yes, Mrs Woodruff,' both women said as they bobbed a curtsey.

*

The servants' hall at Albany House was a larger affair than at Oatlands and more luxurious in keeping with the status of the house. The room was warmer and the fireplace much bigger than at Oatlands. The kitchens were in a separate block which meant that the mouth-watering aromas of the duke's and duchess' meals did not permeate the servants' hall as they did at Oatlands. That was a plus for Will who had a 'fancy for fancy food' as he often joked, which made everyone groan. The chairs were more comfortable although still wooden and Will tried to work out why they were more comfortable. He decided it was because they were more substantial, with deeper seats. He noticed though that the butler and the housekeeper had a cushion on theirs. There were two sideboards and dressers instead of the one sideboard they had at Oatlands and they were of a higher quality. But even though, Will decided, he preferred the Oatlands servants' hall. It felt like home and this didn't.

Also, breakfast was a more chaotic affair than at Oatlands with so many staff coming and going. They came in at different times depending on their duties, so there was always food available. Will was a little wary of Mr Faraday, the tall, rather thin but distinguished butler, who was the opposite of Mr Sweetman in temperament being more austere and serious, which made Will nervous; however, he stood up and asked for permission to speak.

The butler gave him a disapproving look but nodded.

Will cleared his throat dramatically. 'I know the weather today is atrocious and we are all in a turmoil here with so much happening, but I would like to take this opportunity to announce some good news.' He looked over at Mercy who was smiling broadly. 'I would like to announce that I have the pleasure to be engaged to Miss Mercy Batchelor and to say that I am the happiest man on earth.'

A murmur of congratulations filled the room and many of the men made comments like, 'Lucky man, William,' coupled with one or two indistinguishable murmurs which Will ignored.

Everyone congratulated Mercy and some of the women even said, 'Lucky woman, Mercy,' and Mercy decided to keep a close eye on them when Will was around.

The butler stood. 'Now, now, settle down everyone. Congratulations to William and Mercy. It is nice to have some good news for a change. Do you have thoughts on when you will marry?' He addressed Will.

'Well, Mr Faraday, sir, we would like to marry in Weybridge so that our friends and family can attend. We are hopeful of a summer wedding.'

The butler smiled and looked more human and approachable. 'Ah, yes, a summer wedding is indeed a good thing. Weddings in winter can be a cold affair for everyone. Well, I wish you all good luck and I will inform the duke whenever the opportunity is suitable.'

'Thank you, Mr Faraday, sir,' Will said as he looked over at Mercy and smiled, unable to hide his happiness. He had no idea of the shock to come.

*

Not long after breakfast Will was summoned to the duke's office to replace Edward who had been sent out into the foul weather on an urgent message from the duke. The duke's important meeting was still in progress and another footman was needed.

Rather him than me, Will thought with satisfaction, pleased it was Edward who'd been sent out in the storm. Serves him right, he thought. He deserves to get a cold, with a bit of luck!

He made his way up the stairs carrying, as instructed, a tray with several more pots of coffee and hot chocolate. The butler took the tray off Will and went through the extravagant, over-large door to the duke's office. As he came out he pulled the door closed and while the lock clicked it didn't catch and he failed to notice when it slipped open a little.

'Ah, William, you will stand outside the door until you are needed. The duke is meeting very important people today and the meeting is private so you stand outside and the duke will summon you if he needs you.'

'Yes, sir, Mr Faraday, sir,' Will said to his retreating back.

As Will took up his position he realised he could hear most of what was being said if he concentrated hard. He knew it was wrong but he couldn't resist it. There was a row going on with several raised voices and Will positioned himself to the best advantage to hear whilst standing to attention should anyone pass by. There had been many such meetings of late and Will had no reason to think this would be any different: a lot of chat and not much action, but the next sentence turned his blood cold and caused his stomach to lurch up into his chest.

'For God's sake, sir,' the duke barked, 'the King of France was guillotined yesterday morning. We *must* come to an agreement. We cannot go on squabbling. We must be *decisive*.'

Will froze. My God! Those Frenchies have gone and done it, he said to himself. The unthinkable! He recognised the Prince of Wales' voice. 'We cannot allow sovereignty to the people – which is what this revolution is all about – to take hold here.'

'Too true,' an older voice Will didn't know, agreed. 'We tried that when we executed Charles 1 and look what a farce that turned into with Cromwell and his Commonwealth sending our country to rack and ruin. Much worse than anything the king had done beforehand. Chaos and anarchy reigned – the Commonwealth, my arse. Within eleven years we had Charles' son on the throne. This country is royalist and must stay so.'

'Hear, hear. We must never let that happen again,' several voices concurred.

'Agreed,' more voices echoed.

'That Declaration,' the same older voice continued, 'adopted in France for the Rights of Man and the Citizen, damn it to hell. What rubbish. Look where it's led. Give power to the peasants and this is what you get. This means war.'

'Gentlemen!' the duke admonished. 'France has not declared war on us.'

'Not yet,' another strong voice admonished the duke in return.

Who were these people, Will wondered. They must be very important if they speak to the duke like that. He felt indignant on the duke's behalf.

'War will certainly come, there is no doubt,' the prince said loudly, his voice full of authority. 'Frederick must be appointed as Commander of the Expeditionary Force immediately!'

Well done, sir, Will thought. He was getting to like the prince the more he saw of him.

'Pitt is against it. Very against,' someone said.

'The king is all for it. In fact, is insistent,' the prince replied in that same voice.

'But our prime minister—'

'To hell with Pitt,' the prince shouted. 'You politicians must talk him round. Tell him the king is for it and remind them that Frederick is the only man able to do the job. Don't forget that he has been educated and trained to be a soldier and commander since the age of sixteen. AND under the guidance of the Duke of Brunswick – who, in case you have forgotten – is regarded as one of the most successful generals of our age. AND Frederick has fought abroad many times so has vast experience of how these foreign armies operate; their strengths and weaknesses. AND he has the highest status, being the second son of our king. AND he is also the son-in-law of our ally the King of Prussia. That social rank will mean a great deal on the field of battle to both officers and men. There is no doubt he is the man for the job.'

'But Pitt points out that, with respect sir, the Duke of York was not covered in glory during his earlier campaigns abroad,' someone dared to say.

'That was because he was very young and inexperienced, operating under extremely difficult circumstances and let down by his allies,' the prince shouted, obviously furious. 'Frankly, sir, I challenge anyone to do better under the same circumstances. AND sir, he is now older and more experienced – that is my point. He has learned from his mistakes; benefited from them. He knows these countries and their soldering. AND, sir, I am not defending the duke because he is my brother but because I believe it to be the truth. AND tell me this, man, who else is there?'

'There's Cornwallis.'

'Indeed, Cornwallis is a superb commander but he is Governor General of India and is there right now. He cannot be in two places at once. NO, sir, it is the duke who is the best man here.'

'I don't think Mr Pitt will agree—'

'I told you, man,' the prince said, exasperated, *'it is your job to persuade* Pitt and the other ministers especially that foreign secretary, Grenville and that fool of a home secretary, Dundas. We need the duke because we have so few soldiers. We do not have enough of them to fight a war with France therefore we need the help of mercenaries from Hanover and

Hesse. These men will follow Frederick because of his standing as I have explained and they will respect his orders because of it. The success of this campaign will depend on this, believe me.'

'We have a formidable navy with 600 ships and 100,000 men to man them. I don't see why we couldn't transfer some of those men to the army.'

'But this is not a war of *water,*' the prince sounded even more exasperated. 'We need every one of those ships and sailors to defend us because we're an island country, if you hadn't noticed.' The prince's tone was contemptuous. 'Therefore, everyone accepts this kind of strength in the navy. But the army? We cannot give that kind of strength to the army. Look, let's be honest here. This country has had a strong hostility to the idea of a strong standing army since Oliver Cromwell and his bloody Commonwealth. No one wants to go back to the days when he kept this country in thrall to a repressive military regime. He became a Caesar in the end. No one wants to risk that.'

'His Royal Highness is right,' a new voice full of confidence said reasonably. 'We don't want to risk a large army in this country. Therefore, we must rely on mercenaries and our links to Hanover and Hesse make their men ideal for our purposes. I agree, the duke is the best man for the job.'

The duke's voice sounded loud and clear. 'And I want the job, gentlemen. Believe me I am a man of reason and I know my soldiering. I would not say this if I didn't believe it wholeheartedly. I agree with my brother for all the reasons he has stated that I am the best man for the job.'

A cheer went up and shouts of encouragement flowed.

That same reasonable voice of a moment ago said, 'As the duke so rightly said France has not declared war on us. But, I agree, we must be prepared. This matter has to be decided right away, we cannot prevaricate any longer.'

'Thank you, general,' the prince said. 'Let us take a vote. Is every man here of the opinion that the Duke of York should be appointed Commander of the Expeditionary Force to defend our country should France declare war on us?'

A loud chorus of, 'Hear, hear, agreed,' went around the room.

'Any dissenters?'

Silence.

'Then it is agreed,' the prince said. 'We need to have a meeting with Prime Minister Pitt immediately. I have a message from the king. He told me that if we came to this very agreement he gave me leave to invite Mr Pitt to come to the king today or tomorrow at the latest, together with everyone of yourselves for a meeting to resolve this. So, ministers, please go back to parliament and arrange for Mr Pitt to attend his majesty post-haste.'

'Agreed,' went around the room like an echo and the door was pulled open so suddenly Will jumped as the duke appeared in the doorway looking as serious as Will had ever seen.

'Thank you, gentlemen,' he said as he shook hands with each of the departing men. Will recognised a few but not all of them. Generals and politicians and advisers made their way purposefully down the stairs and out into the rain.

Will breathed a sigh of relief that he hadn't been caught listening and if the duke noticed the door was ajar when he opened it he didn't react in any way. Hopefully, he was too distracted to notice Will convinced himself as the duke walked away from his office with his arm over his brother's shoulder.

As Will entered the now empty room he decided to open a window to clear the fug of stale breath and cigar smoke as he collected the pots and cups and saucers onto the large silver tray. He started down the servants' staircase and couldn't help thinking again that he was so glad he had decided to stay in the duke's employ and not become a soldier. He was right in the centre of things here and he loved it. For as long as he could remember the taverns he frequented had been full of the news from France and everyone had an opinion on whether the French King, Louis XVl, would follow the example of the aristocrats who had been guillotined. But no one in this country knew it had actually happened. No one but the rulers and me! The thought made his head spin as he realised his position. *Damn, damn, damn! Why did I listen?* This knowledge is not mine to know so I cannot tell anyone. But it would be in the newspapers tomorrow, he was sure. Then everyone would know, so he could tell Mercy now, surely? She was his fiancée. He couldn't keep secrets from her and more to the point he didn't want to keep any from her. But then he stopped dead, mid-stair, as he realised he couldn't tell Mercy either. He would be breaking his promise to keep everything he saw and heard in the house confidential. That was expected of all royal servants. Loyalty was everything, especially this kind of knowledge. And then, like an apparition, Mercy was in front of him coming up the staircase carrying a pan and brush. She looked up and smiled and as the staircase was narrow, turned and went back down the few stairs she'd just climbed.

Should he tell her? He slowed his steps, giving himself time to think. It's now or never. Make your decision, man. And then he realised he'd be dismissed for sure if it leaked out he'd listened in on a private meeting of the duke's and then talked about it to others. And Mercy would never forgive him for that – for getting dismissed and for being disloyal. And then he was level with her.

'Has the meeting finished?' she asked and then looked around and seeing no one else gave him a quick kiss on the cheek.

He took a deep breath and smiled. 'Indeed it's finished.'

'Was it all fine? Did you manage up there on your own?'

He hesitated only a moment. 'I was not privy to the room. I was waiting outside, but my darling Mercy, this tray's heavy, so please forgive me I must go and put it down before I drop it. See you later.' As he turned he hoped Mercy had not seen the relief on his face.

*

As Will suspected, the news of the beheading was all over the servants' hall at breakfast the next morning. Excitement was coupled with panic as some believed war was imminent. Everybody talked at the same time.

'Settle down,' Mr Faraday commanded. 'Eat your breakfast or you will be good for nothing all morning.' He looked around the room as everyone settled, with many of them trying to disguise their excitement but failing.

'What's going to happen, Mr Faraday, sir?' 'What will happen to the duke?' 'What about the duchess?' 'Will this mean war?' 'How could they kill their king?' 'Who decides something like that?'

'Enough!' the butler said. 'I don't want any more talking. Eat your breakfast and get on with your duties. Yours is not to know why or how or anything else unless it has to do with your duties. Do I make myself clear?'

'Yes, sir, Mr Faraday, sir,' everyone said, a few not too enthusiastically.

Will had sat through the whole thing rigid with anxiety as if everyone would know he had already known this. He glanced over at Mercy who was white with shock. Neither of them spoke a word.

*

Later that evening Mercy managed to whisper to Will as he took his break in the servants' hall. 'Come outside. I must speak with you.'

She walked quickly in the moonlight thankful the rain and wind had stopped but finding it hard to breathe easily in the frigid air. Will followed until they found a quiet corner near an outbuilding and she put her arms around his waist and hugged him. 'I'm frightened, Will. What's going to happen? Everyone's talking about it and most think this changes everything for us here.'

'What do you mean, for us here?'

She pulled away from him, looking up at his face,

the anxiety on hers showing clearly in the moonlight. 'Unrest! I'm talking about unrest! Civil disorder! People doing the same thing as in France and causing chaos here ... in our country, *in our* country ... people trying to start a revolution *here*.'

He was taken aback. This wasn't like Mercy. She sounded panicky and she never panicked. That was one of the things he liked about her. 'And have you any proof this will happen?'

She looked at him levelly. 'Have you any that it won't?' He had to laugh a little at that which infuriated her. 'Don't laugh. I'm serious.'

'You listen to too much gossip, my darling.'

'No, you don't understand.' She broke off and breathed deeply, gathering her thoughts. 'Please listen and do me the courtesy to acknowledge that I know myself. And I am frightened of the future.'

He took her in his arms and hugged her close. He kept his voice soft, she needed reassuring. 'You know yourself better than I know myself. I have the greatest faith in you, you know that.' He stroked her forehead, she always liked that, it was soothing she'd told him. 'Of course, I'll listen, my darling. Take your time. Tell me what is in your heart.'

Mercy stepped back from him so she could look directly into his eyes, her own showing her despair. She caught hold of his hands. 'I'm pure, you know that.'

He nodded, surprised, unsure of what was coming next.

'But, truth be known, I want to lie with you, to stay with you all night, to know the joy of that now in case we all die if the events in France come over here.'

Before he could stop them the words tumbled out, *'Mercy! What are you saying?'* Shock had taken the place of surprise. He felt his world and his values spinning. Should he say what he was thinking? He couldn't shake the mental image he had of a naked Mercy in his bed but his roommate would be only a few feet away in the other bed.

'Mercy, look … we cannot – you know – be together all night here with our roommates there too. I couldn't do it, Mercy. Not with people looking on.'

She let go of Will's hands. 'No, silly, not like *that*. No. I think we should … well … get married. Now, as soon as we can.'

'What! Here, in *London?'* He was floundering. 'What about family and friends, they are mostly down in Weybridge still.'

'I know, I know. I'm being selfish. I know you want your parents and friends. I have friends too I want to be at our wedding, but honestly, I feel so frightened and I wonder if … well, you know, if the same kind of unrest happened here as in France would our royal family be in danger? People are saying we'll be at war soon. They're saying all sorts of things and I don't know what to believe.' She wiped away a tear. 'Damn! I don't want to cry, I want to understand. I want to be able to talk about these things with you and we have no chance to talk to each other during the day, we're too busy. We could only talk at night – in bed – and to do that we have to be married. We'll get our own room. Will … I need your strength, your love – your manliness. Marry me now. Marry me for me – for us – not for family or friends.'

He stroked her hair. 'Good Lord, Mercy, you know how to talk well. You've never spoken like that before. Are you sure?' He didn't know what to think.

'Do you think I'm joking?'

He thought if only he could tell her what he knew. The duke may be going away in charge of our army and who knew what the duchess would decide to do. Stay in London or go back to Oatlands. He had no idea and couldn't say anything. But he did know he didn't want to miss this chance; if Mercy wanted him then who was he to say differently?

He smiled and his love for Mercy shone out of his eyes. 'Mercy, my darling Mercy, you know I'd do anything for you. If that's what you want then, yes, yes, yes. We'll ask Mr Faraday for permission to arrange for a special licence as soon as possible. That would be the fastest way to wed. Yes, a special licence.'

Mercy burst into tears and clung to him and all he could do was to try and calm her. He had wanted Mercy in his bed as soon as he'd seen her in the kitchen of Oatlands. He felt so much love for her he thought he would burst.

CHAPTER TWENTY-TWO

February 13th 1793 was blessed with a full winter sun and a clear blue sky. A day for the angels, Will thought, as he walked up the main thoroughfare to his wedding at their local church, St George's, Hanover Square, Mayfair. His hands had shaken that morning as he'd struggled into his best clothes and almost gave up trying to tie his white lace cravat but that was nothing to the build-up of shakes which were now taking over his body. 'I've never been so nervous. I don't know what's wrong with me. I didn't expect the shakes like this,' he said to James, his best man.

'You do look a little pale, you're not going to faint on me are you, like a maiden at her deflowering?' James laughed at his own joke.

'You'll get deflowered if you're not careful,' Will said tartly.

'Come on, old fellow,' James said kindly, putting his arm around Will's shoulder. 'Let's get you to the church. You don't want to get there after the bride, do you?'

'Indeed I do not.' He shivered in the cold, crisp air. 'I hope she's wearing something warm, it's a deceivingly bitter day.' He hunched over slightly against the cold as they made their way as fast as they could amongst the crowds of people, carts and animals using the same roads. Newly built Mayfair may have been but it didn't take long for the lords and ladies and their families to move out of the polluted centre of London and into the good air of Mayfair. Shining carriages with coats of arms vied for space with gentlemen on horseback, servants on errands and delivery people with their loads. It was the place to be and be seen and Will felt good about himself and about his surroundings. He was living in the best part of London and was about to be a husband and a husband with pride in his wife and in his place in the world.

St George's Church loomed up in front of them and as Will looked up at the tall, elegant building with its roman pillars and beautiful round clock tower soaring above them he felt his nerves increasing to an almost unbearable level.

'It surely is a big church,' James said, looking up. 'I never fail to be awed by it when we come to service on Sundays.'

'And it's a totally different feeling to come here to be wed. Before, it felt good to be inside such a magnificent building but now it just frightens me.' Will took out his handkerchief and wiped the sweat gathering on his forehead despite the cold. 'I feel so small.' He looked at James. 'How can I, the poor son of an ordinary soldier, be marrying in such splendour, you tell me that?'

James frowned, taking him seriously. 'You know full well it's because you work for the Duke of York and it is your parish church as well as his. It's simple.'

Will shook his head. 'Simple? Life is mysterious. I was not born to this. This is a church for the high-ups. No wonder I'm nervous.'

'For goodness sake, Will,' James said, exasperated, 'you come to this church every Sunday for worship. We all do. The difference today is that you will not be sat at the back with the other servants and poor folk but up in the front pew where the duke and duchess always sit. That's got to count for something hasn't it? Make it special.'

Will didn't reply.

'Come on, old friend,' James cajoled, putting his arm around Will's shoulders, 'let's get you inside. It's a pity no one can be spared from the house to come and see you wed. So many things happening today it's bad timing. But look on the bright side, let's hope some of the brethren will be curious enough to see who will choose to marry on the unlucky thirteenth, and in February too!'

'The date chose us not we the date as you well know,' Will replied tetchily. 'Who would *choose* this date to be wed? It was the only one free until next month and Mercy … well Mercy …'

'Wants to wed now, yes I know. It is a mystery to me what she sees in you, but then I am a man so what do I know? You obviously have talents hidden from me, thank the lord.' James laughed.

Will ignored his taunting. 'I wish I wasn't so nervous. Look, tell me James, tell me true now, is it a bad omen do you think? Marrying on the thirteenth? Tell me what you think.'

'Come on, Will … less of that, and truth be told, no, I don't believe it's a bad day. It's just another day. How many thirteenths have you lived through and nothing bad happened to you? So make it your day. Your special day and nothing to do with bad omens. Come on, let's go inside out of the cold or we'll catch our deaths.'

'Bad choice of word, James,' Will glared at him. 'It is a bad omen.'

'You're nervous, that's all. Every bridegroom has doubts. Come on, you're going to marry Mercy not some old battleaxe. She's special she is. Know something? If you don't want her then I'll marry her. I mean it. She's a very special lady; the catch of all catches.'

Will looked at James, hard. 'I think you're serious! You keep your rotten little hands off my wife, you, you—'

James smiled at his friend. 'Then come on let's go and make you a respectable married man. But remember, I have second dibs on Mercy and there is a queue behind me of other men looking enviously at you.'

'That's enough! And if you so much as look at my wife in any lecherous way I'll … I'll …'

James laughed loudly and long. 'Come on, let's do the deed.'

Will glared and then saw the joke joining in the laughter. 'You just wait until you marry. I'll get my own back!' He took one more look up at the church and ran up the short flight of steps determined not to be overawed by his surroundings. His footsteps echoed as he marched purposefully down the central aisle with the only other sound that of James' footsteps following him. As Will walked towards the altar he looked over the high-backed pews to see if anyone was there. The doors to each pew were shut tight, they were all empty. He felt relief for himself but was sad for Mercy as he knew she wanted people to see her wed. All brides did, he knew that much about women but their wedding was done in such a rush they had no time to organise anything and the house had been and was still so busy they were lucky to get this time to themselves.

They took their place in the front pew and sat in silence. Will looked up at the enormous painting of The Last Supper which filled the wall above the altar and shuddered. He hadn't been so close to it before and it put the fear of God into him. It made him feel small, a man of no power or influence and he wondered what effect it had on the duke when he sat in this very same pew. A vastly different one to his own, he guessed. He felt a hand on his knee and jumped.

'Your legs are going up and down like you're demented. Calm down, man,' James whispered.

'I can't stop them. I'm as nervous as a vicar's daughter on her wedding night.'

'And that's exactly what you'll be, my good friend, if you don't calm down or you'll be no use to Mercy tonight.'

Will was about to swear at James when a voice boomed above him.

'Good day, gentlemen,' the vicar said, standing in front of them. 'All ready are we?'

Will jumped at his sudden appearance. He'd been so wrapped up in himself he'd not noticed his arrival.

'The bridegroom's nervous,' James said.

'Don't worry, William,' the vicar said kindly. 'All bridegrooms are nervous.'

Will's smile was weak as he concentrated on controlling his shaking limbs. 'Have you still got the ring, James?'

'Yes, it's still in my pocket,' he said, taking it out

and showing him. 'Now, calm down. Nothing will go wrong.' He was cut off by the chimes of the clock resonating around the church.

Will counted ten. It was time but where was Mercy? He looked behind him towards the door but it remained shut. Five minutes later it was just as resolutely shut. 'Where is she?' He said into the air as he shot out of the pew and started to pace. 'She's not coming. She's changed her mind. I knew it. I knew she was too good for me. What shall I do?'

'Calm down,' the vicar said, his breath coming out in white puffs in the cold air. 'All brides are late. It's tradition. Don't worry, William.'

If anyone else tells me to calm down I swear I'll take a swipe at them, Will thought.

James stood up and took Will's arm. 'Sit down. Look, let's be frank here, I've seen how Mercy looks at you, there is no way on earth she is not going to be here. Just as the vicar says, all brides are late. It wouldn't be a proper wedding if she turned up on time, now would it?'

Will sighed from the depth of his being and shut his eyes as he sat back in the hard, unforgiving pew and thought of Mercy.

*

Meanwhile, Mercy had been making her way through the busy thoroughfares with her bridesmaid, Anne. They were both wearing their best clothes and Mercy's deep blue dress complimented her long, thick auburn hair with its wayward curls. Some of the housemaids had made her a crown of snowdrops and small ivy leaves together with a posy of snowdrops with a few delicate trailing strands of ivy. Wearing her crown and holding her posy in front of her told all passersby she was a bride on the way to her wedding. Many smiled at them, and some wished Mercy good luck, but on a few occasions they had to jump out of the way of inconsiderate riders and raucous soldiers.

'Good lord,' Anne said. 'It's not ten in the morning and I swear they're drunk.'

'Well, as long as they stay out of our way. I think we ought to hurry up as it's much too cold to dawdle, busy streets or not.' They hurried ahead but a while later Mercy said, 'I'm getting out of breath. On second thoughts, let's slow up a bit as I don't want to arrive at the church door panting or the vicar will get the wrong idea.' She laughed far too loudly for the street.

'Mercy! How could you!' Anne said before she saw the funny side too.

'I'm sorry, I'm nervous. I never thought I'd be so nervous. It's Will I'm marrying not some monster who is forcing me. It should be the happiest day of my life and yet I'm as anxious and nervous as a frightened kitten. It doesn't help that my worst nightmare has come true and we're at war on my wedding day.'

'You're right. It's not a good feeling. It's only been two weeks since France declared war on us but people are as frightened as I've ever seen them, it's been like a plague spreading fear and panic and each day seems to make it worse.' She caught hold of Mercy's arm to avoid some boisterous soldiers. 'Except,' she said with disapproval, 'for the soldiers who seem to be celebrating war.'

'Soldiers have different priorities to us. They like fighting.' They turned a corner and Mercy stopped and clutched Anne's arm. 'Oh, Anne, I don't want a revolution to start up here. It would be unbearable. Where will all this end? I'm so frightened. That's why I wanted to marry now, just in case.'

'I know.' Anne held Mercy's hand tight. 'But I think you worry too much. Don't forget, the duke has been appointed to command our forces. He'll make sure we beat the French, never fear. Just concentrate on today and your wedding. It's your special day you can't let world affairs ruin it.'

'You're right, you're always right. You're so sensible. I'll not think of it until tomorrow. Oh, goodness, now my legs have started shaking.'

'Hang on to me, it's not so far now. Will's waiting for you, just think of that.'

'He will be there, won't he, Anne? He won't stand me up at the altar?'

'You're not serious, surely! You know how much he loves you. He'd do anything for you, you know that.'

'Yes, you're right again. He'll be there. I must be sensible.'

'Look,' Anne said, pointing. 'I can see the clock tower of the church rising up above the other buildings.'

'What time is it? Can you see the clock?'

Anne peered. 'It's fifteen after.'

'*Fifteen after!* We are well late. My husband-to-be may not be conscious by now. He was very nervous yesterday, you know. I've never seen him like that before.'

Anne laughed. 'I'll risk repeating that he does like to dramatise everything and has always been like it even when he was little. But he'll be all right. It will do him good to wait for you.'

371

At last, they stood in front of the church. 'Those columns make one feel so small and in awe,' Mercy said.

'They are meant to. That's why they're there,' Anne said whispering into Mercy's ear, 'to overawe the wayward congregation.'

Mercy couldn't help laughing. 'Well, there are certainly a lot of wayward people around here. Come on then, Anne, my soon to be sister-in-law, let's refuse to be cowed by church or world events. I am Mercy Batchelor, soon to be Mercy Dresser and I am marrying the best man I've ever met and will soon have the best sister-in-law anyone could desire.'

'Flatterer.'

'Let's go and do the deed,' Mercy said as she stepped inside the porch. She waited while Anne took off both their cloaks and put them on the wall-pegs and adjusted Mercy's crown of flowers, hair and the pleats of her dress.

'There, perfect! You're a very beautiful bride.'

'Thank you. You look beautiful too.' She smiled as Anne went forward and opened the inner church door and then took her place behind Mercy who composed herself by shutting her eyes and taking two deep breaths. As she exhaled the last breath she opened her eyes and stepped through the door and into the church. And there was Will, in the distance, facing her, standing full-square before the altar. The sun's rays shining through the stained-glass windows illuminated his well-built figure and strong legs accentuated in his white breeches. He's like a god standing there, she thought, but he's not, he's my Will and he takes my breath away. She couldn't resist whispering to Anne, 'He's a handsome devil.'

'And he's waiting for you,' she whispered back. Footsteps made them both look to the side as a tall, thin man approached them. He was dressed in deepest black apart from his white cravat. The church warden smiled as he reached them. 'Are you ready, Miss Batchelor?'

'I'm ready, sir,' she smiled back. He raised his hand to the organist as the signal for the music to begin and held out his arm to Mercy which she took gratefully. The church was infused with the building crescendo of organ music. She turned to Anne unable to hide her delight. 'Good Lord, Anne, Will must have arranged for music, the sneaky so and so.'

'Come, Miss Batchelor, your husband-to-be is waiting,' the church warden whispered as he pulled gently on her arm. They walked slowly down the aisle with Anne following on behind as the organ's music resonated around the stone walls increasing its power and volume and penetrating into Mercy's very being. Her nerves tingled and she was filled with joy and pleasure as she walked slowly towards Will, never taking her eyes off him.

*

Will didn't hear the music or see anything other than Mercy walking towards him. He was transfixed.

'You shouldn't look,' James whispered. But Will ignored him.

By the good Lord, she's beautiful, Will thought as he watched her slow progress and the sun shone through the windows casting a colourful, almost religious glow, over her. He felt all his nerves dissolve and a deep calm of contentment took him over. He smiled as she approached and their eyes locked. He held out his hand and time changed into slow motion with the seconds stretching out like minutes as Mercy came to him and took his arm, their eyes making their own vows.

'Dearly beloved, we are gathered here—' the vicar's loud, clear, bell-like voice echoed around the church and the next thing Will remembered was signing the marriage register and Mercy's smile as she took the pen from him and signed her neat signature below his, followed by James' and then Anne's as witnesses.

'Congratulations on your marriage, Mrs Dresser,' Anne said. 'I want to be the first to call you that.'

'And I'll be the second,' Will said as he took her hand and kissed it. 'Mrs Dresser, welcome to the Dresser family.'

'Yes, Mr and Mrs Dresser, all good luck in your married life and I expect to see you in church as usual this Sunday,' the vicar said, smiling.

'I'll escort you out, Mr and Mrs Dresser,' the church warden said very politely as he ushered them gently towards the door. 'Good luck in your new life together.'

And then they were on the street with the cold biting into them, but Will and Mercy were still arm in arm and had eyes for only each other.

'You paid for the organist to play,' Mercy whispered to Will. 'What a wonderful surprise. Thank you, thank you, my darling husband.'

'One of Mr Handel's compositions,' Will whispered back unable to suppress his smile. 'But don't ask me which one, the organist chose it.'

'If I could just interrupt you love-birds for a

moment, I know when I'm not wanted,' Anne joked. 'I've done my bit, now it's your turn. I'll leave you now and get back to the house as James and I are both needed. But you, my two dearest people, have the whole day to yourselves – and I don't want to know what you get up to!'

'Just a minute, not so fast,' James said, his eyes sparkling with mischief. 'I'd like to take the honour of being the first man to kiss the bride.' He kissed Mercy on the cheek.

'Hey, less of that,' Will objected but James was already making his way down the street with Anne. They turned and waved enthusiastically.

'Wait 'till I see him later,' Will said, laughing.

'He means no harm,' Mercy added as she waved back just as enthusiastically and then put her arm through Will's.

'Well, Mrs Dresser. It is well cold so do we walk in the park as we talked of or get back to the house and explore our new married quarters?'

Mercy laughed. 'That makes it sound rather grand for a servants' room that we can now share together. I have a better idea. Let's go to a good inn and have an early lunch, I'm starving. And,' she said with a wink, 'I think we ought to book a room for the night.'

'What, not go back to the house?'

'I don't want to be reminded of what is going on there. I want to forget we're at war. And we don't need to go back. We've been given the night off and a very generous wedding gift from the duke and duchess. Let's go and spend it, you only get married once and I'm ravenous for the food of the table and the food of love. Come on, let's live dangerously. Dangerous times bring dangerous deeds.'

'That's my girl, no, my wife,' he said unable to contain his grin. 'I'm going to have to get used to that and I hope to get used to everything else married life entails. Come on, let's go. I can't wait. Sure you want to eat first?'

CHAPTER TWENTY-THREE

'Come on, Mercy, hurry up. We'll miss them if we're not careful.'

'You couldn't miss them if you tried. Don't fuss.'

'Well, everyone is already gathered outside and ready to leave. I don't want to have to run after them.'

'I'm ready, don't worry, I'm ready,' she said trying to be positive. Will offered her his arm and they made their way from their room to the servants' access at the side of the house. As they stepped outside a cacophony of voices reached them in the icy air.

'Lord, what a racket. Everyone must be talking at once,' Mercy complained.

'Quick, let's join them,' Will encouraged as he guided her gently around the corner and suddenly the darkness turned into an arena of soft yellow light from the glimmering lamps and torches held aloft – smoky and sensual – dancing around as the torch holders moved, picking out the people and buildings in low light and sinister shadows.

'There must be fifty of us!' Will whispered to his wife as they joined their colleagues. 'I can feel the excitement, its sending shivers down my back.'

'I wish it wasn't quite so early. Six of the clock on a late February morning is a time to be indoors, not going out on a walk across half of London in the dark, and it's freezing!'

'Well, you're well wrapped up. You'll warm up as soon as we get started. Come on, join in the fun.'

'Fun! I'll never understand you men. Oh, look, there's Anne. 'Hey, Anne,' she called out and waved.

Anne made her way through the throng of people. 'You're late. I was beginning to think you lovebirds were going to take advantage of staying abed while the house was quiet.' She laughed. 'You've only been wed two weeks after all.'

'I wouldn't miss this for the world,' Will said, grinning.

'You men! You're all alike,' Mercy said. 'A bit of fighting and you're like boys in the nursery.'

'But, Mercy, aren't you excited? Anne asked. 'I can't wait to see the spectacle. It'll be thrilling and King George and Queen Charlotte are coming too, and the Prince of Wales. Oh, it'll be magnificent.'

'You feel it, Anne,' Will said, 'so why don't you, Mercy? The excitement … what it's going to be like … how will they look … will it all go to plan? It's the unknown that fascinates. I've never seen anything like we are going to witness.' He put himself between them. 'Come on, ladies,' he said, smiling and offering them each an arm. 'Let's go off to war!'

Everyone set off together and the noise levels increased with peals of laughter and good-natured shouts ensnaring everyone in the joviality of the moment. From the forecourt of the house they turned into Piccadilly in the direction of Horse Guards. Many people were already making their way down the wide thoroughfare with the light from their torches casting Piccadilly into long and short shadows like something supernatural. The frosty air and the torchlight made everyone's breath look like miniature clouds appearing and disappearing in equal measures as songs started and were picked up by others.

'It's like a festival,' Mercy said, 'and I'm not sure it should be.'

'Come on, Mercy,' Will cajoled, 'everyone's been talking of this for the past few weeks. We're going to give it to those Frenchies. Everyone's excited and it's such a relief that something is finally going to happen. And do you know what? The duke's a canny man giving his staff leave to witness the troops going off to war. Everyone else is welcome to see it so why not us? I've never seen people so animated. Atmosphere and spectacle give people confidence. It's what the country needs right now. It will all be reported in the papers tomorrow.'

'Well, I suppose you're right,' Mercy admitted reluctantly. 'It certainly gets under your skin.'

'And the more people who come, the merrier and more impressive it will be.'

'You should be a politician. That was a good speech, Will.'

'Thank you, Anne,' he said, taking his hat off and making an extravagant leg as if she were a duchess in a ballroom.

'He's like that, though, isn't he? Will started up again. 'The duke loves the army and is enjoying his new power. Why shouldn't he let his servants join in this historic moment and see him in all his glory? I'd do the same in his position.'

Mercy guffawed. 'What? You? Made Lieutenant-General and Commander of the Expeditionary Force, like the duke?'

'So that's what you dream at night, is it, brother

379

dear!' Anne teased. 'You're still dreaming of the army.'

'We all have to have our dreams,' Will said, joining in the jesting. 'It's Lieutenant-General and Commander of the Expeditionary Force or nothing for me.'

The two women burst into laughter. Recovering, Mercy took Will's arm. 'You know, you were right all along. I'm sorry,' she said, giving him a peck on the cheek.

'I'm very pleased to be right, my darling wife, but can you enlighten me as to what I was right about?'

'All this,' she said, indicating the scene with a sweep of her arm. 'I know we've talked about the revolution in France and what it means to us here and—'

'We've talked of nothing else, it seems to me,' Will jumped in with a smile.

'I know I've been upset by the events and the threat of war. But now, here, with it all happening, well, the fact that we're doing something to defend ourselves and our way of life, well, if I'm honest, it's biting into me, to be part of this ... the excitement ... the opportunity to tell the French what we think of their revolution and—'

Mercy caught her breath as she got jostled by some rowdy men, drinking and shouting some obscenities about the French as they went by.

'Hey, have a care here,' Will shouted at them, 'this is my wife your—'

She clutched his arm. 'Leave it. I'm not hurt – it's part of the whole atmosphere – I'm enjoying it Will. I'm ashamed to say it but it's true. I'm getting carried away with it all. Oh, come on, Will, I can't wait to get to Horse Guards. Where's Anne?'

'Did I hear my name?' Anne had to yell from behind as the noise was so deafening.

Mercy and Will turned. 'Anne, come quickly,' Mercy said linking her arm into Anne's and then Will's. She laughed as she shouted, 'Let's go to war and give it to those Frenchies.'

Anne and Will joined in. 'Yes, let's go to war and give it to the Frenchies,' they sang out in great merriment as they made their way to Horse Guards.

They were jostled some more by the growing crowds as they approached Horse Guards but the merriment continued and they found a good place outside the parade ground. 'We're in time to see it all, look, the troops are coming out of the building.' Will said in great excitement.

'I wish it wasn't so dark,' Mercy said, 'I can't see much.'

'But the flickering torchlight makes them look wonderful,' Anne replied, 'not quite real … and the shadows look so sinister. It's thrilling.'

Two thousand soldiers lined up precisely in neat, straight rows with the white of their breeches glowing in the torch light surrounding the parade ground. The light was not strong enough to pick up the red of their tunics, making them look black and mysterious. Their breath came out in multiple puffs like steaming kettles on the boil. Every man looked fit and healthy and a force to be reckoned with.

'LOOK, HERE'S THE DUKE ARRIVING ON HIS HORSE,' someone in the crowd shouted and a general exclamation of admiration went around as the impressive figure of the duke appeared riding his black stallion, his own uniform sparkling in a profusion of gold braiding and brass buttons. A large group of his fellow officers rode behind as the crowd exclaimed:

'He looks magnificent!' 'He can beat those Frenchies.' 'Put them in their place.' 'We'll win this war, you wait and see'. 'Send those Frenchies off.' 'Give them a lesson they'll never forget.' 'Hear, hear.'

Cheers went up.

As the cheering subsided, Will said to Anne, 'I heard that three regiments had been decided upon to accompany the duke as the expeditionary force but they needed volunteers from other regiments to make up a shortfall of soldiers in the chosen regiments. The duke gathered all seven thousand guards on the parade ground and spoke to them. He then explained that volunteers were needed and every man stepped forward as one. Every single one of them,' he repeated in awe.

'I'm not surprised. He's that kind of man. He knows how to command.' She looked at him, puzzled. 'But I heard that only two thousand men were going with the duke? Is that right? That's not many to fight the French, is it? What about the seven thousand who volunteered?'

'Ah, but the duke will be in command of the foreign forces too, and there's many thousands of them. Our lot will be joining the Dutch soldiers in Holland already fighting the invading French. We'll show them a thing or two, you wait and see.'

'Yes, I see … I think. Oh well, the duke knows what he's doing.'

At last dawn broke and a weak sun slowly

appeared struggling to illuminate the surroundings, finally gathering strength into a bright orange, bathing the parade ground in shimmering light.

Someone bellowed, 'LOOK! HERE COMES THE KING.'

Everybody turned and craned their necks to see King George and the Prince of Wales arriving on horseback with a dozen mounted officers leading the way, followed by the royal coach with the queen, the Duke of Clarence and three of the princesses inside. Another dozen officers followed the coach.

'It's a pity the duchess refused to join the royal party,' Mercy commented to no one in particular.

'She made it clear,' Anne answered, 'that she didn't want to see the duke going off to war as her spirits were sorely depressed by it. They have already said their goodbyes.'

'Mmm. I can understand her feelings,' Mercy answered looking at Will whose eyes were shining bright and his body taut in barely contained excitement.

The crowd cheered and clapped as the royal party rode past. 'LONG LIVE THE KING,' went around the crowd like a mantra as the two men trotted into the parade ground and the duke rode up to greet them. The duke, the king and the prince were in full military uniform and as the sun got stronger it highlighted the extravagant braiding and epaulets beloved by royalty and worn by each man. The still-rising sunlight caught their scabbards, making them sparkle like jewels at their sides.

'Oh, look,' Anne said, as she jumped up to try and see more clearly, 'the king is inspecting the troops.'

'I can't see,' Mercy said as she stood on tiptoe, losing her balance as the crowd jostled for a good view.

'Let me help you,' Will said, taking hold of her arm and steadying her, 'you too, Anne.' He stood between them and offered each his arm so that they could stand on tiptoe without overbalancing.

'Thanks,' Mercy said. 'I wish I had your height, I'd be able to see everything much better.'

'Then, my darling wife, you'd be a footman and not a maid.'

'Oh, I'd love to be a footman. It's got to be better than being a maid.'

'Shh, you two,' Anne hissed as they, and everyone else, watched in fascinated silence as the troops marched past the king in slow time led by six drummers.

'How do they make the horses stand so still?' Anne asked. 'Look, the king, the duke's and the prince's horses have hardly moved since the soldiers started the march past.'

No one answered, so completely involved in the ceremony were they. As the last of the men marched past the king the duke rode forward and positioned himself at their head, followed by the king and the prince riding side by side behind the duke and then the royal coach. Half of the mounted officers rode ahead of the duke to lead the way while the other half followed directly behind the coach for protection. They moved off with six drummers following and the soldiers marching six abreast behind them, the crowd following on in great disarray and jubilation.

They left Horse Guards with the drummers beating time and marched passed Charing Cross and down the Strand. The day was now crisp and clear with a blue sky full of gently floating white clouds. The ice on the ground and on the windowpanes of the houses didn't stop people from leaning out of their windows, awoken or alerted by the noise, and waving whatever they had to hand, stockings, clothing, caps, hats and scarves in a rhapsody of colour and movement and shouts of 'God save the King' and other indecipherable comments. Many overcome by the excitement rushed out of their houses to join in the great explosion of joy and jollity in the street, knowing the fight back against France had started.

Anne, Will and Mercy kept their arms linked so as not to be separated in the growing crowds as they continued to follow the troops.

'I've never seen anything like this,' Mercy said in great excitement.

'Look over there,' Will said, 'that's Covent Garden at the end of that side street and look, I swear all those people swarming down are stallholders and, if I'm not mistaken …' he peered, 'their customers too. Good lord, well, I never, they've all left the selling and buying of fruit and veg and are joining in. Hope their stalls are still there when they get back.'

'I don't think they care too much,' Anne said, 'looks like they've been drinking for a while.'

'And look,' Mercy said laughing, 'they're giving their tankards of ale and goodness knows what else to some of the troops.'

'Well, they're known for their early tippling at the Garden,' Will said, longingly.

Inns opened up along the route and did a roaring trade as they sold beer and spirits on tables outside their premises. Bakers too went out on the street with their buns and pies and the glorious aroma filled noses and made mouths water as people bought more than they needed and gave some to the troops who called out their thanks. Maids ran back and forth from bakeries with trays to replenish the stock as more and more bakers, their wives and even their children bore trays hanging from their necks and selling out almost immediately.

The parade continued down to St Clement Danes Church where the bells were ringing out in a continuous merry peal.

'Look,' Will cut in, his extra height giving him a good view, 'the clergy are blessing the royal family and the troops as they pass the church.'

'What's happening? Quick, tell me,' Mercy urged him.

'Well, the duke, king and prince have nodded to the clergy but haven't stopped and the men, by the look of it are behaving in a more-or-less orderly fashion, as far as I can see.'

'Won't last long,' put in Mercy. 'Bet you they start on the grog again as soon as they pass them.'

Will laughed as the mood became ever more infectious and exuberant, the excitement growing like a contagion. 'Well, hold on tight as they are starting to push a bit from behind. Keep close now.' A little while later, he said, 'We're just passing into Fleet Street and, good Lord, there are so many people there'll be no room for the soldiers.'

Anne put her hands over her ears as cheers and shouts erupted like a volcano of sound and people waved scarves, and hats went into the air, and others jumped up and down to get a better view as the parade passed down Fleet Street, cutting a swath through the crowds who dispersed merrily before them.

'Come on, don't dawdle or we'll lose our place and get left behind. What's that they're shouting?

Give 'em what else and—'

'Yes, I heard them, thank you, Will,' Mercy teased. 'We don't need you to repeat low-life bad language.'

'Inventive though, you have to admit.'

'People are as drunk as lords,' Anne said, looking around at the ever-growing crowds.

'Watch your language in front of royalty,' Mercy jested.

'I wouldn't mind a drink or two myself,' Will added.

'It's too early,' Anne chastised him.

'I know, but it's a special occasion. People have been plying the soldiers with tankards of ale and goodness knows what else for ages. I'm half tempted to go and pretend to be a soldier and get my fill too.'

'Don't you dare,' Mercy said severely and Will laughed and winked at her.

'My feet hurt,' Mercy said with feeling. 'I should have worn more comfortable shoes.'

'Well, my darling, you would insist on wearing your best ones.'

'Big mistake, I agree.'

'It's not my feet it's my back,' Anne joined in. 'I wish people would stop jostling so much it jars every time.'

'Would you rather not be here, you pair of complainers?' Will asked with smug smile that said he was suffering from nothing but a longing for a drink.

'No!' They both shouted at the same time.

'No, no, no, we would not have missed this for the world, would we, Anne?'

'Not for the world. This is a once-in-a lifetime experience.'

The people were drunk on relief as well as alcohol after the months of anxiety with the possibility of the rampaging in France becoming a reality here. The sight of the soldiers, of the royal family, defending their country and its way of life was inspiring and created excitement and an exuberance few people had felt before. It was catching, like a plague few could resist, but unlike a plague it promised life and health and a prosperous future.

The great noise from the crowd rose and fell like waves on a stormy sea as it rose up to a crescendo and then dipped before rising again in the full voice only jubilant people can attain. Some were still in their nightclothes with greatcoats or cloaks over the top so anxious to join in were they. A man in a nightcap and fur-trimmed dressing gown was doing a drunken jig with a man in rags who smelt like a sewer drain on a hot day. It was like the party to end all parties so raucous and uninhibited were they. Even the queen hung out of the coach window and waved joyously at the crowd and someone thrust a tankard in her hand and to the surprise of everyone she drank the contents down in one and started waving enthusiastically again. The king and queen had taken a lot of criticism for their staid and boring ways. It must have been emboldening and encouraging to them to see their subjects so supportive to the royal family. Everyone needs encouragement, even queens.

'Good lord,' Anne said. 'I can't believe this. Look, look there,' she said clutching Mercy's arm. 'One of the staggering soldiers has fallen down and I do believe he's dead drunk.'

Spectators laughed at his plight as his mates tried to haul him to his feet but they too fell down too drunk to help. 'What a disgrace,' Anne added, but fascinated just the same as someone came rushing forward with a cart containing a few sacks which he threw out carelessly, carried away by the moment. Everyone laughed as he and his assistant picked up the soldier and laid him none too carefully in the cart followed by some of the other drunken soldiers until the cart was full. They then started pushing the cart along with the rest of the soldiers.

'I'm not sure that they'll make it to the ships at Greenwich let alone Holland,' Anne said.

'The king and the duke and the Prince of Wales are all enjoying it,' Mercy answered. 'If they don't mind I don't see why we should.'

'You've got good eyesight being able to see them at the front.'

'I saw the duke accept several tankards, drinking them back in one. The prince too, but he has to be more careful as he's riding next to the king.'

'No, the king wouldn't like that too much. He's always watching Prinny for bad behaviour,' Will joined in.

'Don't call him Prinny. We're royal servants, we can't call him that,' Mercy reprimanded him.

'Even though the rest of the country does?' Will shot back good naturedly. 'But never mind, whatever we call anyone is not important but what is important is that we have reached Blackfriars Bridge. This is as far as we go, ladies, the Thames is our barrier. While the soldiers go on through the countryside to Greenwich and the ships awaiting them, we, my dearest wife and sister,' he looked at each of them, grinning, 'have our own work awaiting us.' He stopped walking and was immediately jostled as he looked around. 'Mmm, we may have some difficulty getting through the crowds as everyone seems intent on going over the bridge. But we will prevail. Keep a hold of me and I'll lead the way,' he said as he turned and led the women to the edge of the crowd. 'It's a little less crowded this side, come on, I don't know about you but I'm starving. Keep a hold of me, come on. Let's leave the duke to do his job and we need to go and do ours.' He put his arm around Mercy. 'Aren't you glad you came?'

'I wouldn't have missed it for the world. You were right. It's been marvellous ... but—'

'But what?' Will said looking concerned.

'I do have to wonder what the future holds for us now.'

CHAPTER TWENTY-FOUR

Albany House had become an empty space since the duke had left, echoing forlornly, or so it seemed to Will. The non-stop activity that had continued throughout its rooms, the rushing about of footmen and servants upstairs and down was replaced by a quietude; a smoothing of the waters. The life led by the duchess was as far from the duke's as could be. A passivity now prevailed, as if the house had let out a great sigh and resumed its life with slow steady breathing.

Most of the staff were grateful for the reprieve, especially the housemaids and kitchen staff who had struggled to keep up with the cleaning and non-stop food and drink demanded by constant visitors and meetings and parties. For the duke loved a party and that was his way of relaxation after a heavy day's work. A large dinner followed by cards and excessive gambling and drinking revived the duke much more than a night's sleep. No matter what time he went to bed, he was up early, getting in the way of the housemaids work and demanding breakfast before the rooms had been cleaned from the extravagances of the night before. Will missed this; the underlying atmosphere of expectancy, urgency and the unknown.

Now, callers were mostly other ladies calling on

the duchess, leaving their cards in the hope of an audience or good friends of hers offering company as she mourned the departure of the duke. Although the duchess also liked entertaining and giving and attending parties she was not as enamoured of it as her husband and was not inclined to socialise except with her intimates at this moment. This, as far as Will was concerned, was boring. He no longer waited on great men of the state but on the wives, widows and daughters of lesser men as and when they were admitted by the duchess.

'I miss it, Mercy, you know,' he said as he climbed into bed one night and snuggled up to her.

'Oh, for goodness sake, get your cold body away from me until you warm up.'

'Come on, warm me up. You're like toast.'

'Do I have any choice?' she said, relenting and putting her arms around him. 'Come on then. It's nice, being cuddled up like this. Are you happy you're an old married man now?'

'Hey, less of the old.'

'Well, you have been married for a month.' She kissed his cheek. 'It seems like an age, don't you think?'

'It certainly seems like we've always been like this. I can't remember a time when we went to our separate beds,' he said, caressing her.

'Life has changed so much since we came here.'

'Well, it's certainly a different life now the duke's gone. Do you think the duchess will go back to Oatlands soon?'

'I hope so. I so want to go back. I used to like it in London when I worked here for the duke but now I've got used to the quiet and beauty of Oatlands – and met you of course – I think I'd like to bring our children up there and not here in busy, polluted London.'

He pulled back, looking at her in hope. 'Mercy! You're not, are you?'

'No, of course not. It's way too early for things like that. I'm just saying what I feel I'd like to happen.'

He took her in his arms. 'In that case, we could try and see if we can make at least one of those things come true.' He kissed her gently and before he knew it he'd forgotten all about London and Oatlands and so had Mercy.

*

A few days later, everyone settled themselves in the servants' hall for dinner as Mr Faraday commanded, 'Attention please,' from his chair at the head of the table. There were several sighs, all muffled as no one wanted the butler to see they thought more of their food than of him.

'Before we settle down to dinner I have an announcement.' He cleared his throat importantly. 'Her Royal Highness, the duchess, has informed me that she will return to Oatlands shortly.' A mumble of indistinct voices coupled with sage like nodding greeted this news as if everyone had already guessed. 'I know it's been rumoured for some time that this is what she would do, it is now official. Servants who came up to Albany House with the duke and duchess from Oatlands will return there with her.'

Will glanced over at Mercy and smiled. Her look of pure happiness gladdened his heart. He looked over at Anne, who was smiling as broadly as his wife. The two women in my life, he thought. Two women he loved and would do anything for. And if it was to go back to Oatlands and live a quiet life there he would do so. But at the back of his mind was the thought that the duke would return and then, well, who knew what would happen. Life was so unpredictable. But for now, Will was content.

*

Will and Mercy strolled along hand in hand through the woods of Oatlands basking in the hot summer sun.

'It's been good to be back here,' Mercy said, as she let go of Will's hand and swirled around in front of him, arms outstretched. 'Look at the beauty of this place. The Thames just over there,' she pointed through the trees, her arm making a great arc which continued to encompass the rest of the land. 'And the trees are so thick and healthy, unlike the paltry ones in London.' She looked around breathing in the fresh, clean air deeply. 'Oh, Will, my darling Will.' She threw her arms around his neck and kissed him passionately. Then, in a very Mercy like way, she pushed him away from her and said, 'I've got a secret,' and gave him a look of satisfaction.

'Oh?' Will answered, determined not to be sucked in.

'Do you want to know it?'

'Mmm, maybe?' he said with an air of indifference.

'Oh, you, you're infuriating sometimes.'

'Well, are you going to tell me or not?' He couldn't suppress his smile.

'What's the thing you most want?'

'Mmm, to suddenly become a royal duke and have everything I want?'

'Well … maybe you will be the equivalent of a royal duke to some little creature in the future. He, or she, may look up to you with awe.'

'*Mercy!?*' He dragged out the word as a form of chastisement coupled with a question.

She looked into his eyes and ran her finger down his cheek in that way she had which gave him shivers. 'You, my dear husband, are about to be promoted. You will not only be a husband but a father also.'

'A *baby!*' He took hold of Mercy's hands and looked into her eyes as if the truth was there. 'We're to have a *baby? I'm going to be a father!*'

'Your face is a picture,' she said, smiling a satisfied smile and running her finger down his cheek again, 'a picture of incredulity and utter pleasure. Oh, my darling, yes, you will be a father.'

He took her in his arms and whispered so softly into her ear that his voice was almost lost on the air. 'And you, my darling wife, will be a mother and the best mother in the world as you are the best wife in the world.'

'Hold me. Hold me close,' she said suddenly serious as she clutched him closer. 'Tell me, tell me true now. We'll be all right, won't we? We'll be all right here, at Oatlands, with the duchess? I worry about the future, the war and children and … and … well, we will be able to cope, won't we?'

He hugged her hard and long, kissing her neck and caressing her back as if he had a child already who needed comforting. 'You're a difficult woman to understand sometimes, but that's why I love you so. And I'll make you a promise from the bottom of my heart. Yes, my love, we'll be all right, although the world is changing and will never be the same as it was. The war with France; the guillotining of King Louis, the continued imprisonment of Queen Marie Antoinette … oh, my darling, it threatens us all. But look at it another way. Look at what excitement there is in the air. The unknown is beckoning. Our child is coming, that's our future and we have to make a successful world for our children. We live in great times – times of change. We are part of that. Never forget that, my darling.'

AUTHOR'S NOTE

Frederick, Duke of York, the beloved brother of the Prince of Wales, later Prince Regent and then George IV, decided to use Oatlands House in Weybridge, Surrey, as his country residence in the late 1780s. However, this is not a book about the duke so much as about his servants and their love of the duke and of the house of Oatlands itself.

My interest was first piqued when, doing a family history project, I discovered my five times great-grandparents were servants (footman and maid) at Oatlands for over twenty years, and possibly, though unproved by documentation, it was either my six-times great grandparents or maybe my six-times great aunt and uncle who also worked at Oatlands as porter and his wife. The only documents I have of him are his entry registration of joining up to the Coldstream Guards from Derbyshire and the Chelsea Hospital record of a pension when he was invalided out with 'gouty and rheumatic complaints,' over twenty years later as a sergeant in December,1787.

My imagination took over and although this novel is fiction I've kept to the historical facts as much as possible and interwoven them into the lives as I imaged them of my ancestors. How did they get to work for the duke? After all, you do not just go and knock on the door of royalty and expect to be employed. You must be vouched for I would imagine. During my research I realised that when my possible six times grandfather was in the army, the Duke of York became the Commanding Officer of his regiment, The Coldstream Guards. There was the connection!

All the records I have of my ancestors at Oatlands are from the Household Accounts where their names and wages are recorded, plus the marriage of William and Mercy at St Georges Church, Hanover Square, London. The baptisms of their children, all eleven of them, are recorded at St. James Church, Weybridge as are the burials of William and Mercy.

Where a few facts have been altered somewhat it has been for the benefit and flow of the story.

The history of the Duke and Duchess of York is well documented and I have included some of their story in this novel. Research and my imagination have helped me to create the lives of my ancestors in this world long gone by. What was it like serving the duke and his brother, the Prince of Wales, who often visited him at Oatlands. What was it like to live in a royal house and how did it affect the servants' lives?

Frederick, Duke of York, is famous because of an underserved jingle.

The grand old Duke of York
He had ten thousand men
He marched them up to the top of the hill
And he marched them down again.
And when they were up they were up
And when they were down they were down
And when they were only halfway up they were
Neither up nor down

This jingle was probably circulated after the duke's death. It refers to the Campaign in Flanders and specifically to the battle of Turcoing in 1794 where the duke was unjustly blamed for the unsatisfactory outcome of the battle. In fact, the duke received a letter of apology from the emperor, Francis ll, expressing his satisfaction with the way the duke had removed his men from danger.

The Duke of York was an experienced and respected soldier who became the Commander-in-Chief of the British Army, a post he held for thirty years. He reorganised the nation's forces putting in place structural training and logistical reforms which enabled the British to defeat Napoleon. He founded Sandhurst which promoted professional and merit-based training for future commissioned officers in place of the buying of commissions as well as a school for the children of British soldiers.

Thackeray describes the duke as follows: "Big, burly, loud, jolly, cursing, courageous; he had a most affectionate and lovable disposition, was noble and generous to a fault, and was never known to break a promise."

He was a man of his time and class, but at the same time, was a man of principle and kindness in areas where this was not usual. His brother, the Prince of Wales, deeply loved and admired him and they were very close throughout their lives. Unusually, the duke's marriage was not arranged by interested families or governments looking for advantage in another country, but by the duke and Princess Frederica falling in love with each other. In his youth, the duke spent seven years, mostly in the area of Germany and Austria, fighting and learning his trade as a soldier. In the summer of 1791 he was in Berlin because of unrest between Prussia and Russia over Turkey. The crisis passed quickly and this gave him time to think more of Frederica, whom he had met many times before. He wrote to his tutor, General Grenville:

"You knew for many years that the Princess Frederique has been a flame of mine, and you will not forget that when we left Berlin four years ago I then told you that I should be very glad to marry her if it could be brought about. The different events that have happened during the last four years have hindered me till now from declaring myself, but still I can safely say I never lost sight of my object … I have no doubt of being perfectly happy. The Princess is the best girl that ever existed and the more I see of her the more I like her."

He also wrote to his friends at the time, "I do not say she is the handsomest girl ever formed but she is full enough for me and in disposition she is an angel. Every day I am more attached and more convinced that I could never enjoy any happiness without her."

After a few years of marriage, the childless duke and duchess started to lead separate lives as suited their personalities. The duchess disliked London and London life and preferred the quiet of Oatlands while the duke spent most of his time in London taking care of his duties in the army while taking advantage of all the entertainments and distractions money, status and a capital city could offer. However, they remained very close and continued to love each other to the end. The duke spent quite a bit of his time at Oatlands together with his friends and the duchess joined in the socialising enthusiastically whilst keeping her decorum. The duke died in 1827 of dropsy.

The Duchess of York was well loved by her servants, the people of Weybridge and others for her lack of superiority, her generosity and her friendliness. In later life she is described by one visitor as, "A little animated woman, talks immensely and laughs still more. No beauty, has bad teeth."

Charles Greville, who knew both the duke and duchess well, describes the duchess as, "Clever and well informed. Liking society and disliking all form of ceremony while preserving a certain dignity of manner. Her mind is perhaps not the most delicate; she shows no dislike to coarseness of sentiment or language, and she is seen to be very amused with jokes, stories and allusions which would shock a very nice person. But her own conversation is never polluted with anything the least indelicate or unbecoming. She is very appreciative of little attentions and annoyed if anybody appeared to keep aloof from her or to shun conversing with her."

Her charity was widespread and she took a great interest in the children of Weybridge and arranged for them to be better clothed and educated under her own supervision. Later, apprenticeships were arranged for the boys and small marriage portions for the girls. Every Sunday the children were invited to Oatlands where she personally served them cake and wine and took great enjoyment from it. The old and sick were also taken care of. She was regarded as eccentric because of her love of animals. She had over thirty dogs at one time as well as animals from all over the world living in the grounds of Oatlands, including a Brahmin bull, Australian wallabies, rare goats, fowls, peacocks, monkeys and parrots and was, "never more delighted to receive gifts of yet more."

When she died of a chest complaint in 1820 Greville wrote, "Probably no person in such a situation was ever more really liked. She was deeply regretted by everyone." She left £12,000 to her servants and to some of the children of the poor she had educated.

The villagers of Weybridge erected a memorial to her on the village green which is still there today and she is buried at the local church of St James.

Oatlands still stands today as a hotel but is greatly altered since the duke's time, although it is still an impressive and interesting building. The surrounding estate was sold off and is now covered with housing and roads. Guests at the hotel have included Emile Zola, Anthony Trollope, Edward Lear, and of course, the author of this book.

Finally, a further note about my ancestors:

I have changed most of the names of my ancestors. While this may sound rather drastic or disrespectful I had to always keep in mind the flow of the novel. The family name at this time was the rather harsh and unattractive name of Wilcockson which I felt pulled the reader up somewhat rather than blending in to the background as it should do. Also, as was the fashion at the time, children were named after their parents and, unfortunately, everyone in my family tree at this time had the same first names, William and Mary. I was forced therefore to change most of the first names too. I kept the names William for the footman and Mercy (interchangeable with Mary), his wife and apologise to the rest of my ancestors for having to change theirs.

I cannot trace any reliable records of William Senior (porter) or his wife after he retired from Oatlands but I did find William Junior (footman) and Mercy working at Horse Guards for the duke during the last years of their lives. They worked in the Quarter Masters General's Office as "Office-keeper" and "House-keeper". They died, probably in post, within four months of each other in 1819 both in their late forties. Mercy died first and her remains were taken to Weybridge for burial in St. James Church and so was William four months later. One has to wonder if some disease outbreak was to blame or whether Will died of a broken heart. Also, who arranged for, and paid the not inconsiderable amount, to transport the bodies from London to Weybridge and why?

Anne (Mary, of course) became "wardrobe maid" to the duchess. I interpret "wardrobe maid" to mean lady's maid. She was loyal until the end and died unmarried in 1813 aged 44 just a few months after her name disappeared from the accounts, presumably she had to abandon her post because of illness. She is buried in St James Church, Weybridge.

For readers wishing to delve deeper into research of this time here is a list of the books I found most useful.

The Biographical Memoir of His Late Royal Highness Frederick, Duke of York and Albany by John Watkins. Printed in 1827 and made available in reprint by Harvard University Library.

The Noble Duke of York – The Military Life of Frederick Duke of York and Albany by Lieut-Colonel Alfred H. Burne, D.S.O. Staples Press, London

The Grand Old Duke of York – A Life of Prince Frederick, Duke of York and Albany 1763-1827 by Derek Winterbottom. Pen and Sword Military. ISBN 9781473854770

A Soldier in the Seventy-First, From De la Plata to Waterloo 1806-1815 by Joseph Sinclair. Frontline Books, London ISBN 9781848325616

Eavesdropping on Jane Austen's England – How Our Ancestors Lived Two Centuries Ago by Roy and Lesley Adkins. Abacus ISBN 9780349138602

The Grotto Makers, Joseph and Josiah Lane of Tisbury by Christina Richard. The Hobnob Press, Gloucester. ISBN 9781906978549

Weybridge Past by Neil White. Phillimore & Co Ltd., Chichester. ISBN 186077086X

A Short History of Weybridge, M.E. Blackman & J.S.L. Pulford. Walton & Weybridge Local History Society Paper No. 29 1991

Royal Elmbridge E Royston Pike. Esher District Local History Society, 1977

Life in an Eighteenth Century Country House by Peter and Carolyn Hammond. Amberley ISBN 9781445608655

Behind Closed Doors, At Home in Georgian England by Amanda Vickery. Yale University Press ISBN 9780300168969

John Macdonald Memoirs of an XVlll Century Footman 1745-1779 by John Macdonald. The Broadway Travellers Series, Harper and Brothers, New York and London (no ISBN)

The Footman's Directory and Butler's Remembrancer 1823 Originally printed by the author and sold by J Hatchard and Son, Piccadilly, 1823. This facsimile reproduction by Pryor Publications, Whitstable and Walsall ISBN 0946014701

The Diary of Thomas Turner 1754-1765 Edited by David Vaisey. Oxford University Press ISBN 0192818996

Life Below Stairs – In the Victorian and Edwardian Country House by Siân Evans. National Trust ISBN 9781909881648

Printed in Great Britain
by Amazon